A failed grad student.
Toddler twins.
A celestial war.

The fate of the world lies with two little girls...

...she looked closer and saw them coming unbound. A maelstrom of fire was contained within their shapes, leaking from their linked hands, and the boundaries that kept them human were fraying...

What Others Are Saying:

"Lovely worldbuilding and an unusual heroine surrounded by strong relationships and good intrigue kept me reading Matchbox Girls until well past my bedtime. Tzavelas has created a winning story universe and I'm impatient for the next book!"
—CE Murphy, bestselling author of *Urban Shaman* and
The Queen's Bastard

"An intriguing debut urban fantasy with intricate and deep wordbuilding and engaging characters in the heroine and two young girls. Children who are pawns in a game of power and the keys to the future...."
—Robin D. Owens, bestselling author of *Enchanted Again*

"You want to read Matchbox Girls because it will devour you. It will consume you. It will wrap around you and it will colonize your world with its shapes and symbols and its faces."
—Jenna Moran, creator of the hit RPG Nobilis

matchbox girls

Chrysoula Tzavelas

First edition published 2012.
Second edition published 2015.

ISBN: 978-1-943197-05-7
eISBN: 978-1-943197-01-9

Cover art by Ravven
www.ravven.com

Book design and composition by Kate Sullivan
Typeface: Adobe Caslon

Editors: Kate Sullivan and Ellen Harvey

Proofreaders:
Rose Martino Bigelow
Matt Hydeman
Sarah LaBelle

www.dreamfarmer.net

For my mother, who believed in me,
and my son, who made me understand.

-one-

Marley woke up, reaching out of a forgotten dream for her cellphone, knowing that she couldn't miss this call. Half-asleep, she fumbled at her nightstand, knocking a bottle of pills and three books over and onto the floor. Then she rolled over to stare at the phone, which wasn't ringing. She frowned. Why had she—

It rang.

"Yeah?" she mumbled into the phone as she fell back onto her pillow again, putting her arm over her eyes to block out the late morning sunshine streaming in her window. The sky had that baked-on brilliance that said it was already too hot to imagine doing anything outside.

"Marley, come get us?" She heard a small child's voice, beguilingly familiar but unexpected. "It's scary here."

Marley sat up and glanced at the caller ID on the phone. Despite an unlabeled number, she identified the voice: Lissa or Kari, the twin nieces and wards of her gorgeous friend Zachariah. Almost daily, she met the twins and their guardian at the nearby park where Marley went to read and they went to play.

"Kiddo? Where are you? Did you get lost somewhere?" The children were preschoolers, young enough to get seriously confused if they decided to set out on an adventure.

"At home, but Uncle Zach isn't here. He said, 'Call Marley!' if we ever can't find him." A second voice on top of the first said, "Come get us, Marley!" There was a shrill edge to the voices that pulled Marley to her feet before she was entirely aware of it. The trickle of worry became a flood, twisting her stomach into knots.

She took a deep breath, forcing the anxiety down. Her meds were on the floor. Cradling the phone against her ear, she opened the bottle and swallowed a pill. Then she started looking for clean clothes. "Where did he go?"

The voice closer to the phone said, "We don't know. We were in our room and he just—"

The second voice said, "We do know! He went into his study to use the phone and he didn't come out! We've looked for him and he's not playing!" That was Kari, identifiable from the energy in her speech.

"I'll come over and help you find him, all right?" Still holding the phone, she struggled into a pair of jeans and jammed her feet into some sandals. She paused to run a finger down the back of the kitten sleeping on a pile of overdue bills, letting the soft touch center her. Then she lifted it off the stack of envelopes and found her car keys.

She'd never been to Zachariah's home, but his address was somewhere on her computer, shut down due to brownouts the day before. While it booted up, she tried to get the twins to tell her more about their day. But they weren't interested in chatting.

"We don't want to stay here. It's scary," Lissa insisted.

Finally, Marley found and printed out the address to Zachariah's house, and took another calming breath. The twins were playing a game, probably. They were little kids.

Little kids were mischievous. She was surprised to discover they knew how to use a phone, though, let alone knew her phone number. Zachariah was probably in the backyard. Almost certainly. Waking from a black dream to their phone call was just a coincidence. But best to make sure. "Well, what's scary about your house?"

"Things under the bed."

"Shadows that go thump!"

"The roaring in the walls."

"The bells behind us."

"Whatever took Uncle! Please hurry, Marley!"

The first item on the list almost made Marley smile, but the raw fear in their voices by the end of the list had her rushing to the door. Because what if he'd really left them alone? "It's okay, sweethearts. I'm sure it's okay. Your uncle probably just had to run an errand and thought you wouldn't notice he was gone. I'm on my way over, and I'll stay with you until he gets home." She clattered down the steps of the old brick building and out to her car.

There was sniffling on the other end. "Do you really think so?"

"Absolutely," she lied as she started her car. She couldn't imagine the emergency that would make Zachariah leave his two little nieces alone; he was devoted to the kids. Still, better to try to imagine that than worry about the alternatives. Deep breath. The anxiety wouldn't fade away. She was crazy. But she had to manage despite it for the girls.

"I've never been to your house before. Why don't you describe it to me so I know what I'm looking for?"

"Okay," said Lissa. "My side of our bedroom is pink! Kari's side is lavender. That's like purple, but faded."

That wasn't what she'd had in mind. But it kept the twins distracted and on the phone with her, so it sufficed. When a squabble broke out between the sisters, she felt a flash of amusement. She embraced it. Anything but the dread that could so easily paralyze her.

There was a warning beep from her phone. Oh, no. Oh, yes. She'd forgotten to charge her phone the night before, just like always.

Marley raised her voice to cut across their argument about pastel rainbows. "Girls, my phone battery is about to die. I'll be there in ten minutes, all right? Just wait for me. Don't do anything—" The phone turned off.

Swearing, Marley yanked the earpiece out of her ear and threw it on the seat beside her. Now the twins didn't even have her voice to keep them company. And she had no easy way to fend off her own crazy worries.

She couldn't afford to pull over and have a panic attack. Instead, she turned the radio up and rolled down the windows of her little car as she wove through L.A. traffic. The blue sky was tinted by a brown haze of smog mixed with smoke. The fires that sometimes swept the San Gabriel mountains had started up once again a couple of days ago. Marley inhaled deeply, filling her nostrils with the stench of August traffic, and tried to identify each scent: gasoline, charred rubber, hot asphalt, dust, and the tang of fried food. Sensory distraction. She couldn't smell the wildfire smoke yet.

News of an accident came on the radio, and she changed the station. She did her best to ground herself in the here and now, to be mindful of what was and not worry about what might be. It was something her doctor had recommended as a way of fending off the anxiety attacks, and usually she couldn't do it. But this time, two children depended on her. It was so rare that anybody or anything really needed her. It gave her focus. It wouldn't last—it never did. But all she had to do was hang on until Zachariah showed up again.

She managed to distract herself so well with the details of palm trees and the number of sports cars on the road that she almost missed the turn for Zachariah's home. It was an expensive neighborhood, near the Huntington Library, with landscaped green lawns and enormous homes bordered by Italian cypresses and shaded by carefully tended olive trees. Zachariah's home was a Mission-style structure behind a wall that protected an emerald lawn. His red SUV was parked in the long driveway.

He'd come home. Or the kids had been playing a prank on her. Thank heavens. She'd find out what was going on, at least.

But as she stepped out of her car, the front door flew open and the twins scurried out to wrap their arms around her waist. "You came!" said one of them. They were tiny children, dressed in identical denim shorts but with different colored tops so clueless adults could tell them apart. They both had long auburn hair tied up in pigtails with ribbons that matched their t-shirts.

"Zachariah's car is here," she pointed out to them after she bent to return their hugs.

"We know that!" Kari put her hands on her hips. "I said he went into his study and didn't come out. I did!"

Marley remembered that, but she'd dismissed it out of hand; the twins had such active imaginations. "Well, let's go look in his study. Maybe he has a secret door." He didn't, she knew, have a job outside the house. She wasn't sure he had a normal job at all; she had the impression that a trust fund paid the bills so he could devote all his attention to the twins. He seemed to have a full schedule shuttling them between a dizzying array of art and dance and music classes, along with playdates at the park where Marley had originally met the family.

She took the girls' hands and let them drag her up the veranda stairs and into the house. The inside was as lovely and well tended as the exterior, with polished wooden floors and plush, pale carpets. It was also so air-conditioned that she was glad she'd worn jeans.

The twins dragged her down the hall, past the wide staircase and what looked like a formal sitting room to a door standing ajar. "This is the study," said Lissa. She pulled her hand from Marley's and laced her fingers together, fidgeting.

Nervousness twisted through Marley; she shook her head in irritation at herself and pushed the door open. The only way to know what was beyond was to look and see.

It was a very old-fashioned library, dark-paneled and windowless, with bookshelves covering most of the walls. One lamp illuminated the heavy, antique desk, and another created a warm circle of light around a leather armchair. Marley, who'd dropped out of her grad program in English lit, was immediately envious.

But there was definitely no Zachariah. She glanced down at the twins and then untangled her hand from Kari's. "I'm going to look around. Maybe I can find a clue to where he went."

The twins stared up at her, lip-biting reflections of each other. Then Kari shrugged. "Okay. But don't you leave us here." She absentmindedly took Lissa's hand and they watched, framed in the doorway.

Marley wanted to examine the bookshelves, but that was the curiosity of a bibliophile more than anything else, and she knew it. Instead, she went to Zachariah's desk. There was a slim, curved computer screen to one side, so elegant and subtle that, at first, she thought he didn't have a computer. Since it was turned off, it wasn't nearly as interesting as the cellphone lying on its side in the center of the desk. She picked it up as she continued looking around. Other than the computer and the phone, there were books neatly arranged between stone bookends on one side of the desk and ordinary mail and writing supplies on the other side. The books were a mix of economic studies and paperback science books, with one collection of fairy tales at the end.

The cellphone was a sleek black bar that lit up when she touched it, displaying a picture of a lightning storm. "Did you call me from this?"

"No, we have our own phones!" Kari came into the room, fishing a bright green flip phone out of her pocket.

Marley raised her eyebrows. It was smaller than an adult phone, and when she opened it, it only had five buttons other than the arrow keys: a silhouette of a house, a man, a woman, and two keys to start and end calls. The house button had been inexpertly colored pink with a marker. The branding on the phone announced it as the Senyaza Beacon. "How did you dial my number?"

"Uncle Zach put your number in here, see?" Kari pressed the "woman" button and Marley's name and number flashed on the screen.

That startled Marley. Until now, she hadn't really wondered about why the twins had called her in particular—she'd been too busy trying not to panic. The twins seemed very attached to her, even though they mostly saw each other at the park or on lunch dates. But surely Zachariah had other, more important people to program into a dedicated button on the twins' phones. Surely?

She didn't really know what her relationship with Zachariah was, other than one of the few bright spots in her life. While they'd flirted some, they'd never been on a date without the kids. Sometimes he looked at her with such intensity that she shivered. But the girls had teachers, and knew other parents—people with a much better idea of how to take care of children in an emergency. Marley could barely take care of a kitten.

She bit her lip and scowled down at Zachariah's phone, searching out the contacts list. It was as long as she would have expected, full of names and businesses. None of them shouted out Very Important. She flipped over to the recently called list, and scrolled through the shorter list of names. Today: Corbin. Grendel. Yesterday: Annalise. Tia. The day before: herself. A number without a name.

The missed calls list was even more opaque. A call from Senyaza Corp. A call from an unlisted number. A call from—what? Instead of a number, a strange black and white image flickered on the screen. It reminded her of animated tribal art, and after only a few seconds, it made her eyes water. She looked away.

She thought she should call some of the numbers, and find out if anybody knew what happened to Zachariah. Perhaps somebody had called him away, and picked him up. But she couldn't call strangers and ask about Zachariah with the twins staring at her expectantly.

"Does anything seem out of place to you guys?" Kari's mouth opened and Marley quickly added, "Other than Zachariah being gone." Kari's mouth closed again.

"That." Lissa pointed across the room, to the small round table beside the armchair. "Book's out of place and the ball is new. We're supposed to put books away." A large book was on the table, and on top of the book were a thick golden candle and an iridescent glass ball the size of Marley's fist. The positioning was very strange; surely the candle would damage the book if it was ever lit. And something about the ball bothered Marley; it seemed no more substantial than a soap bubble. In the relentlessly tidy home, the odd arrangement seemed both deliberate and out of character. The back of Marley's neck prickled.

"Pretty ball. Can I play with it?" Kari moved closer to the tableau.

Marley snapped, "Stop, Kari. I'll look at it." Then she closed her mouth tightly. She hadn't meant to sound so harsh.

The words had just slipped out, before she'd even thought them. But the little girl froze obediently. Marley moved past her. The orb looked like it might roll off the table and pop from an unwary breath. As she stepped closer, the hairs on her arm rose. There was a barely audible sizzle.

She lifted the candle off the book. That was enough to knock the ball off as well, and she caught it in one hand, or tried to. As soon as her fingers touched it, it burst into a puff of dust. There was a bright light and a flash of heat near her hand.

Marley blinked. She blinked again. Between blinks, the room changed. For just a heartbeat, she saw the table knocked over, the computer thrown off the desk, the rug askew and crumpled on the floor. A voice whispered, "Come and play." And everywhere, there were the dried leaves of autumn.

She blinked once more. Everything was tidy and straight, just as it had been when she entered.

Almost everything. The candle in her hand was burned halfway down, and the book on the table was gone.

-two-

Marley stared from the candle to the table and then looked at the twins. They stood close to each other, both looking at Marley with interest, their fear apparently forgotten. Carefully she put the candle down and rubbed at her eyes. "Where did the book go?" She might have mistaken the state of the candle but the presence of the book? Never.

Kari looked around as if trying to spot it, while Lissa cocked her head, staring at the floor. Then she said, "Somebody put it away?"

Marley blinked down at her. "Who? When?" Lissa just shrugged, staring back up at her with big blue eyes.

Marley blew out her breath. The kids were cute when telling her about their toys or an adventure, but trying to get useful information out of them was like deciphering a language last studied in junior high. She examined the bookshelves, trying to extract the title of the missing book from the image in her memory. She was good at noticing books. There'd been a curlicue font on the spine. "Something Tales," she thought.

Books filled every shelf, edge to edge. Apparently Zachariah didn't ever leave books out when he was reading them. *Or he never read them*, a cynical little voice suggested.

Out of the corner of her eye, Marley saw something move. She stared hard at Zachariah's desk and at last decided it must have been the screensaver on the computer, just barely visible from this angle. It hadn't been off after all. She looked away and spotted the single gap in the rows of books.

Or perhaps he only uses one book at a time, she continued the argument with herself, walking over to the gap. It was at least as wide as the large book had been. Near the back, something pale glimmered.

The shelf was just above eye-level, so she rose on her toes and reached in. Dust puffed out. A tube of paper was tucked into the back, tied with a silver ribbon. It seemed like pages torn from a book, with that heavy, solid paper found in commercial journals. It was covered in the same dust—or was it ash? She caught a whiff of wood smoke.

Marley stared at the roll of paper for a long moment. The feeling stole over her that she was standing on the edge of a vast ocean, a strange surf washing her toes. What had just happened?

Come and play.

Something moved at the corner of her vision again, dark and low to the ground. She glanced up, her skin prickling, and saw only bookshelves.

At the door to the study, the twins stood holding hands again. "Marley? What's that roll?" asked Kari.

Marley shivered. She wanted to get out of this house with its strange shadows and the strange thoughts they inspired. She crossed to the desk and put Zachariah's cellphone into her purse. "I don't know. Let's go back to my place and I'll call some people and we'll find your uncle."

Lissa brightened. "A slumber party?"

"Uh," said Marley. "Sure."

"Okay! I'll go pack!" Lissa ran out of sight.

Kari lingered in the doorframe, though, watching Marley. Marley turned the rolled pages over in her hand. If she was imagining the moving shadows, then it was probably nothing more meaningful than a lost collection of laundry bills. It was certainly too dusty to be anything recently handled by Zachariah.

Marley put the roll down. She *wanted* it to be laundry bills. And she wanted to get away from this windowless room with its moving darkness. She wanted to find somebody else, somebody who knew what was going on. Zachariah must have been insane to make her a point of contact for the kids. He *knew* the state her life was in. She liked the kids, but she wasn't in any position to look after them.

"Where's your mother, Kari?" Zachariah had never said anything direct about the twins' mother. She'd picked up the impression that she was away rather than dead, though.

Kari shrugged. "Dunno."

"If I can't find your uncle, is there somebody else I should call? A neighbor? A teacher? Another uncle?"

Kari gave her a confused look. "There's just Uncle Zach. He said to push the lady button for you if we couldn't find him."

Marley mulled that over. The thing was, Zachariah *wasn't* insane. He was one of the most practical and prepared people she'd ever met. So what was he thinking? "What sorts of things does he say about me?"

"He says you're very pretty and very special and he wishes you weren't so sad all the time."

Marley said, "Oh," then mumbled, "That started off well, but now I wonder if maybe he's been talking to my mother."

Kari frowned. "What?"

"Never mind!" Marley said quickly. "Let's go see what your sister is packing." She followed the tiny girl upstairs to the bedroom the twins shared.

Lissa had pulled out a backpack as large as she was and was stuffing it full of toys. Marley found herself attempting to convince both children that toys weren't the only component of a slumber party. Eventually, she found it was easier to just explore the room and pack for the girls herself, judiciously choosing from among the girls' many suggestions.

Partway through stuffing a favorite blanket into a miniature duffel bag, something else occurred to Marley: Had Zachariah, always so prepared, *expected* to vanish? He'd warned them to call her. She wished she could get answers from the children on the matter. Yet it was clear they barely understood the situation as anything more than a new and semi-frightening game.

It was that question, though, that made her stop by the study on the way out of the house and pick up the rolled sheaf of papers again. A very quick glance showed her that it wasn't a laundry list; the pages were densely filled with handwriting that was incomprehensible at first glance. She rolled them up again. The bundle was weird, and so was Zachariah's disappearance. Even if it was creepy, she couldn't ignore it.

She also took a sheet of stationery and wrote a note to Zachariah, explaining that the children had called her and where to find them. She left the note on the table in the entryway and went outside, leaving the door unlocked behind her.

As she was loading the girl's stuff into the back of her hatchback, the girls peeked in the windows of her car. Kari said, "You don't have seats in your car!"

At first, Marley was puzzled. Of course she had seats. Then she remembered that babies and small children were supposed to ride around in special booster seats.

"Nope. You can ride in the grown-up seats, though."

The twins exchanged looks. Lissa shook her head. "No, Marley. Have to have carseats." She sounded absolutely convinced of this. "Can't ride in a car without carseats."

Kari said, "*We* have carseats. They buckle in." She pointed at Zachariah's SUV. Marley peered in the window and saw a matching pair of miniature bucket seats installed on the back bench. She tried the door.

"It's locked. Do you know where the keys are?"

The twins exchanged another wide-eyed look. "In Uncle's Zach's pocket," Lissa said.

Marley pressed her fingers to the bridge of her nose. She hadn't had a chance for breakfast and she was starting to miss it. Eyeing the house, she wondered if she could convince the kids to come along without the carseats. She really didn't want to stay here; whatever had happened to Zachariah could happen again. She pushed that thought away reflexively. But she did want to go home, where it was safe, and where she had breakfast and her medication.

She tried all the other doors of the SUV, just in case. They were all locked. So she leaned on the hood and looked at the tiny girls. They were whispering to each other, arguing.

Lissa raised her voice. "If you don't, Kari, she'll leave us, too!" There was a touch of hysteria to Lissa's childish syllables, and Kari looked frightened and guilty.

I burned the kitchen down. Will you leave now, too? Marley flushed at the surge of memory and shook her head. "Never," she said fiercely. "I'd never do that to you." She'd spent too much of her own adolescence dreading the same thing.

Lissa gave her a frustrated look. "But we need our carseats."

Kari gave a little shriek and turned to face the SUV door. "All right!" She gave Marley a sulky look and added, "It's a secret. Uncle Zach doesn't know."

Then she touched the door. The click of the internal latch unlocking was very loud. Kari hauled on the door handle and the door popped open. With a defiant look, she scrambled up into one of the carseats and sat in it, arms crossed.

Marley opened her mouth. She closed her mouth. Finally, she unglued her tongue from the roof of her mouth. "Can you hotwire the engine, too?" At the girl's blank look, she rephrased. "Can you start the car, too?"

"No!" said Kari. She looked like she was about to cry.

Marley peered at the door. It didn't seem to have any high-tech sensors. "Can you unlock other doors? Like the door to the house?"

"She can," whispered Lissa. Kari shot her an ugly look.

Marley's mouth went on using autopilot while she scrambled frantically for a real thought. "We have to put the seats in my car. Let's figure out how to unstrap them."

"There's pictures," Lissa said, pointing at the side of Kari's seat.

So there were, little pictorial instructions printed on the plastic. For a few moments, Marley concentrated on straps and buckles. When she had the kids buckled into their carseats in the back of her hatchback, she sat down in the driver's seat and leaned her head against the steering wheel. Then she got out of the car, went to the house, and locked the front door. If she had to get back in, she didn't need a key—she had Kari! She paused at the SUV long enough to reach inside and snag Zachariah's car cellphone charger before relocking the vehicle. In her own car, she fussed at plugging it in and connecting her phone for a moment.

Lissa said timidly, "Are you mad, Marley?"

Marley sighed and started the car. "No. Just surprised." Missing uncles and strange visions and secret powers in little kids—it was a lot to absorb. All she could do was concentrate on the details she could influence: where they would sleep, what they would eat, how she'd keep them from breaking her stuff. Charging her phone.

She was keenly aware of her anti-anxiety medication finally kicking in; it let her relax and let go of concern over the strangeness of the morning. Without the medication, she'd be a quivering ball of panicked indecision, convinced the worst imaginable horrors were going to happen and overwhelmed by her inability to stop them. Crazy. *With* the medication, the constant nagging fears all drifted away, banished into a distant blur somewhere over the mental horizon. It was just as hard to get work done and bills paid while medicated as it was while crazy, but at least she wasn't panicking about it. That was something. Some mornings, like this morning, it was everything.

-three-

Some things, though, had to be taken care of as soon as possible, even if it was difficult. Marley flipped open her phone and dialed the number of Branwyn, her roommate. She had no idea what to say, but thought the more warning she gave of the impending preschooler infestation, the better.

When Branwyn answered, Marley said, "Action Girl, I think I've ended up in your plot by mistake." They'd known each other since before junior high, and by now the old games were reflex.

"Research Girl, is evil afoot?" Branwyn responded around a yawn.

Marley's gaze flicked to the image of the twins in the rearview mirror, each looking out a window. "I don't know. I hope not."

"Use your magic visor, Research Girl!" Branwyn cried. Her voice dropped to a quieter register and she added, "So what's up?"

"I have some guests that will be staying with us for a bit. Combined ages: around eight."

"So what you're saying is: I should cancel the naked kegger I was just now dreaming up. That's fine, I can do that. Is it the kids of your park boyfriend?"

Marley made a face. "He's not…yes, them."

"Where's he, then?"

"I'm not sure."

Thoughtfully, Branwyn asked, "Is he at a kegger?"

"Branwyn! What is it with you and keggers today?"

"Guys at work. It's fun to say. Kegger. Kegger." Branwyn rolled the word across her tongue.

"He's more of a James Bond martini gala guy, anyhow, I think."

"Oh, we could do that. The gazebo. With action figures." Branwyn paused, and then said with the faintest hint of accusation, "Except we can't. Because now we've got the preschoolers. While he's off drinking all the martinis."

"Actually, I almost hope that's true." Once again, Marley pushed away visions of other situations Zachariah could be involved in. She injected a cheery note into her voice as she added, "On the bright side, there's no deposit for kids!"

"Strange but true. Maybe we can sell one to pay the pet deposit for your cat."

Marley had rescued the kitten that now lived in their apartment from the shrubberies under the apartment window almost a month ago and named it Neath. She'd promised Branwyn, who already paid most of their shared bills, that she'd come up with the pet deposit the apartment required herself. Her income from book reviews and the occasional magazine article was so unsteady, though. And it was so hard to get out of bed most days…

Marley hissed into the phone, and then said, "Don't joke like that when they can hear you. It's a sensitive situation. I'll give you the details later."

"When they aren't listening to every word you say? Fair

enough. You remember Smile Girl's coming over tonight, right? She has gifts from Europe for us." Smile Girl, or Penny to the rest of the world, was the third member of their little trio. They'd drifted through high school together, and stayed close through college and beyond.

Marley frowned. "I thought she wasn't back until Thursday. I mean, that's great, but—"

"It *is* Thursday, Marley." Branwyn sighed.

Marley winced. "Oh. Right."

There was a banging on the other end of the line. "We'll talk later, all right? I have to run." The phone clicked off.

Marley drove the rest of the way home in silence, with the kids lost in their own thoughts. Once she parked and turned off the engine, though, that changed.

The girls unstrapped themselves from their carseats before Marley had gotten her own seatbelt off, and a back door flew open. Kari shaded her eyes, looking around the parking lot. "Where's your house?" The lot was small, with both covered and uncovered parking. There was a Dumpster in the corner nearest the road. Her nearby apartment building rose up six floors, with fire escapes leading from the higher apartments. Neatly groomed flowering shrubberies lined the walk to the mailboxes and brightened up the woodchip beds.

Lissa banged on the back of the car. "Open up! I need my stuff!"

Marley pointed out her apartment's window to Kari as she opened the trunk. She filled her arms with the twins' belongings, and then juggled them until she had a free hand to grab her own things. Lissa carried a stuffed penguin.

Marley looked around for Kari, who had vanished. She blew out her breath, tried to look around with the eyes of a preschooler, and then marched over to the dumpster. Kari was around one corner, inspecting a stinking, stained armchair.

"Hey, you." Marley said. "Stay near me." She looked

around. Now Lissa was gone.

But not gone far; she was kneeling down in the wood-chips outside the door Marley had pointed out, showing them to her penguin. "Go to your sister, Kari," she ordered, and walked after her, feeling like a sheepdog.

Once she got her own door open, the twins brushed past her into the interior of the apartment. Then Lissa stopped dead, blocking the door. "It's hot in here," she announced, like one faced with an insurmountable problem.

Marley maneuvered around her and dropped all their stuff in a heap on the couch. She debated trying to explain to the child that she didn't have the air conditioning resources of their uncle, and decided to go with a simple, "Yes," instead.

Lissa looked up at her and then spotted the calico kitten Neath on the back of the couch. "Kitty!"

"Marley, where's the bathroom?" called Kari from the hallway.

Marley ran both hands through her hair and hurried to Kari, showing her the open door two steps away. "Do you, uh, need help?"

Kari said cheerfully, "Nope!" and shut the door in her face.

She turned around, and found Lissa hugging Neath to her like the kitten was a plush doll. "Lissa, no, don't hold her like that!"

Still squeezing the cat, Lissa gave her a puzzled look. Marley took a deep breath. Then she rescued Neath from Lissa's embrace. Quietly, she sat the girl down and showed her how to pet the kitten gently. Neath sat in Lissa's lap, staring at her with amazed kitten eyes.

After a few minutes, she moved on to showing Lissa how to entice Neath to play by waving a cat fishing pole.

It was the splashing of water that made her realize that Kari had been in the bathroom for a while. She went to the bathroom door while watching Lissa and Neath play, and called, "Is everything all right?"

"Yes! Um, where are the towels?"

Marley pushed the door open. Kari stood on top of the toilet lid, leaning over the sink. The faucet ran steadily. She'd pushed down the stopper and the sink was overflowing.

The little girl gave her a guilty look. "It's so hot. I just wanted to splash."

"Did you consider turning off the water?" Marley leaned over and did just that.

Kari's wide eyes looked startled. "What?"

Marley shook her head and sighed. She dragged a towel off a rack and dropped it on the floor. Then she picked the damp girl up. She turned around, holding Kari under one arm like a sack of cat food, and almost had a heart attack.

Neath was on top of one of the tall bookshelves that lined the walls of the living room, an impressive but not unusual feat. Lissa had apparently been inspired, though. She was almost to the top of the same bookcase, cat fishing pole clenched between her teeth. Near the top, she'd paused to look at the books on the high shelf, and with a frightening clarity, Marley could see her grip slipping.

Still holding Kari under her other arm, she dove forward. She wasn't anywhere near close enough when Lissa's grip slipped entirely and she fell backward, clutching a book in one hand.

Pain spiked in Marley's head as she stumbled. Lissa seemed to rotate mid-fall, so that she was oriented feet down, rather than head down. Marley had seen Neath do the same thing, but this didn't seem nearly as coordinated.

Lissa thumped to the floor on both feet and then fell onto her butt. "Ow," she said, spitting out the cat fishing pole. Then she inspected the book she'd grabbed. "Uncle read this to us!" she said, and looked up. Her grin faded as she saw Marley on her knees.

Marley released Kari and fell to one side. She rolled over and stared up at the ceiling, waiting for her racing heart to slow down. "This is crazy. How do kids survive childhood?" She thought about that. "How do *parents* survive childhood?"

"I'm sorry, Marley," cried Lissa. "Look, I'm being good." She scrambled over to the couch where Marley had left her and sat down again. "Kari, you clean up your mess! Don't you make Marley angry." She hugged her penguin.

Kari grumbled something and went back to the bathroom. Before Marley could roll to her feet and follow her, because she suspected good intentions meant *nothing*, Kari reappeared again, holding a medicine bottle.

"Are you sick, Marley?" She shook it and a few remaining pills rattled.

Marley grabbed it away from her. "No. Those are so I don't get sick." She thought about that and then added, "And they're only for me. You don't take any medicine, pills, or candy in this house that I don't give you, all right?"

Kari gave her a quiet look and nodded once. Then she went past Marley to climb onto the couch and sit beside Lissa. After a minute, she stuck her thumb in her mouth.

Marley leaned against a wall, looking at the two miserable little figures. Then she looked at the apartment's living room. Three of Branwyn's art awards had been knocked off the shelf Lissa had been climbing, and she brushed them off and put them back.

She snuck another glance at the kids. She couldn't make them just sit on the couch all day, even if they seemed willing to try. They were clearly nervous and worried about the situation. Her own worries about abandonment were too different to give her any idea of what to do next.

She went to her phone and texted a query to Branwyn, who had six younger siblings to Marley's own one. A response came back: *Do familiar things.*

That was how, forty minutes later, she found herself pulling into the little lot of the nearby park the girls usually visited, carrying bags of fast food.

It was a pleasant place, with live oaks mixed with palms along a jogging trail that passed some volleyball courts. Hardy grass struggled to remain green in the blistering summer heat. There was a truly magnificent playground, which was probably why Zachariah originally brought them there. It usually had more kids than it did today, but Marley was glad to find it nearly empty.

After lunch at a picnic table, Marley sat on a bench with an unopened book beside her. This was familiar, all right. The only thing missing was Zachariah himself, sprawled on another bench chatting with her, or hunched over a sleek palmtop computer. She usually enjoyed the role of part-time observer and playmate, while Zachariah was the one really responsible for the twins. Dammit, where the hell had he gone? These weren't her kids!

Marley thought about that for a moment, and then fumbled for Zachariah's phone. Now was the right time to start investigating those numbers. She opened the phone and looked at the recent calls again. Some of the names were really odd. But she was familiar with Senyaza Corporation, at least; it was one of the big transnational electronics companies. She'd picked up the idea that he had business with them, maybe even worked for them as some sort of contractor. If so, he probably had friends there.

She tried the number, and reached a computerized operator that instructed her to state the name or enter the extension of the person she wanted to reach. She hesitated, and almost hung up, before saying, "Zachariah Thorne."

There was a click. The computer voice said, "I will connect you to the Department of Special Investigations and Threats."

Another voice picked up, this one a recording of a man

with a faint British accent. "Hey. We're all busy fighting monsters right now, but you can leave a message by pressing 1. Do remember to tell us the name of the scallywag in question."

Carefully, Marley hung up. She wasn't sure if that meant Zachariah worked for this Department of Special Investigations and Threats, or if they considered him a "scallywag," and in any case, she wasn't desperate enough to leave random messages. Yet.

She frowned, flipping through the phone contact list, trying to decide who to call next. The idea of telling random strangers that Zachariah had vanished and she had his children did not excite her. Who knew how they'd react?

As if reading her mind, a voice behind her said, "Kidnapping is a federal crime, you know."

-four-

Marley looked up. A man stood behind the bench, gazing over the playground. He was clean-shaven, with blond hair. His hands were in the pockets of an expensive grey suit.

"Were you talking to me?" Marley asked, wondering when he'd shown up. There was a white minivan sitting beside her car in the parking lot, with a figure in the driver's seat.

His eyes, blue like the sea, flicked to her, and a smile crooked one corner of his mouth. "Yes. But I don't want this to end up in the courts, do you?"

Marley stood up. "What the hell are you talking about?"

The man's smile faded and he looked exasperated. "The children, Miss Claviger. The ones you kidnapped from their uncle's home."

Marley stopped breathing. Then she inhaled and snapped, "Who the hell *are* you?"

"The designated guardian of those children in the event that Zachariah Thorne is unavailable to care for them. Jeremy White." A business card materialized between his fingers.

"I didn't see your name in his phone." Without taking

her eyes off him, Marley raised her voice, calling to the girls. When they ran over to her, she said, "Do you two know this man?"

They shook their heads, pressing shyly against her sides. She looked up at Jeremy White again, narrowing her eyes.

He sighed. "Whether they recognize me is irrelevant to whether or not the courts do. But if you release them to me now, I'll make sure no charges are pressed." He reached out for her hand.

Marley looked down as he slid the business card between her fingers, and saw "Attorney at Law" printed under his name, and his expensive watch, and a swirling tattoo peeking out from his shirt sleeve.

Through numb lips, she said, "How did you even know he was gone?"

"He called me. Right before he left." He smiled and added, "From his house phone."

Kari said eagerly, "Why did he go?"

Lissa added, "Where is he?"

The lawyer directed his smile at the kids. "He's on a plane flight right now." He glanced up at Marley again. "He'll be calling tonight to talk to the kids. I was supposed to pick them up from the house earlier, but I was... delayed." He frowned and then shook his head. "To be honest, I'm looking forward to finding out what's going on. He was distracted when he called me."

Marley felt cold, despite the blazing sun. What he said made sense. He'd already convinced the children; she could feel them pulling away from her. But she wanted to find a hole in his story. "How did you know I had them?"

His teeth showed again, not unkindly. "You left a note."

"Oh." She'd meant that for Zachariah. And she'd locked the door. Hadn't she? She felt thick and stupid. His smile was really beautiful, and he was being so patient with her. What had possessed her to just take the children anyhow? Zachariah *must* have had a different plan; he knew how incompetent she was at running her own life these days. The children had a trust fund; with trust funds came lawyers, and a whole slew of people to take care of what needed taking care of.

She felt dizzy. "Did you know their mother?"His smile faded, and his blue gaze went far away. For a moment, it felt like Marley had been released from a crushing pressure.

"Nineveh," he murmured, and his gaze snapped back to Marley. "Yes. A very special young woman." His broad smile returned. "Perhaps Zachariah's finally tracked her down."

The sense of pressure returned. He was so believable. So genuine. Those blue eyes were drowning her.

But she'd had a chance to breathe, for just a moment. She fought back. "I want to see some kind of documentation."

He gave her a concerned look and said, very quietly, "You're the one who kidnapped them, Miss Claviger, and I'm the lawyer. All I need to do is call the police. That would be so upsetting, don't you think? And unnecessary, too."

Then he knelt down and held out a hand to each twin. "Ready to go talk to your uncle?"

Kari and Lissa seemed mesmerized. They stepped away from her.

Marley's world cracked open. The sky howled above her. She stumbled and fell against the bench, bruising her hip. The pain became a flash of vision: the twins crying and screaming, furious and fading away. The pain throbbed again and the vision vanished, a shout of despair burning Marley's throat. She panted and squeezed her eyes shut against the spinning around her.

When she went to rub her face, she realized she was holding each girl tightly by a wrist. They nuzzled up against her. A tiny hand pressed against her cheek. "Are you sick, Marley?" asked Lissa.

"Do you need your pills?" asked Kari. She looked over at Jeremy. "Can she come with us? She's our friend."

Her pills. Maybe it was time to up her dose again, she thought blearily. She hadn't had an attack that vivid since high school, before she'd started the medication. Those attacks had never faded quickly, but this time the screaming fear that had overcome her was gone already, leaving just the physical after-effects of the adrenaline rush. Score one for medical science.

"What pills are these?" asked the interested voice of the lawyer. "Are you ill, Miss Claviger?"

"No!" She glared up at him and maintained her grip on the girls. Now she could see the face beneath the sweet concern that was painted on like clown makeup. Under the glow of good intentions, he was impatient, careless, and stressed. *The twins had been told to call her.* She ran her mind over the previous conversation and found more questions, more inconsistencies that troubled her. Zachariah's cellphone. The children's ignorance. But none were so disturbing as the overwhelming pressure she'd felt when he looked at her.

"No. You're lying, Mr. White. About something... maybe about everything. Go away. I'm going to take care of the girls until their uncle comes for them." *Somehow.*

He looked taken aback. "That could be a while." She shrugged. He studied her and then shook his head. "No. I can't trust you. You can't even stand up straight. Do you really want to fight me on this? Because I'll win, and it won't be good for you."

Marley raised her chin defiantly. "Bring it." She realized another man had moved in from the other side of the park, lurking just out of earshot. The new guy was tall, dark-haired, and ragged-looking, just like the crows that took to the air ahead of him. He stared at her so intently that she thought he must be associated with the lawyer. An enforcer. There was somebody in the minivan, too, draped over the steering wheel. She remembered her vision of the study in disarray and wondered if the lawyer meant a real, physical fight, right now. *What had happened to Zachariah?*

Jeremy moved closer again and dropped his voice to a near whisper, as if he wanted to make sure nobody overheard them. "Believe me, Miss Claviger: You do *not* want to fight me on this. My allies are more dangerous than you can imagine. They are also exceedingly powerful. If you cooperate, we will compensate you for the inconvenience you've suffered thus far."

"No!" Once again, his urging seemed genuine, and Marley couldn't bear it. She rose to her feet and ducked around him, pulling the kids after her. Why, oh why was the park so empty of the normal family groups? Would the people at the baseball diamond hear her if she screamed?

Jeremy White followed her, as if he didn't believe the conversation was over. She went to her car and opened it, pointing inside. Kari balked. "I want to see Uncle Zach. I'm tired of this game."

"I can take you," said the lawyer quickly. "Miss Claviger can come, too. I'm sure Mr. Thorne and his companions would like to speak with her. We've plenty of room in the van. Or you could follow us."

"Uncle Zach can call us, Kari. And I'm sure he will when Mr. White tells him I'm being stubborn." She looked nervously at the lawyer as he put his hand in his pocket, but he only pulled out a smartphone.

Lissa leaned to Kari and whispered, "Marley's the one who will take care of us, Uncle Zach said. And that man is weird. Look at..." and they both looked up at Jeremy. Kari frowned. Then she turned and climbed inside the car, Lissa following her. Marley shut the door and turned to look at him.

"Gonna make any calls on that? Direct to Zachariah?"

He glanced at the phone, tapped the screen, then said irritably, "I said he was on a plane right now. And not the sort that allows incoming calls." He studied her in apparent puzzlement. She stared back, as fiercely as she could. Finally, he shrugged. As he resettled his jacket, the tattoo flashed again. "We'll meet again, Miss Claviger."

"Bring a bailiff next time."

He touched two fingers to his brow in an absentminded salute as he turned away.

She watched him until he got into his vehicle. He had a discussion with the other person, and then the van drove away.

After it was out of sight, she looked around the park again. The other man had vanished as well, and she wondered if he'd even been involved. Probably not. Maybe his presence had even encouraged Jeremy White to leave. She felt a twinge of guilt for thinking the worst of him.

"Are we going home?" Lissa asked.

Marley weighed her options. "No. We were only going to leave if that man didn't. You can go play more."

But she didn't just sit on the bench watching after that. She stayed close, and she studied every adult who entered the park through narrowed eyes.

-five-

Penny, I'm so happy to see you!" Marley held the apartment door open so her friend could manhandle two large shopping bags into the living room. The twins, sitting at the table eating dinner, watched curiously.

"Yes! I'm glad to be back. I really missed all the local comforts, and you guys." Penny put the bags on the floor and paused to look over Marley, so Marley returned the favor.

Of course, Penny always looked good. She wore expensive makeup, chosen to subtly accentuate her bronze skin and enhance her brown eyes. Her clothes, as always, were stunning: a blue wraparound skirt and an off-the-shoulder white blouse accented with chunky gold jewelry. Shoulder-length dark hair curled artfully around her face, and her fingernails, when she pushed it away, were recently manicured.

"You cut your hair," Marley remarked before hugging her. "I think it looks good."

"I'm still getting used to it," Penny confessed. "Sometimes I'm not sure it was a good idea. But you—look at you. Branwyn said you're taking care of Zach's little girls?"

Marley twisted her mouth in a half-smile. "Something

like that. They're eating dinner right now. They asked me for macaroni and cheese. That seemed reasonable, right?"

"It's on every kids' menu in the country."

"Yeah, that's what I thought. But guess what Zachariah never lets them eat?"

Penny looked puzzled. "What, never?"

Marley smirked. "He gives them 'cine fredo' instead."

Penny considered. "That makes sense, actually. Kind of European. I didn't see a lot of kids' menus there. But how'd you find out?"

"It turns out four-year-olds, even really bright ones, aren't very good at lying. Come on, I want to introduce you."

Penny looked the girls over. "Being that adorable should be a crime. My mother would flip. How can you tell them apart without the different shirts?"

Marley said, "It's a knack. You'll get the hang of it. Lissa, Kari, this is my friend Penny." She pointed at each of them as she named them. Both girls looked shyly down at their dinner.

Then Penny pulled out two boxes from one of her bags. "I just got back from a trip and I brought presents for everybody, including you two. Do you want to open them?"

Shyness was secondary to opening presents, it seemed. The girls bounced out of their chairs to seize on the wrapped packages. Each box contained a butterfly-winged fairy fashion doll. Kari immediately pulled out all the accessories, while Lissa took hers back to the table to examine as she finished dinner. Unprompted, Kari whispered, "Thank you," and Lissa looked up, blushed, and echoed the statement.

"Well done," said Marley, to both Penny and the girls.

"I picked them up on my way over," said Penny, pleased. "Here, this is for you."

Marley opened a box to reveal a thick burgundy book. Its cover was fine leather over wood, and the blank pages had the look of handmade paper. She inspected the binding and smiled, then turned to the fragment of handwritten verse inside the cover.

Cobbles like scales
on a dragon's back
she sleeps, chained by concrete
her dreams secrets swallowed long ago
in another world she wakes
and these constructs fall away.
But what

"You didn't finish it," she commented.

Penny looked down, the flush of embarrassment in her cheeks only visible to an experienced eye. "It wasn't very good anyhow. I only wish I'd realized it before I tarnished your gift. I thought about getting you something else, but—" She paused and then said, "But did you see the paper? I watched them make a book just like it in Rome. You would have loved it, Marley."

Marley smiled again, running a finger down the spine. Bookmaking and its history had fascinated her through high school and college. Even though she'd dropped out of grad school when she realized just how little application her literary studies had to the real world, she still appreciated the props of the field. It was nostalgia for her youthful daydreams, but sweet all the same.

She kissed Penny on the cheek. "It's lovely. Thank you."

"When is Branwyn coming home? I can't stay too late."

Surprised, Marley said, "No? I thought we'd hang out, order pizza, and you could tell us about Europe." She'd hoped for that, for some normality in her day.

Penny smiled, radiant. "Well, I'd been planning on it, but a guy I met in Rome called me this afternoon. He's from

L.A., too, and now that he's back in town, he wants to have dinner with me tonight!"

"Oh, that's great!" Marley tried to hide her disappointment, but Penny's smile faded.

"Are you sure? I mean, I didn't know about the kids when he called. I do want the scoop on how you ended up babysitting them, you know."

"Not quite sure of that myself," Marley muttered. The day had taken on a dreamlike quality that seemed far away from the whoosh-whoosh noises the girls were making as they flew their fairy dolls around the table. "I wanted to get your help with something, though."

She fumbled around until she came up with the sheaf of pages she'd taken from Zachariah's study. She'd opened it again after coming home from the park, hoping against expectation that it was actually a useful legal document or something similar. Instead she'd found... strangeness. Strangeness she hadn't had time to investigate before the twins had needed her help with something. "I found this under mysterious circumstances, and you like puzzles, so I wanted to see what you made of it."

Penny flipped through the pages, each one covered in black marks that looked like handwriting in an unknown alphabet. "Is it a cipher?"

"I have no idea. Is it? For all I know, it's just really bad handwriting."

Penny smiled faintly and rotated the pages to examine them from different angles. "It's not the Roman alphabet." She peered at the black markings from the side. Then she frowned and flipped through the pages again. "Is this some kind of holographic thing?"

"What do you mean?"

"I think I just saw the marks move." Penny flipped through the pages again and frowned, running her fingers over the paper. "Probably just my imagination. Look, you can see how the dots and marks curl together. An optical illusion, maybe. Could be part of deciphering it."

Marley peered over her shoulder. The swirling markings didn't seem any different to her, but she hadn't studied them closely before.

Something dark moved at the corner of her gaze. She turned her head sharply and for a moment, it seemed like the swirled black designs had burned into her retina, flashing over her vision. She blinked and the afterimage faded away.

"Neath," she called, and on the opposite side of the room, the cat meowed from her perch on the dining room table.

"What is it?" Penny asked.

Marley muttered, "Optical illusions."

When Branwyn came home, Marley put the sheaf of papers away and conversation turned back to Penny's European adventure. Marley tried to pay attention, but between keeping an eye on the twins with their butterfly fairies and looking frequently into the corners of the room, she only seemed to catch one word in three.

Penny didn't notice. She was aglow, jubilant over being home again, thrilled about her upcoming date. While Marley couldn't keep track of her anecdotes, she enjoyed her friend's radiant happiness. It was so rare.

Branwyn was more attentive. She commented on Penny's stories and more than once, Marley looked up from peering into the shadows to see Branwyn watching her thoughtfully. Finally, the sun set and the oppressive heat of the day loosened its grip. Penny noticed the time and made her escape, promising to call them both the next day.

Branwyn closed the door behind Penny and turned to Marley. "Why don't we put the girls to bed on the pull-out sofa and then talk?"

Talk. Why did the promise of a future talk never bode well? Still, Marley was grateful for the assistance of somebody more familiar with children while she worked out the bedtime routine. There were baths and stories and tucking in involved.

Lissa tugged at her sleeve while Marley was snugging the sheet down. She didn't say anything, but looked deep into Marley's eyes, as if trying to find something.

Marley kissed her forehead. "It'll be okay."

Lissa wrinkled her brow. "That man today... He said he knew Uncle Zach. But he was mean to you."

From the other side of the bed, Kari said, "He was yucky."

Marley chose her words with care. "He was pretending something was true and got confused, that's all." Branwyn, crouched on the other side of the sofa bed, listened as keenly as the little girls.

Lissa's fingers tightened in Marley's sleeve. "Don't leave us. Don't leave us anywhere." Her voice was tiny.

Marley wrapped her fingers around Lissa's hand. "I won't. I promise." Her adoptive mother had made the same promise, and oh, how Marley had tested it. She suddenly decided Zachariah was going to be in *so* much trouble when he got back. "Your uncle will come back soon, and he'll probably have presents for you." She'd damn well make sure of that. "So curl up and sleep and we'll see what tomorrow brings. Okay?"

Lissa's other hand tightened on her new doll, and then she released Marley and rolled over. "G'night."

Marley went to the other side and repeated the goodnight kiss and whispered, "I'll be in the other room if you need me."

Branwyn followed her into her bedroom and half-closed the door behind her. She kept her voice low as she said, "At least they have each other."

"At least my second mother never actually vanished on me. I feel so bad for them," countered Marley.

Branwyn grimaced. "What do you think happened?"

Marley studied her friend. She had naturally red hair, but since high school, Branwyn had chosen to dye it exotic colors. This month, her hair was green, and the color intensified her eyes. But no matter how she dyed her hair, Branwyn always *looked* like a redhead. Not only that, she looked like the kind of person who caused trouble.

And it was true. Branwyn was chronically unable to resist involving herself in trouble. She'd been arrested more than once for being involved with illegal protests or unauthorized explorations. It drove Marley nuts, but now that attitude might be useful. "I don't know. It *looks* like he just walked away. Leaving behind his cellphone and his car. Which..." Marley hesitated and then concluded with, "Doesn't seem like him. And there are weird things..."

"Such as?"

"Just... incongruities. Things out of place. I'm probably making a mountain out of a molehill. Don't worry about it."

Branwyn blew out her breath in exasperation. "You're being as vague as Penny was about this Jeremy guy she's on a date with."

"Jeremy?" Marley shook herself as a nasty feeling uncurled. She'd forgotten something. Two Jeremys in one day? "Jeremy. Did she say his full name?"

"Jeremy White. A lawyer. But she wouldn't say how she met him or what they did together." Branwyn's annoyed look faded as she met Marley's eyes. "What?"

Marley sank down onto her bed. "Oh God. That's got to be a coincidence, right?"

"*What?*"

"That guy the kids were talking about. He wanted to take them away from me, tried to convince me he was their guardian. He introduced himself as Jeremy White."

"Their guardian. But you didn't believe him?"

Marley shrugged helplessly. "I'm sure he was lying. Incongruities, you know?"

"I wonder what Zachariah was involved with?" Branwyn's mouth twisted with worry. "I wonder what *Penny's* involved with."

Marley hunched her shoulders. "All I know is that something bad will happen to the twins if I don't take care of them." It slipped out before she could stop herself. She tried so hard to keep the crazy to herself.

Branwyn only looked at her solemnly. "All right." She hesitated. "This sounds like a big time investment. I don't want to add to your stress, but we need to do something about Neath. If we're keeping her, we have to pay the deposit. The apartment manager keeps reminding me, every morning."

Marley rubbed her eyes. "Yeah. I'll handle it soon, I promise. Somehow." A check from one of the sites or magazines she wrote for occasionally might be in mail. It was possible.

"I could just pay it, Marley. I have a credit card. Or we could send her to my family; I already asked Mom and she'd love a kitten she didn't have to keep once it became a cat. Just until you get things together."

"No!" Marley fought down a surge of frustration. "No. Thank you. I want to do it myself. I can't depend on other people for everything." The kitten had just appeared one day, meowing in the hedge below her bedroom window. As soon as she'd picked the tiny creature up, the kitten had nestled into her hand and begun to purr. Marley had thought then that maybe if she couldn't get her life together for her own sake, she could do it for another, for something else that needed her. Nobody really needed her book reviews, her silly articles; nobody needed her abandoned graduate work in literature. But that little body depended on her. Nobody had ever depended on her like that before.

After a moment, Branwyn said, "We have two weeks until rent is due. I can put the apartment manager off until then. But if you don't have the money, I'm going to pay it myself. I can't lose the apartment over this."

Then she patted Marley's shoulder. "Don't look so despondent. Two weeks is a long time. L.A. could burn down. You could be arrested for child stealing. The Russian mafia could kick down our door. It could all be so much worse!"

A little smile crept across Marley's face. "I suppose so."

Branwyn stepped out of the room and returned a moment later with Neath in her arms. "Here's your motivation."

"Thank you."

"Good night, Marley."

"Good night, Branwyn."

-six-

When Marley was a child, nightmares had stalked her sleep, making her rest uneasy and waking a misery. This continued until she trained herself to wake swiftly and immediately distract herself with the tasks of the morning. To never, ever think about what she dreamt; if something triggered a flash of dream-memory, it was safest ignored. Her sleep was still uneasy, but at least once she woke up, she was fine.

One of the side effects of the anti-anxiety medication she took was that it buried dreams, and so for the last few years, her sleep had been far more peaceful.

But now she dreamt again.

She lay in a four-poster bed, dressed in a high-necked nightgown, in a bedroom that she recognized but did not remember. Her childhood memories crowded the shelves that lined the walls, and on the floor there was a rug woven of her kindergarten lessons.

She sat up, languid, as if she'd spent a long time sleeping, and looked around the room further. A rocking chair was draped with her baby blanket, and a chest at the foot of the bed was crayoned with clouds and trees. On the chest sat Neath, watching her carefully.

Marley stretched. "You don't belong here, do you? I never had a cat growing up." She felt weak, as if she was flexing muscles she'd never used before.

The kitten tilted her head attentively, the same way she listened to Marley when it was close to dinnertime.

Marley beckoned to Neath. It was odd that she was dreaming, and odder that she was aware of it, but she was not uncomfortable. She felt totally relaxed, better than she'd felt in years.

The cat ignored the summons and shifted her gaze to the bottom of Marley's bed, ears swiveling. A moment later, Marley heard it, too: a tiny grunt, as of somebody squeezing through a tight space.

Something was hiding under her bed.

When she'd been very small, sometimes she'd leap off the bed to avoid grasping hands, or huddle under the covers and worry about sharks in the sea that masqueraded as a floor. But that had been in her real bedroom, in her little single bed with the princess frame. This was the bedroom of her mind. If she was safe anywhere, she was safe here. She knew this, and trusted it.

She leaned over the edge of the bed and peeked under. "Hello?"

There was a glint, and a sparkle. Then a small shape crawled out from under the bed, shaking its head, amidst a puff of dust. "Not what I expected," it said, in a pleasant, boyish voice. Neath arched her back and hissed.

Once clear from the bed, it stood up and inspected itself, glancing at bare arms and leaf-clad legs, and then twisted around to look at the dragonfly wings on its back. "But it'll do. Greetings and salutations, fair lady."

Marley blinked. "You're a fairy fashion doll." But that

wasn't quite right. It was male, to start with, and quite alive. Neath began to growl.

Lips far more expressive than a doll's twitched in response. "It's too soon for that conversation, don't you think? We've haven't even intro—oh shit!" The little figure disappeared under a biting, clawing kitten.

Marley watched in concern. She'd never seen Neath angry before, and it was different from how she played with her toy mouse. There was a flash of bare chest under the kitten. A green leg kicked. Curses mingled with the yowling. A tiny fist plunked Neath on the nose and the sprite scrambled away while the kitten looked at herself cross-eyed. Crimson scratches glistened on his torso.

Then Neath refocused and leapt again. This time, he was ready, rolling with her and kicking out with both legs. The kitten squeaked breathlessly as she tumbled off him and failed to land on her feet.

Marley intervened, scooping up Neath. "Hey," she said mildly. "Don't hurt my cat."

The sprite glared up at her. "Don't 'hey' me! Who's the one bleeding here?"

Neath hissed.

"Bleeding—and winged! Fly away." She stuck her tongue out as the sprite gave her a startled look. It seemed like the right thing to do in the environment. "What are you doing here, anyhow?"

"Right, introductions." He looked over his shoulder at his wings again. "I wonder if these things work." He flicked one with a pointy-nailed finger, and it quivered. Then they whirred to life and the sprite lifted into the air. "Whee!" He buzzed around the room.

Neath started growling again. It was a strange sound, much smaller than a dog's growl but far more menacing. The sprite paused in midair and pointed a finger at Marley. "You keep that cat away from me, or I'll go right back where I came from."

"Why doesn't she like you?"

"Do you think I know? Do you think I spend a lot of time around great gawky cats longer than I am tall? Silly thing can't even land on its feet. Who ever heard of a cat not landing on its feet?"

"She's just a baby," said Marley defensively. That baby's claws were sinking into her hand quite painfully, though. "Maybe you'd better introduce yourself before I let her go again."

"That would be a mistake," the little figure snapped. Then he took a deep breath. "But you're right. Fine! I am the great fairy Tinker Chime, here to—what? What?" Marley was giggling.

She fell back onto her bed, still holding Neath to her chest. "Chime? Like, a bell? I love this dream!" He looked so affronted that she had to work hard to stop herself from bursting into peals of laughter. "Sorry, Chime, you were saying? Here to...?" And she snickered again, unable to stop herself.

The great fairy Tinker Chime hovered over her head, near the canopy of the bed. "You're not very nice. I've probably found the wrong dream and you're not the one with the important destiny."

Marley gazed up at him thoughtfully until the pain from Neath's claws forced her to shift her grip. The cat squirmed away from her and stalked to the edge of the bed, where one of the posts led up to the canopy. Chime shot out from under the canopy and up to the ceiling.

"She can't fly, glitterbrain," Marley called after him.

"Yet! She can't fly *yet!*" called back the piping voice.

"Oh, come on. Tell me about this great destiny. Fair warning: You probably do have the wrong person, though. Action

Girl's down thataway." She pointed *yonder.*

A tiny pair of intense violet eyes peeked over the edge of the canopy. "To be honest, at this point, we'd take even a decent destiny. Maybe even a mediocre one."

"Desperate times!" She watched Neath crouch, her tail lashing back and forth. "You'd better talk fast."

Chime somersaulted into view, hovering beyond the bed. "My lady, you are called on to rescue—"

And the dream shattered, torn asunder by the gouge of pain in her back and gut. For a moment, she saw Chime's mouth moving, before he and the bedroom around him shriveled like paper in a fire. Then it all blew away, nothing more than dried wisps of grass. Beyond stretched a desolate sunless wasteland, where nothing moved. A thousand eyes watched from the heavens and the moon was a clockwork machine with a face she could not read. She took a step forward and fell through, into stars—

Marley opened her eyes. One twin had her head butted up against Marley's back, while the other had her feet planted in Marley's stomach. One of them was snoring lightly. She hadn't noticed them crawling into bed with her, and she wondered vaguely when they'd done it. Neath was nestled next to her head.

She sighed and adjusted herself and the children so she wasn't in danger of twinjury, and closed her eyes again. She could remember the dream with Tinker Chime clearly, more real than a childhood memory. But when she tried to recapture the light-hearted state of mind and return to the dream, all she could see was the wasteland, and all she could hear was Neath's growl.

-seven-

The children dragged Marley from bed far too close to dawn, ignoring her sleepy complaints. Branwyn, already up, laughed at her.

"Did you encourage this assault?" Marley settled onto the barely used sofa bed, legs crossed, and ran her hands through her tangled hair. Her eyes fell on the box one of the fairy dolls had arrived in, and she remembered her dream again.

She picked the box up and turned it over. There was a picture of each doll in the toy line on the back, but they were all girls. No little fairy boys, which she thought showed a lack of imagination.

Neath settled into her lap. Marley blinked. Branwyn was talking. "Yup. I also fed them breakfast while you were sleeping the morning away." She was already dressed and ready for work. The twins, Marley noticed, had made their own dressing choices: Lissa was in one of Marley's own t-shirts, dress-sized on her, while Kari had chosen a violet swimsuit.

"Thanks," Marley said grudgingly.

Branwyn continued, "The wildfires are worse today. They've started talking about evacuating certain areas. Keep an eye on it. I'm taking this—" she hefted a duffel bag "—to work, just in case." With that, she left, abandoning Marley with the two preschoolers.

The morning passed. Chaos occurred.

It was a beautiful day despite the fires charring the mountains. A nearly annual occurrence, the danger they represented to the civilized parts of the Valley varied from year to year. Right now, they were a television worry compared to the continued mystery of Zachariah's disappearance. Marley tried to listen to the news on the radio as she navigated her way through some errands, but the chatter of the girls in the back seat drew her attention. They hadn't liked changing clothes at all and she was anxious to keep them in good moods.

Their last errand was to the Pasadena Central Library. She wanted to do some research while the girls entertained themselves in the children's section; Penny and Branwyn didn't call her Research Girl for nothing. Finding a library was always her first recourse when she ran into something new, although it had been months since she'd felt inspired to research much of anything.

The reference librarian suggested the encrypted book was a prank or prop, which Marley rejected purely on gut instinct. She spent an hour moving back and forth between the stacks and a bank of computers, and finally collapsed into a chair, rubbing her eyes in annoyance. She'd learned nothing about Zachariah, a little about Senyaza Corporation, and quite a lot of utterly useless information about encryption techniques. She could have spent all day there, but the twins were getting bored despite their basket of books.

Lissa knelt on a chair at a table, pretending to read in a voice too loud for a library, while Kari sat under the table, playing with her doll and listening. Marley moved to their table to quiet Lissa and smiled to herself as she noticed that the book, full of pictures of a pixie's adventures, was upside down. The little girl noticed Marley and abruptly fell silent.

"Would you like to go back to the children's section and I'll read this to you?"

Lissa shrugged and pushed the book across the table. Marley glanced at the open page as she picked it up. She frowned and ran her mind back over what Lissa had just been saying.

"Can you really read, Lissa?" She'd been more fluent than Marley had believed possible in somebody who wasn't even in kindergarten.

Lissa shrugged again, acquiring a familiar uncomfortable expression. "I dunno."

Kari scrambled out from under the table. "She can!"

Marley said, "It's all right if you can, Liss. It's very good! I just didn't know."

Lissa addressed the table sulkily. "Can't. Not properly. Real reading is with all the letters."

"Oh." Marley frowned. "You've got the book at home, then? You've memorized it."

"No...?" said Lissa uncertainly. "Kari just found the book and wanted to hear the story."

"Because it's like the dolls Miss Penny gave us," explained Kari. She glanced sideways at her sister. "Reading is reading, Liss."

Lissa hesitated until finally Kari poked her viciously. "I just say what the book tells me. That's all."

Marley realized that Lissa's body language was identical to Kari's right before she admitted she could open the SUV. There was another secret here. She shook her head in wonder and said brightly, "Let's check it out so you can finish reading it at home."

As she started to the self-checkout counter, her gaze fell on a man sprawled in a soft chair, who was looking at her. He had a worn paperback closed over one finger. Something about him was familiar. He seemed lanky, even sitting down, with unkempt black hair and shadowed eyes. He wore hiking boots, faded black jeans, and a worn grey t-shirt.

He met her eyes and stood up.

Marley's breath caught in her throat. He'd been at the park the day before, eavesdropping on her conversation with Jeremy the lawyer. At first she'd thought he'd been Jeremy's ally and then, when the lawyer had left, she'd thought he was just a passerby.

There was an intensity in the way he stared at her that made her certain she'd been right the first time. She dropped her gaze quickly and hustled the children with their books to the manned checkout station. He followed her.

She attended with rather less than half an ear to the librarian's idle conversation as she scanned the books. From the corner of her eye, she could see that the tall man had paused a couple of yards away, still looking intently at her.

She took a deep breath as the librarian slid the books into a bag for her. What could actually happen, surrounded by the patrons and staff of the library? If he made a scene, they'd kick him out. Better to have a bad encounter inside than out. So she wandered over to the New Books section, towing the kids after her, and waited until he approached her.

His voice pitched low, he said, "Miss, I need to talk to you."

"No," she said firmly, giving him only a cursory glance. "Go away."

He stared at her, mouth tightening, "I know you're one of Zachariah's allies. I know you're trying to keep the kids safe. But—"

"I said no," Marley repeated, raising her voice. "Please leave me alone." She looked over at him again. It was a mistake.

He shimmered, as if tears were pricking her eyes. Her

stomach twisted and crimson crept across the blur of her vision until the man's face was covered in blood. Something bad was going to happen soon. The idea—no, the *understanding*— slammed into her head like a spike: *He would die soon.* The frustration on his blood-washed face was the beginning of a path that led directly to... emptiness.

She swayed, trying to gulp down the panic. This hadn't happened in years, and it had rarely been this bad. She squeezed her eyes shut until she felt the insane certainty recede. She knew it was insane; hadn't she had visions like that growing up, visions which were no more likely to come true than a horoscope? For a moment, the light over his head seemed very bright, and then all was a blur again, from the real tears in her eyes. "I'm sorry," she gasped out, and turned and fled.

Five steps away, she realized Kari had slipped out of her grasp and was standing four-square in front of the man, staring up at him defiantly.

"Kari!" she cried. The little girl jumped and then raced after her, grabbing her hand again.

They made it through the science fiction section to the library foyer before he caught up with them, darting past Marley as she juggled books and children to stand in front of the second set of doors, blocking their exit. He spread his hands. "I'm not going to hurt you."

Just outside the library entrance, a teenage girl sat on a bench, holding in one hand the leashes of three good-sized dogs that lay at her feet. She turned from watching the parking lot to peer through the glass windows of the foyer. She looked from the tall man to Marley, and frowned.

Marley fumbled at the inner doors behind her, ready to retreat into the main library again.

"I'm not going to hurt you," he repeated. "But those people out there might." He pointed out at the parking lot.

She couldn't watch him and look at the parking lot at the same time. He lifted both hands as if to show they were empty, and then pushed the door open and went outside. When it swung shut behind him, she quickly scanned the parking lot.

It wasn't even half-full on a day like today, and the minivan from the day before leapt out at her. She could see two people inside it. It was right next to her car. On the other side of the minivan, a sky-blue sedan's doors opened and people spilled out and began milling around both the sedan and the minivan.

Marley's shoulder blades touched the wall of the foyer, and she found herself sinking down it. Lissa climbed into her lap as soon as she was sitting on the ground. "What's going on?" the little girl asked. "Are we going home?"

Marley squeezed Lissa with one arm, and pushed herself back to her feet, sliding the girl onto her feet again. "Soon. I just have to talk to this man." As if he heard her, he opened the foyer door again.

Kari turned around. "You said no. Why? How are they going to hurt you? Will they push you down? Or hit you?"

He looked down at Kari and said, "Maybe. They might take her stuff, too."

Kari turned serious eyes to him. "Why?"

The tall man opened his mouth to answer and then hesitated. He shrugged. "I don't know." He raised his eyes to Marley. "I know them, though. I know who... sponsors them."

Marley looked at him sidelong. The overwhelming certainty that he would die soon did not reoccur, although she still vaguely felt that something unpleasant would happen. *That* feeling, at least, was one she was used to.

She peered out through the window again. The people surrounding the minivan were laughing and horsing around with each other. They were young and casually dressed, clean-cut and well-groomed. "Sponsor? They look like college students."

An unexpected smile briefly quirked the corner of the man's mouth. "You could say they're interns."

"Uh-huh. Scary, dangerous interns. And what do you want?"

"For starters, I'd like to find Zachariah." There was an edge to his voice.

"So would we. I'd like to have a little chat with him about his idea of advance planning." She looked outside again. Some of the college students were watching them. So was the girl with the dogs.

"How did you end up with his kids?"

She transferred her gaze back to the man. "You know what bothers me about you? How you found me at that park yesterday. How both you and that other guy found me, if you're not working together. I mean, I left Zachariah a note, but I didn't include a last name, an address, or an intended schedule. So, okay, if the lawyer guy has been watching Zachariah for a while, the park was a pretty good guess. We meet there a lot. But you just asked me how I ended up with the kids. Which was in the note. So how did you know I was involved? How did you know to find me yesterday if you didn't see the note? Something doesn't make sense here."

He stared at her, his eyes wide. His mouth opened, and then closed again.

Marley looked back out the doors. "On the other hand, that's the same van Lawyer Jeremy was in yesterday. Which makes me quite uninterested in buying any magazine subscriptions, or whatever they're selling."

He cleared his throat and said, "I can distract them."

"How sweet. I'll just bet you can."

He frowned at her and shook his head. Then he went outside and spoke to the teenager with the dogs. Marley shifted her weight uncomfortably. She'd believed the teen was just a random observer, just like she'd hoped the tall man was a random observer the day before. Marley wished the girl didn't look so young.

Kari whimpered. "I want Uncle Zach back."

Lissa took Kari's hand and stared out the window. "Somebody made him go away."

Shocked, Kari said, "Nobody could do that."

"And Marley's scared of people out there," Lissa continued, in a dreamy voice.

"What?" said Marley sharply. "No, I'm not. I was just surprised." Kari glanced up but Lissa didn't seem to hear her.

Something clunked in the library ventilation system, and Marley could suddenly smell the wildfire as if she were right beside it. Outside, the tall man and the teenager stopped talking and looked around, and the dogs sniffed the wind. The tall man looked at Marley and frowned again, and then nodded to the teen.

The girl slipped the leashes off her three dogs, and then snapped her fingers and ambled in the direction of Marley's car and the minivan. The dogs raced ahead of her while the dark man followed behind.

Marley crouched down and put an arm around each of the twins. "We're going to play a game. We have to get to our car and get inside without the people next to the van noticing."

Lissa looked over at her. "I don't want to play a game," she said, her voice flat.

Marley hesitated. Something about Lissa's voice made her ask, "What do you want to do?"

"Make them go away."

Kari laughed suddenly. "Look at the doggies!" At the same time, there was a chorus of barking.

Two of the dogs had scrambled onto the roofs of both the sedan and the minivan, and were barking hysterically down at the college students. The third dog was growling at Lawyer Jeremy himself as he stepped out of the car, while the teenage girl pulled vainly on its collar. The tall man was waving his hands in the air dramatically. Somebody shouted.

"Come on!" said Marley. She picked up Lissa around the middle and kicked the door open. She almost started to run, but then she remembered that running attracted attention. So she walked. Briskly. Lissa hung from her arm, a sulky dead weight, while Kari trotted beside her. The chaos around the vehicles attracted a flock of crows that circled only a few feet above, adding to the assault of sound. The noise seemed to be seriously hampering the college student trying to use a cell-phone. A few yards from her car, one of them turned.

"Hey—" he began, and the brown dog on top of the mini-van landed on top of him, growling.

Marley froze for a moment, the real cries of fear trigger-ing an instinctive need to help. Then she squeezed her eyes shut, shook her head, and kept moving.

As she unlocked the door and piled the children in, the cries became angry swearing and shrill demands. "What the—get—move—Hey!" She didn't look over. Instead, she put her seatbelt on and started the car.

Nobody stopped her. Nobody flung themselves in front of her car. Nobody tried to open the door. She wasn't even sure if anybody noticed.

As she pulled into traffic, she glanced in the rearview mirror. The dark man was walking across the parking lot again, and the teenage girl and her dogs were nowhere to be seen. The college students were all clustered in a tight huddle as Jeremy climbed back into the van.

Marley looked at each of the twins in the mirror. Kari met her eyes and said solemnly, "Bad doggies."

Lissa, looking out the window, said in a tone of satisfac-tion, "Yeah!"

-eight-

By the time Marley got home, her thoughts on the encounter at the library had become a confused mess of speculated motivations. The tall man had been almost convincing in his desire to help her. But the knowledge he didn't explain and those dogs that had attacked the college students were both troubling. Was setting your dogs on people the act of a good guy? And the college students hadn't seemed threatening or thuggish; they'd had the cheerful demeanor of those out to do good and unburdened by moral ambiguity. But they'd had Lawyer Jeremy, and there'd been so many of them.

She finally concluded that the whole thing was impossible to sort out based on the available information, and settled for being glad that she'd gotten out of it. She even found a moment to be reassured that Jeremy was relying on college students rather than the police. That was mysterious in and of itself, but supported her belief that whatever Jeremy was up to, it was No Good.

Penny waited outside her door, smiling.

"Penny!" said Marley. "You would not believe the morning I had. There was this guy—"

Penny's eyebrows went up. "You too?"

Marley remembered Penny's date with possibly-Lawyer Jeremy. "No, not like that. More like—he said he knew Zachariah, but he was—" She shook her head. "It was complicated. How was your date?" She unlocked the door and gestured for Penny to go inside.

Penny danced through the door and picked up Neath from the back of the couch, twirling her around. "It was lovely. He missed me! Which was more than I expected. We spent hours over wine, just talking."

"Yeah? What about?" Marley watched the kids settle down to play.

"Oh... stuff. Me, my friends, his friends, the places we went when we were in Rome." Penny collapsed on the couch into a graceful pile of limbs. "He knows some fascinating people. He said they all really liked me, too."

Marley always thought that Penny worried a lot more about people liking her than was necessary. But Penny was rarely convinced anyone believed she had intrinsic worth. In high school, her money and busy parents had made her the envy of other students, but Marley had often seen how little there was to envy. "What did you two do in Rome?"

"Oh, we went to clubs. Dancing. A couple of parties." Penny smiled. "I wasn't sure if he was actually interested in me or just being nice while killing time. He flirted with me, but... well, he kept introducing me to other people and then leaving me with them for a while." She considered. "He's very busy, though. He's on the board of this private charitable organization. I think they build bridges or something." She rubbed her left wrist and frowned. "I had the strangest dream last night."

"So did I," said Marley. "A fairy doll wanted me to come save his flower kingdom. What was yours about?"

"Light," Penny said simply. Then she shook her head. "I don't remember. I don't even know why I thought of it. Anyhow, I can't wait for you to meet Jeremy. I'm dying to know what you think of him."

Marley regarded Penny steadily for a moment. She hoped, oh so desperately, that it was an innocent coincidence. The sick twisting in her stomach believed otherwise. But when was that ever right? She couldn't rely on an anxiety disorder to make decisions for her.

Finally, she sighed. She couldn't make it better, but she could make it a lot worse by remaining silent.

"It's funny, because I met a Jeremy White yesterday. A lawyer. He was interested in the disposition of the kids. A common name, I guess."

Penny's eyes widened. "Really?" Then she looked away. "My Jeremy didn't recognize your name when I mentioned you." She paused. "What did you think of the one you met yesterday?"

"He was..." Marley searched for the right word.

"He was bad," said Lissa, without looking up from the paper she was coloring on. Marley blinked. When they were quiet, it was so easy to forget the children were there and probably listening. Lissa went on, "So many bad guys."

"Well, my Jeremy is good. He runs a charity!" Penny said firmly, and then seemed to realize she was talking to a small child. "Lots of people have the same names, after all. There are probably dozens of Jeremy Whites in L.A." Lissa didn't respond, and Penny looked up to meet Marley's eyes. "So how are you doing? How's work?"

Marley blew out her breath. "Intermittent. Been a bit distracted the last couple of days, but I have to get something out soon. How about you? Did you get any more writing inspiration in Rome?"

Penny blushed. "A little, then I got stuck again. But I was

talking to Jeremy last night and he suggested…" She fell silent abruptly. Then she said, "I had some interesting design ideas, too. Of course, it's Italy—that's why I went there."

Gently, Marley asked, "You told him about your writing?" It wasn't a subject Penny talked about to most people. Throughout high school, Penny had written, Branwyn had illustrated, and Marley had been their sole audience.

Penny shrugged. "I like him, Marley. I want this to work. I… feel like I'm part of something when I'm with him. Part of something, but… special, too." Penny's expression turned derisive, one corner of her mouth twisting. "A special snowflake. It's dumb, I know. But things fall apart enough on their own. So, don't…" She shook her head and fell silent.

For a long moment, the ghosts of old conversations thronged the air. Marley listened to them.

She looked at her own anxieties and demanded of them: *What do you want me to do? I can't make her do anything. All I can do is be here afterwards.* And then, taking into account current events, added, *Possibly metaphorically speaking, writing letters from Cellblock 2-A.*

Her misgivings had no words of their own in reply, so she said to Penny, "All right. I won't." And from somewhere inside, she found a smile to share with Penny. Penny returned a little smile of her own.

Kari appeared at Marley's elbow, holding her fairy doll and a container of dental floss. "Put this on her," she ordered, and thrust the dental floss at Marley. "She's naughty. She keeps trying to run away. She needs a leash."

Marley blinked at Kari, and then down at the dental floss. But Penny spoke before she could. "That's not a good leash. But I know what to get." She disappeared into Branwyn's room and reappeared holding a spool of white ribbon and a pair of scissors.

"Put it 'round her neck." Kari gave the doll a kiss. "You

can't trust fairies. They're fun but trouble." She sounded like she was quoting something she'd heard somewhere.

"Please, I object to strangled fairies," Marley said. "Put it around her waist instead."

"Leashes go 'round the neck. Like the doggies."

Penny shifted her gaze between Marley and Kari. "It's called a harness if it goes around the body. They even make harnesses for little kids." She tied the ribbon in a cross over the doll's torso, then snipped off a long tail.

Kari looked dubious, but she took the doll back. After inspecting it, she wandered off to bother her sister, dragging the doll behind her.

Penny's faint smile had real pleasure behind it now. "What else can I do to help?"

Marley looked around. The mess in the apartment seemed to reflect the disorganization in her head. There were plenty of things that needed doing, but—

"I know!" Penny announced. "How about I take the girls out to lunch and give you an hour or two to work? You said you had to get something done."

That was a good idea.

No. No, it wasn't. No sooner had Marley considered the idea than a wave of nausea and panic swept over her. It was the same as the day before, when the lawyer had tried to take them away.

"Hey, what's the matter?" said Penny sharply. "Why are you looking at me like that?"

With an effort, Marley dropped her gaze to the carpet and breathed carefully, waiting for the internal visions of misery and doom to fade away. It was the screams heard by her mind's ear that faded last. Her own screams.

"Sorry," she whispered. "Panic attack." She looked up in time to see Penny's face change, the warmth shuttered away.

"You don't trust me."

The sick feeling didn't fade, though. "That's not it. I don't want—it seems like—" Marley fumbled for an explanation. She had to find an explanation because she couldn't let Penny take the kids away from her.

"Don't worry about it," said Penny. She stood up and grabbed her purse. "I should go, anyhow. I just remembered I have something to do myself. It was good chatting with you."

She stalked to the door while Marley sat curled in on herself on the couch, wretched with confusion. Penny yanked the door open, then turned to Marley, doubt playing across her face. She almost spoke. Then she stepped outside, and there was nothing but the door.

Kari reappeared next to Marley. "Uncle says at least angels are honest. If you can get them to talk to you. Will you put a leash on Lissa's fairy too?"

-nine-

The apartment was stifling. Marley tried to think about Zachariah. She examined the ciphered book fragment again, watching the way the patterns seemed to waver and move when she stared at them for too long. She threw herself from couch to computer chair to dining room table, but all she could do was rehash the conversation with Penny in her head.

At last, after peanut butter sandwiches and medication, she decided to go out again. She considered the possibility of the Interns of Evil reappearing, and realized part of her hoped they would. She wanted somebody associated with all this *this*-ness to yell at.

Marley scolded herself and found Branwyn's extra can of pepper spray. The anti-anxiety medication made her reckless sometimes, especially when she upped her dosage like she had just now. She forced herself to consider the idea of taking her car to a different park. After a careful, thirty-second examination of her choices, she concluded that if she wanted to be stealthy, leaving the car where it was, taking the back exit from her building, and walking to the local park was the best option.

The back door of her apartment complex led to the laundry room and the dumpsters. It was always smelly, but today the whiff of smoke in the air overwhelmed the other odors. A firefighting helicopter flew by, tilted like a swollen mosquito, and she tracked its progress toward the mountainside until it faded into the haze.

As they walked, Marley said to the twins, "This afternoon's game is: run away from anybody over the age of ten who gets close enough to touch you. Except me. Don't run away from me."

Lissa said, "Something bad is happening, right? All these bad guys." She sounded more thoughtful than scared.

Marley hesitated and then said, "Yes. But it's too hot to hide under the bed."

"Hah!" said Kari to Lissa. "I told you the fire was part of it."

"What?" said Marley. "No, no. That's just nature. Everything gets so dry." She tried to remember what it had been like to be so young that the forces of nature had been anthropomorphized to her. She had vague memories of believing that earthquakes came from the sea's jealousy of the coast, but that was it.

"But you're not supposed to hide under the bed if there's a fire in your house," said Kari seriously.

"That's... that's true. I was just referring to the summer, though."

"It was sticky back at your house."

"Mmm," Marley said, because what else *could* you say to that? Looking down at Lissa, she asked, "Are you scared, Liss?"

Lissa was quiet for a moment, and then shrugged. "I will throw rocks at them."

Kari giggled. "Yeah! And bugs! And dog poop!" She

looked shocked and pleased by her own daring.

Marley, who had been present for a park lecture from Zachariah on why dog poop was yucky and shouldn't even be poked with a stick, sighed. "I'd rather you just ran away."

Kari seemed to ignore her entirely, while Lissa just shrugged. They walked along in silence for a few moments, until they came to the edge of the park. As far as Marley could tell, the place was utterly empty. It wasn't entirely a surprise given the wildfires and heat, but it was a relief.

"There we go," she said. "Nobody to throw things at. Please, *please* come to me first if you think that would be a good idea. Now go play."

She followed them into the playground. While Kari wouldn't let go of her harnessed fairy doll for any reason, she otherwise played as she always had. Lissa, in contrast, was quiet and uninterested. But after ten minutes of Marley's enticement and encouragement, she relaxed and began to show signs of enjoying herself.

It was nice, until Marley looked up from Lissa's smile and realized a familiar figure had appeared in the park.

It was neither Lawyer Jeremy nor Tall, Dark and Nevermind, but the teenage girl with the dogs. She was throwing a Frisbee that two of the dogs chased, while the third lazed around in the grass, ears pricked toward the playground activity. The girl seemed to be paying no attention to anything else around her, but Marley was not convinced.

She looked around the park to see who else had shown up. There was still nobody near the playground, although a ball game seemed to be assembling on the distant diamond. On the other side of the park, a pair of women strolled along the jogging path.

The girl's back was to Marley, making it impossible for Marley to catch her eye. She snapped her fingers at the dog watching her, a chocolate-colored retriever. Its tail waved slowly, but it didn't move.

Finally, she cupped her hands around her mouth and called, "Hey, you! Girl with the dogs!"

The girl looked around and then waved. Marley beckoned her over. Much to her surprise, the girl immediately dashed across the grass to her, all three dogs following in her wake.

"Hi!" she said. Marley looked at her with narrowed eyes. The kid looked to be maybe fourteen, with a mop of curly dark hair and big hazel eyes in a brown face. She was pretty in a way that almost seemed airbrushed, which wasn't uncommon in L.A., but did usually require makeup.

"Who are you?" Marley finally asked.

"Is this about the dogs? Because they are totally under control." She made a hand gesture and all three dogs sat down. Her words were followed by a hopeful grin; her teeth were very white.

"That's nice. That's good. But I already saw that today. However, now I am asking for your name," Marley said.

"Oh! I'm Annalise Audot. Call me AT." She grinned again, but there was a hint of nervousness beneath the cheer.

"Why are you following me around, AT?"

AT looked like she'd just been asked the one test question she absolutely knew the answer to. "Corbin asked me to help keep an eye on you."

"Is that the tall man from the library?"

"What, he didn't even tell you his name? What a dork." AT rolled her eyes and raised a hand in despair at such neglect. "Yeah, him."

"Where is he now?" Once again, relief flashed across AT's face, and Marley wondered what questions *would* worry the girl.

"He went to look up something. I think he wants to figure out what the bad guys are planning."

"See? Bad guys," said Lissa, from somewhere behind

Marley's leg. "I said."

Marley looked around. Kari was playing in the woodchips near the edge of the playground, while Lissa was crouched in the grass a few feet behind Marley. She clutched a sizable stone in each hand, but didn't seem ready to throw them. Marley hesitated and then let it pass.

Instead, she fished for a question that would make the dog girl nervous. "Where's Zachariah?"

A serious shrug. "I wish I knew. I can't f—" she cut herself off. "He knows stuff he didn't tell Corbin."

"Uh-huh. And what makes those other folks the bad guys?" AT stared at her like she'd asked something ridiculous, so she clarified. "Maybe I'm the bad guy. Maybe *you're* the bad guy."

AT shifted uncomfortably. "Um. They're the bad guys. If you knew what I knew, you'd agree. But I can't explain," she added hastily. "It's complicated."

Marley was pleased; that was more information than she'd actually expected to get. Secrets. Complicated secrets!

Lissa, who had crept forward, tugged on Marley's pants leg. "Kari's throwing stuff."

Marley turned in time to see Kari on the far side of the playground, chucking a piece of wood bark at the pair of approaching women. It fell far short of them, but the little girl had a supply of ammo in her shirt.

"Kari, no, stop it!" Marley called, moving toward her. The strolling women paused. They were middle-aged, and reminded Marley of her own adopted mother, with short, neatly managed hair and quietly stylish clothing. There were almost certainly women who had experienced the idiosyncrasies of small children before.

Except one of them looked honestly frightened of Kari, while the other one was absolutely expressionless. The frightened one fumbled in her handbag, a large, pale leather affair.

They both had identical handbags, which was... strange.

Marley's stomach churned. Something was wrong. She shouted, "Hey!" and her jog became a sprint.

It seemed like a tidal wave of dog poured around her as AT's animals sped past, but she barely noticed. Kari was looking back at Marley, confused. Beyond her, the woman was shaking something out of her purse. No. They couldn't. Who would...?

Kari started to run. There was a cracking sound, and another, and another.

Everything seemed to happen at once, but Marley could order a few things: the sting of pain in her arm before she saw the gun in the blank-faced woman's hand, pointed directly at her. The yawning feeling in her mind, like her ears popping after a long flight, before Kari tripped and rolled and came to her feet again, still fleeing. More cracking, but the guns were obscured by the dogs. Blackness sprayed through the air.

Then the women were down and the dogs, previously silent, were snarling on top of them. AT dashed past her to kick at a woman's hand.

Kari cannoned into Marley, and she realized she was on her knees. Hesitantly, still aware of the yawning, open sensation in her mind, she felt her head. Was she dead? What had just happened? Where had the guns come from?

Her skull seemed whole, but the rest of the world seemed... different. It was as if she'd discovered distance, as if a television image had suddenly become the view from a window. Marley shook her head, and the feeling faded as she focused on Kari. The little girl seemed uninjured, although there was a smudge of dirt on her face.

Marley raised her hand to wipe at the smudge, and realized there was blood running over her fingers. She stared at it.

"Marley, you're hurt," said Kari, wonderingly. "You're bleeding." She pointed at Marley's upper arm. Marley felt at it with her other hand. The stinging she'd barely noticed became a searing ache as she touched the edges of a long cut.

"Bang, bang," said Kari. Her eyes widened. "They shot you."

Lissa, standing only a few yards away, said, "Bad guys." Her voice was clear and cold. It rang in the empty vastness in Marley's head and her vision rippled and distorted. The world broke into a riot of kaleidoscopic images. After a moment of utter disorientation, Marley realized every person she saw was refracted and layered upon themselves, filling up the new distance.

But there were only two images of Lissa. One image wavered and glistened, with small shadows crawling over it; just looking at it made Marley's stomach churn. The other one seemed normal: Lissa the little girl. Beyond the child, the two women lying passively on the ground had their own pair of refractions, one muddled with the long grey-blue shadows of grief, and one swirled with silver-limned night. Faint lines of light linked the images of grief to Lissa's nauseating refraction.

Lissa walked toward the women. The dogs holding them down tumbled off them as if blown by a gale-force wind. Their claws scrabbled at the ground, but they couldn't regain their positions. AT, crouched down near the women, stared at the child. Her eyes widened with shock as she struggled to keep her own balance.

The women on the ground lay still. The one who had been frightened of Kari was terrified now, and her handbag had a hole blown through its bottom. There were lines around her eyes and a dog bite on her hand. Her mouth was moving but no sound emerged.

"You bad guys should just go away," said Lissa. She tossed her stones.

The golden light that burst around them was like the sun

had come out from behind the clouds. It cast no shadows; it suffused everything until there was nothing to see. It was blindness without end.

But the kaleidoscope vision remained.

Marley saw the two images of Lissa waver. The nauseating one strengthened, and the line that connected her to the fallen women thickened. Static began to devour the images of the women. They cracked and fragmented, until they were pitted and worn like a rock face under a sand wind.

Then great golden wings folded around each woman, a shield against the devouring. The static faded away.

The light spoke.

Foolish. But you were loyal and true.

My loyal servants shall not be lost while I yet endure.

What was will be again.

The light faded slowly. There was only one strong image of Lissa left, and the glass of the kaleidoscope was clear and undistorted.

The grass and playground reappeared out of the light. The women were gone.

In the silence that followed, Lissa stomped over to where the women had been, and kicked at the pile of clothes remaining. A dog whined and huddled, licking its flank. It was the black dog, Marley realized, and it had been shot, just like her.

She touched her arm again absently, but her questing fingers only found a dull pain and a scab.

"I fixed it," said Kari, smiling up at her. Both her hands were smeared with blood. "I fixed it." For just a heartbeat, Marley thought she saw static around Kari's hands, too. But she blinked, and it was gone. The blood was shocking enough, in any case.

AT stood up slowly. She had many refracted images, too many to count. Marley pushed the kaleidoscope vision away, flinching, refusing to see the refractions.

"You should... you need to get out of here," said AT. Her voice was unsteady.

"What happened? Did that just happen?" Marley stood up herself.

"Didn't you hear me?" AT cried, her voice shrill. "You need to get out of here. Those were gunshots; the cops will come."

Doubt flickered across Marley's mind. "But... the light... those women..."

AT kicked a gun across the grass, savagely. "Let the cops worry about it. Let Senyaza worry about it. You have to go, before somebody else shows up. The cops will separate you from the kids."

Marley grabbed Lissa, who seemed calm and satisfied, by the hand. "What about you?"

AT glanced at the black dog, which was being licked by his friends. "I need to take care of my dog. I'll find you later or something. Go, go, go!"

They'd *shot* her. Suddenly, Marley needed no further urging. She took hold of Kari with her other hand, and she ran.

-ten-

Habit guided Marley's rushing steps home, while the fog of dissociation gently drifted through her mind. It's inevitable, when faced with something incomprehensible, to try to cast it in a familiar framework. When that fails, when no explanation suffices, just write it out of history: a glitch, an anomaly. Let the habits of normalcy prove that it didn't really happen. Would the world go on just as it had, otherwise? Palm trees and dark birds under a hazy blue sky. A helicopter whirring by, the distant sound of somebody's stereo. Somebody, somewhere, laughing. Her door, her key.

She wanted things to be normal. She moved around the apartment, picking up all the belongings the twins had scattered. There was no thought that went with the actions. Her thoughts were all busy shuffling the deck of her memories. *Pick a card, any card; I'll make it disappear.*

But the magic trick wouldn't work. It couldn't work. Normalcy had wandered out of her life the day before, with the phone call from the twins. And some parts of it all were just too close. Her arm ached. When a door slammed somewhere outside, she froze. Aloud, she said, "That was just a door slamming. Just a door."

But she walked across the room to the bathroom, closed the door behind her, and sank down to the floor. "Boom," she whispered, and she remembered the crack of the gun.

They'd shot her. She felt it again: the sting in her arm, and her terror, not for herself, but for Kari. They'd wanted to kill her. Dead. *Boom.*

After a few moments, she realized she'd bunched a towel up against her face because she was sobbing and she didn't want the twins to know.

Unsteadily, she stood up and ran the faucet to splash water on her face. Then she twisted and began to inspect her injury. It seemed half-healed already, but the blood that had run down her arm was crusted into the edges of the wound. Cleaning the actual injury seemed impossible without assistance and a commitment to potentially re-opening the wound, so she settled for just cleaning the rest of her arm. Then she stuck four strip bandages over the strangely scabbed area, so it didn't look quite so hideous.

When she was done, she felt a bit better. The state of the injury itself linked to a whole sea of questions. But there'd be time to worry about those later. At least, there would be if she could avoid being shot at again.

The twins were both sitting outside the bathroom door when she opened it, staring up at her with wide, worried eyes. "Hi," she said, and stepped over them to find some clean clothes.

"Don't send us away!" burst Kari. "We'll be really, really good."

Marley paused in the process of buttoning up her shirt. "Why do you think I'm sending you away?"

"You packed up all our stuff!"

Marley glanced over at the couch. So she had. "All of us are going. Together." But the expressions on both little faces remained dubious.

Marley sighed and sat down on her bed. "Come here and sit beside me; I want to tell you a little story." When they were snuggled up next to her, she went on. "When I was a baby, my first mommy decided she didn't want me. So she left me at a hospital, and I got a new mommy, and a daddy, too. My new mommy loved me very much, but I was always worried she was going to give me away, especially if I misbehaved. But she never ever did. Whenever I was difficult, she just gave me a hug, like this, and told me how lucky she felt that she got to be my mommy. Just like my new mommy wouldn't send me away, no matter what I did, I'm not going to send you away, or go away from you. We're going to go find Zachariah together." She looked between their faces, hoping they had followed at least the essential point.

Kari said, "Where's your second mommy now?"

"She lives south of here. It's a bit of a drive, but whenever I want to go home, I can."

Lissa said, "Why did your first mommy not want you?"

Marley flinched inwardly, but her voice was calm as she said, "Nobody knows. Most likely she couldn't take care of me very well and wanted me to have a better life." She ignored the child's voice raging inside: *She could have done it through proper channels, she didn't have to just abandon me.*

Both twins were quiet, absorbing the story. Marley hugged them again and stood up to pack her own bag. She didn't know where she was going, but she knew she couldn't stay in the apartment, waiting for her mysterious enemies to come to her. The pair of women had been moving toward her home from the park.

She stole a glance at the children while she unzipped a backpack. Kari was quietly repeating the story to her doll, changing it so it was the doll who never left her. Lissa was watching Marley with a solemn, thoughtful gaze.

Marley hoped that the kids would never experience as

much of the angst-filled side of adoption as she had. When she'd been nine, an unexpected baby brother had joined the family in the traditional way. By the time she was twelve, she and her parents had become aware of all the ways that her brother's heredity made him like her parents. In comparison, all the ways she was different stood out as they never had before.

Her mother, a screenwriter, and her father, an effects programmer, could share their love of stories with her, but they couldn't teach her extroversion, or not to worry so much. They taught her to be practical, but they couldn't teach her to be cheerful. They couldn't teach her to be *tall*. She was just so different, and she'd realized it right around the time puberty hit and made things *really* complicated.

She'd always known she was adopted; the evidence of the fostering process was too omnipresent in her very young childhood to just ignore. The story she'd told the twins was one, with some wording changes, that her parents had told her. Her parents had been quicker to assume the best of intentions on her birth mother's part. But by thirteen, Marley no longer believed them. Heredity clearly influenced a lot, at least as much as upbringing. Her brother was her mother and father mixed together! And she was—what was she?

No matter what anybody told her, teenage eyes could see The Truth. Anybody who gave a baby up for adoption was wicked in the eyes of society. Adopting parents were heroes, but those who gave their children up were poor, which meant lazy, or unready for a child, which meant irresponsible—and they were almost certainly sexually active without being married, which was the most basic definition of a bad girl.

Her adolescence had been a battlefield. She was so intent on proving that she'd been born unlovable that if it had just been her versus her parents, she probably would have succeeded in wrecking her life. But fortunately, she'd had Branwyn, and later Penny, to help stabilize her. They'd proved, over and over again, that some people thought she was worth caring about, even people who hadn't invested as much as her parents.

As she'd grown up and failed to convince her parents to reject her, the battlefield had faded away. Didn't they all? And as the tempers of adolescence cooled, she realized and accepted that nothing could convince the woman who had raised her to stop being her mother. But that didn't heal the wounds inside, scraped raw by constant teenage worrying at the question of her birth, and worrying at the truth of what she'd inherited from her genetic parents. It simply made her adopted parents saints.

Guilt twisted inside her. She didn't visit them enough. When her parents came to visit her, she had a good time, able to appreciate her family as she couldn't ten years ago. But the old house was the site of too many fights, and too many tantrums she hadn't yet forgiven herself for. They laughed about the new kitchen in the old house, which replaced the one she'd set on fire. But she couldn't laugh. Maybe if she'd been theirs biologically...

She shook her head, shook away the bad habits that clustered around her like flies. As she'd told the twins, she could go home anytime she wanted. But that wouldn't be today, especially not with who-knew-what after her.

Lissa suddenly asked, "Are we taking the kitty?"

Marley blinked. "Absolutely," she said. "Thank you for reminding me." Between the threatened evacuations from the wildfires, and the bad guys, she had no idea when or if she'd be able to get back. She wasn't leaving *anybody* behind.

She looked around her apartment, searching out the cardboard cat carrier, and realized that, as Lissa had inadvertently pointed out, there was more to leaving than just responding to an initial instinct. She thought it was dangerous to remain at the apartment, and she wasn't the only one who lived there.

She'd have to talk to Branwyn. She thought about it a bit more. At least it gave her a short-term plan more focused than "running away."

It took longer than she liked to load the children and the cat, along with supplies for a few days, into the car. The girls were obedient, but too helpful, and the cat... a small cat can get places one would rather not stick one's arm. Marley did her best not to think about it.

After the kids were strapped in, she moved around the outside of the car, studying the tires and wondering how to tell if the vehicle had been sabotaged somehow. She felt the old familiar anxiety rise up, and hard on its heels came a realization: the medication had burned out of her system.

Her thoughts were sharper and more focused than they'd been for a year or more. How had that happened?

But she had no time to worry about it, because the kaleidoscope sight fractured her vision again. Neighbors walking through the parking lot rippled with a half-dozen variations on themselves, all wounded or scarred. But the twins, looking out the back window at her, were unchanged, without refractions.

The sight calmed her. The anxiety vanished before it could become a full panic attack, and the kaleidoscope vision vanished with it.

Marley let out her breath. Then she got into the car and started it up, quickly, before the anxiety could resurface. Without medication, the world seemed like it was sustained by madness. Ordinary people got through life by believing in an illusion: that life was safe; that *it*, whatever *it* was, couldn't happen to them. But to someone, somewhere, it did. It *could* be her or her loved ones. And there was nothing she could do about it. Oh, there were sensible precautions that anyone might take. But anybody who really thought about the randomness of the world would build a bunker, or else eventually go insane. And nobody seemed to want to hide in a bunker.

They'd shot at her.

And then they'd gone away.

Marley shifted in her seat as she nudged the car into the beginnings of rush hour traffic. The kids were playing quietly with their dolls in the back seat, while Neath curled up tight in the cat carrier in the passenger seat footwell.

Her gaze went back to the kids. She didn't want to think about what else had happened at the park, but it kept intruding on her thoughts. That light, and the terrible expression on Lissa's face. The voice, and the empty clothes after the light faded. Where had the women gone?

She forced her thoughts away. Stuck in traffic wasn't the time to try to understand what had happened, or ponder her brain's health. Instead, she turned up the radio and listened for news of the wildfire, and for the traffic report.

She listened to the list of road closures as the traffic crept forward. Then, as the DJ went on to talk about some celebrity news in much more detail than he'd given to the natural disaster, Marley noticed a white minivan two lanes over.

Panic exploded through her. She couldn't see the driver or the plates but it didn't matter. It *could* be them, and here she was, trapped in traffic. She couldn't go forward or backward; she couldn't even change lanes.

It took every bit of willpower she had to not unbuckle her seatbelt and fling herself out of the car.

She hunched over her steering wheel as her breathing got faster and the traffic crept forward. She let the car coast forward a few yards. Her breath rasped and the panic slipped out of control again. What was she doing in a car? She was stuck in a tin can on an assembly line of death. They all were, and nobody could get out.

The kaleidoscope vision returned. Instantly, the clogged

freeway became a panorama of catastrophe. Every car she could see was wreathed in a dozen possible disasters of flame and twisted metal and half-glimpsed body parts. Even the loud radio seemed to merge into the hallucination, with guitars screaming like tortured souls.

Marley sobbed, pressing her head against the steering wheel. Even with her eyes closed, the image of the worst pile-up imaginable wouldn't leave her. So many people, so many possible bad choices. How did anybody survive?

The blast of horns around her cut through her misery and she realized space had opened up before her. Squinting through her eyelashes, as if that could drive away the kaleidoscope vision, she let the car creep forward again. She stared at the road. She couldn't get out, or go back, or get off the highway. All she could do was go forward. The kaleidoscope vision flickered off and on erratically. What was wrong with her?

She was at the heart of the traffic jam now. A patrol car was on the shoulder, behind a long, sleek black sports car. The officer and the sports car driver were both standing between the two vehicles.

And it was all wrong. The officer was rigid, while the other man was relaxed and confident. He had one hand on the officer's shoulder, in a friendly sort of way, and he was speaking. There was a maelstrom of disaster wreathing the officer, but it wasn't nearly as awful as his expression. The twisted horror on the officer's face was so vivid that it shocked Marley out of her panic.

Then she saw the other man through her kaleidoscope vision, and a jolt of terror brought the panic back again. Instead of a rotation of variations, there was only a vortex, a spiral of oblivion. A gaunt framework of bone wings sprouted from his back, reaching forward to enclose the officer lovingly. The form of the man himself seemed like a paper mask pinned over something all the worse because she couldn't see it. Whatever its appearance, it was a monster.

Her knuckles turned white on the wheel. Like an animal scenting prey, the monster turned his head toward her car, pausing in his speech. He met her eyes. And he smiled, showing lots of teeth.

Her hands dropped into her lap, boneless. *Poor mad thing*, said a voice that was brother to the voice at the park. *If you come to me, I'll make it all go away.*

Marley couldn't help herself. For a moment, she imagined peace. Then, in the rearview mirror, she realized the twins were staring at her.

Something white-hot blazed through her. She would not allow anything to happen to them! She had to protect them; nobody else could. It was a rock-hard certainty, backed up by her visions of destruction and death. Only with her were they safe. If that was madness, she couldn't fight it. She could only go forward.

She forced the kaleidoscope—the catastrophe vision, as she was starting to think of it—away through sheer willpower. The highway went back to normal, and once again, the driver on the side of the road seemed like an ordinary man. Except that he was still looking at her, a faint smile on his face.

Traffic moved again as the people ahead stopped gawking. She raised her middle finger at the monster as she drove by. He winked back at her.

Ahead of her, the freeway opened up.

-eleven-

Branwyn worked at a large garage, fulfilling the paint and body shop jobs. When Marley pulled into the parking lot, she noticed that the place wasn't as busy as it'd been on previous visits. The promise of ash pouring from the sky did not encourage new paint jobs. All the same, she parked on the far side of the main building, out of sight of the street. Then she grabbed the cat carrier and shepherded the children into the office.

The waiting area was empty and recently straightened, with neat stacks of magazines on tables between steel-framed chairs and the little water cooler area freshly supplied with paper cups. Branwyn's feet were on the counter, obscuring the rest of her as she leaned back, reading a magazine. The radio played softly from under the counter.

"And here I was worried about distracting you from work," said Marley.

Branwyn looked up, startled, and then sat forward. "Hi there. Hi, kids!"

The twins peeked around Marley's legs, mumbling. Then Kari spotted the water cooler. "Oooh!" she chirped, and trotted over to it.

"Don't make a mess," Marley warned, and nudged Lissa encouragingly to join her sister. When she turned back to Branwyn, her friend's gaze was on the bandages over her injured arm.

"What happened?"

Marley shifted the cat carrier to her other hand and rubbed her forehead. "It's a long story. I've had a pretty incredible day."

Branwyn perked up. "Oh yeah? Tell me about it? A *Newsweek* from last month is pretty dull."

Slowly, Marley shook her head. "I'm not even sure what happened."

Branwyn raised her eyebrows. "Well, what happened to your arm? I mean, you managed to put some Band-Aids on it, so you must have noticed it."

Marley hesitated. But it was Branwyn. "I got shot."

"No way!" Branwyn's chair rocked backwards, but she caught herself on the counter before she fell over.

Marley plunged on. "And that's why I want to borrow the keys to your studio. And you shouldn't go home, either. I think it's dangerous."

Branwyn slung herself over the counter. "Wait, who shot you? They were at the apartment?" Her green eyes were wide.

It's Branwyn wasn't enough. She couldn't find the words to explain the utter strangeness of the park, even to her. "I—I don't quite know. It was at the park."

"What did the cops say?" When Marley didn't immediately answer, her eyes narrowed. "You didn't call the cops. Or 911."

"You're not exactly a fan of the authorities yourself, Bran. And they would separate me from the girls, which would be... bad. It was just a graze."

"Yeah, but guns... Well, what happened to the gunman, then?"

"They... went away." She tried to squeeze shut memory's eyes on that awful devouring static, and the speaking light.

Instead, she watched Branwyn's face tighten. "You're not telling me anything. Are you in shock? Sit down. Put your feet up."

Marley fumbled for words as she sat down. *I'm being stalked by a group of people with supernatural... a pair of older women attacked... and there was a girl with some dogs...* No. Branwyn was open-minded, but Marley couldn't bring herself to describe what she didn't understand. "I don't want to talk about it here. Maybe tonight, after I've had some time to process it?"

Branwyn stepped closer and investigated the bandages on Marley's arm. Her gaze slid over to where the kids were getting water all over the floor. "Hmmm." Her eyes flicked down to the cat carrier Marley was still holding. Then she fished a keychain out of her pocket and slid off a key. "Do you want me to leave work and take you there?"

Marley closed her fingers over the key, feeling its warmth. "No. I survived getting here. I'll be fine."

Branwyn hesitated, then nodded. "All right. I have some errands I need to run after work, but I'll be there later."

"Oh, and I wanted to rent a car."

Branwyn stared at her, then said, "I wish you could tell me why, Marley. Loaners are technically for customers."

"Shall I go outside and key my hood?" Marley snapped. Then she took a deep breath. "I'm sorry, Branwyn. I don't even know if I'm being too paranoid or not paranoid enough. But somebody *shot at me.*"

Branwyn put her hand on Marley's head as if checking for a fever, and then hopped over the counter again. "Yeah. Let me see what I can find."

Marley focused on the twins splashing in the water they'd spilled. She suddenly realized she'd even seen Kari deliberately turning a cup upside down. "You two, cut that out. And clean it up."

Lissa, who'd been drawing in the puddle, gave her an inscrutable look before grabbing some paper towels. But Kari kicked a foot across the puddle and then stomped it to make a teeny-tiny splash. "It's. Too. Hot."

Marley blew out her breath. "Yes. It is. We all agree. And if somebody goes to get some water and slips and falls because you made a mess, they'll hurt themselves. And if you clean it up, you'll cool down. Everybody wins."

"The studio's air conditioning is imaginary. Won't that be a charming scene?" said Branwyn. "I've checked out a car for you. One of the premiums."

Marley gave Kari the stink eye until she abruptly giggled and started moving water around with a paper towel. Then she turned to Branwyn and fished out her emergency credit card.

Branwyn gave her a scornful look. "Put that away."

Marley was acutely aware of the mini-lecture she'd just given Kari on responsibility. "Bran, I need to—"

Branwyn's look became positively unfriendly. "You want a different car because you think you're being followed. Do you know if they can follow your credit card, too?" Branwyn shook her head as she typed into the computer. "In my opinion, Marley, you're definitely not being paranoid enough."

Branwyn's art studio was one of a set on an unfinished third floor over a pawn shop, and it was breathtakingly hot. The local air pollution was so bad Marley could hardly see or smell the smoke from the wildfires. Smog clung to the heights of downtown, sucking the life out of what seemed like it should have been a busy, interesting street. But it was quiet on the block outside the studio, and felt as empty as a ghost town. Branwyn apparently liked it, but Marley had never understood why.

There were three ornate black metal box fans in the studio, functional works of art created by Branwyn herself, and once they were turned on, at least there was a hot breeze to dry their sweat. More bits of twisted metal and spools of wire were piled around a long table littered with tools. There was also a utilitarian shower, and a sink large enough to bathe a small child.

Marley filed that thought away for later. For the moment, the twins seemed content to pant on the couch, exhausted from the strange day. Even Neath flopped bonelessly on the floor, too hot to explore. Marley understood the feeling. Once she had the fans pointed at the couch, she sank down beside the girls and her eyes seemed to drift closed all by themselves.

She dreamt first of her idealized bedroom, and a doll-sized fairy waving at her. "There you are! I've been waiting for you for an oak's age." Dream-Neath leapt off the bed, pinning the fairy to the floor. A sparkle devoured the walls of the bedroom. Then, even though there was a muffled, "No, come back, get this thing off me—" from the fairy, Marley was back in the park, reliving the nightmare from earlier in the day. That happened nine or ten times, until Marley was viewing the events through a review column she was writing. "Too post-modern for my tastes," she wrote, and shoved the scroll through the keyhole from *Alice's Adventures in Wonderland*. It stuck there, because it wasn't the key.

She woke up, feeling as if her head had been buried in sand.

The girls were still asleep, taking long, deep breaths that suggested they wouldn't be waking up anytime soon. Marley went to the window and looked out. The mountainside was mostly a charred black, with spots of orange where patches of fire still found fuel. The main line of fire was out of sight, hidden behind the cityscape. That meant the fires were bad this year. Marley wondered if maybe this year, all the warnings and evacuations and careful fallback plans would be justified. Then her wandering gaze passed over a familiar figure leaning against a wall across the street.

It was the man from the library, the one who'd helped her escape it and had otherwise been so uninformative. There were big black birds at his feet, and on the building around him. Marley glanced at his face and met his eyes; he was staring directly at her.

She swore and ducked away from the window, her heart pounding. How had he found her so quickly? He wasn't the most frightening thing that could have appeared outside her window, yet if he'd found her, surely Jeremy the Lawyer and his interns could, too? But she thought of Kari opening a locked door, and the monster in man's clothing on the highway. She had no idea what the rules of the world were anymore.

She peeked around the window frame. He was still there, still looking up at her. His hands were crammed into his pockets, and he looked angry. Marley bit her lip and then stopped suppressing the catastrophe vision. A wheel of possibilities wreathed the tall man. Death was still on the wheel, but it was no longer the most prominent future. Instead, an image of loneliness painted into a forest of self-loathing was clearest in the stack, though not pinpoint sharp.

Marley caught her breath. Why? If this vision was some kind of precognition, why did she only see bad things ahead of everybody she looked at? Everybody but the twins. She turned to gaze at them. Cherubic in their sleep, they still seemed utterly safe to her, as if nothing could harm them or tarnish the possibilities of their future.

When she looked back outside, the man across the street was gone, although the flock of black birds remained. Several of them seemed to be looking up at her window. She blinked at them, trying to determine if that was actually true, or a trick of the late afternoon shadows. Then there was a creak in the hall outside the studio, and a soft knock on the door.

Marley raced over to the door. It had no chain, just an ordinary lock on the knob that she was suddenly very happy she'd remembered to turn. She leaned her shoulder on the door, and waited.

"Hello?" came a masculine voice, muffled by the door. "I wanted to introduce myself. We met at the library. My name is Corbin Adair."

"And why were you outside my building, Mr. Adair?"

The floor creaked, and the door moved a tiny bit; Marley realized he was also leaning against the door. His voice, when he spoke, was uncomfortably close. "Watching over you."

"Right. Because you're oh-so-helpful. I forgot. I still don't know why, though."

She could practically feel the frustration in his voice as he said, "Because I don't know what else to do."

An unexpected sympathy swelled within Marley, but she crushed it ruthlessly. "And how exactly did you find me?"

The pause from the other side went on too long. Finally, he said, "I don't want to explain it like this. I don't think you'd understand."

Marley pressed her lips together. "Really. Give me some credit, Mr. Adair; I'm not an idiot."

"Did you understand what happened at the park today? AT told me about it."

"I understand that some people shot at me, and I don't know why, or who sent them. Was it you?"

"No! *Damn* it!" There was a thump on the door, at about head-height. "Look, whether or not you believe me, we want the same things: to find Zachariah, and to protect those kids. And I expect you want to survive the next few days, but who knows if that's actually true. God knows I've been wrong before."

Marley bit her lip. "Are other people going to follow me the same way you did?"

"No, absolutely not. And if they tried, I'd know about it."

She raised her eyebrows at the door. "You're that certain? Well… good." She closed her eyes. "Still not going to let you in, though. You know how it is. I'm a helpless woman with some kids to protect, and you're a big, strong, deceptive man who won't explain himself to me."

There was a snorting sound from the other side. "I'm going back to keeping watch. If anybody else does show up, I'll warn you, and distract them."

"My friend Branwyn is coming over. She has green hair. Don't you touch her." Then curiosity drove her to add, "How will you warn me?"

The door shifted again as he moved away from it. His voice drifted back. "There will be wings at your window."

-twelve-

At first, Corbin returned to his position across the street. But, apparently, he didn't like the view, because as the sun sank below the skyline, he moved to the near side of the street. It was just out of Marley's line of sight, unless she pressed her cheek to the screen, which didn't feel very pleasant. So she gave up on watching him watching her, and turned her attention to the waking little girls. Tepid showers soothed grumpy tempers admirably, and afterward she watched them play with the cat among Branwyn's projects and wondered what to do about dinner.

When Branwyn showed up, she called Marley's cellphone rather than knocking, and Marley opened the door to help her with the armful of fast food bags she was carrying. They exchanged meaningful glances that meant "food first, before the little girls eat us," and settled down for a hamburger picnic on the studio floor.

Marley, who'd been thinking about what to tell Branwyn, started the conversation. "Do you remember those stories your great grandmother used to tell us? Black dogs and white cats and horseshoes? And the magpies?"

"All her superstitions from the old country? Yeah." Branwyn smiled briefly at a memory. "Two magpies to the right is lucky! Never ask a fisherman where he's fishing!"

"And all the stuff about fairies. That old story about a world under a burning mountain, and trooping fairies on the move."

Branwyn nodded. "And a covenant requiring a tithe to Hell. Yes. What about it?"

"I've just been thinking about it. She really believed that stuff—it wasn't just stories to her."

"People 'really believe' all sorts of stupid things," Branwyn said. "At least she had the excuse of being born a long time ago."

"You mean, before we knew it was all stupid things?"

Branwyn's eyes narrowed. "Before people were educated enough to question what they were told. Are you leading up to telling me that Zachariah was stolen away by fairies? Because he's about forty years too old for that."

"No! I'm not. And he's not that old. I'm thinking about angels, actually, and not because of Zachariah. Angels and demons and why so many people believe in them. But they don't believe in magic. How does that make sense?"

"Doing as you will creates a bigger burden on the conscience than doing as you're told." At Marley's questioning look, Branwyn sighed and continued. "People want a higher power to blame, so they don't have to be held accountable for their own actions and decisions. The strength and authority comes from outside them. Magic, of the wizardly variety, represents personal responsibility. So that's the fantasy." Branwyn's mouth twisted in disgust. "It's the same reason big corporations are so popular."

"But you don't believe in magic *or* religion," Marley pointed out.

Branwyn took a bite of her veggie burger, chewed it, and

swallowed. "Or big corporations. That's because I don't need a metaphor to help me take responsibility. I believe in me."

"It isn't just because religions encourage the faithful not to believe in magic?"

"Personal responsibility. But while we're on the subject... Penny called me this afternoon. I went to see her after work. She'd been crying."

Marley lowered her gaze. "What was wrong?"

"Well, apparently you told her that her new boyfriend was using her to get to the kids, for one." Branwyn paused for a moment and then went on.

"And thinking over her date last night makes her wonder if it was true. She said it was 'too perfect.' Actually, she said it was 'more perfect than she deserved,' but this is Penny, so I ignored the latter bit." She frowned. "But he called while I was there, and she... transformed. Talking to him made her happy like I've never seen before. It was strange."

Marley chewed on her lip again. "What was she like, after?"

"Happy and confused. She said Jeremy told her she had a higher purpose in his organization, which she laughed at, but... I could tell she really liked the idea." Branwyn scowled. "I think Lawyer Jeremy's pulling Penny into a cult."

Marley eyed her friend and thought of a group of happy, well-dressed young people. "I could believe that. What did you say to her?"

Branwyn looked irritated. "Nothing. That sort of accusation makes me sound like an overprotective mother. But I'd love to prove to her that the bastard is just using her."

"Break her heart for her own good, you mean." Marley shook her head. "I'd rather he just... went away."

"Me too!" chirped Lissa, who was listening intently.

Marley gave her a look. "You go play with your sister."

"She's listening too! Right, Kari?"

Kari, dangling a makeshift fishing pole before Neath, said, "Right! Fairy lawyers!"

Marley rolled her eyes and dug out a pair of picture books from her hastily packed luggage. When she'd settled the twins on the other side of the room with Lissa reading aloud to Kari, she returned to Branwyn.

"Did you see that guy outside? Dark hair, loitering outside the building?"

Branwyn perked up. "I did. Is he one of the bad guys?"

Marley made a face. "You're as bad as the kids. And I don't know. He says he isn't. I'm not afraid of him like I should be, either. And I keep wondering if it's... I dunno, Stockholm syndrome or something. Because there's no reason not to be afraid of him. Just because he says he's on my side doesn't mean anything."

Branwyn eyed her. "Yeah. About that. What's going on?"

Marley launched into the abridged explanation. "My theory is that Zachariah has some information that a 'business rival' wants, and his gang is trying to kidnap the kids to give them some leverage over him. And I think the authorities are compromised in the whole deal, so I can't go to them."

Branwyn's expression was very dubious. "And the gunmen who just 'went away'?"

"Oh! There were other people around. Including this girl with three really big, aggressive dogs. I think they got spooked into shooting before they were ready, and then ran. Everybody could see their faces and everything." Even as she spoke, Marley felt a pang of guilt, and she busied herself cleaning up the remains of dinner. Branwyn didn't want to hear about flashes of wings and light—that much was clear from their earlier conversation. And for all Marley knew, she was telling the truth. Maybe the flash of light had been a hallucination brought on by shock. Not talking about it until she understood it better was the responsible solution.

She heard Branwyn stand up, and then suddenly the taller woman was hauling her up by her injured arm. "Hey, ow, what are you doing?" Marley demanded. When Branwyn ripped the bandages off, it didn't hurt as much as Marley feared because they hadn't adhered completely to the scab over the half-healed wound.

Branwyn ran her hand over it. "What the hell is this? Come on." She tugged Marley over to the big sink. "Soak your arm here and we'll clean that up." She started the sink filling. Then, conversationally, she said, "My friend Stephen got shot once. In the leg. It took a chunk out. I saw it the next day. After a doctor had stitched it up, sure, but it still looked raw." She shot Marley a look, her green eyes blazing.

Marley remembered Kari touching her arm, patches of static swirling around her fingers, saying happily, *I fixed it!* "I have no idea what happened. Maybe it wasn't actually a bullet. I really don't know, Branwyn! Don't look at me like that."

Branwyn pushed her arm into the water, pulling it down until it was submerged to the shoulder. "You know something. You're too honest."

"I don't *know* anything, when it comes to that."

"And too philosophical, too. That guy outside? You're not afraid of him and he says he's trying to help you? Maybe it's actually true. Not everybody has a hidden motive."

"The other people following me around do. Lawyer Jeremy does. They haven't presented me with an affidavit of their intentions. They just shot at me, Branwyn. And I don't know why. I'm sorry."

Branwyn gently rubbed at the crud around the main scab. "Well, something certainly happened to you. That's going to be some scar."

Marley craned her neck to see the injury. Washed clean of all the extra dried blood, her arm still had a dime-sized dent in it, covered with a moist, half-healed scab. She raised her eyes to meet Branwyn's gaze. The blaze of emotion had faded, at least a little. Softly, Branwyn said, "I keep wondering if I missed seeing this injury over the last week or two. But I'm sure I didn't. I wish you trusted yourself enough to tell me what you're not saying."

Awkwardly, Marley shrugged. "I've told you what I'm pretty sure of, and what I've speculated. That's what's important."Branwyn's face closed up, and she released Marley's arm. "Yeah. But it's not everything. I'm used to deciding 'important' for myself. And since you're asking me to stay away from my home because of this..." She shrugged, and put a new bandage on Marley's arm. "You haven't been this reserved since we were kids and you were upset about your brother."

"I haven't felt this crazy since then, either," Marley muttered. It just slipped out. She looked up at Branwyn, but Branwyn was walking away, over to the kids. With a cheery voice, she invited them to play with her art supplies, her back to Marley.

ʒ ʒ

Branwyn hauled out a dusty old sleeping bag from the depths of her car, and claimed the floor, leaving Marley and the twins to dogpile on the couch again.

As Marley snuggled the twins down into the couch, Kari said, "We know about fairies! Uncle Zach told us."

"Did he?" asked Marley, wondering if she'd be able to sleep tonight.

"Uncle Zach said that all fairies are lawyers. Can't trust 'em!"

"But they like gifts. And they keep their promises, basically," added Lissa.

"And they live backwards. I guess that's why you wear your shirt inside out?" Kari said.

"No, Uncle Zach said that was just a useless superpower," corrected Lissa.

Kari hugged her doll. "And they wear leashes. Because otherwise they're naughty."

"They loovvvvve games. And they're basically imps."

"You're imps," laughed Marley. "Close your eyes now."

They both closed their eyes, but Kari's popped back open. "Marley? Why did those people want to hurt us? Why did they hurt you?"

Marley's smile faded. "I don't know. I think it's because..." and she paused, her mind racing as she searched for something appropriate to say.

"Sometimes people get confused and scared by things they don't understand. And they want to make the confusion and scariness go away, by making the thing they don't understand go away. I think maybe those people didn't understand why we were running toward them and they wanted us to go away." She was aware of Lissa listening so hard her ears seemed to have grown, even though her eyes were still closed. "But they chose the wrong way to do it."

"So it was an accident?" asked Kari.

"Kind of, yeah."

"Okay," said Kari, and turned over. But Marley thought Lissa stayed awake for much longer.

The temperature that night was almost reasonable, although there was a red tint to the light pollution that made the night that much less comfortable to sleep in. "Just pretend it's the world's biggest campfire," suggested Branwyn, before she put her headphones on.

Marley expected that she'd have trouble sleeping, but the gentle breathing of the twins, and Neath's contented purring near her head, knocked her out before she had time to worry about it.

And once again, she was in the dream room.

Tinker Chime the fairy fashion doll was waiting for her. "Just passing through again?" he said acidly. His arms were crossed and his tiny foot tapped on the air. "Don't mind me, I have all aeon. It's not as if captivity can crush my people's spirit any more."

Happiness tickled Marley like champagne bubbles in her soul, but she resisted it. "You again? Where's my cat?" She felt around under the bed and encountered a paw. Even in her *dream*, Neath was tuckered out.

"Why are you so *unfriendly*?" complained the fairy. "Most people would be delighted with an encounter like this."

"I don't believe in fairies," said Marley, flatly.

"Oh! Ow!" Chime pressed his hand to his chest and drifted to the ground. "A mortal wound!" He landed on the carpet, one arm flung dramatically over his head. One eye opened, then the other. "Just kidding."

There was an angry yowl under the bed, and Neath slunk out. Chime leapt into the air again. "You woke the beast!"

Marley swatted at him. "Good! Maybe she can make you go away!"

"That would be the wrong choice," said the fairy, and his voice was so serious that Marley remembered her own words to the twins, back in the waking world.

"I don't care," she said defiantly. "I don't need this bullshit invading my *dreams* as well as my real life. I should be able to get a good night's sleep. I *deserve* a good night's sleep."

"You *are* asleep," pointed out Chime. "That's the magic of dreams. And this isn't bullshit. It's very important! The fate of my people rests on your action and goodwill!"

"It's *totally* bullshit! The world is supposed to make sense. People aren't supposed to disappear into thin air. Wounds aren't supposed to be healed by the touch of a little girl. And crazy people aren't supposed to shoot at small children!"

"Why not?" The fairy flew closer to her face.

Marley glared. "Because." She picked up Neath and cuddled the cat close. "The world's complicated enough. Don't you roll your eyes at me!"

The fairy drifted backwards, out of reach. His worried eyes scanned her face. "If your world is so complicated, what's the addition of a couple more complications going to cost you? Do typhoons and microwaves bother you? They're *very* complicated."

Marley started to respond and then tripped over her tongue as she actually thought about the question. Then, begrudgingly, she said, "But I don't know if the new things are... a microwave or a typhoon or a hallucination." Even as she said it, she realized that was *an* issue, but *not* the biggest issue making her so angry with the world.

The fairy shrugged. "Mortals can't make typhoons."

"Well, humans did these things."

"Did they? You sure? Well, humans are talented folks." The fairy smirked.

Marley's irritation at the fairy returned. "I saw them. *Children.*" As she said it, a great shudder passed through her body. "These are tiny kids, and they can do such unbelievable things." She again saw the terrible expression on Lissa's little face, as she told the women with the guns to *go away.*

The devouring static stretching from Lissa to the women, at the same time as a similar static enfolded Kari's hands on Marley's arm.

And then the wings had come, and the ringing, otherworldly voice had spoken—but that, and all it implied, didn't bother Marley nearly as much as the children. Forces she couldn't guess at wanted them, and she *knew* it wasn't to coerce Zachariah. They were amazing all on their own.

"They're so *small,*" she said. "And so young. How can they possibly be aware of what they're doing? And I've made them my responsibility." The thought made her angry, not at the twins, but at a world which had taken advantage of her weak spot to saddle her with more than she had any idea how to handle. "That doesn't mean just keeping them safe. That means... teaching them. That means if they hurt anybody, it's because I let them do it. How can I teach them if I don't even understand what they're doing?"

"Find out more?" Chime turned so he was floating on his back. He sounded bored.

"How?" Marley demanded.

"How should I know? However your kind passes on lore. Or do you think these babes are something new? Uncharted territory?" A miniscule eyebrow arched. "I mean, personally, I don't think you should worry about it. There's much more important things going on. My people, for example."

"Real children trump dream people, Tinkerbell."

The fairy made a sour face. "*Her* friend was much more amenable to adventure than you are."

Marley ignored him. *Wings at your window.* "Some of them seem more friendly than others. I could at least find out why they're so interested in the kids."

Neath squirmed out of her arms and began stalking in a circle under where the fairy floated. He cast a displeased look down at her. "You can keep hunting me, beast, but it isn't going to keep me away. In fact, if she fails my people, I'll be here *forever.*"

Marley mused, "I wonder if Zachariah knew."

The dream began to disintegrate around her as Neath leapt straight up. The last thing she heard was a peevish fairy voice saying, "But more likely, she'll end up *dead*, and those precious children with her."

-thirteen-

Marley woke up to morning sun, and the rattling of the studio shower. She blinked for a moment, trying to remember where she was and what she was doing. She turned her head and the sight of Branwyn's big custom box fan helped her place herself. Still, she wouldn't have been surprised to see the fairy fashion doll sitting atop the box. She wondered if Tinker Chime was a representation of her subconscious, triggered by late-night fairy conversations, and if so, what it meant that he was a tiny, but attractive, male. But she did feel better about the twins and their strange abilities now. Dreams weren't always bad.

Lissa was wedged between her and the back of the couch, while Kari was on the floor, her knees tucked up under her body and her rump in the air. After carefully disentangling herself from the girl, Marley stepped toward the window. And paused. A black bird—a crow or a raven?—was perched on the windowsill, looking into the studio with one shiny black eye. It turned its head to one side, and then scratched at the screen. She could barely hear the scrape over the rattling of the shower and the roar of the fans.

It had something clutched in one foot, something white. A scrap of paper? She hurried over to the window and leaned against it, turning her head. Corbin was gone. Unexpected disappointment rose up, which she ignored as she turned her attention to the bird. It hadn't flown away at her approach, although it had hopped along the ledge when she leaned on the screen. "What do you want?"

It opened its mouth silently, then lifted its foot, thrusting the scrap of paper against the screen.

"Oh! Sorry." Marley felt embarrassed talking to the bird, but even more embarrassed that she hadn't realized its point before. But Corbin always seemed to be with birds, and even in the normal world, birds carried messages. She worked on figuring out how to open the screen. As she did, the shower turned off and she could hear Branwyn moving around behind her.

Finally she got one of the latches bent enough that a corner of the screen popped open. Immediately, the bird's foot thrust through the gap and released the scrap of paper. Marley snatched it up as the raven launched itself into the air, with a caw that sounded like laughter.

You're right. You deserve to know everything I do. Call me.
                                                    –Corbin

There was a phone number printed next to the name. It looked familiar.

While she was trying to remember where she'd seen it, Branwyn said, "I'm going on into work today. Since there's nothing better to do. If you don't call me every few hours, I'm going to call the cops." Marley turned to look at her. "Or worse." Her friend's green hair, spiky when wet, seemed to match her tone. She really didn't like being excluded from what she assumed was an adventure.

"I'm going to find out more today, Branwyn."

Branwyn shrugged. "Good." She turned away and then turned back. "I hope you don't think you're protecting me or something stupid like that."

"No." Marley said it, but her treacherous thoughts said, *Maybe a little.* "I just don't want to spread my own confusion."

Branwyn grumbled, "Yeah. Research Girl. At least it's not Penny's excuse." She left, shutting the door quietly behind her.

Marley stared at the door for a moment. Then she found her cellphone in her purse, right next to Zachariah's phone. "Oh!" she exclaimed, and then glanced guiltily at the twins. She took both phones and went to the far side of the studio. Then she turned on Zachariah's phone and scrolled through the call list. There it was, Corbin and his number, called the day Zachariah had vanished.

Before she thought about it too much, she pressed the call button. The phone rang twice, and then a bewildered voice said, "Zachariah? What the hell—"

"It's me," Marley said. "I have his phone."

There was a pause. "Oh. The girl with the kids. Marley."

"Yes," she said patiently. "A bird gave me a note signed by you."

"Yeah. I'm sorry, I just woke up." Marley felt a twinge of irrational annoyance. How could he be watching out for bad guys if he was asleep? And why had she been relying on him to do that? He continued, "Is everything all right?"

"Nothing has changed. I'm calling because you said you wanted to explain things. And I'm ready to have things explained."

"Right. Can we meet somewhere?"

Marley glanced at the kids, who were stirring. "I'm still not comfortable letting anybody I don't trust too close to the kids. Not after yesterday."

Another pause. "This will be harder, then."

"Why? Talking is talking, and phones are safer."

"Because seeing is believing, and I'm just a voice in your ear." He sighed. "Where do you want me to start?"

"Who is Lawyer Jeremy working for? Who's behind the people shooting at me? What happened to Zachariah? What's your connection to Zachariah? I saw that he tried to call you the day he vanished."

"Yes. I was busy at the time." Corbin's words were clipped. "Trying to save my friends from the clusterfuck he sent them into."

Marley frowned. "What?"

"I'm sorry. Yes, he called me, presumably to find out how we were doing on a task he'd set myself and my friends. The answer there was 'poorly'."

"What was the task?"

He hesitated. "We were trying to protect something from somebody who wanted to steal it. We failed. I think the same somebody is now trying to get the kids."

"You're being very vague," Marley observed. "Do you think I won't understand big words?"

"So prickly. Look, how much do you know about the Backworld, and the Geometry? Have you even heard of nephilim or the war in Heaven?"

She almost hung up the phone right then. Her thumb even twitched. "I took geometry in high school. Nephilim are mythological giants that were washed away in the biblical flood."

"So you don't know anything. About your—about magic, and the secret side of the world, I mean," he added hastily, and then paused. "Are you still there?"

"Yes. Sooner or later you're going to say something meaningful. I'm waiting for it."

"Are you sure you don't want to meet somewhere?"

"Are you kidding me? Convince me you're not a paranoid schizophrenic first."

"I don't think that's possible over the phone. Not quickly, anyhow. And you don't sound inclined to give me a lot of time."

Marley blew out her breath. "What is it with you and birds, at least? Why are they always around you?"

"They're my friends," he said mildly. "They've always been the friends of my family. Look, I'm going to tell you more about what we were doing for Zachariah. And I'm going to put it in a way that will make sense to you. And then I'm going to change the perspective a little. All right?"

Marley silently rolled her eyes. "Go on, already."

"Zachariah was a friend. He asked me to go with some other friends on a mission: to interfere with an organization attempting to steal an important object. He said this organization was planning on using the object to unlock a barrier preventing the organization from accessing great power. My friends and I—we failed. We didn't anticipate the force they sent in. And my friends were badly injured. After getting them someplace safe, I came back to discover Zachariah was missing, and the organization's primary agent had sent his servants after you and the kids as the next step of the plan. Zachariah didn't warn us about that. I don't know what they want with the kids, yet." By the end of the story, Corbin's words had become clipped and angry again.

"Maybe Zachariah holds the last part of this key you mentioned? A final password or something? And they want the kids in order to extort it out of him?"

"Unlikely. I don't think Zachariah had any significant role in the creation of the barrier. No, I think they want the kids, and Zachariah was in the way, which is why they're after you now."

Marley let this sink in, and said, "And the perspective

changer?"

"The agent is an angel," Corbin said bluntly. "The barrier prevents his kind from directly manipulating humanity."

Marley remembered again the wings in the light, and the ethereal voice. "I was afraid you were going to say something like that. An angel. An *angel*? From Heaven? God's messenger?"

"Maybe once upon a time, but they ran out of new messages long ago. Now they make their own decisions, just like us. Usually, they're more subtle than this. And the primary agent in this case, an angel called Akaterin Ettoriel, doesn't have the profile of a powermonger. None of this makes sense, which is why I'd really, really like to talk to Zachariah."

"Of course."

Corbin didn't continue, and she let the pause drag out while she tried to figure out what to say next. She'd decided she wasn't going to hang up the phone, even if it seemed like the most sensible option. Sense had flown out the window the day before.

She watched as Kari sat up and looked around. Silently, Marley pulled out a bottle of water and a box of graham crackers and offered them to the child. The practical act grounded her.

"Are you still there?" Corbin said.

"I'm not sure how to feel about running away from something like that," she said conversationally.

"There's a lot you still don't know. Are you sure—you're taking this better than I expected," he said. "You really didn't know anything?"

"I hardly know anything now. You didn't mention a Backworld or any geometry, for example. But it's an explanation. It's as good as anything. I was afraid what I saw was a hallucination. Though maybe it'd be better for all of us if I *was* crazy. Don't you think?"

His voice became low. "No. Whether or not you were crazy wouldn't change anything. You're not, though. Whatever's happening to you, you're not." There was a warmth to his voice that startled Marley. "Zachariah was cruel to you."

She was startled. "No! We're friends."

"He kept secrets from you. Things he *really* should have shared. At the very least, he should have told us about you. My family was right about him."

"There you go talking about your family again; what's that about? How is it you and Zachariah are in the business of opposing angels? Are you Satanists?"

A bark of laughter buzzed the phone. "Satanists! No. God, that's really funny. No. We oppose angels mostly because what they really want to do is get rid of us."

"And why is that? What are you?"

"Us? We're their children."

-fourteen-

"**N**ephilim,**"** Marley said, after a moment. "Not washed away in the Flood. Not *myths*."

"Mmm. No. No more than angels." He fell silent.

"You're the child of a—What does that even *mean*?"

"Well, when an angel loves a mortal very much—"

"Please! Don't joke!"

Mildly, he said, "It's not entirely a joke. Angels, of all the celestials, can be particularly fierce in their passions. It takes a lot to lure them out of Heaven and into breaking the Precepts. But in any case, it means we're partly human, and partly celestial. We inherit powers from our celestial side, and we don't age like humans. But we're not immortal like angels are, either."

"Don't age... How old are you?"

"Me? I'm only thirty. I'm also third generation; my father is... much older."

"And Zachariah? He's also a—uh. Is he old, too?"

"Ancient." She could hear the amusement in his voice, and she didn't like it.

"How about that girl with the dogs? AT? Is she also 'family'?"

"Yes. And she's sixteen, before you ask. She should be keeping an eye on your building right now."

Marley was aghast. "She's a kid. Why would you involve another kid in this?"

Corbin's voice sharpened. "She involved herself, and she's been involved in more frightening things. Her *life* is a more frightening thing. Don't worry about her."

"Right." Marley watched Lissa roll off the couch, stand up, stagger over to her sister, and take Kari's graham cracker. Kari's lip trembled.

Suddenly, she was ready for the conversation to be done. *Angels. Nephilim. Immortals.* "Well, I have to go be a foster mom now, so nice talking to you. Thanks for the info."

He paused, then said, "All right. It's a lot to take in. I'll let you think about it." She was about to hang up when he blurted, "Marley! They can't find you like AT and I can, but they *will* find you. You're not going to be safe where you are."

"Is there someplace I *will* be safe?"

"Just... keep moving for now. I'm going to try to find out why Ettoriel wants the kids. And I'm going to see what help Senyaza—uh, the family business—can provide."

"Right." She clicked off the phone and closed her eyes, letting Corbin's stories swirl around in her mind. Then one of the twins squealed in anger. She sighed, opened her eyes, and pushed into the fray.

There was, she reflected an hour later, only so fast that she could get the twins moving in the morning without scaring them or making them unreasonably surly. She wondered if experienced caretakers had any tricks, or if it always took this long to, say, get kids out to preschool. If the twins knew, they weren't saying.

Once she'd herded them out to the sidewalk and deposited most of what they'd taken upstairs back in the car, she stood back and looked around. The haze of smoke from the wildfires painted the sky with yellow, and there was hardly anybody out on the street. A block down, on the corner, she saw AT sitting sideways on a bus bench, all three dogs sprawled around her.

She was reading a magazine, some kind of teen thing, but she looked up as Marley approached and smiled. "Hi."

Lissa pressed close against Marley's leg, but Kari pulled away to go investigate the dogs. "Your doggie was hurt before."

A shadow passed over AT's face. "Yup. But he's better now. You can pet them if you'd like. They'll be nice." The black dog, the one who'd been shot, yawned hugely as Kari patted his head.

Marley put her hand on Lissa's hair. "Thank you. For yesterday, I mean. And, er... keeping watch now?"

AT's friendly smile returned. "Sure. I'm happy to help. Corbin called me and told me you two talked."

"Have you... has anybody... has it been busy?"

"Nope. I bet they're still figuring out that you swapped cars. That lawyer's people, anyhow. They're not big creative thinkers."

"How did you find me?"

AT patted the red dog curled up on the bench beside her. "Dogs have an amazing sense of smell. Especially mine."

"Oh. Right." Marley stood still, uncertain of what she wanted to say.

While she was wondering, AT tucked the magazine into a backpack and pulled a knee up under her chin. "So, Corbin finally introduced himself, and gave you his number."

"What? Yes. He told me about the... person after us.

Something Ettoriel? And, uh, nephilim." What was easy to talk about indoors on the phone felt strange and alien outside and face to face.

AT tilted her head, looking up at her. A lock of curly hair fell into her eye, and she shook her head to toss it away. "Akaterin Ettoriel," she said absently. "Corbin's a nice guy. Too serious. Kind of angry sometimes. But he's been a friend since I came to Senyaza. Hey, are you dating Zachariah?"

Now thoroughly off-balance, Marley said, "What? No? I mean... no."

"Hmm. But you're pretty close to him? Enough that he sent his kids to you?"

"Well... that was unexpected. *Really* unexpected. And kind of weird. Why are you asking about this?" The girl grinned at her and she felt irrationally defensive. "We're friends. A man and a woman can be friends without dating." *Even if I had hopes...*

AT's smile widened. "That's great. Friends is great. I'm all for friends. And you're not dating anybody else?"

"No, and why does that matter?" With bad grace, she added, "Do *you* have a boyfriend, since we're being nosy here?"

AT laughed, as if Marley had said something really funny. "I wish. But that won't happen anytime soon." She hopped off the bench. "So did you just want to say hi?"

"I wanted to see what you had to say about this Ettoriel guy." A casually dressed man approached them, earbuds in his ears, and Marley found herself turning her body so Lissa was behind her, and stepping closer to the dogs. The man veered around them without ever really looking at them, and continued down the sidewalk. Lissa peered after him, and then joined Kari in petting the dogs, whispering to them as she did.

AT barely glanced at him. "Dunno much about him. I haven't had much experience with the angelic side of the celestial equation. I've heard the name a couple times before. And of course there was that messed-up scene yesterday. I never expected things to go down like that."

Marley scanned the street for more passersby, and put the bus bench between her and the street. Then she shook herself. She'd barely heard what AT said, she'd been so distracted. "How do you know if it's somebody dangerous? The dogs again?"

AT had watched her change position without comment. "They can help, sure, but angels mark everybody who works for them. It's visible with the Sight. Which," she added with a look of dawning realization, "you don't have. Crap. You make sure to ask Corbin about that next time you see him, and he can set you right up. I would, but I don't have the tools." She shook her head. "Wow, no Sight; that must suck."

Marley was briefly distracted by the idea that a capital-s Sight was like a pair of sunglasses. But then she recalled the catastrophe vision. It flashed across her perception, but she was becoming more adept at suppressing it, and only saw enough to feel confident that horrible doom did not currently lurk in AT's near future.

"What's it look like?" she asked hesitantly. "Because I have some kind of new perception..."

"Do you? Awesome! An angel's mark is a symbol over their heads, usually. What do you see?"

"Disasters," Marley said bleakly. Lissa hugged her leg again before returning to her pretend conversation with the dogs.

AT scrutinized her, then said, "That blows." She brightened. "Maybe Corbin can help you out with that, too. He's got some serious skills. He's, like, a Geometry hacker."

"That'd be great." Marley's phone beeped as a text message arrived. It was a note from Penny.

Sorry about yesterday, I shouldn't have run out on you like that. I was scared. Forgive me? And she remembered Penny saying, *I dreamt of light.*

Marley stared at her phone for a long minute. "Tell me more about this angel mark?"

AT looked curiously between the phone and Marley. "Well, it's a symbol, kind of like zodiac symbols. It means their soul belongs to the angel's house. The angel's connected to them. Mostly angels only talk to people they've marked. That's about it, really. It's kind of a celestial bar code."

"But the angel puts it there? Is it permanent?"

AT laughed a little, although Marley didn't understand why. "Kind of. De—other celestials can remove it or replace it, and it's harder to claim a soul if the soul is actively unwilling."

"So it's not mind control or anything?" Marley persisted.

AT gave her a thoughtful look. "The mark itself isn't."

Marley stared at the ground gloomily. Of course it wasn't. No mind control was necessary to turn Penny's head, just an attractive man who could convince her for a moment that she was beautiful. If Jeremy White hadn't been so interested in the children, Marley wouldn't have even considered sinister motives or methods. It would have just been Penny, trying once again to find herself in someone else.

She wondered what she would see if she looked at Penny with the catastrophe vision. But she already knew the answer to that, because the catastrophe vision had been there all along, suppressed by medication and misunderstanding. She could remember now what had been there since the beginning. This relationship Penny had found was bad, bad, *bad*. It was going to destroy her, and it wasn't going to be by breaking her heart.

"If they have the mark, do they know about the, uh, angel who marked them?"

AT shrugged. "Everybody knows about angels, even if they don't believe in them."

"But you said it was easier if they were willing to be marked." Marley paced along behind the bench.

"Yup. But that can just be a willingness to be part of something, or make a commitment. Like being baptized, or taking an oath." She watched Marley's restless movement, her head cocked. "A lot of my relatives are very much against marking, but I'm not sure it's really a bad thing. For mortals, anyhow. I mean, we don't *know*. It's how they get to Heaven when they die. It's the safe option." AT looked apologetic. "Sorry I'm not making much sense. I have a friend who's really into free will, and she says part of free will is knowing you can give it up."

Marley had no idea what to make of that. So she focused on what was important. "I have a friend, too. I think she's involved with this supposed angel's group, but she doesn't know it. And it's going to go badly for her. I can *see* it, see a disaster waiting for her. Or I could yesterday, anyhow. I need to go see her, see if there's anything I can do for her. I know she won't hurt me, so the worst she could do is pick up the phone and call her new boyfriend, right? And if you were outside, you could watch out for anybody showing up."

The teenager sprang to her feet. "Wow. And this is a friend we're talking about? A good friend?" When Marley nodded, she said, "Oh." She stared down at her feet for a moment, then said, "Let's go see her." One of the dogs tilted its head at her and made a complicated growling whine. AT put her hands on her hip and said to the dog, "You *cannot* abandon friends in a situation like that, or else you will totally lose them to the other side." Another growl. "I just know. You be quiet. Ignore him, Marley. You head over there and I'll meet you."

-fifteen-

On the way to Penny's, Marley made some phone calls, first leaving a message for Branwyn and then letting Penny know of her plan to visit. Penny sounded normal on the phone. But that was one of her skills, along with finding a pretty smile for strangers even when she was empty inside.

"Are we going someplace not so hot, Marley?" asked Kari from her booster seat.

"Absolutely. Penny's house has an excellent air conditioner. And a big TV with lots of videos."

"The angel lady?" asked Kari, and Marley's skin prickled.

"Angel Penny," corrected Lissa.

"She's just Penny," Marley said, a little more sharply than she meant. "She doesn't want to be somebody else." Which was, she knew, the biggest lie she'd told the twins so far. Penny wanted to be *anybody* else. In college, she'd tried out six majors. She spent thousands on clothes and subscribed to dozens of magazines dedicated to helping her figure out who she was on any given day. Marley and Branwyn had become accustomed to it. She'd always been there for them, no matter what else she was pursuing, and it was the least they could do.

But—Angel Penny? Where did that lead?

Penny had an adorable Craftsman house on Orange Grove, purchased by her trust fund when she turned twenty-one. Although it was a lovely home with a gorgeous porch, Penny had been to Marley's place far more than Marley had been to Penny's. Penny loved to decorate the house, and hated to spend time there. Her mother, the big producer, sent photo shoots and film crews by occasionally. Like Penny in her childhood and adolescence, the house had been an extra in a number of movies. But while Penny was eventually able to convince her parents she didn't want a career in front of a camera, the house had no such ability. The house represented everything they wanted for their daughter.

They rarely came to visit her there.

As Marley parked the car, AT loped around the corner of the block. Two of her dogs had vanished, and the third one, the red female, was on a leash. "Nice house," she said, as she approached Marley.

"How'd you get here?" Marley asked. "Do you have a car? How can you track me by scent in a car? Where are the other two?"

AT only smiled. "They're around. Go see your friend; I'll hang out here and try to get a look at her. Keep a lookout, that kind of thing." She faded back to the curb.

As Marley looked at the house again, her phone rang. When she fished it out and looked at it, the number was unfamiliar. And she almost answered it, before she remembered Branwyn saying, *I don't think you're being paranoid enough.* She stared at the phone until it stopped ringing. A moment later, the message icon lit up.

Was listening to messages safe? She had no idea. Then Lissa said, "Was that Uncle Zach calling?" and Marley just had to find out.

It wasn't Zachariah. It was Jeremy White. "Hello, Miss Claviger. Sorry about yesterday afternoon; some of my assistants were hoping to curry additional favor with our employer." He didn't even bother to try to sound honest. "I was personally hoping to give you one more opportunity to willingly surrender the children before my employer assigns the retrieval to somebody more experienced in direct action." There was the sound of paper shuffling. "Call me back in the next hour if you'd like to avoid said direct action. I have to say, this guy is a real beast."

"No," said Marley flatly, putting away the phone. "Not Zachariah." And she marched straight up to Penny's door.

Penny answered the chiming doorbell with a hostess's smile, a wall of cool air coming with her. "Come in. I hope you don't mind that the place is a mess."

"There's no mess that these two can't improve," Marley said gravely, as she ran a critical eye over her friend. To mundane vision, she looked normal. Despite the churning in her stomach, she kept the catastrophe vision suppressed until she could at least sit down.

Penny smiled down at the twins, and then looked over Marley's shoulder at AT, who was loitering on the sidewalk inspecting her dog's feet.

"Who's that?"

"Just a kid I met yesterday. She has friends in the area," Marley said.

" ...Okay." Penny frowned and moved aside to let them in. The twins flowed past her into the coolness.

Kari said happily, "Hello, angel lady," and then glanced up at Marley. Marley remembered her sharpness and forced a small smile for the child.

As she moved through the door, Penny waved a hand at AT and said, "Does she want a drink or anything? It's really hot out. I hope the poor dog's feet aren't getting burned." She paused and added, "It's just that she's staring at me."

Marley looked. AT was, indeed, staring at the two of them, a strange look on her face. Then she met Marley's eyes and shook herself before dashing down the street.

"See, she's fine," said Marley. But she wondered.

Penny touched her hair, her mouth, her collarbone, smoothed her skirt. "I wonder what she noticed," she said, as she closed the door.

"More likely me than you, Penny. Last night I found a sticker on the back of my shorts. A glittery fairy sticker. I didn't even know we had stickers, but there it was." Marley looked around the house, which seemed as spotless as usual.

Penny's mouth quirked up in a smile, and she looked down at the twins. "I have some stickers. Oh, and I thought you might be interested in some of the movies I have. Want to see?"

The twins looked at each other and then offered enthusiastic agreement. Soon, they were bickering over a pile of animated movies, trying to decide which one to watch. Penny looked at them with a fond smile.

"They're cuties. I almost wish they were mine." She squeezed her eyes shut and shook her head. "But only almost! It'll take an amazing guy to convince me to have kids."

"Not Jeremy?" Marley asked quietly.

Penny's smile turned vague and distant. "I'm not *that* impressed by him. Hey, have you made any progress on that puzzle booklet? The one you showed me the other day?"

At first, Marley had no idea what she was talking about. Then she exclaimed, "Oh!" as she remembered the strange book fragment she'd been researching at the library the day before. It seemed like a lifetime ago, when a coded book and an absent friend were the weirdest things in her life. She fumbled in her backpack for the sheaf of papers. "I haven't had a chance to study it since yesterday."

It was a good way to occupy Penny so Marley could release the catastrophe vision. Maybe if she really studied the images, she could find clues to avoiding the disasters. They couldn't be guaranteed; the freeway hadn't actually turned into a hellscape of screams and twisted metal. That she might be delusional instead of tapping into the Sight mentioned by AT was an idea that did occur to her, but what could she do about it? She was more worried about Penny noticing and getting upset again.

Penny flashed her a smile. "I've just been thinking about it and I wanted to see if any of my new ideas would apply. And maybe it will help solve your mystery." She perched on the edge of a chair, flipping through the pages.

Lissa came over to her and whispered, "Marley, Neath really wants out of the cage."

Marley looked over at the cat carrier. The kitten was pressed up against the holes in the box, her fur fluffed. Reluctantly, she shook her head.

"There's too many places to get in trouble here." *Especially if we need to leave in a hurry.* The kitten yowled indignantly in response.

Lissa looked around. "Okay. This house is sad anyway." She went back over to watch the video her sister had started.

Marley settled back on the couch, studying Penny in the chair opposite. She took a deep breath, and stopped suppressing the catastrophe vision. And because she was prepared, she didn't gasp, or cringe in horror.

One of the future echoes of Penny was empty, like the shell of a building after a fire had passed through. Another was swollen with harsh light that seemed to be burning painfully through her skin. A third wore a statue's peaceful face, eyes closed, with wings folded on its back. All three were very strong, backed by other images too faded to decipher.

Bubbles of hysteria tickled Marley's mind. Where was

the good? Why couldn't she ever see a good thing? Did it not exist? Or was she simply so twisted she couldn't imagine it? She drew in a deep breath, and flicked her gaze away before the hysteria escaped.

Once again, the sight of the twins soothed her. They were safe, their images stable and fixed. Any dangerous destinies before them were distant and washed out, impossible to comprehend. As long as they were near her, they would be well. But *why* did she feel that way so strongly? Why was she so confident she could protect two mystery kids she'd known for less than a year, and so filled with grief at the sight of one of her best friends?

It was illogical, and it was stupid. She struggled to push the lying, useless catastrophe vision away. Penny had been there so often for her over the last ten years: comforting, accepting, encouraging; sharing secret dreams and private fears. Marley, Penny, and Branwyn, a trio. Writer, illustrator, reader. None of the stories had been amazing, but as the only audience of the collaborations, she'd felt intimately involved. More than once, the promise of a new story had been all that kept Marley from rash decisions and rasher actions. It seemed like such a small thing in recollection, but it had mattered so much at the time.

"Is this another copy of the cipher?" Penny asked, tapping the sheaf of paper with a pencil.

Marley wiped excess moisture from her eyes and stood up. "What? No? Why do you ask?"

"Because there are complete words scattered throughout now. Look, here. Little things like 'the' and 'he'. More than one 'he,' in fact." Penny smiled to herself.

Marley peered over Penny's shoulder. Sure enough, every few lines, she could discern a whole, short word. There were also legible letters mixed in with the twisted symbols that covered the rest of the pages. Penny flipped through the pages and used her pencil to point out a capitalized 'I'. "A novel or a diary, I think."

"That makes sense, given the type of paper," Marley agreed. "And it *is* the same paper, as far as I know. It's just been tucked in my backpack. Can you use the unencrypted text to decipher the rest of it?"

"Maybe. Probably not; it's more of a visual encryption. But I don't think it matters." Penny looked up at her, eyes shining. "I think it's decoding itself. Isn't that amazing?"

Marley stared at her and then stared at the papers. Slowly, she said, "I guess that's one word for it."

"I can't wait to see what it's about." Penny flipped through the pages again, peering closely at the writing. "It's like watching a countdown on the web. You just keep coming back to it, imagining what the end result will be. Do you think it's associated with some movie launch? A viral advertising campaign?"

Marley hesitated. "No. I found it at Zachariah's place. I thought it might be related to his disappearance."

The glow of Penny's mood abruptly dimmed. "Oh." She glared at the stack of papers, and then put them down on the end table. Standing up, she paced over to the window before turning to look at the cartoon the kids were watching. Marley waited a few minutes, then finally tucked the sheaf of paper away in her bag again.

When Penny spoke, her voice was quiet enough that Marley had to move closer to understand her.

"It makes sense, you know. That Jeremy would just be using me. I'm an idiot for not seeing it earlier. Why else would a man like that hook up with a vacation fling?"

Despite the pain in Penny's voice, relief washed through Marley like cool water. The catastrophe vision flashed on and off, just long enough for Marley to see the winged marble statue overlaid over Penny. Its eyes had been closed before, but now they were only almost-closed. Light leaked from beneath the lids.

Penny kept talking. "But he's part of something good. That charity I mentioned, he called it Bridges. I really felt connected to them. I mean, at first I thought they were a bit silly, especially after I saw their little ritual. Very, uh, Old World, you know? Branwyn would mock it. But ever since then, I've felt... better about myself. Like I was part of something real." She rubbed her wrist and took a step toward Marley, her expression intense.

"The thing is, Jeremy's part of that, too. He may be using me, but... he led me to this good thing. So I don't think he can be all bad."

Marley tried for gentleness as she said, "Yesterday at the park, some people shot at the children and me. Jeremy may be involved with something good, but he implied threats against me when we spoke, and then his own people shot at us. So I think he's involved in something bad, too."

"Shot at you..." Penny whispered. Then, "Did they mention him? Is there any reason to assume they're connected?"

Marley shrugged. "He left me a message a few minutes ago mentioning the attack. He said some of his coworkers had gotten overenthusiastic. So you can see how the appearance of guns means I'm a bit less concerned with your love life right now. Just so you know." She offered a smile and knew as soon as her lips turned that it looked fake. "I trust you."

Penny bit her lip. "Yeah. Enough to let me take the kids out to lunch while you take a nap?" She repeated the offer from the day before, pointedly.

Marley remembered the panic attack brought on by her friend's earlier suggestion. This time, the catastrophe vision showed her more: the twins, no longer stable and safe, but burning, and the light they shed as they burned cast the shadows of wings. And on Penny, the eyes of the marble statue were half-open and gleaming with gold.

Penny's own expression darkened as she watched Marley's face. "Yeah, I didn't think so." She turned to the window.

Marley crossed the remaining distance between them and touched Penny's arm. "There's more going on than I can explain, Penny. It's not about trust. It's about knowing that I can protect them. Knowing it even though I don't even understand how. Everything feels like that book right now. The world's suddenly become completely incomprehensible and I'm trying to make tiny pieces of it make sense. And I'm not very good at it."

Penny turned her head just enough for Marley to see her profile. "You could be right. I mean, I feel really good about Bridges. I feel like, yeah, maybe Jeremy's a bastard, but he can be... redirected. But yesterday I was willing to believe Jeremy wanted me for myself. I don't trust myself. You know what an idiot I am."

Marley's hand clenched into a fist. "Stop it, Penny."

Penny shrugged. "Fine." A stricken look crossed her face and she whispered, "I really don't want you to leave, Marley."

Still irritated, Marley said, "I'm not going to leave you just because you get involved with a guy or a cause, and you know it." She softened her voice. "Tell me more about this charity?"

"Bridges. I'm sure you've seen some of their little logos around, attached to buildings or movie posters or whatever. They build stuff. Shelters and so on. And they counsel people..." Her voice trailed off as she stared out the window.

Marley frowned. "They sound kind of familiar."

"Oh, they show up in the tabloids sometimes, and on gossip sites. A lot of celebrities are involved. I think it's a status symbol." Penny turned toward Marley again, her eyes huge. "But they do real things. They have a..." she paused, and then finished defiantly, "A patron angel."

"Ah," Marley breathed. "Oh, Penny."

"Don't you say anything! You can be a skeptic all you want, but I've dreamt of him. Every night, lately." Pink suffused her olive skin. "Dreams I don't want to wake up from."

Marley suppressed a snort of unexpected laughter. *Her*, be skeptical. If only she could afford to be. If only doubt would make all this just go away. Instead she said, "What if it's Bridges who wants the children, Bridges who Jeremy is representing?"

Without hesitation, Penny said, "Then give them to him. They're the good guys, Marley. I'm certain of it."

Marley stared at her, aghast. "But I was shot. They actually hit me. Good guys don't shoot innocent babysitters!"

"Then maybe they weren't part of Bridges!"

"But there were wings, Penny. Wings, and a light, and a voice. They were protected from..." Marley bit off the end of that sentence and then said, "I saw wings. So I'm no skeptic. Believe me."

Penny looked at her, her breath indrawn. She started to speak, and then stopped, and then started again. "Maybe Zachariah's using you just like Jeremy's supposedly using me. Maybe Zachariah's the bad guy. This is an *angel*, Marley."

Marley lowered her gaze. It was possible. She thought of the way the twins had been instructed to call her in an emergency. That probably qualified as using her, although she still didn't understand the motives behind the action. And Corbin had been very vague on the nature of angels, other than their animosity toward his own people. Probably, with a few infamous exceptions, they were good. Did that make *her* the bad guy, too? For protecting children from the disaster she was sure otherwise lay ahead of them?

"Do you know the angel's name?"

Penny's mouth moved silently again, before she said breathlessly, "I should call Jeremy! I'm sure he'll come over and—"

Marley raised her eyebrows in surprise. "What? No, don't do that. I don't want him to know we're here."

The strangest expression moved across Penny's face, a sort of desperation. "Yes," she whispered. Her eyes closed, and she took a deep, gasping breath. When her eyes opened again, her face was calm. "You're right, I shouldn't. I won't. And I do know the angel's name."

Uncertainly, Marley said, "Are you all right?" Penny shrugged, so she added, "What's its name?"

Penny lowered her gaze. "His name is Akaterin Ettoriel."

The statue overlaid over Penny opened its eyes completely.

And when Penny raised her eyes again, they gleamed gold.

-sixteen-

Penny's face flickered, changing subtly. She brought her arms up to stretch slowly. Then she wrapped them around herself, rocking from side to side. "You," she said. As with her face, it was Penny's voice, but smoothed and perfected.

Marley stumbled backward, terror racing through her, devouring her ability to think. The catastrophe vision showed her two things of note: that the statue was moving in close synchronization with Penny, and that the vision of the light burning through Penny's skin was much more immediate. It was too much; she shut the vision down with a violence that made her head ache. Outside, dogs began to bark.

"Marley," said the thing inside of Penny, as if savoring her name. "You've been a trouble, but it needn't be this way." It held out Penny's hand. "Give them to me."

A small hand closed over Marley's fingers: Lissa. Kari stood on Marley's other side. Somebody shouted in the animated movie behind them.

Marley gripped Lissa's hand and fumbled for Kari. "Go to hell," she whispered. "And get away from Penny."

It inclined Penny's head. "I might yet. There are consequences for all actions. And yet it must be done, else all our little squabbles will end, and silence be the only winner." Penny returned to hugging herself. "This one invited me in. She wanted to be part of something great, and so she shall be."

Kari dodged Marley's hand and took a step forward. "What's happened to the angel lady?" Penny's gaze stayed silently fixed on Marley, never even flickering to the kids.

Marley said, "She's sick. Get away from her. Come with me. We're leaving." She stepped backward again, grabbing at her backpack and slinging it over her shoulder. "Kari!" Kari jumped and ran over to the door.

"No," said Penny. "You're not."

"Marley! The door won't open!" cried Kari.

Something dark moved in the corner of Marley's vision, first on one side and then the other. It was eerily familiar. She suddenly had the feeling that the room was crowded; that there were many, many beings pressed into it, watching her, just beyond her ability to see. The barking outside took on an enraged quality. Her nose stung with the smell of wildfire smoke.

Marley raced to the door, grabbing the cat carrier along the way, and wrenched at it herself, before frantically turning the deadbolt back and forth. The door simply wouldn't move, as if an invisible weight was hanging onto the other side.

Penny remained where she was, her head tilted to one side. There was a concerned expression on her lovely face. "It will be better this way. This one has a beautiful soul, fragile and precious. I will use her if I must, but completing the valence event will save her." A hand stretched out again. "You, too, might have been beautiful. I can see you through her eyes. And so I will mourn you."

Marley muttered, "I gotta say, Penny, you're really creeping me out." She tugged on the door again and then went to a window. Outside, the street seemed empty. Where was the barking coming from? A shadow flickered to her left, then her right. There was something below the window frame that she couldn't quite see. Dread crawled up her spine and made her look away, back at the living room.

Lissa let go of Marley's hand. Her fairy doll sailed through the air, hitting Penny on the side of the head. "Get out," the little girl shouted. "I don't want you here no more!"

Penny blinked and shuddered. "Marley?" she said, in her own voice. "I should have done it. I should have called Jeremy. Then you would have gotten away from here."

Kari yanked on the door again, but it still wouldn't open. Marley said, "Penny, Penny. Oh, sweetie, no. Don't do this."

Penny smiled, an expression so sweet and joyful that it broke Marley's heart. "I won't let him hurt you, Marley. He's not evil, you know. He's good; he's not one of those who fell. You're just on different sides. You can work it out if you try..." A tiny frown creased her brow, and then all expression smoothed away. The light that only Marley could see intensified, devouring the edges of Penny's image.

"He's hurting you!" The scream ripped its way out of Marley's throat. "He's destroying you!" And something happened, in that bruised spot in her mind where the catastrophe vision waited. She tried, without quite knowing how, to make Penny safe, as the twins were safe; to take Penny into her hand, under her care. To shelter her under wings she'd never grown.

Whatever she was trying recoiled back onto her. Pain radiated through her head. Through a red fog, she heard the angel's version of Penny's voice say, "She is not a child, to accept your barriers, nephil. She has chosen to accept me."

Lissa threw a scented candle at Penny. This time, Penny caught the missile in the palm of her hand. She turned her head to look at the girl and Lissa squeaked in fright. Kari ran over to her sister, grabbing her hand.

The lights flared and then died as the power to the house surged. The sound of the animated movie cut out mid-song. The stink of burned electronics merged with and then overwhelmed the wildfire smoke. There was a barely perceptible sizzling in the air, and the sense of dozens of invisible watchers fled. The barking dogs were suddenly very close.

The front door thudded, and then sprang open. Corbin stood beyond, his hair wildly disheveled. He held what looked like a small rubber ball in one hand. He scanned the room, then cursed. "Get out of here," he snapped, and stepped into the room, away from the door.

The sizzling atmosphere stilled, and Penny turned to look at him. "You. Nobody minds getting rid of you."

"The feeling's mutual," Corbin mumbled, and started bouncing the ball. "But not today." It bounced surprisingly well, given the carpeting, and each thump of the rubber seemed to tremble across Penny's features.

Marley shook the twins, who were staring at Penny as if mesmerized, their hands tightly clasped together. They both looked up at her, and then scrambled for the door. She took a step after them, and then turned to Corbin. "What about Penny?"

"You leaving *now* will be the best thing you can do for her." Corbin made a shooing motion with his free hand. At the same time, Penny launched herself at him, grabbing at the ball. He dodged to one side. Marley stumbled backward out the door, unable to look away. Corbin said, "Stupid," and flung the ball at the wall. Penny scrambled after it, while Corbin ran for the door, pushing Marley ahead of him and pulling the door shut behind him.

For a moment, they were very close. She could see the grey flecks in his dark eyes, and how his eyes widened as she looked at him. One hand still on her waist, he put the other on the doorknob, holding it closed. "Keep going," he said roughly.

She stepped back, her heart thudding with adrenaline. "Thanks."

AT stepped out of thin air beside the twins, who were getting to their feet in the yard. The sound of barking followed her, although Marley still couldn't see any actual dogs. AT sliced her hand to one side and the barking stopped. Then she helped Lissa to her feet. "Get to the car, you two."

Both girls looked at Marley, and she nodded. After glancing between AT and Corbin, she ran after them, waiting for the door to open and not-Penny to come out after her.

She didn't make it two steps before something shimmered in the air before her. As if sketched quickly on the air by a ballpoint pen, the shape that appeared there was formed of straight lines and gentle curves, and enclosed by a pair of slowly moving rings.

Light flickered through it. Then, just as AT had a moment before, a man stepped through a shimmering in the air.

He was the biggest man Marley had ever seen, but perfectly proportioned, as if he'd been constructed on a slightly larger scale. He had bronzed skin and well-cut, sun-bleached hair. Mirrored sunglasses hid his eyes, and he wore khakis and a buttondown shirt. None of it coordinated with the sleek, complicated-looking gun he carried in one hand.

"Oh, shit," said Corbin. "Him." But adrenaline was already propelling Marley past the newcomer to scrabble at the car door. From her peripheral vision, she saw the big man look around, then dodge as Corbin threw something small at him. Then she was in the car. A quick glance showed her the twins were already inside, even if they weren't in their seats.

She started the car. As soon as the engine came to life, she reversed and slammed on the gas. The car thrust backwards a few yards before there was a jerking thud. In the rearview mirror, the big man staggered. Then he turned and looked at her. She ground the gas pedal into the floor, trying to knock him off-balance again, but it was like she'd backed into a wall.

Then several rubber balls bounced off the trunk of the car, scattering in all directions, and the giant turned his head to track them. AT tumbled into the car behind the twins and Corbin threw himself into the front seat.

"Good, go, drive! While he's distracted." Corbin was out of breath. Marley didn't need to be told twice. She shifted gears and peeled away from the curb, the car jouncing unpleasantly until she got straightened out on the road.

She drove faster than she would have thought sane a few days ago, until they were out of Penny's neighborhood and onto the tangle of city streets beyond. For a while, taking random turn after random turn was oddly soothing; if she didn't know where she was, how could anybody else find her?

Finally, Corbin said, "Slow down. Don't attract attention." He was holding Neath's cat carrier in his lap.

In the back, Kari was sobbing while Lissa sniffled. Both twins were sitting in their seats with the straps loosely in place. AT sat between them, patting Kari on the back. She briefly met Marley's eyes in the rearview mirror. "I'm sorry. I thought your friend looked odd, but I didn't realize what it meant until too late."

"How is it you two keep finding me, and how is it different from... whatever happened there?" Marley realized her voice came out sounding flat and ugly, and further realized she didn't care.

Corbin, staring out the window, said, "AT's dogs can track you through the Backworld. It's a gift. I ask the birds. Her method is faster, so sometimes I just ask her."

"And that guy? Who the hell was he? I hit him with my car and he barely noticed!"

"Absolven. We met him before, my friends and I, when we were trying to protect the Ragged Blade. He came out of it better than they did. He's nephilim like us. He's very old, and has a long history as a black sheep. Like Zachariah—but Absolven's always been honorable and honest. Except now he's working with Ettoriel." He leaned his head against the window. "None of this makes sense."

"How did he find us? He showed up out of nowhere. I can't hide from that. I don't even know where to start." Just thinking about it sent panic rushing through Marley.

"Slow down," repeated Corbin. He was still looking out the window. "He can't just show up where you happen to be; he has to know where you are or have a signal he's following to use the Backworld to travel to you. And most of us can't just enter and exit the Backworld wherever we happen to be. He had help. That glyph..." Marley could hear the frown in his voice.

"Yes, what was that thing?"

"I don't know. I think..." and he shook his head. "I don't know. I'd like to, though."

Marley felt a surge of irritation. "Don't you know anything? Maybe it's okay for you, but not knowing is going to get me killed." Her internal critic nudged her and she thought, *Is this how Branwyn felt? Crap!*

In the back seat, AT cleared her throat. "If you'll just pull over up here somewhere, I'll get out and go cause some trouble for that Absolven guy, see if I can figure out what's going on with him."

Marley gave a hostile look to the anxious face in the rearview mirror, unwilling to put up with teenage bravado. But then she remembered AT appearing out of the air, just as the man called Absolven had. She might look like a teenager, even be the same age as a normal teenager, but she was also one of these nephilim people. And Marley was realizing she had no idea what that really meant, no idea what the scope of the supernatural powers involved was. "Is that a good idea?"

she directed to Corbin.

Corbin didn't lift his head from the window. "I guess so. She's pretty hard to slow down. As long as she isn't stupid."

"I've used up my stupid for the day, I hope," said AT. As Marley pulled over at a curb, she said, "Again, I'm really sorry about your friend. I truly didn't expect that. "

"It's not your fault she's gotten herself in trouble again. But I remember what you said. The mark can be removed, right? The connection broken?"

AT looked stricken. She said, "Corbin?"

Tiredly, he said, "I'll explain it to her. Go."

AT muttered, "So sorry." Then she squirmed past Lissa, and was out the door.

Marley watched her vanish around the block. "What's going on? Why was she apologizing so much?"

"Can I explain it when we're someplace less exposed? I can direct you to a hotel associated with Senyaza. It has some features that should help you hide from even Ettoriel himself for a few hours. We could talk more easily there, and I could set you up with the Sight. Then you can see some of what I see, and draw your own conclusions."

"I'd like that," said Marley. "I really would."

-seventeen-

Penny called and she was kind of hysterical. She tells me that some man broke into her house and kidnapped you with a bouncy ball." Marley could imagine Branwyn cocking an eyebrow as she asked, "So, are you kidnapped?"

"No. Bran—"

But Branwyn went on. "Then another guy, Hercules with a gun, I think she said, showed up and started talking to her like she was a goddess, bowing and refusing to look at her and stuff. She finally got him to leave by telling him to take a nap or something, and then she called me. She wants me to come stay with her, in case he comes back again. So... a bouncy ball?"

"I have no idea. There may have been a ball," said Marley. She was sitting on a queen-sized bed in a large hotel room, watching the children build a fort with the extra pillows, some blankets, and the couch. The distraction of the hotel room had prompted Kari to recover from her sobs, at least. Neath prowled around the room, happy to be free of the cat carrier. "I went by and she was going to call Jeremy, and I was having trouble leaving until Corbin showed up to distract her.

Penny was... she was acting weird, Bran. It was really strange."

"I'll just bet. Corbin, huh?" said Branwyn. "I see. But since she seems to want me around, and you clearly don't need me, I'm on my way to go take care of her now."

"Um," said Marley. "Hold on." She went to the open polarized-glass doors that led to the balcony, where Corbin was staring at a pair of ravens on the railing. "Hey, Branwyn is going over to visit Penny. Is that... I don't want Penny *and* Branwyn to get into trouble."

"This is the green-haired girl? I don't think Penny or... I don't think she's in any danger from Penny. Not if she wouldn't normally be. Most angels don't like to hurt humans without a good reason, and Ettoriel is even more principled than most. According to my database. I wish I knew why..." He shook his head. "Anyhow, Penny must be influencing her passenger toward restraint since you weren't hurt either. A friend to remind her of herself might help her hang on longer." He held out his hand to one of the birds, and it snatched something off his palm.

Thoroughly disturbed by everything Corbin had just said, but picking out the crucial information for her current needs, Marley uncovered the phone again. "That's a good idea," she told Branwyn.

"I'm so glad you think so," Branwyn said dryly. "Where are you, anyhow?"

"At a hotel, at the moment." A hotel with no visible name, a sleek five-story building on an anonymous downtown street, with a burly doorman and a gated lobby. Senyaza was apparently not only a privately held multinational electronics corporation, it was an organization of nephilim, focused on enabling them to "survive and prosper" in a hostile world. Or so Corbin said.

Suspiciously, Branwyn said, "How are you paying for a hotel? Remember what I said about credit cards?"

"Um... I think the guy with the bouncy ball is paying for it." He'd given the clerk a card of some sort, at least, though it hadn't had any logo that Marley recognized.

"Give me the address," ordered Branwyn.

Marley read off the address from a piece of stationary, and added the name. "Hotel Gigantes #3. But I don't know how long we'll be here. Maybe only a couple of hours."

Branwyn blew her breath into the phone. "If Penny didn't need me, I'd be on my way there already. But at least this way I know where to start looking if you vanish."

"Bran, I know I'm acting strange, but—"

"You're not, really," Branwyn interrupted. "I thought you were at first. But you're acting just like you do whenever you aren't sure you're right. If it didn't seem so dangerous, I'd be delighted to see you acting so *normal*. But it *is* dangerous, and if you vanish, I will never, ever forgive you. I will hunt you down like a *dog*. In fact, what am I thinking? Penny's safe at home. I could call her mother to look after her—"

Marley imagined Penny given more excuse to act like an empty doll, as she so often did around her mother, and shuddered. "Penny really does need *you*, Branwyn. If you can stop her from getting pulled further into whatever's got its hooks into her, that would help me, too. Probably. I'm hoping to find out as soon as I get off the phone with you."

"See, I felt all warm and fuzzy at the 'helping you' part, but then you went on with the 'probably' and now I'm all 'she's not telling me stuff again,' and pissed off. Should have stopped while you were ahead, Mar."

But Marley could hear the affection in Branwyn's voice. She said, "The more I hold out, the more you'll believe me when I tell you the full story."

"Or the more likely I'll think it's a huge prank."

"A prank? I wish. Gotta go. I'll check in later."

She rang off, and spent a moment wiping moisture away

from her eyes. Then she tucked the phone away before looking up at Corbin as he re-entered the room. "Hey. Everything
okay with the birdies?"

"They're going to get some information for me. And keep
watch, of course." He met her gaze, his dark eyes assaying
her. Marley was suddenly conscious of how haggard she must
look, and how on the edge she must seem.

She tried for a relaxed smile, to show her self-control was
fine. "So that stuff you just said outside? It was all kinds of
messed up. Can we start with that?"

He leaned against the wall, studying her face further.
"Normally angels just mark people and then talk to them," he
finally said. "Ettoriel's moving into Penny's soul. Possessing
her. They don't usually do that because it eventually destroys
the victim, mind and soul."

"AT said that marks can be removed. Can this?" She
asked the question, but she was already thinking about how
AT's repeated "I'm sorry" had sounded like condolences rather than an apology. Rage, cold and sluggish in an unfamiliar
environment, began to stir.

"Exorcisms don't work," he said bluntly. "Once he has a
foothold, the celestial controls the process." Then he hesitated. "Mostly. I slowed it down some, earlier, by disrupting the
numina flow. But I can't stop it. Only Ettoriel can do that,
and only in the early stages."

"And it's going to destroy her? How?" She wanted precise
answers to focus her anger.

"I've heard the process likened to burning her soul away."
He shrugged. "As for her mind, there aren't that many minds
that can survive cohabitating directly with a celestial, especially without a soul to stitch to. The mind becomes fragmented, dominated, and eventually shattered."

"So he's got the equivalent of a supernatural gun to her
head, not just her heart," Marley said quietly. It was true; she

knew it was. Hadn't she seen it? The rage grew, flowing into the little spaces in her mind where anxiety normally nested. She suddenly understood the appeal of revenge; it was control, applied retroactively. *Perhaps I cannot stop you from destroying my friend, but I can make you regret it.* And there was no room for worry about methods or power differentials, about how Ettoriel was an angel and she was a failed grad student. The rage scoured all those spaces, clean and pure.

Corbin blinked at her and muttered, "Wow."

Lissa was suddenly standing on the bed, one hand on her shoulder. She peered closely into Marley's eyes until Marley said, "What is it, kiddo?" Her voice came out thick and low.

Lissa touched Marley's forehead. "You lit up."

Corbin said, "You can see it?"

Lissa ignored the question to say, "Why doesn't she see, Mr. Bird Man?"

Corbin studied Lissa. "I haven't taught her how yet."

"When are you going to do that?" the little girl demanded.

"In a little bit."

"Okay." As swiftly as she'd come, Lissa returned to the pillow fort. Corbin watched the twins for a moment, fidgeting with something he'd pulled out of his pocket.

"What's going on?" demanded Marley.

Corbin gave her a sideways look. "What happened to you just now?"

She narrowed her eyes. "You told me that Penny was going to have her soul eaten by a lunatic angel, and I got angry about it. Then, you said 'Wow'."

"I did? Damn it," he said. "Well, for me, your halo just lost most of its tarnish."

Shock flooded her, overwhelming even the rage. "M-my halo?" She sat down on the bed. "That's probably a technical term, right?"

Corbin crouched down in front of her, taking her left

wrist into both his hands gently. "Motherfucking Zachariah," he muttered. "Yes, but it means about what you'd expect it to mean."

She forced a brief little smile. "Tinkly golden ring over my head?"

"Not quite. Here." He cupped one hand over his eyes and drew it away, then placed the cupped hand over Marley's eyes. When he pulled his hand away, she could see...

more...

Corbin caught her as she instinctively jerked backwards, trying to dodge the beams and strands and bars of light that filled the room. "It's called the Geometric Sight. I designed it to appear like a heads-up display, overlaid on your actual vision. To deactivate it, imagine the outline of a circle, a triangle and a square, all on top of each other, and then separate them. Reverse that to reactivate it."

Marley barely heard him. Many-colored light had transformed the world: Objects had auras, and faint lines connected the auras to other auras. Corbin himself was a mass of lines and blazing circular nodes, far more complex than any of the simple objects in the room. The hand near her face had a circle of white light on the palm, and inside the light was... complexity. Smaller lines and nodes of every shape, interlocking like the gears of a clock. She couldn't understand it. Then Corbin drew his hand away and she focused on his face. There was a circular node on his forehead and another hovering near the top of his head, but her attention was immediately caught by the crown of light glowing about eight inches above him.

The silvery nimbus was only vaguely ring-shaped, and in the center it darkened until the core was a miasma of shadows. She gaped at it for a moment, reaching her fingers out to touch it. To her surprise, she felt a tingle when her fingers brushed where it appeared to be.

Corbin, still holding her left hand, smiled. "There's another one down there," he said, pointing. She looked down at the matching glow wreathing his feet. "They come in pairs. Some art gets it right."

He continued after a moment. "If you see somebody with the halo and the chakra nodes, that means they're nephilim. If someone only has the chakra nodes, they're mortal. If they only have the halo, they're the vessel or construct of a celestial creature."

She turned her head to the twins, who were both watching curiously. They had both the halo and the circular nodes. But while Corbin's nodes were each filled with gem-like colors, the children's nodes were all empty.

"Okay," she managed. "What about everything else?"

He stood up and pulled her to her feet as well. "We'll get to that. But first..." He gently drew her over to the full-length mirror next to the bathroom door. She flinched as a line of light crossing from the door to the window passed painlessly through her head. "What do you see?"

She looked at her reflection. She had a series of circular nodes—chakras, she remembered Corbin calling them—running down her body in a line. Two of them were filled with tinted, complex light. And over her head and at her feet, glowing like the moon and its reflection, were a pair of halos.

-eighteen-

I'm... not mortal?" Marley fought against the blankness in her mind. "Does this mean one of my biological parents was an angel?" Suddenly she remembered the not-Penny addressing her as *nephil*. It'd been convenient to ignore that at the time.

"Or one of your grandparents. Somewhere in your family tree, somebody attracted the attention of a celestial. I take it there are some missing branches?"

"All of them. I was adopted." She shook her head wonderingly. "I always figured my mother was a..." She noticed the twins watching her in the mirror. "Somebody in a lot of trouble," she finished.

"Hmm," he said.

She flinched, imagining what lay under that noncommittal sound. Quickly, she said, "What did my, uh, halo look like before?" At the moment, it was tall and clean. While there was a shifting shadow at the heart of Corbin's halo, hers seemed to have a whirling brightness that made her uncomfortable to study.

"The day before yesterday, it was suppressed almost entirely. Veiled, we call it. If I'd passed you on the street, I wouldn't have noticed you. Yesterday afternoon and today, it was... blotched." He sounded puzzled. "Dark, dull spots, with very little fire. I don't think I've seen anything like it before."

"But how can I be like you guys? I don't have any super-powers. No dogs or ravens."

He raised an eyebrow. "I'm not so sure about that." He glanced down at the thing that had reappeared in his hand. It looked like an elaborate keychain ornament, all cubes and rods moving over each other. Flashes of light cast shadows onto his face.

"I'd know better than you, wouldn't I?! What's that you're playing with?"

"This is a fragment of a celestial Machine. I borrowed it from the Senyaza Repository. I wanted to see what it could tell us about the kids, maybe give us a clue as to why the angel wants them in particular." He turned it over in his hand, and there was a silken sound. "No idea what it was for originally, but it's been... useful in the past when it comes to newly found nephilim and the trouble they cause. Item number 41, informally known as the Lullaby Plaything." He held it out to her.

Marley didn't take it, even though she longed to poke at the little toy. "Celestial Machine? Angels have machines? What for?"

"Heaven has Machines, anyhow. Huge, amazing things, or so I've read." He glanced down at the Lullaby Plaything again, fidgeting absently with it. More little flashes of light, faster now. "What makes its way out isn't as impressive. Possession of them is important to the angels. I think the Machines do all the real work, myself. But all we really know in general is that they exist, they're powerful, and they're the only things that can stop a celestial from reincarnating when they die. When celestials war among themselves, they use a few of them as weapons. This is just a tiny piece of one."

Angels can die. Marley filed that away and stared at the moving rods. "So somewhere up there, the celestial Machine in charge of spring threw a bolt and is now is going 'clonk'?"

Corbin smiled. "Maybe. I mean, probably not. They're not that obvious. But if anybody really knows, they're not telling. This one, we've studied some. It has a calming, focusing effect on the nephilim who play with it, and the little laser show can suggest the nature of a nephil's heritage, what domain their celestial forebear was associated with, and so on. Take it, it won't hurt you. When you're convinced of that, give it to one of the kids."

Marley took a calming breath, and then picked up the Lullaby Plaything by one of the metal rods. A cube at the end of the rod rotated as if on a pivot, and another rod, connected to the first near the other end, slid down. It really did look like an engaging little toy, the sort of thing her father would have in his office. She prodded a third rod. Its cube started spinning, with a gentle clicking sound. Small colored lights bloomed on each of the cubes, and dotted the rods. They were pleasantly soothing and she gazed at them for a moment, until her breathing deepened.

Unobtrusively, her catastrophe vision activated. It was a peaceful device, without the intent to harm anybody. It certainly wouldn't harm the twins, although its own fate in their hands was obscured somehow.

Her nose tickled. The campfire scent that had overhung everything for what felt like days now was replaced by the strong ozone tang of thunderstorms. She glanced at the window, but the sky was clear. She turned an inquiring look on Corbin, and recoiled. He was watching her closely, analytically, and his own personal array of catastrophes hung about him like a suffocating cloak. She yanked her gaze away, fumbling with the Lullaby Plaything as she rejected the vision.

The lights on the celestial toy dimmed, and the clicking spin of the moving cube slowed.

Eyes on the carpet, she stalked past him to the twins' blanket tent. "Hey, kids." Corbin's Sight overlay showed her the lines of light blazing down their curved spines, and hollow circles of light, seven of them, dotting the central line. Their halos were identical radiant stars with sparkling motes mixing between them.

"Wait," said Corbin. "I knew you had a gift. AT said you had a unique sight. What do you see with it?"

Corbin's impersonal, diagnostic tone scraped against already sensitive nerves. "It's a curse, not a gift," she snapped. "I see the bad things that might happen to somebody."

"Why did you suppress it? I'd like to see it in action more so I can integrate it into the Geometric Sight."

"Why? I don't want to use it. It's deceptive. Useless. Mostly what it shows doesn't happen." Before the Lullaby Plaything had activated it, she'd been pleased with how she'd kept it utterly suppressed since the encounter at Penny's.

"Oh." He stared at the ground. "Sometimes celestial powers have trouble manifesting properly within a human framework. It can feel like a curse. But if you—"

"No," she said flatly.

"So you don't actually *want* a superpower." He rubbed the space between his eyes, his face drawn and tired.

She shrugged and held out the celestial toy to Lissa. "Here. Play with this," she ordered.

Confused, the preschooler took the device. She prodded it much as Marley had done, and all of the cubes started spinning. Kari squeezed out of the fort beside her and reached out to brush a finger across the glittering lights. The clicking of the cubes became a choral hum, like the long tones of a water harmonica. The light brightened until it was a flickering aurora. Then the Lullaby Plaything rose into the air until it was near the ceiling, twirled once, and soundlessly, peacefully exploded. The rods and cubes scattered everywhere, thudding into the furniture and carpet.

Corbin ducked a cube that flew past his head. "Uh." His eyes were wide.

Marley looked at him inquisitively. "Not supposed to happen?" She bent down and picked up one of the rods. A cube came tumbling out from under a bedspread and bounced up into her other hand, and then tugged itself over to the rod as if by magnetism. They snapped together. The little girls, unfazed by the exploding plaything, oohed appreciatively.

Corbin said, "That wasn't in the documentation, no."

Lissa looked up. "Did we break it?"

Corbin stared down at her. "I hope not."

Kari squeezed out from behind the table. "Here's another piece." She held a cube hopefully out to the rod Marley still held, but nothing happened. Her face fell. She patted it against the other cube a few times, until Lissa took it from her.

Tilting her head, she said, "It needs to rest for a while." She carefully put it on the table and then scurried around the room finding the other pieces. After piling them on the table, she took the rod Marley held and added it to the collection. "There. Now it can take a nap."

Corbin was still staring at the remnants of the Machine. "Corbin?" said Marley. "Are you all right? Are you going to get into trouble?"

He shook his head. "That was really weird. But for all I know, maybe the kid is right. As for trouble... I'm *already* in trouble. This is at least interesting trouble." He shook his head again. "I'm more worried about how tired I am than trouble from Senyaza. I should have gotten more information from that."

Kari said, "Maybe you need a nap, too!"

He mustered a smile. "Nah, I'll be fine."

Kari shook her finger at him and then ducked back into the blanket tent. Lissa lingered outside, patting one of the cubes. Marley watched her for a moment and then turned and threw herself on the bed, covering her eyes. That gave her a close-up of the line of light running down her arm, but when she actually closed her eyes, the—what had Corbin called it?—the Geometric Sight faded away. She said, "This 'detect-if-they're-an-angel' vision is pretty good, even if the Machine test didn't work. It'll tell me if someone's marked by an angel, too?"

"Yes. The mark appears in the place where the halo would be."

"That's great," she said. "That's a useful superpower, I think. Doesn't impact the rest of your life, either."

"Marley—" he said, and stopped. When he spoke again, she could hear the frustration in his voice. "Are you really hoping to go back to your old life when this is over? Do you think you can make it all just... go away?"

She took her arm off her face and looked at the ceiling. "What? People trying to kill me? Exploding children's toys stolen from Heaven? A monster inside my friend? I sure hope so."

"I meant what's inside of you—what you are—and you know it."

"Can we just not worry about the catastrophe vision, please? I've got it under control at the moment. We don't have the time or space for me to turn into a screaming, weeping wreck, here or on the highway." She shuddered reflexively as a flash of the nightmare of multiple driver consequences flashed before her mind's eye.

"I'm pretty sure there's more to it than that," he said tiredly. "You should be able to influence what you see."

"No, I can't!" she snapped, and sat up. "I tried, with Penny! When I saw that thing inside her, I tried to make her safe. And it didn't work. There is no safety. Except for them." She pointed at the blanket fort as Lissa vanished into it, and realized she'd gotten very loud.

He stared at her silently, his eyes shadowed. Finally, she said, "If there are angels, are there also demons?"

"There are. Why do you ask?" His voice was perfectly neutral.

"Because if Ettoriel doesn't let Penny go, I'm going to make him regret it. And I bet demons would be the folks to go to for help there. You said angels could die."

Cautiously, Corbin said, "Machine Blades can end a celestial. And my people have developed a way to kill them, but it's not as permanent."

"How impermanent?"

"Something eventually appears with the same name, and the same tendencies, but without any of the memories of the previous bearer of that name."

"That sounds pretty good," said Marley, with vicious satisfaction. "How is it done?"

He spread his hands. "Somebody performs complicated magic near the celestial's avatar or hidden core. The spell tethers the three parts of an angel—spirit, numina, avatar—together. While the tether is maintained, damage to the avatar or numina can affect the spirit, which is normally immortal and untouchable. It requires a solid team of my people to bring down a celestial, because the celestial needs to be heavily distracted or else they'll disrupt the spell."

"But you do it. You kill the immortal."

He shrugged. "My team is out of commission right now after trying to help Zachariah. And angels aren't our primary targets, so much. Not these days. There are other kinds of celestials that are more overtly dangerous."

"Demons," she said. "And I bet they're pretty interested

in fighting angels, eh? Maybe they'll help me, if your people won't."

Both amused and taken aback, he said, "You know, most humans just aren't worth a Faustian revenge bargain."

She pointed a finger at him. "You shut the hell up. Sounding like you're something other than human. Aren't you part angel and part human? Well, so far, the humans are worth a lot more than the angel. So as far as I'm concerned, there's human, and human-plus."

"Perhaps I'm part demon, instead. Still human-plus?" He looked at her expression and a number of emotions crossed his own face. "Not that it matters. Someday you're going to meet a demon and you're going to be surprised. Try not to be too attached to your preconceptions or you'll get into trouble. They usually aim to please."

Marley gave him a killing look, and stalked over to crouch down in front of the blanket tent. "Everything all right in there?"

Kari and Lissa were huddled together, clutching their dolls.

"You were yelling," Kari whispered.

Guilt stabbed Marley, refocusing her frustration and irritation on herself. "I'm sorry. I didn't mean to upset you."

Lissa said, "I want Uncle Zach back. When is he coming back? Can he come back now?" She curled up on her side, and stuck her thumb in her mouth.

"Not right now, but soon, I hope." She dropped the makeshift tent flap and turned away, wishing she had another answer to give the two pairs of sad eyes. Corbin hadn't moved from where he'd been standing, even to turn his head.

"I'm sorry," she said to his back. "There's just so much I don't know, and Penny's in so much danger, and my other best friend is going to hate me soon because I can't tell her what I don't understand, and these poor kids are so lost..." She trailed off, thinking about Zachariah.

Corbin's near hand clenched into a fist. "I don't believe he didn't know what you are."

"What?" she said, off-balance.

"Zachariah. He knew you were nephilim, an isolated one that Senyaza hadn't found. He must have known. And he chose to keep you ignorant. He could have explained all this and more, and he didn't. He could have given you days to acclimatize, weeks to learn."

"I'm sure he must have had a reason—" But she suddenly didn't know why she was defending Zachariah.

"Oh, I'm sure he did. Just like I'm sure he had a reason for sending my friends and me off to get our asses kicked while keeping us ignorant as to the real reason. Because he's a selfish secret-loving bastard."

"I think even if he had clued me in, it wouldn't have protected Penny," she said quietly. "Why are you angrier at him than at the angel who actually hurt your friends?"

He crossed his arms and turned his head, but didn't turn around. There was a pause, longer than Marley expected, until finally he said, "Because angels trying to kill nephilim isn't unexpected. It's part of their philosophy. They want us all to go away. We... embarrass them. But nephilim have survived by cooperating. It doesn't matter if your ancestors were angels or demons or kaiju or fae—we're all nephilim together. That's what Senyaza is all about. Senyaza doesn't trust Zachariah, but I gave him a chance. And now my friends are all in the hospital. And I *know* there's more going on than he shared."

"I see," Marley said quietly. "And where's Senyaza now? I thought you were going to get their help."

He finally turned around, spreading his hands again. "I'm it. Apparently there's something major going down in Europe, so I got a promotion. So to speak." He hesitated. "And somebody upstairs is pissed about the kaiju hunters being incapacitated. They *really* don't believe anything Zachariah is involved in is good for Senyaza."

"Lovely," said Marley. "What does a promotion mean?"

He sat down. "Not much. I got access to this place, and to the Repository. Some people answered some questions when they might previously have told me to go away. I don't normally have much status, as the junior auxiliary member of the kaiju hunters... Anyhow, Ettoriel's doing some weird stuff. He shouldn't need children for what Zachariah claimed he was trying to do. But I don't think he's doing that anyhow. All the database remarks about Ettoriel say he's... decent. Subtle. Not our friend, but not genocidal either."

"What's he supposedly trying to do, again?" Marley knew he'd mentioned it, but somehow it had gotten lost in the flurry of new information. "Destroying my friend isn't decent," she added.

"I know," said Corbin. "It's desperate. Zachariah said he wants to destroy the Hush. Break down the wall we built so that the angels and demons and kaiju couldn't directly control human events anymore. They try it sometimes, but Ettoriel has never been involved before."

"What were you trying to protect from him?"

"You mean before you and the kids?" He sighed. "A ritual artifact called the Ragged Blade. Profoundly useful for cutting directly through lines of the Geometry. And, of course, for killing people."

"A Machine Blade?"

"No. Something created by a human wizard, long ago. Ugly thing. There's a story that it could cut a victim right out of the world, in the proper circumstances."

He yawned, and then yawned again, wider this time. "Look, you've got a lot to think about. And look at. Play with the Sight some. I haven't had enough sleep for a week, so I'm just going to stretch out here for a few minutes. And then I'll explain to you about the Geometry and the Hush and magic. Make a list of questions, if you want." His eyes closed as his head touched the bedspread-covered pillow.

Then one eye opened. "Order something from room service when you're hungry. Don't go outside. I'll wake up if anything happens. But nothing should. A whole lot of nothing, at least for a day..." His eye closed again.

-nineteen-

Room service didn't knock on the door. Instead, the front desk called her and told her there was a cart outside her room, to be collected at her leisure. As she hauled the cart in, she saw a figure at the far end of the hall, unlocking another room. He had the nodes and the halo of a nephil, although his halo was dim, and he paid no attention to her. She saw another figure from the window, without a halo, but with each of his nodes infused with a complicated, shifting light. He got into a car and drove away, and she realized later that she couldn't remember anything about him except the richness of the circles of light. That was when she decided maybe she should experiment with turning the Sight off and on.

As she and the kids ate, she poked at the Lullaby Plaything. The pieces all clumped together as if magnetized, but it wasn't in the delicate, engaging construction it had previously been. Instead, it was just a vaguely spherical chunk of components, like all the pieces had been mashed together. Marley tried to pull a rod out, but it resisted her, shifting in her hand as the clump tightened. It reminded her of Neath when the cat didn't want to wake up, and she put it back on the table. If it was a heavenly Machine, that might make it practically alive. Perhaps Lissa was right and it was only resting. She hoped for Corbin's sake that was true, even if it hadn't been very useful to them.

Later, as Corbin continued to sleep, she took a shower. While the smoke from the fires hadn't started making it hard for her to breathe yet, the endless haze seemed to have permeated her skin. She felt like she hadn't been clean in weeks. While scrubbing, she discovered that the wound on her arm was almost entirely healed. That changed the experience a bit.

She came out of the bathroom, combing her hair and trying to convince herself to let Corbin link her catastrophe vision to the Sight, to discover the twins arguing about something. They stood in a puddle of blanket, Kari grasping Lissa's hand with both of hers and speaking rapidly; Lissa looked furious. They both looked up guiltily, and Kari fell silent. She pulled away from Lissa and went to stare out the polarized window.

"What's going on?" asked Marley. She tried to sound casual, but the suppressed vision trembled like a captured bird. *Yes, so noted, disaster lurks*, she thought to it sourly.

"Does the lawyer man know where Uncle Zach is?" Lissa asked. "The one from the park. He said he did."

Marley paused mid-comb, struck by the question. "I suppose he might."

Lissa persisted, "Or is he gone like our mommy? And your mommy?"

Marley's fingers clenched on the comb, the sharpness sweet next to the pang inside. "No. He'll be back again, I'm certain of it. It just may take a while."

"And then he'll make it all better." It was a statement from Kari, not a question. Lissa turned to stare at Kari's back.

Marley hesitated and then crossed to stand beside the little girl. "What do you think he'd say right now?"

Kari's face screwed up, and in a grumbly voice, she said, "We're not gonna run from them. We're going to make them run from us."

Marley put her hand on Kari's head gently, and wondered if that attitude was why Zachariah was missing. "I prefer the term 'tactical maneuvering'."

"Tactile grooving, right. That means we're gonna go—hey, it's that guy." Kari pointed out the window at the parking lot.

It took a moment to spot him among the cars in lot, especially since she didn't know which "guy" Kari was talking about. It turned out to be the enormous man from outside Penny's house, the one Corbin called Absolven. He didn't have a gun this time, but was otherwise unchanged. Penny had described him as a "Hercules," and the description seemed to fit; there was something of the classical Greek god to him. He was walking among the cars in the parking lot, looking at them carefully.

Marley moved Kari away from the window. Corbin was still stretched out on top of the bedspread, fast asleep. He'd only moved enough to fling his arm over his eyes. She touched his shoulder gently. "Corbin, wake up."

He shifted slightly, and she stepped away in case he was a violent waker. But when he lifted his arm, his eyes were already open and clear. "What's going on?"

"Absolven is outside. He's looking at the cars in the parking lot."

Brow furrowed, Corbin glanced at the bedside alarm clock. "I slept too long."

"You said we had a day! I mean, God knows, somebody should get some sleep around here."

He rose to his feet and brushed past her to look out the window. "The protection against finding you here via magic delays a celestial by about a day. Absolven probably just used logic. Hell, he's probably used this place himself in the past." He leaned on the glass, squinting. "You might as well come over here. We can make this an educational experience."

"He's not going to look up, see us, and shoot us? He had a gun earlier."

"Such a modern girl. Absolven wouldn't dream of killing somebody he couldn't look in the eye. C'mere. Activate the Sight and look at him."

Marley gave the twins a sharp look as she joined Corbin. "You two stay away."

"All right. So you've noticed the lines and nodes? We call the lines the Geometry. Nodes are formed when lines join up; the more nodes something has, the more sentient it is, up to seven nodes or so. The old idea of chakras comes from this. Those who know how can open up a few more. Enchantments of various sorts can be tied to a node. The usual sort are semi-permanent enhancements we call charms. The Sight is a charm, the most basic there is. Most people in the supernatural scene, mortal and otherwise, have it. Other charms provide other enhancements."

"Where do they come from?" Despite her rising anxiety, she tried to study the man moving around below. His seven circles each radiated a different color.

"They're either constructed by Geometry manipulations, which are best done in a controlled ritual environment, or they spark from an object a celestial has prepared—relics and talismans and that sort of thing. He has the Sight in his highest circle, which is normal. And in the second circle... You can see how the golden flare has a shape within it, the beak and claw and wings?" She could see more than that: the complete image of a restless griffin, lion's tail lashing. Corbin went on quickly, "That's a glamour. Absolven isn't actually human in his natural shape, but faerie glamours are so good they convince the inanimate world as well as mortals. I wonder what he traded for that..."

"You said something about that before. Fairies as well as angels and demons?" Marley shook her head. "Are there werewolves and vampires, too?"

The expression on Corbin's face was neutral. "Monster stories have their source." He hesitated. "Look, in the end, there are only celestials and mortals and us. The Fallen behave in a number of ways, based on what they believe about their Creator. Those beliefs reshape them, but they're all variations on the same basic template: spirit, numina, avatar. It all adds up to trouble."

"How does this stuff not make it onto the six o'clock news?" She watched Absolven vanish behind a large van, her pulse picking up as soon as he was out of sight.

"The Hush. And its prototype, the faerie Covenant. Anyhow, Absolven's other charms are all angelic blessings, save the glamour and another one. That one..." He frowned, as if concentrating.

Marley remembered her reflection. "I have two, I saw. You gave me the Sight—and without a ritual environment? But what's the other one?"

"I just duplicated what I had, rather than custom-building something for you. And yeah, I noticed that. I meant to investigate." He transferred his gaze to her and brushed his hand over the top of her head, barely touching her. Then his fingers twitched, tangling lightly in her hair. She shivered.

His gaze refocused on her face, his fingers sliding down to her temple and brushing her cheek. Then he cleared his throat and pulled his hand away. "It's a celestial beacon, I think. Maybe from Ettoriel, to aid in tracking you? Have you touched anything he might have blessed?"

"What? Something from him? Lawyer Jeremy's business card, maybe?" Marley rubbed at her arms, and then brushed at her forehead, as if she could wipe the thing away. "Can you get rid of it? That sounds really bad."

"Not here and now, no. You can't just casually remove other people's charms and enchantments." He coughed. "Well, I can't. There are those who can."

"Who? Can't we find them?" Panic was rising in Marley and she suddenly saw no reason to stop it. A beacon? On herself, not a bag she could lose somewhere, not a hat, not a physical item at all. Somebody had reached out and put a marker on her soul and there was no way she could remove it. A moment ago, the concept of magic had seemed fascinating and alluring, even in the midst of danger. But now she felt violated. Now she wanted nothing to do with it.

"I'll look into it," he said, in a soothing voice. "It'll be okay. We'll just keep moving once we get out of here. Ettoriel can't keep up this kind of effort forever."

"But it's already done its job! His hunter is out there and we're stuck in here." She turned back to the window, scanning the parking lot frantically for the glamoured nephil.

"Oh, I've escaped him more than once before. I'm not expecting much challenge if we're just trying to esca—" He blanched suddenly and turned to look out the window. Marley heard the hysterical cawing before Absolven stepped around a large truck. This time, he was holding a raven with one wing bent at an awful angle. Carefully, he put the bird on the hood of the truck. It fell over helplessly, pecking at its legs, and Marley realized they were bound together.

"That bastard," Corbin whispered. "That last charm... it makes him invisible to birds. They never had a chance to get away." Absolven vanished around to the back of the truck again, and returned with another crippled, bound bird.

Corbin wrenched open the sliding glass doors next to the window. "Corbin, what are you doing?" Marley whispered. The catastrophe vision twisted and churned, fighting against her suppression, desperate to show her something dreadful.

"I have to save them. They're my friends. He's hurting them, but I can fix it if I get them away from him."

"Corbin, it's a trap. He's trying to lure you out." It didn't take foresight to figure that out.

His breath huffed out. "I think it requires some subtlety to be a trap. The right word is 'challenge.' What an absolute bastard." Then his teeth flashed. "I was going to have to send him off anyhow. Don't worry. A flock of ravens can chase off an eagle." He stepped out onto the balcony and then, unbelievably, hoisted himself over the railing and dropped, three stories.

-twenty-

Marley ran to the railing despite herself, just in time to see Corbin rolling to his feet. He limped into the parking lot and ducked behind an SUV. Absolven was still standing near the crippled birds, eyes raised to scan the hotel. Nobody else was outside. Smoke had rolled down the slopes of the mountain while Marley was distracted, and now the haze in the parking lot made distant cars faded and unreal.

She glanced inside, where the children had come to the door, Kari holding a floppy Neath. Then she closed the glass door on them, so the smoke wasn't drifting inside. It scratched her throat when she breathed, and she hoped it was better down on the ground.

She grimaced. Who was she kidding? It didn't matter if the smoke was better on the ground; Absolven was going to catch Corbin and end him. She opened the door again and dashed back inside, slamming it shut behind her. She grabbed the phone off the nightstand and dialed the front desk. This was a hotel run for supernatural types; surely somebody could do something to help Corbin. But the phone rang and rang, until finally a voicemail message picked up and apologetically told her that they'd call her back just as soon as possible.

Could she find somebody else? Another guest of the hotel? How would she convince them that helping Corbin was worth their time? She ran to the window again. Corbin was not visible, but Absolven was strolling east across the lot. His shape flickered, and Marley could suddenly see the griffin underneath the glamour. It was larger than she'd imagined, far bigger than either a lion or an eagle. It looked like it could eat lions for breakfast. Cars seemed to cringe away from his wingspan and each footfall should have made the ground shiver. She remembered: Once, the nephilim were called giants.

If anybody was going to help Corbin, it had to be her. She knew the catastrophe vision wasn't fixed in stone. Maybe she could go down there and distract that thing while Corbin attacked it. Or maybe she could be on hand to provide first aid until some kind of emergency services could arrive. That could make a difference, right? The voice of reason in the back of her head pointed out that the tiny first-aid kit, combined with her own rudimentary skills, might save a choking person but wouldn't be much use with disembowelment, which is what those rasping claws looked good at. And what would stop the griffin from eating her if Corbin was disemboweled? How well had she protected herself so far?

She ignored the voice. Doing something was better than doing nothing. Doing anything was better than gnawing off her own hand in helpless fear.

But the dry voice continued: And what about the children? Corbin said to not leave the room.

Corbin is an idiot who went into a clear trap. To save a friend? Like you're doing? She hated that the voice was her own.

She stopped and looked at the children. Were they still safe? She slipped the leash on her foresight.

And her first instinct was *Take them with me. They will be safe. No matter what happens out there, they'll be safe if they're with me.*

But she looked closer and saw them coming unbound. A maelstrom of fire was contained within their shapes, leaking from their linked hands, and the boundaries that kept them human were fraying. Was this the future or the present? After seeing the angel inside of Penny, she was no longer sure.

"Marley? Why are you looking at us?" Lissa asked.

"I'm worrying about what to do next," she said.

The cry of an eagle mixed with the yowl of a cat cut through her thoughts. Neath came alert and quivering, claws digging into Lissa's arms until she yelped and let go of the kitten. Marley looked out the window in time to see Corbin running through the parking lot, Absolven loping after him. Corbin scattered something behind him that sparked as Absolven moved over it. He shrieked and leapt to one side, his paw smashing down into the pavement, eagle wings catching the pale smoke and shoving it forward. Corbin stumbled, and staggered to one side before vanishing behind another car.

Opening the single duffel bag she'd brought up, Marley fumbled for the pathetic first-aid kit she'd packed. She ran into the bathroom to gather up some towels, and noticed something unusual on the wall: This hotel room came with its own first-aid kit, and it was a lot more impressive than hers. She wrenched it off the wall, barely noticing how easily she tore it away from its bolts.

"We're going downstairs to help Corbin," she announced to the kids. She remembered a fire exit a few doors down. That was good, a useful thought, because she wasn't jumping over the balcony. She was crazy, not suicidal.

Kari brightened. "Fight the bad guy?"

"Save Corbin," she corrected. "You two stay very close to me. But if I say run, you run, and if anybody tries to hurt you, you do whatever you can to them, you hear? Anything you can." She strode to the door, towels bundled around the box from the bathroom.

A hero's death is not an option now, little fool, whispered a voice, sliding into her mind like a scalpel. It was familiar, but it wasn't hers. *Stay. Don't be too stupid to live.* It was the voice she'd heard on the highway, as she passed a roadside scene, the voice from something that had looked like a paper shell of a man inhabited by a monster. She looked around wildly.

The man who was a monster underneath sat in the armchair in the corner of the room. The black spiral still spun over his head, and the monstrous wings spread around him like a dark aurora. She blinked and pushed away the symbolic imagery of the catastrophe vision, leaving only the more technical Sight Corbin had given her. Then she could see that he had none of the colored nodes of a mortal, only the black wheels at his head and feet. The dark halo sucked at her gaze, inviting her to lose herself in its lazy black spin. But to ordinary vision, he looked so normal. Dark hair, clean-cut, just pretty enough to not stand out in Hollywood. Just a man.

Except when she looked in his eyes.

She released the first-aid kit and towels from trembling hands and moved to put herself between the kids and the dark celestial. "Who are you?"

"Wherever you go, you're already between them and the world," he said, in a mortal's voice. She liked it no more; it was deceptive. On the phone, he might be human.

She didn't bother with more questions. "Out into the hall, kids, let's go."

But before she could take even a single step away, he'd risen from the chair and captured her wrist, in a grip as strong as self-hatred. It hurt. He stroked the knuckles of his other hand down her cheek, tender like a lover. Nausea flooded her. "I'd say you shouldn't be afraid of me, but I'd be lying," he whispered.

Run, she tried to say. She tried to move her mouth in the shape of the word, to whisper it. But her mouth wouldn't listen to her. It stayed firmly closed, her teeth clenched together.

"But I'm already inside you." He tapped his thumb over her mouth, and she retained just enough will to jerk her head away. "I know how cruel you are to the woman who raised you. And about the skiing trip in high school. The girl you could have saved from that terrible accident. If you'd only listened to yourself and warned her. If only..." His hand slid down her neck and his fingers went around her throat like a necklace. "But even then, you already longed to be emptied. To be devoured..." Marley's knees sagged under her as she fought her way through the tidal wave of emotion his words unleashed, but he held her up. Old guilt and new terror merged together.

Then a little voice cried, "You let her go!" and it was lemon juice over raw wounds. She gasped, blinking back tears, and a blur resolved itself into Kari standing beside them, small fists clenched. A yard behind her, Lissa pressed her back against the wall.

"Sit down, children," said the man calmly, not taking his nightmare eyes off Marley's face.

"Let her go!" It was suddenly a lot hotter in the room.

The man sighed, and looked down at the kids. "Children, *sit down.*" The command was so palpable that Marley would have ended up on the floor if she wasn't still caught in his grip. Lissa slid down the wall, but Kari remained standing. Her eyes widened and her brow furrowed and she leaned forward, as if setting her weight against something.

Marley realized that the man's grip on her wrist had become only as strong as iron, a mundane thing. She pulled and twisted, and at first it simply hurt. So she recovered her balance instead.

Then Kari sagged, and sank down to the floor. The man smiled. "Good children. Go and sit on the bed." As obedient as the beaten, they both scrambled to the nearest bed. "Now, we were talk—" But Marley exploded with sudden fury, kicking and yanking on her arm and clawing at his face with her free hand. He caught her other hand, was unmoved by her kicks, and he kept smiling.

Until a tiny, yowling bundle of fur and claws landed on his back. The iron in his grip was brittle. It broke. Sobbing, Marley collapsed and scrambled away, even as the man arched his back and cursed, reaching around to grab Neath from behind. He looked at the spitting, flailing calico kitten and said, "I see," derisively before tossing the cat on the bed with the children. Neath promptly hopped off the bed and onto Marley's shoulder. Her claws were painful pricks that helped Marley focus.

"Run," Marley gasped. "Run, run, run." Her voice was breathy and nearly gone. But the twins just sat there, huddled together. "Oh, please run," she begged them. Lissa buried her face on Kari's shoulder and started whimpering. Kari stirred, sluggishly, raising her gaze from the bedspread.

The man stepped over where Marley was tangled up in herself, putting himself between the door and the rest of the room.

"No," he said calmly. "Even if the security in this place has been damaged, you are still safer inside this room than out."

"W-why?" Marley asked. *How could that be possible?*

"The angel would appear here now that he knows your location. If he could. But he can't." This time his smile showed teeth. "Because I got here first. I'm here to help, you see."

-twenty-one-

The idea was so ludicrous that it drove all thought out of Marley's head. She stared at him. He smiled at her and leaned against the door. Neath's claws kneaded on her shoulder. Carefully, she stood up. "You're serious."

"Absolutely. I don't want anything happening to the little dears. As long as they don't piss me off." He winked at the kids.

"You're a demon," Marley stated. She took Neath off her shoulder and cuddled her.

His eyebrows lifted. "Don't mistake me for them. I haven't the principles of that kind."

Marley tried to figure out what this meant, and then gave up. He was supernatural, he was the most awful thing she'd ever encountered, and he had some delusion that he was better than the alternative. That was what mattered. "Why? Why isn't anybody noticing what the hell's going on?" she muttered.

The monster smirked. "Glamour's a powerful thing when unleashed, sweetheart. Glamour clouds the world, makes her lie. And the next morning she hates herself and tries to pretend nothing happened. The freak out there has access to a *lot* of glamour. Everybody in the hotel not in this room is busy staring at the pretty lights right now."

Outside, there was a hoarse cry that sounded like Corbin. Marley flinched. She wanted to crawl onto the bed with the children and cower. Instead she raised her chin, acting like she wanted to feel. Old advice of her mother's. "Why would you want to protect them?"

His smile broadened. "Rumor has it they'll make all my dreams come true someday."

"Oh my God. What could something like *you* dream about?" Marley whispered.

"Exactly," he agreed. He looked past her. "The raven child is losing. I'll have to deal with the freak myself when he claws his way in here. Not that I expected much else." He yawned.

Marley's mouth shaped words, but she couldn't force them out, until they were exploding out of her in a shout. "Do it now!" Neath's claws bit into her arm.

He looked at her in surprise. "Do what now?"

"Go deal with that thing, if it's so easy! Before Corbin dies!" Outside, the sun was setting. Was it evening already? But the sky was the color of blood in the smoke-choked twilight. The crimson light gave everything a strange glow.

"That might be amusing," the monster admitted. "But no more amusing than staying here." He eyed her. "Perhaps much less so."

It was so hot in the room. Even with the sliding glass door closed, the smell of wood smoke and sulfur scratched her nostrils. He was enjoying her fear. She had never hated anyone so much. He was forcing her helplessness down her throat and she was choking on it.

But he wasn't touching her anymore. She was no longer trapped in his hand. A little voice in her head pointed this out, over and over again, until finally it sank through the fear.

Why was that? He'd so clearly enjoyed it.

There was no time to reason things out. Dropping Neath, she flung the door open and ran onto the balcony. The griffin was perched on top of a car, the top bowing in from the weight of the creature. She saw a glimpse of Corbin, blood on his arm and face, and then the griffin leapt. There was a crash of metal, a muffled whomp, and a billow of dark grey smoke. Both Corbin and the griffin staggered out of the smoke in different directions, Corbin coughing weakly.

The monster's hand was on her arm again, pulling her away from the edge of the balcony. "No," he said in irritation. She glanced at him angrily and realized, *I'm more afraid for Corbin than I am of him. And he doesn't like that at all.*

Without thinking, she smashed her hand against his face. She felt the crunch, and had enough time to wonder at how easily a nose broke. Then a new jolt of fear raced through her as he barely seemed to notice. He caught her hand with his free one. He didn't cry out, didn't flinch, even as blood gushed from his nose. But the fear was followed by a thrill: He was bleeding. Even if he didn't seem to care, his body was mortal; it could be wounded.

She yanked hard on her trapped arm, pulling him toward her and off his center of gravity. He flowed rather than stumbled, keeping his balance with the same physical mastery that let him absorb a broken nose without a wince. She didn't care. She kicked with one foot and stomped with the other, aiming for his knee. Maybe that would break as easily.

He crouched. Something complicated happened. Air whooshed past Marley's head as the world rotated.

She was dangling over the balcony, prevented from falling only by the monster's grip on her arm.

"You are an idiot," the monster growled. A drop of his blood spattered on Marley's face.

"Do it!" she said. Maybe she'd handle the fall as well as

Corbin did, she thought wildly.

He stared down at her, emotions warring across his face. She could see the conflict so clearly. Here was a creature, un-imaginably old, and totally unused to having his will thwart-ed by the likes of her. He really wanted to let her fall, she could tell. But he also didn't want her hurt. That was what her subconscious had noticed. He was like a dieting man in front of cheesecake he'd promised himself he wouldn't eat.

"Marley!" the kids screamed, appearing at the balcony door.

And here comes cheesecake filled with razor blades, thought Marley spitefully. *Try to eat them and you'll choke on your own blood.* She didn't even know what the thought meant.

His mouth tightened as he glanced back at the kids. Then he yanked her arm up, so hard she gasped, lifting her high enough that her feet hooked the rail of their own accord. He caught her under her legs and then set her down on the nicely solid surface of the balcony.

As soon as he did, the twins moved toward her, falling over her in their eagerness to make sure she was all right. Neath twined between them all. Then they turned toward the monster.

He jammed his hands into his pockets, staring down at them. Once again, the temperature seemed to rise. This time, Marley felt a prickling across her skin, as if random parts of her body had fallen asleep. There was a pressure rising be-tween the three of them and the monster. She didn't know what was happening, but it felt like a weight was pressing down on her, and like she was sprouting spikes from her skin in response. She shifted uncomfortably and gathered the chil-dren closer. They were both distracted, their entire attention focused on the monster, their faces blank.

The monster shook himself and his stance shifted slightly. Marley's prickly, spiky feeling vanished. Quietly, he said, "Go inside, children. We'll all go inside."

Marley gave them a little push, and they seemed to wake up. After a look up at her, they stumbled back through the door, Lissa picking up the kitten again as she went. He watched them and then looked at her, tilting his head toward the door. She gave him a feral smile. "What do you think?" She held up her hand, the palm still smeared with his blood.

"Fucking Christ," he exploded. "I think that this isn't going to end until this entire block is a smoking crater. If I break up the fight between your boyfriend and the freak, would you please go sit on the bed like a good little girl until it's over?" He didn't wait for an answer, but faded away into a shadow, just as he'd arrived.

"No," said Marley, anyhow. She had never felt less like being a good little girl. "You two stay inside, though, just in case. No, further inside. Play with your dolls."

"I threw my doll at the angel-Penny," protested Lissa.

"Then watch TV!" Marley was already scanning the parking lot eagerly, trying to find the monster, or Corbin. It was easy to see the griffin, who was crouched on another car, wings flapping lazily. She finally found Corbin, on the far side of the parking lot. Even from that distance, she could see his awkward, hunched posture, as if he was braced against pain. He shouted to attract the griffin's attention, and it leapt toward him, using its wings to turn the jump into an extended glide.

As it closed, Corbin's posture changed, straightening as the wounded hunch dropped away. He brought his hands up and light flickered between them. The griffin flinched and the glide turned into a tumble. Thunder boomed as its wings frantically pounded the air. Then the creature plowed into a Lexus SUV.

And pushed itself to its feet again. Its beak opened and a raucous stream of noise hardly identifiable as language, let alone individual words, emerged. Corbin hunched to one side again, and Marley's heart sank. She'd hoped he was faking before to keep the creature off guard. This was it; she knew it, even with the catastrophe vision suppressed. This was Corbin's last stand. He was going to die keeping this creature away from her, and it wasn't even the guy directing the hunt. Despair washed over her.

Tsk, said the monster's mind-voice. *The angel won't even appreciate the flavor.* He stepped out of shadow behind the crouching griffin, and said its name. *Absolven.*

The griffin jerked, midstep, and reared back even as it spun. As if hearing a whisper from across the room, Marley could distantly feel the monster speaking to Absolven. She twitched in reflexive sympathy even as she fought to again suppress the feelings he'd awakened. She'd asked for his help, demanded it, knowing he was a monster.

The griffin shook its head and closed its wings tightly. A shimmer, and it was a man again, oversized but limping. He stepped backward once, still shaking his head, and glanced between Corbin and the monster. Then he looked directly over to where Marley stood on the balcony and a scowl twisted his face. Inclining his head in a shadow of a bow, he turned and strode away. The monster called something after his retreating form, but Corbin interrupted, his voice harsh. Hands in his pockets again, the monster turned to him, but Corbin shook his head and started limping back to the hotel.

The monster fell into step beside him, loose and relaxed. He didn't seem to be talking, but with every step, Corbin's movements became tighter and more defensive, as if he was withdrawing inside himself. He stumbled, and the monster caught his arm. Corbin jerked it away, and stumbled again. The monster said something. "...reasonable... carry you..." Corbin glanced up at the balcony and Marley quickly turned away. If he didn't want an audience while he accepted the monster's help, it was the least she could do.

She went inside, wondering if she'd made the wrong choice. Would Corbin have actually preferred death to the monster's assistance, as his body language seemed to indicate? But how could she have known that? How could she have known they'd know each other, as they seemed to? She didn't have time for Corbin to die a heroic death, anyhow. She opened up the hotel's first-aid kit and unpacked antiseptic and other supplies.

"Is Mr. Corbin okay?" asked Lissa. "Is the bad guy gone?" She slipped off the bed and came over to hug Marley's leg. The TV was on, but tuned to a weather station both girls were ignoring.

"He's hurt, but I think he'll be okay." Marley wondered who they considered the bad guy—the griffin or the monster. "Did you know the man who was just in here?"

Tears filled Lissa's eyes. "No," she whispered. "He was scary."

Marley dropped some gauze and wrapped her free arm around the little girl. "Yes. He was."

Lissa whimpered into her shoulder, "We couldn't make him go away."

Kari, on the bed and holding her doll close, said, "He's too big. They're all too big. I couldn't open the door." Marley blinked and then realized she was talking about the door at Penny's, the one Ettoriel had been magically holding closed. *I wonder if Senyaza has child therapists in their super-powered ranks*, she thought uneasily. "You're both still very little. It's okay. You don't have to be as strong as grownups."

"The fire says we could be," Lissa whispered.

"What?" Marley blinked and pulled the girl away to look at her. "What says you could be?" Lissa just shook her head. "Listen to me. Things are awful right now, but it isn't up to you to fix it. Anyone who tells you otherwise is lying to you. They're part of the problem. The only thing you should be doing is staying safe."

"Nobody else is fixing things," said Kari sulkily. That hurt. While Marley was still staring at her, trying to find something to say other than a plaintive *I'm trying*, the door to the room opened.

Corbin was back and the monster was still with him, half supporting him, half dragging him.

-twenty-two-

Here he is, sweetheart. Safe and sound." The monster smiled crookedly as he released Corbin's arm. Lissa scrambled back onto the bed beside Kari, as if she thought the monster would reprimand her.

Corbin sagged immediately and Marley leapt to help him to a bed. He folded his fingers over her hand. "Marley," he said, his voice urgent. "Did you offer him anything to get him to help me?"

"What? No!" She wondered, *What could I have offered him that he couldn't have just taken?* "I did punch him in the nose, though."

Corbin stared at her and then broke into a broad grin. "You're beautiful."

Marley's face felt warm and she turned to gather up the first-aid supplies. "What is he, anyhow?" she mumbled.

"We call them kaiju. Big monsters. Generally speaking, they want to destroy the Creator's work, in a variety of nasty ways. My friends in the hospital try to keep their numbers low."

"I'm right here, you know," said the kaiju, aggrieved.

"That's a problem you could solve anytime," snapped Corbin.

The kaiju ignored him to address Marley. "You could at least say thank you, sweetheart."

"Do you have a name?" she asked him, as she inspected Corbin. He had several wounds on his arm and torso, and a chunk missing from his shoulder. She thought a leg might be injured, too, but she wasn't going to ask him to take his pants off while the kaiju was still there unless Corbin mentioned it.

The crooked smile returned. "I try not to, but they do make paperwork easier. My last driver's license claimed I was Severin something-or-other. I liked the sound of it. Severing."

"He's in the books as the Whispering Dark," muttered Corbin, wincing. "Low priority due to his focus on single targets. Asshole."

"Mmm. Low priority. I've lived a very, very long time as 'low priority,' raven boy."

"Old. And thus, very, very dangerous," concluded Corbin. "As I said, when celestials reincarnate, they retain the same personality but lose their memories of their previous existence. Newborn kaiju are barely more than rabid animals. The longer they're allowed to survive, the better they get at staying alive and wreaking their own particular brand of destruction."

"And see how good I am at staying alive? You owe me *your* life now, boy."

Corbin's jaw clenched. Marley touched his arm and then pulled her hand away. "So what now? Is Absolven gone for good?"

It was Severin's turn to look irritated. "No. He ran away rather than fight. Maybe if *somebody* hadn't stopped me from bringing him down.... well. He'll recover, and return. Humanity makes you people so *resilient*. And of course, the half-breeds must always stick together, even when they're otherwise trying to kill each other."

Corbin's hand twitched and Marley grabbed it, wrapping her palm around his long fingers. After a heartbeat, his fingers curled lightly around hers. Severin noticed, his gaze resting on their linked hands, and his smile made Marley feel dirty.

"Are we running away again?" asked Kari. She was still holding her sister's hand.

"The security of the building has been seriously compromised. The power Ettoriel's flinging around, to shut down an entire hotel..." said Corbin, gazing off into space.

"Compr—?" frowned Kari.

"Shattered. Broken. Shot to hell," said Severin helpfully.

Kari's brow wrinkled. "I thought compromise meant sharing?"

"No, compromise means surrender. That means to give up." Severin smiled over at the kids, and Marley shook herself.

"It has two meanings," she said, and glared at Severin.

He mouthed something at the kids—she couldn't tell what—and all her rage and hatred came boiling back. She suddenly didn't care about old grudges surfacing inside the hotel room. She was ready to press some new ones herself.

Corbin's fingers squeezed her hand lightly, and she took a deep breath. "And yes, we have to go someplace else." Marley paused, looking at Kari's sulky face. "But I agree, we can't run forever."

"It'll be over with one way or another soon enough," said the kaiju. He sprawled in a chair. "The raven boy knows. Tell her, raven boy."

Corbin paused and then disentangled his fingers from hers, running his hand through his hair. "If the angel is planning on doing a major ritual, something that will affect the world Geometry, he has to do it on a specific date. A day and a half from now."

Marley glanced at the date on the weather channel still muted on the television. "August…thirteenth? What's so special about that?"

"It's not an annual event. It's a celestial conjunction, but one that involves the Machines of Heaven rather than stars. A valence day, it's called."

Marley remembered. "Penny—the angel—said something about a valence event."

Corbin nodded, but before he could speak, Severin said, "The Hush was created on such a day. And the Covenant."

Glumly, Corbin said, "Yes. The functions shaping Creation can be altered at a high valence point. Sometimes. Occasionally. They mostly don't stick. We got lucky with the Hush."

"Did you? How nice for you," the kaiju said, as if the topic bored him.

"So is Ettoriel trying to remove the Hush or not? Zachariah said he was, right? But you don't think so?"

Corbin grimaced. "If he was, I'm sure 'Severin' here would be helping him instead of chasing off his servants. Although he is more subtle than the usual kaiju…"

Suddenly the kaiju was in Corbin's face, one finger pressed against Corbin's forehead. "Listen up, raven child. One: I don't care about your precious Hush. It has never inconvenienced me in the slightest." He flicked out a second finger. "Two: I'd rather kill an angel than work with one. Three: *Don't make me change my mind.*" There was a frozen moment, as Corbin and the kaiju stared into each other's eyes from a distance of about six inches. Then the kaiju's mouth curved up into a hard, feral grin. He leaned even closer and whispered in Corbin's ear.

Corbin's reaction was instant: He shoved the kaiju so hard that the creature actually flew away from him and hit the wall. He slid down it until he was crouching on his heels, still smiling. No, not just smiling, laughing to himself.

Fresh blood darkened a bandage on Corbin's arm. "Thank you for your help," he said coldly. "Do you have any other plans in that direction we should know about?"

"Well, as long as I'm here, I'm plugging the hole in the security. And if I stay here while you leave, nobody will notice you fleeing the scene, at least for a time."

"Oh, thank God," muttered Marley.

"No, thank *me*," said the kaiju. "Thank my self-control, honed through many years of not being serially murdered by the raven boy's friends. Because you are such a tasty snack that I don't really want to let you get away." He considered. "Either of you."

Marley stepped out into the hotel parking lot. The end-less smoke-twilight had finally turned to night, but that only made the flames easier to see. On the near mountainside, she could make out individual blazes and their fuel: candle flames consuming the chaparral, matchstick flames burning a tiny doll's house. Steam billowed from the fire eating the home as a helicopter fought the hot air nearby, but the weather was too dry and the fire too hot. There was land burning that hadn't burned in a long, long time.

Shouting in the parking lot dragged Marley's gaze away from the distant inferno, and she pressed her back against the wall instinctively. A work crew comprised equally of staff in suits and staff in overalls worked at cleaning up the disaster area the lot had become. She wouldn't have noticed before, but now, with recently educated eyes, she was pretty sure magic was going on. The hotel staff and occupants had woken up from the glamour that had kept them from knowing of the conflict outside, and now they were cranky and confused. It was, she gathered, unusual even among the supernatural set to blink and realize you'd spaced out through a mythological monster tearing up the place.

Her rental car, at least, was fine, tucked in a corner away from the main swath of destruction. Had Corbin moved the fight away from their escape vehicle on purpose? She turned to ask him as he came out the door behind her, but then thought better of it. He was still sullen and cold, not quite rude but definitely unfriendly. Whatever the kaiju had whispered in his ear had transformed him.

The kids trooped out behind Corbin, but Severin the kaiju had stayed in the room. When Marley had left, he'd been on a bed, snickering at a gory action film. He'd waved without bothering to look at her, a dismissal from his attention, and she'd been glad of it. But she wondered if he'd show up again. If he did, she hoped it would be in a place with more room to run.

They loaded up the car and left in silence, directed around the recovery work by an angry man in a nice suit who seemed simultaneously furious that they were leaving, and glad to see them go. Corbin had spoken and then argued with a similarly dressed man who had appeared at the room door as they were preparing to leave. Explanations had been demanded, and Corbin had turned the demands back on the concierge with aggressive, angry remarks about the hotel security. He'd been furious, and the kaiju had laughed at him, and that had made it worse.

Marley peeked at Corbin from the corner of her eye while they waited for the light to change at an empty intersection. His mouth was tight, his jaw hard, as he stared out the window.

"If you look in my backpack, right back there, there's a sheaf of paper I wanted to ask you about. Next to the Lullaby Plaything. A folio of a book. I'm pretty sure it has some kind of enchantment on it. That's possible, right?"

He gave her an unreadable look and then rifled through the bag until he found the papers. He glanced at it and then flipped through it. "It's encoded. Locked to a specific key. The owner's touch, probably."

"But it's decoding itself, look and see."

Corbin shrugged. "Where did you get it?"

"At Zachariah's house. It seemed odd. Out of place. As if somebody wanted me to find it." It seemed obvious now that some kind of magic had been present.

"What's the point of wanting you to find a book you can't decode? Oh, right, you said this was at Zachariah's house." He made a disgusted sound. "With time and the right resources, I could remove the encoding. But it's not going to happen in the next couple of days."

Lissa, quiet and withdrawn since the kaiju had returned to the hotel room, suddenly said, "Can I see?"

Marley felt Corbin looking at her inquiringly. She said, "Not—not right now, sweetie."

"It shouldn't hurt her. It's a passive working."

Marley shook her head. "The magic may be harmless, but the words might not, and I told you, it's decoding itself."

Corbin glanced through the pages. "He said. I kind. Really good. Cat."

Marley blew out her breath, suddenly exhausted. "Look, I don't understand magic, and I don't understand everything the kids can do. The Lullaby Plaything didn't react the way you expected it to. Until we can explain that, I really don't want to let them play with other things I don't understand." She met Lissa's gaze in the rearview mirror. "Sorry, sweetie."

The little girl looked away, out the window. Again, Marley felt uneasy. She didn't know how to deal with children who were angry at her. Her friends, she could coddle and scold and snap at, but the dependence of these children was too new.

"I told you, it's just an encoding. It's not going to react strangely to them, because it only exists in two states, on and off."

"Then why is it decoding itself? Did somebody install a dimmer switch?"

Corbin frowned at her and then down at the book. He remained silent for a while, his fingers twitching. Marley continued driving, making her way to a fire evacuation shelter they'd identified before leaving the hotel. It wouldn't be comfortable, but it would be a place to rest, and both Corbin and the kaiju had assured her that the angel would have personal and magical difficulties hunting her amidst so many humans. *Angels want to protect humans*, whispered the kaiju's voice in her memory. *And the raven child's precious Hush will limit the angel's abilities to act without harming them. The glamour he's borrowed can only go so far.*

A crowd wouldn't stop you, she'd observed, and she'd been proud of how steady her voice had been. *You and that cop on the side of the highway, in front of all those people.*

I chose my prey carefully.

"The spell isn't degrading," Corbin announced, as they drew close to the evacuation center and the traffic thickened. "It's just very, very slowly unlocking."

"Not keyed to the owner, then."

"You sure it's not yours?" he asked, and she couldn't tell if he was teasing or not.

She gave him a puzzled glance. "Why would you think that?"

He almost smiled. "Because then I could still be right."

Then they were caught up in the parking chaos and the evacuation center check-in. The expansive lot was filled with RVs and trailers, some of which seemed to provide food service. Volunteers guided the traffic to empty spaces far, far away from the evacuation center itself. The fires were just a blaze of orange light on the night-shaded mountain from there, although the smell of wood smoke was inescapable.

The evacuation center itself was a stadium, filled with row upon row of cots, with tents down less-busy corridors. Families had set up house on many of the cots, pulling them closer together in little family groups. A subtitled news channel was displayed on one of the big overhead screens, while on another, an animated movie played. A lot of people were lying down, but there didn't seem to be much sleeping going on.

Corbin fidgeted with the encoded book while Marley checked in. As soon as she herded the kids to the cots they'd been assigned, he drew her attention to it once again. "I wonder if it's reacting to specific celestial genetic proximity." He half-gestured at the girls, who were bouncing on a cot.

"You mean, like the Lullaby Plaything did?"

He frowned at her. "I meant, if it's linked to a person, it might also be set to be decoded by their offspring. Which would be why it's decoding now."

Exasperated, Marley said, "Is there any way to *test* that?"

"We could hand it to one of them and see if direct contact finishes the process."

Marley considered this. "You said genetic proximity. Wouldn't a strand of hair work for that?"

Corbin stared at her. Then, his words coming slow and distracted, he said, "Properly prepared it might. Just harvesting from the hairbrush would make the current decoding continue even away from the offspring, but I don't think it would accelerate much. I said genetics, but it has as much to do with the personal Geometry of the individual. A little bit of that is contained within shed hair, but not enough without refinement." He lapsed into silence, still looking intently at Marley.

"Proper preparation. There's a lot of that in this magic of yours..."

He shrugged, looking away. "Some things take time. Some things don't. If the kids are related to the key, testing that won't take any time at all."

Marley took a deep breath and looked past the habit of anxiety to the catastrophe vision that had trained it. There was uncertainty around the twins, a wobbling she couldn't quite identify, but between Kari and the encoded book, there was nothing worrying.

She let out her breath. "Kari, want to help us with an experiment?" Kari bounced off the cot and over to the adults, looking up in interest.

Lissa, who had been paying attention, said, "Why her?"

Marley hesitated before telling the truth. "It will give you nightmares. But not her. And no, I don't know why." She glanced at Corbin, nodding for him to go ahead.

He crouched down to face Kari, and took her hand. He touched one of her fingers to the paper.

Even from where she was standing, Marley could see the writing on the top page writhe. It lasted only a few heartbeats before it settled into words she could read. Then a flash ran over the page, like the glare from bright sun. As it passed, the words faded away.

"Whoa, whoa, whoa!" said Corbin, yanking the book away from Kari's touch. He crouched over it, muttering to himself, his right hand poking and pressing like he was interacting with an invisible touchscreen.

"It was locked," said Kari, looking on with interest. "You wanted it unlocked, right?"

Marley dropped a hand on her shoulder. "I thought we did." She could hear the hint of hysterical laughter in her own voice. "Well, it's not like we've lost anything we previously had."

Corbin said, "I'm working on it. I think I can save most of it..."

"Do you know what happened?" Marley sat down on a cot and let both girls snuggle up beside her.

"She hacked the charm. A brutal, nasty attack on its definition. The charm had a provision for a brute force attack, which was to destroy the contents." His fingers continued to move as he talked, and he didn't look up.

Kari stiffened under Marley's arm. "I was trying to help! Why are you so mean?"

Corbin did look up then, surprise on his face. "What? How am I mean?"

Big angry tears slid down Kari's face. "You said I was a brute and nasty!"

Marley pulled the little girl completely into her lap, hugging her, but glanced at Corbin to see what he was going to do. He looked flustered and irritated. "It was praise. You're very talented. Later, I'd really like to know what you did."

Kari sniffed. "I said. I unlocked it."

Corbin mumbled, "Later. Right now, I need to work." And he bent his head over the book, and said no more.

-twenty-three-

So Marley read the twins a book about Thumbelina, complete with extended critical discussion between the twins about princes, wings, and moles. When they were done, Corbin held out the papers to her.

"I did save some of it. There's quite a lot more readable than what we had before, anyhow."

Marley took it. "Is there anything useful in it?"

Corbin shrugged. "It's the diary of a high school girl. She talks about boys a lot. I only skimmed it, though. Maybe you can read it more closely?"

"What are you going to do?"

He ran a hand through his hair. "I want to go talk to somebody who might be able to explain to me why the kids are so... talented and interesting. AT is on her way here to stay with you while I'm gone."

"Not somebody you can just call up, I take it?"

"Not with a cellphone, not if I want reliable answers."

She looked at him carefully, wondering if what he was about to do was very dangerous. The catastrophe vision unfolded—

"Stop it," he said. His voice was so harsh it shocked her. "I don't want you to look at me like that. Yes, it might be dangerous. It has to be done anyhow." He turned away.

Bewildered hurt flowed through her and she stared at his back. "Fine."

"I'll call you or AT with what I discover tomorrow—actually, later today. Try to get some rest while the kaiju is still distracting the angel."

She watched him walk away, and then busied herself convincing the girls to lie down and rest. Lissa wanted to take Neath out and play with her, and refused to understand that wasn't possible. The volunteers at the evacuation shelter were overlooking very small pets, as long as they were contained, and Neath herself showed no interest in crawling out of her box. Marley had prodded her all over and she didn't seem injured from her encounter with the kaiju, just worn out. AT slouched over, dog-free. "The dogs are around," she said, when Marley raised her eyebrows. She looked tousled and cranky. "I heard the big guy found you anyhow. I'm sorry. Not really sure why Corbin asked me to come over, given how little help I've been so far."

Marley bit her lip. "I appreciate your company."

"Yeah. Did Corbin take off already? Wow, he must really be confident." AT looked around.

"I think he was angry, actually," Marley said. "Although I don't know what he had to be angry about."

"*You* sound angry. Did you two fight?" AT's mouth tugged down into a frown.

Marley looked away. "I'm going to take a look at this book Corbin and Kari decoded. We're hoping it will have some kind of useful information."

AT shrugged, and stretched out on a cot, propping herself onto her side and pulling out her cellphone. She began tapping at the screen, apparently prepared to entertain herself.

Marley settled onto her own cot. A wave of exhaustion crashed over her, and she wondered what time it was. The middle of the night? Had it only been three days since the twins called her? It felt so much longer. One day she was a marginally employed, depressed, anxiety-ridden writer; the next, she was protecting strange little girls from the angel who wanted to claim them and kill her. Kill her *and* all the other part-angels, which she happened to be.

Even reviewing the terror and weirdness of the last few days didn't decrease Marley's vast desire to sleep. But she couldn't give in yet, not when there was the mysterious book to read. She'd had plenty of sleep in the past few days. She could cope a little longer.

She thumbed through the book. It *was* a diary, undated but with stars and moons doodled between the entries. The entries that remained were on lined paper. But in many places, the diary was blotched by emptiness. Both writing and lines had faded away, leaving only naked white paper behind.

A quick preliminary flip-through confirmed that the diary seemed to be written by a teenage girl, and primarily documented her experiences with some boys. Marley was reminded of Penny, at first, until she caught a phrase: "the nameless man." She flipped back to the beginning. It was blank. She carefully turned pages until she found the first patch of remaining text.

I saw another strange man today. But he wasn't as creepy as the nameless man. This time, I knew his name, but he didn't. He was looking around like he was lost, and he was very pretty, so I stopped to see if I could help him out. He told me he was looking for somebody but couldn't remember who, or how he got there. He didn't have a wallet or any kind of identification, so I walked him over to the Westgate Shopping

Center lost and found. I almost told them his name but I decided that would probably get me into more trouble than it would help him. I hope he's all right. I've already nicknamed him Cat.

The next page was there, too.

The stray Cat was exactly where I found him yesterday today. Same clothes, same pose, everything. Creepy deja vu at first, but then he saw me and smiled. Ashley was with me today and she squealed and giggled and told me I didn't say he was so hot. Well, no, not in so many words, it's not like she needs encouragement.

Anyhow, the Cat told me he thought I could be a lot more helpful than the people at the lost and found. "There's just something about you," he said. Uh huh. Right.

That's when I called him Cat. It's actually part of his name. He didn't react like somebody who'd been faking forgetting his own name, though. So I took pity on him and asked him what he did remember.

He said he remembered a man who had stolen something from him. He had to find that man again in order to get back whatever he'd lost. The man's face was burned into his memory. Ashley loaned him her art pad and a pencil, and he sketched a picture.

He was a very good artist. I did know the face. It was the nameless man from the other da

And that entry abruptly ended. Marley glanced over to where Kari lay curled on her side. She was watching Marley sleepily. Marley found a small smile for the little girl. "Go to sleep."

"Sorry I was nasty," Kari whispered. She sighed. "I want Uncle Zach back. I don't like all this."

"We'll get through this together," Marley said. She was

very aware that it wasn't the same as "we'll find him" or "he'll be back soon," and she suspected Kari knew it. But the little girl just sighed again and closed her eyes.

Marley bit her lip and turned her attention back to the book.

I looked up Cat's full name on the internet. I didn't find anything reliable.

We ended up spending the day together. He's so full of... joy. I told him that and he said he wasn't, except around me. He says he's lonely and lost when I'm not around. He hates not knowing who he is. I thought again about telling him his name, but... I can't. I've gotten into enough trouble over knowing names I shouldn't know.

* * *

He moves like a dancer, but food confuses him. He really liked the pizza, though.

* * *

I can't tell if he knows about kissing or not. I'm too nervous to find out!

* * *

I asked him today if he could just move on with his life. I really like him. But it's like there's a huge wound in him. He says he knows he's not like the other people around us, and it hurts him to try. I do know what it's like to be different from everybody else. We have that in common. It's probably part of why we like each other. But I can't even bring myself to tell him about Mother and why I think I'm different. I'm not ready for things to change yet.

* * *

Today I found myself at this strip mall I'd never been to before, with a grubby park behind it. I didn't know why I went there at first, I was just wandering around and I felt this... emptiness sucking me in. I could hardly not follow it. HE was there. The nameless man. He was just walking around the building, stopping every so often to look at it. I went quietly over to the park and sat on a swing. I was kind of scared... ok, I was really scared, but I couldn't think of a REASON, one that made sense, to be scared. Just because I didn't know his name, or he was able to trick my name-sense before... and just because Cat was looking for him...

He looked like he was the same age as Cat, maybe 20. They almost looked like brothers, both tall and slender. He was scary but he just didn't seem DANGEROUS. I didn't worry that he was going to grab me and throw me in a van, or chase me down. He had this purposefully casual style, you know, with a sloppy tie and a rumpled shirt? But his sleeves were rolled up neatly.

He walked around the building touching it here and there, and then stepped backward into the park. Then he turned and looked at me. He just... looked at me for a while. At first I tried to pretend I wasn't looking at him but that was pretty stupid, so I stopped. It really bothered me that I didn't know his name, so much that I almost asked him what it was. But I hated the thought of giving in like that. Eventually, he walked close enough to talk to me. He said, "The blond guy you've been hanging around with... you should stay away from him. He'll hurt you when he remembers his name again."

Who the hell was he to tell me who to hang around with? That must have shown up on my face, because he kind of shrugged and turned away. So I said, "I know his name already."

He turned back again and looked me over, just like he'd been inspecting the building. Then he asked, "Why haven't your people taken care of you?" I had no idea how to answer that, and it was pretty clear he wasn't actually talking to me, either, no more than he'd talked to the building.

I had to say something, so I said, "What do you know about my people?" What did "my people" mean, anyway? Only then it occurred to me that maybe he knew my mom.

But he said, "I know your blond friend doesn't like them very much."

I decided to attack. "Don't YOU know his name?"

He laughed. "Oh yes. I've got it here, safe and sound." He tapped his head, and then crossed his arms, looking at me like I was a zoo exhibit again. I was starting to think he WAS dangerous in the normal ways, and if he got any closer I was running for the stores.

But I wasn't done asking questions, as long as he stayed away. "So you did do something to him! Why?" I can't believe I asked "why" instead of "what." But that's what I asked and that's what he answered. He said, "He would have gotten in my way. I'm investigating something interesting." He trailed off, like he was thinking about something else. "In any case, what I did won't last. You'd best not be around him when he remembers who he is." And then he just turned around and walked away.

I decided not to tell Cat about this. I wouldn't be telling him anything he didn't already know, except that he might not like me when he remembers himself. And I want to think about it for a while. I'm afraid of exactly what that guy said. But surely if he was cruel or violent, it would show up even now, wouldn't it?

There was half of an entry, faded at the top, talking about one of the diarist's female friends and her sexual misadventures, and then another entry that was just one line:

Cat likes kissing.

Marley stopped reading the diary long enough to put her head in her hands. She wanted to reach into the past and shake the writer. She flipped to the end of the diary, which was, unsurprisingly, blank. Had it been blank before? She couldn't remember. She thought about asking AT to read the diary instead; the writer was probably a nephil just like Marley, forgotten and overlooked by her own people. But she had no idea what to make of the amnesiac Cat, except that making out with him seemed like a bad idea.

I'm careful. I'm watching him. I really, really like him. He's sweet and gentle and noble. He always wants to do the right thing. He's been protective of me but he trusts me, too. He really trusts me. I hope I'm doing the right thing.

Cat quit his job today because they wanted him to ignore some kind of underhanded deal. He just couldn't do it. But then he got another one almost right away. He's just so damn pretty. He likes this one more because it lets him move around and look for the nameless guy. That guy must be hiding somehow. I've tried looking for him again, too, and I haven't been able to find the same hole in the namespace that led me to him before.

* * *

My house has rats. My aunt finally got fed up and put traps down recently. One of the traps had a baby rat in it today. I was really depressed about this when I saw Cat. Apparently he's just like his namesake, because while he was nice, he wasn't very sympathetic. He PRAISED me for being so COMPASSIONATE but he said it had to be done, if the rats were damaging the house. That made me cranky, even though I guess he's right. He tried to distract me by kissing my neck, but I wasn't in the mood.

There was a big drawing of a rose on the next page, and several rows of the entry-break doodles before another entry, and then several blank pages. Marley wondered how much time was passing between entries. There were a few brief notes about the diarist's friends. Cat admitted he had a job only so he could stay near the diarist and do nice things with her. It was so sweet that Marley felt uncomfortable reading it.

Finally, she came to another long entry, only marred by the fading at the top. It was the last one in the book.

I hope the nameless man was wrong. I have to do it now, or else I think I've lost my Cat.
It's my own fault. We were making out and at one point I was so unfocused I said a larger part of his name. And I never thought it would get the reaction it did. He jumped away from me and started looking around like he'd never seen his own room before. At first he seemed terrified, then angry. He said he remembered more now. Not everything, not where he'd come from. But that he was a "justice-keeper," and the man he was chasing was a criminal. He wasn't human, but he was a protector of humans. Then he started treating me like I was a criminal too. He accused me of collaborating with the nameless man. Of seducing him and keeping him distracted and tangled in whatever the nameless man had done to him. I tried to tell him he was wrong. But I DID keep his name from him. How could I know it would have such an effect? I tried to explain. I just

wanted to be close to him. But he left.

I've been crying all night. Is he right? Did I sabotage him on purpose? I didn't think it would matter. Even when I wasn't scared of telling him my secrets anymore, I didn't know how to start. "Oh, by the way, I've known your name since I first laid eyes on you but I haven't told you." What excuse could I possibly have?

But I think I love him. Or at least, I love who he was before I screwed up. This is what I was afraid would happen. That he'd remember who he was and then he wouldn't like me anymore. I wanted him to be happy, and he WAS happy with me, I'm sure of it. And surely who he was WITHOUT all his memories is who he REALLY is, right? So that person will still be there, even when he remembers everything, even if it's buried underneath everything else? If he loves me, he'll love me even afterward. It won't just go away... it can't just go away. That's not how love works.

But right now he sees me as the bad guy, and I deserve it. From his perspective I AM the bad guy. I had information he needed and I kept it from him. But I STILL have information he wants. I only whispered part of his name and he only got back part of his memory. So if I tell him the rest, he'll remember everything. And I'll prove to him that I'm on his side. And then even if we can't be together, he'll know I love him. So I'm going to go find him and tell him. And if that doesn't work out, at least something good has been returned to the world.

Here I go. I hope you can forgive me, Akaterin Ettoriel.

-twenty-four-

And there it was. Marley was certain that the narrator was the twins' mother. What Corbin had said about the connection between the writer and the decoder, the journal itself, and what the twins had said about their mother being "gone" but not dead—it all made sense. Marley could all too easily see a teenager in trouble abandoning her newborns with a friendly face. It had happened to her, after all.

That Ettoriel was their father, she was less certain about. If he had claimed paternity from the start, Marley would have felt a lot less confident about keeping them from him in Zachariah's absence. That he didn't seemed significant. But perhaps he didn't know?

Marley flipped through the pages again. Even if he *was* the father, she knew he wanted the twins for grim reasons. If he wasn't the father, what was the point of drawing her attention to this book, and why had it been encoded? She wondered how the story had ended. Had the girl—she thought she remembered Zachariah referring to the twins' mother as "Nina" once—had Nina been pregnant when she'd gone to talk to Ettoriel at the end? Had they even had sex? Blasted, cursed vague writing. Or perhaps the significant details had been in the empty pages. There was something ominous and horrifying about the way the diary ended.

With such thoughts, without entirely noticing, Marley fell asleep. She was only vaguely aware of AT taking her shoes off and Neath jumping on her chest. Then she was aware of nothing at all.

With a shock like waking, the fairy Tinker Chime squirmed his way through a wall. Marley held Neath in her arms, sitting cross-legged on the canopied bed.

"I don't like this anymore than you do," said the fairy. Neath hissed, and Tinker Chime flapped his tiny hand at her dismissively.

"Are you *real*?" Marley asked. "Why do I only dream about you? It's very hard to take you seriously when you only show up when I'm asleep."

"You wouldn't like it if we showed up for real. But that doesn't matter! What matters is that without you, we're going to lose everything."

"Even if I agreed to help you, what could I do from inside a dream?" Neath kneaded her lap, purring unhappily.

The fairy grinned. "You'd be surprised at what can be accomplished within dreams. We've found a weapon for you to use against the Dark Lord and it's *so* poetic—"

"Dark Lord. Is this the first time you've mentioned a Dark Lord? Before it was just about peril and your People In Need."

"What did you think we needed rescuing from? A bad case of bellyaches? The Dark Lord, not content with taking everything from us, now enslaves my people. Day and night we toil under his whip. It took all of my people's remaining power to send me to you. And you've kept me waiting so long."

Marley narrowed her eyes. "Why don't you just go to

somebody else?"

"No one else can do it! I was sent to you. If there was a mistake—and oh, I'd love to believe there was a mistake—I'm stuck with it now."

"That attitude isn't making you any friends, you know. Are you really a fairy? I've heard something about fairies—or maybe fae—lately…" Marley tried to remember. The waking world seemed like the dream now.

The fairy watched her with bright eyes. At last Marley said, "The kids talk about fairies a lot. Corbin mentioned them, too. Something about a Covenant…? Do you know anything about that?"

"Is it a covenant if we did not agree?" The fairy's whisper was barely audible. "The Covenant is a fairy tale told by angels. I know nothing of it. I only know there are three locks on three chains that make us prisoners and slaves. Only a very great weapon can break these chains."

Marley rose to her knees. "Are you mixed up with Ettoriel?"

The fairy did a backflip and when his head came up again, a grin distorted his face. "Ettoriel? Who is Ettoriel? We are compelled by the Dark Lord Tibbersnaufer. He uses our own power against us, forcing us to steal people and wreak havoc in the mortal world. Foul, wicked Dark Lord Tibbersnaufer. But we will help you get the weapon! You must come to us and understand it, and then all will be well."

Marley stared at the small fairy, her head spinning. Something was wrong. Something was wrong with him, and something was wrong elsewhere. Neath was stalking the fairy again, and she seemed larger with every paw she slid forward.

Marley remembered Kari's fairy with a leash dangling from its body. *Fairies are trouble. Can't trust 'em. They keep their promises, basically.* Carefully, she said, "Can you swear to tell me only the truth?"

"If I did that, why, I'd have very little to say." The fairy was barely paying attention to Neath, so closely was he watching her. A paw larger than Tinker Chime batted at him and he flitted away at the last second.

Marley rubbed her head. Something was very wrong. She wanted to wake up, but the walls of her dream enclosed her, like the kaiju's grip on her wrist. The fairy was still staring at her intently. The expression on his face was very different than any she'd seen there before, hard and focused instead of cute and petulant. He made a gesture with one hand, as if pushing something away. The fear that rose with the memory of the kaiju ebbed away. The dream entangled her, but only because it wanted to help her, because she was so close to... something.

Something was wrong. Neath was yowling softly, and she was the size of a bobcat.

"Can you swear you're not working with Ettoriel?" Marley managed to say. Her tongue felt thick.

"One weapon, and perhaps another, to break a chain." Chime said. "If you step through the door, you can find us."

Neath lowered her head and shook it. Then she turned in a circle and leapt. She landed on Marley's chest. Marley fell backward, as Neath sank her teeth into Marley's hand.

The dream shattered in a red-hot wash of pain.

Marley sat up fighting. Neath really was biting her hand. Her face was being licked by a dog, and AT was saying, "*Please wake up, Marley.*" The panic in her voice was frightening.

Marley pushed a canine snout away and clutched at her injured hand as she got up. She glanced around and the crazed sense of wrongness crystallized. There was AT, and there was Lissa, but Kari was gone. Neath clawed her way up to Marley's shoulder and clung there.

"*Where is she?*" Marley realized the growled words had come from her own throat. She scanned the room wildly, then planted her feet and looked again at Lissa and AT. Two of AT's dogs had shown up. One, the black one, was lying on the cot beside Lissa, one large paw draped casually over her lap. The little girl looked guilty and frightened. The brown dog was the owner of the tongue that had tried to lick Marley awake. He sat beside AT and gave her a big doggy grin, his tail moving hopefully. AT, however, was worried and guilty-looking.

"She ran off. To find her uncle, Lissa says. Heart is following her and staying close, but I know you've been doing something to protect them and I didn't want to leave to go get her without waking you up first. And then you wouldn't wake up!"

Her calm certainty of the girls' safety as long as she cared for them was gone. Kari was in terrible danger, and too far away for her to do anything about it. Marley had to find her. She studied the room again, desperately aware of how small the little girl was, how hard to see.

AT went on. "She and Lissa were talking and then she just ran off. I got the dogs here as soon as possible but... she'd already just... vanished. I didn't think anybody could vanish that quickly without using magic."

Marley's attention was suddenly laser-sharp. "But no magic was used?"

"No... Heart found her. She's just so small and fast, she was gone in an instant." AT was clearly shaken, but Marley didn't have time for that.

"Let's go get her." Marley pulled Neath off her shoulder and tucked the kitten in her bag, then scooped up Lissa, who immediately started crying. Words trickled out of her between sobs.

"She had a bad dream! She said we had to find Uncle Zach. I wanted to wait for you but she got mad and ran off. Why wouldn't you wake up?"

"It's all right. We'll go get her," Marley said, as much to reassure herself as to reassure the child. But she didn't even know what direction to go, and that was terrifying. A dog bumped against the back of her legs, and AT tugged her by the elbow.

"She's south. I don't know where she's going, but she was across the stadium parking lot by the time Heart caught up with her."

"Can't Heart herd her this way?" Something terrible was lying in wait for Kari, and the horror would travel across the link between the twins and devour Lissa, as well. She could feel it, feel all the futures turning to cinders.

AT glanced up at her. "Kari isn't a sheep. She's ignoring canine suggestions that she turn around, and I didn't want to start anything... negative."

Marley shifted Lissa on her hip and started jogging, dodging around all the people who apparently had nothing better to do than get in her way. Wasn't it the middle of the night? How long had she slept?

She burst out of the stadium entrance into the grey of pre-dawn—although with the smoke, it was more like the dark red of pre-dawn. More cars had arrived overnight, and the lot on that side of the building seemed nearly full. Marley looked around wildly.

AT arrived behind her. "That way," she pointed towards the street on the far south side of the stadium, and the buildings on the other side. Marley shifted Lissa again, and started running.

Behind her, AT shouted, "He's found her, Marley!"

Marley didn't think she could go any faster while carrying an extra forty pounds of preschooler, but somehow she found the strength. Lissa clung to her, curled half around her back, and Marley's feet pounded the pavement. *If I'm part angel, why don't I get wings? I need wings.* She hit the curb of the street and almost tripped over her own feet. Where next? Desperately, she scanned the other side of the road, looking for anything useful.

A black dog flashed past her, hurtling across the street toward a restaurant parking lot southeast of them. Marley picked up her feet again as she recognized the minivan parked there. As she got closer, Kari's head became visible beyond a car hood. A man in a suit was crouched down a few yards away, talking to her. It was Jeremy. A red dog, the one AT called Heart, was crouched between the child and the man, snarling.

Then Marley was close enough, and the detailed sense of Kari awakened in her again. She still wasn't safe, oh no, none of them were safe, but the sense of desolate wrongness vanished. Kari was close enough. She could protect her. It was like a portcullis slamming down between Kari and the rest of the world. Now, at least, there was a chance.

Jeremy didn't seem to notice Marley's protection falling back into place around Kari, but he tilted his head toward her footsteps even as he finished saying, "—can help you, sweetie." He raised a hand as the black dog rushed him, and the dog skidded to a halt and then started barking.

"Get the hell away from her, you bastard," Marley snarled, panting more from adrenaline than the run. She moved closer to Kari, letting Lissa slide down her hip until the child was walking beside her and holding her hand.

Kari turned dark eyes to Marley. "Why don't you want to go find Uncle Zach? You just want to run away and hide. But Uncle Zach is sad without us."

Marley bit her lip so hard she tasted blood. As much as she just wanted to sweep Kari into her arms, she realized she had to be careful. Kari was questioning her, not rejecting her, but if she ignored the child's questions to focus on the more obvious dangers, Kari would continue looking for her own answers, alone and ignorant.

And here, now, that would lead only to darkness. So Marley said, "Your Uncle Zach wants me to protect you. That's why he sent you to me. Uncle Zach might be sad without you, but he'd be a lot more sad if I let anything happen to you." She held out a hand.

For a moment, the world wobbled as Kari hesitated.

Then Jeremy stood up, brushing off his pants. "But I know where your Uncle Zach is. If you come with me, I can take you to him."

Kari blinked and looked at Jeremy. "You do? Did you take him away?"

Jeremy said, "No, no. He had to leave? Remember what I said the other day?"

Marley moved up behind her as Kari said, "No... that's not right. He wouldn't just leave! Give him back!" Something tense and ugly flitted through the air, and Marley felt Lissa's grip on her hand tighten. Kari took a deep breath, looking frustrated, like she wanted to lash out.

Instead, she started to cry. It was the loud, wailing sob of a child who had finally had too much, and was going to let it all out in an extended tantrum. Marley noticed Jeremy shift his weight, as if letting out some tension. "My employer will be arriving any moment now," he said pleasantly, raising his voice to be heard over the wailing and the snarling and the barking. "He's had enough of the delays you've been causing." He tapped his watch in case Marley hadn't heard him.

From behind Marley, AT said, "Be quiet, Nod," and the black dog switched to growling. AT moved to Lissa's other side and took her free hand.

Marley ignored Jeremy and crouched down to put her arms around Kari. "It's okay, Kari. He's being mean." Kari tried to pull away, still howling, her hands on her cheeks. When Marley held her anyhow, she pulled harder, buckling her knees to fall over. Marley sighed and picked her up bodily.

Kari's eyes opened and she gasped, "No, no *no* no! I want my uncle! You're not my uncle!" She kicked Marley in the gut a couple of times and bopped her in the nose, then slumped, still sobbing. "Where is he?" she whimpered.

Abruptly, AT gasped in sudden pain as Lissa kicked her in the shin and dodged away, moving toward Jeremy. Heart sprang up, body-blocking her, and Lissa collided with the red dog. "I can find out," she shouted, pushing at the dog with both hands. Then she slumped and muttered, "I just have to get closer. I can't hear them."

While Marley was still trying to figure out what Lissa was talking about, Jeremy looked up. The ground shuddered and Marley lost her balance, stumbling backward. Was it an earthquake? But the air shimmered, too, wavering in the pre-dawn light like it did on hot afternoons. Jeremy inhaled deeply and AT cursed as she darted forward to grab Lissa again. For a moment, Lissa seemed ready to take over the kicking and screaming part of Kari's tantrum.

The lights of the minivan behind Jeremy came on. The interior lights brightened until they outshone the headlights. Then the driver's side door opened, and the lights dimmed. There was the faint sound of music from inside the vehicle, a mix of electronica and a choir. Someone stepped out of the car, and the shadow he cast had wings.

-twenty-five-

Marley blinked. When Jeremy said his employer was arriving soon, she'd thought he meant the same way Ettoriel had shown up within Penny. Even the twins had paused their tantrums, staring at the van. Marley squinted, peering through the light. When the lights shut off entirely, the parking lot seemed as dark as a closet at midnight. She stumbled backward again and fell onto her backside, still holding Kari close.

The little girl was limp for a moment. Then she tensed, arms and legs curling around Marley so she could cling to her. "Who is that?" she whispered. Marley just shook her head and clambered to her feet again.

The van door slammed shut, but the music still lingered just on the edge of hearing. As Marley's vision cleared, she could see the newcomer standing beside Jeremy. Unlike Jeremy, who was dressed in a nice suit even at this early—or late—hour, the newcomer had on jeans and a black leather jacket. He didn't seem to have wings, despite the shadow pooling around him. He did have a long knife with a jagged edge hanging from a loop on his jeans. The Ragged Blade.

"Thank you, Jeremy," the man said. "I'm sorry you had to face them alone." He looked speculatively over the little cluster of girls and dogs, an overhead light illuminating the planes of his face. His pale hair glimmered like molten gold.

"They haven't been aggressive. But I'm glad you're here, all the same." Jeremy shifted his weight, as if he wanted to step backward but didn't dare.

"As it should be," said the man pleasantly. He'd said enough that Marley could recognize the cadences of Ettoriel's speech, even though before he'd spoken with Penny's voice. "Marley," he continued. "There is no point in asking you to release them from your protection. We've already had that conversation. Even to regain your friend, you won't surrender the children. So let me see..."

Marley flinched. Would he really kill Penny if she didn't give him the kids? Her heart squeezed. "Why are you *doing* this?" she demanded. "How can an... an *angel* do such *evil*?" Her skin prickled.

"Mmm? I do what has to be done." The prickling on her skin increased, and Marley remembered the balcony the night before, when she and the kids had faced the irritated kaiju.

He's trying to take apart my protection, she realized. *Whatever it is I have, my superpower, the thing that keeps them from just pushing me down and taking the kids, he's trying to get through it.* She swore under her breath and wished the shield were a sword. The prickles on her skin began to burn and her thoughts moved into overdrive. She wondered what would happen if she turned and ran. She was pretty sure he'd catch her before she got ten steps. He might not be able to take the twins, but he could certainly hurt her. No, running wouldn't work. She'd been running all this time and it had led her here. She promised herself that if she survived this, she'd get a gun.

But for now, what did she have? A protection she couldn't control. Laughable. At least AT had her dogs. Two of them were here now. But AT seemed as frozen as Marley was, staring at Ettoriel. She clearly didn't think it was a fight she could win. What else was there?

The twins. Even the kaiju had been wary of them, and he'd scared her more than the angel did.

"Lissa," she whispered, her mouth dry. "Lissa, can you make him go away? Like you did at the park?"

The little girl glanced up at her. "The fire says we can make lots of things go away. It roars."

In Marley's arms, Kari said, "The fire is locked but I can open it... Behind the shadows, there's a black land..."

The prickles became more painful and then eased. Ettoriel ran a hand through his hair and frowned. "There's still time left. And there are other ways." He knelt down and placed the palm of his hand on the pavement.

A bitter taste seemed to rise from Marley's feet, through her shoes. All she could think was: *strange*. Then the angel was suddenly, mysteriously, too close. She could feel his presence all around her, as if she'd been locked in a closet with him. He hadn't moved from his crouch, with his head down and his golden hair falling across his face. Marley tried to back away, but her body wouldn't respond. Everything seemed frozen.

His voice thrummed through her bones. "I cherish loyalty, but you don't even know what you're being loyal to. Let me show you what you just tried to invoke." The music behind him changed, moved into a minor key and picked up its beat. The world shifted around her, just as it had an aeon ago when she had inspected Zachariah's study, touched an orb, and seen a flash of the study trashed by a struggle.

She was picking her way through a wasteland. Blackened lumps around her resolved into the husks of buildings; the air was white with ash. There was a creak behind her and she turned to see a swingset in the distance, charred like everything else. One small figure sat on the swing, rocking back and forth, while another sat on a pile of rubble nearby, a thick book open in her lap. There were no other signs of life, as far as the eye could see.

"That is now, if they are triggered while young and barely formed. When they are grown and their destiny comes upon them, there will not be a world left for them to play in." There was genuine anguish in Ettoriel's voice. "I cannot let this happen. They were never meant to be. None of you were. Our crimes have brought this fate to the world, and so we must remedy it. I... will erase them."

Marley struggled to speak, struggled to move. A kitten rubbed against her ankles, and tiny, bright eyes peeked out of the wreckage around her. She drew a deep breath, and the nightmare dissolved. Ettoriel's presence retreated, until he seemed like just a man again. He stood up.

"Run along. I'll take the children to their uncle after you can no longer care for them." His voice sounded different, and she realized that his previous speech hadn't been aloud— it had been for only her to hear.

Marley scowled. The nightmare had been a trick, designed to make her hesitate. She wouldn't. "You 'run along.' I'm not going to just turn—"

Something was wrong. There was a snap and crackling buzz above her, a flare of light, a horrible smell. AT shouted, "Marley!" and slammed into her. She, Kari, and Marley tumbled backward as a power line flopped to the ground, writhing and twisting like a live thing right where Marley had been standing.

Marley scrambled to her feet and backed away, pulling Kari with her. AT moved away just as quickly. Lissa was on the other side of the line, standing very still, staring at it with big eyes. Every time it snapped in Lissa's direction, Marley felt a tickle in her head.

But Lissa was safe. She was *safe*, Marley was certain. The

live wire could not hurt her. Not like Ettoriel could. Still, she said, "Come around the wire, Lissa." She threw a worried look at Ettoriel, fully expecting him to take advantage of the distraction.

But he just said, "We can go, Jeremy. It won't be long now." Jeremy nodded, and they got into the van.

Lissa scrambled around the live wire and threw herself on Marley. Marley held her with one hand, watching as the van left the parking lot. Then she looked at AT, who was staring at her with a furrowed brow. "What the hell was that all about?"

AT shook her head slowly. "I don't know... I think he's done something to you. Put some magic on you. Do you feel anything?"

Marley looked down at her clothes, which were coated in the black, oily dust one gets from rolling around in parking lots, mixed with a very fine ash. She felt filthy, mostly. But... there was a deeper wrongness below the filth. It felt like an ache in a location she couldn't quite identify, someplace outside of her. The bones of the world were glass, and if she wasn't careful, they'd shatter.

She shook her head and tried to force some normality into things. "We ought to report that to somebody..." She nodded at the live wire, and started drawing them all away from the danger zone, to the far side of the lot.

AT got out her phone. "But do you feel anything strange?"

"Strange like seeing lines of magic, or strange like seeing catastrophe kaleidoscopes over everybody that mostly don't happen? Or maybe strange like seeing people dissolve into static? Or a vision of a dead—" Another time, Marley might have given into hysterics. But the anguished expression on AT's face was as good as a slap. She took a deep, gasping breath and rubbed her face. Then, in a subdued voice, she said, "Yes, of course. This time it feels like a really bad medication side effect. It feels like the kind of thing I'd want medication to deal with. It feels like my brain is broken."

AT hesitated and then dialed a brief number on the phone. Quickly, she reported the downed wire and the address, watching Marley the whole time. Marley, who didn't like feeling like *she* was the live wire, inspected the children.

Kari, looking down, seemed barely aware of the world. Miserably, she mumbled, "I just don't like this. It's not fun anymore." And then she wouldn't say anything else.

Lissa said, "He was too heavy. I couldn't make him go away without listening to the fire." She scowled. "And I couldn't tell if he really knew Uncle Zach or he was just pretending." Her shoulders hunched.

Marley pursed her lips. "What does the fire say?"

Lissa glanced up, her eyes shadowed. "It calls me 'spark.' It's hungry, and it wants to be eaten. It wants to be eaten by a bigger fire." She shuddered.

Marley put a hand on her head. "I'm sorry. But we did make him leave, right? Maybe we can do something else, too, like finding your uncle. Is there something you can listen to that will tell you where he is? I mean, something that isn't right next to bad people."

Lissa said, "I dunno."

"Well, think about it and let me know, okay?"

As Lissa nodded, AT said, "Why isn't he answering?" She pressed her phone to her ear, her knuckles white. "I want to ask Corbin about the thing on you but he's not answering."

Marley frowned. "AT, it's okay. The angel showed me a vision, trying to scare me, and it's probably just left over from that."

But AT's gaze drifted to the power line and Marley sighed. "Let's go back to the shelter and pick up our stuff, at least."

They walked down the curb to the pedestrian crossing. As they waited for the light to change, Kari muttered, "Forgot to cross the right way before. Oops."

"So did I. That's because I was worried about you." Was it wrong to put a maternal-style guilt-trip on a preschooler? She lightened her tone. "But we'll do it right this time."

"There weren't any cars, though," said Kari, as petulant as only a small child could be.

There weren't any cars now, either. The light changed. They started to cross the six-lane road. A third of the way across, a black sports car approached. And suddenly, the world was moving too fast. It was going to tear.

Something snapped. She could almost hear the twang.

The black car didn't stop. She saw the driver's face, a middle-aged man, eyes wide with panic. Then she was thrusting herself forward, barreling into the herd of dogs and children ahead of her. The driver must have wrenched on the wheel enough, because she felt the car buzz by instead of hitting her, felt it through her feet and on the back of her legs.

Knees weak, she shouted everybody to the other side of the street. Then she clung to the streetlight. The sports car vanished down the street, dangerously close to the curb and showing no signs of slowing down.

"What the hell!" shouted AT. "I didn't get that guy's license number, but the dogs can track him down."

Marley shook her head. "He tried to stop; I don't know what happened. Maybe his brakes went out?"

AT peered after the car. "I don't like this. He almost killed you."

"It was an accident, AT. I saw his face. He had no idea what was going on."

"And the power line snapping was an accident too, I suppose," AT grumbled, but she seemed to mostly be talking to herself. Once again, Marley mobilized her little crowd and they marched on to the evacuation center. As they went, she peeked in her bag, where Neath was curled up on top of the broken Lullaby Plaything, dozing. One ear twitched, but that was all the attention Marley warranted. It pleased her. At least one being she was taking care of didn't think she was screwing everything up.

The sun was above the horizon, now, and the world was waking up. More people were in the parking lot and the smells of fast-food breakfasts mingled with the smells of coffee and smoke. They went inside the center and returned to the cots that had been assigned to them. The grey dog—Grim, Marley had learned—was curled up on AT's cot, his tongue lolling out as he kept an eye on his surroundings. He sat up and yawned as they approached, and Marley wondered again why nobody seemed to notice the dog. Maybe it was just that kind of situation.

The world was thin and fragile again. A hole would be punched right through and the entire world would deflate like a balloon.

The power went out. For a few seconds Marley was left with the afterimage of Grim's ears flattening. Then the noise level in the enormous space rose, and Marley joined the other caregivers in the stadium in making sure their charges weren't snatched away by the darkness. After a moment, dim red emergency lights and dozens of flashlights made the darkness into less absolute.

"Aren't there backup generators?" AT said.

"Lights out. Why?" said Lissa, her arms wrapped around Marley's leg. The smell of the fire intensified as the ventilation systems stopped working.

"Too much heat, I think." said Marley. "I've never really been sure myself about brownouts."

With a hum, the lights flickered back on, although the big screens against the walls displayed nothing but blue static.

AT looked around and grabbed her bag. She dug something out and pushed it at Marley. "I really don't like that magic the angel put on you. Please, look at it yourself?"

Marley took the compact mirror from AT and unfolded it. "Let me at least sit down. I almost fell over last time I tried this."

She perched on the edge of a cot, with a kid on either side, and envisioned the Geometric Sight activation symbols: a circle, a triangle and a square, merging together. Sitting down had been a good call; hundreds of people were milling around her, each one a collection of lines and circles of light. And there were traceries outlining the building and the objects near her, all tangling together into a mess. But she concentrated on her own reflection. A third circle had been filled in with light. While the first two chakras held a delicate and complex shimmering light, the light throbbed luridly in the third. Tendrils of it extended beyond the chakra itself, moving like a hungry sea creature.

Marley recoiled from the mirror. "That's awful. What is it?"

AT rolled her eyes. "I don't know. I wish Corbin would call me back. I do think it's connected to the power line, though. And maybe that car?"

Marley looked up, at the girders crossing the ceiling high above. "And the power flicker?" A nasty foreboding coiled in her belly.

AT's breath hissed between her teeth. "I'm going to call somebody else I know. She helped me out a lot once. Corbin wouldn't approve, but where the hell is *he*?" She unfolded her phone and speed-dialed a number. Marley took a deep breath, banished the Geometric Sight and started cleaning up the stuff they'd left scattered around the cots. By the time she'd packed up the toys and books and snacks yet again, AT was closing the phone. She looked pale.

"She says that we should go outside, right now. Before anything else happens. Says you should be outside, in a clear, open space without a lot of people who might get hurt." AT picked up a backpack.

Marley scowled. "That's not reassuring. Did she have anything else to say?"

"She said she's on her way." Her hands full, AT clicked to her dogs and headed out of the evacuation center.

-twenty-six-

After dropping everything off at the car, Marley followed AT to the far side of the enormous parking lot. The girl and her dogs headed directly to an expanse not yet colonized by cars. AT was moving swiftly, almost jogging. Marley was a lot slower, limited as she was by the pace of two tired, moping preschoolers.

Marley held a child's hand in each of her own, and wondered if it was physically possible for her to carry them both. They dragged their feet and whimpered and whined so much that she finally picked each one up around the middle and carried them like sacks of potatoes. This, judging from the decrease in whine levels, was better than walking.

It wasn't as exhausting as she expected, either. She felt certain she could even jog while holding them, although the kids would be even more uncomfortable. It was strange. She wasn't in particularly good physical condition, and she could remember struggling with bags that she thought were as heavy as the girls in the past.

She caught up with AT and deposited the girls again.

"Hey AT, are nephilim stronger than humans?"

AT glanced up from her phone. "Some more than others. Corbin says it's something to do with an intrinsic use of the Geometry inherited from our celestial side." She rolled her eyes. "He says stuff like that. We're tougher than humans, too, when it comes to enduring damage and environmental extremes."

"Why haven't I noticed before?"

"Well, Corbin said you were veiled somehow, like your celestial nature was being suppressed. Didn't some other nephil things only show up recently for you?"

Marley smirked darkly. "You mean I only get the perks if I put up with the drawbacks. Of course."

"Do you know *why* you were veiled? It isn't normal."

"I think I've always been aware of... my extra sight, to a limited extent. But I didn't like it. And as I got older, I took medication that really seemed to make it mostly go away."

AT was dismissive. "The first is just ordinary denial, and the second... well, I'm going to hope there isn't actually a drug that can truly turn off who we are, or we're in a whole lot of trouble. It might have disguised the problem, though." She looked down at her phone again.

One of AT's dogs curled up between where the twins had collapsed onto the pavement, nosing them until they cuddled up to her. Neath meeped from within Marley's purse and Marley pushed her back down again. "You can't join them, you're too small." She scratched behind the kitten's ears with one finger, though. "So... tell me about this friend of yours? Another nephil?"

AT said, "Tia. She's... not nephilim."

Marley crossed her arms, looking at AT expectantly.

AT sighed. "She's a demon, all right? Which, yes, I know means she's trouble, but she's helped me out a lot. Without her, I probably wouldn't be here now. At least, not like this."

"So... she's an angel who has rejected Heaven. Which is also what the kaiju are? But demons and kaiju aren't the same?"

"No. They aren't." AT looked away, toward the dawn. "I haven't met many demons, but I know Tia. I owe her a lot."

"Your soul?" Marley guessed.

AT turned on her, eyes blazing. "Nephilim don't have souls, didn't you know? I owe her help, like one often does with an old friend. If you can't avoid acting like a prejudiced mortal, just shut up until she gets here."

Oops. "That was tactless of me. I'm sorry."

"You should be," said AT. "Here she comes now. Try not to let your prejudice leak all over somebody who is only showing up to help you."

A sleek red sports car approached across the pavement. It was going very fast. As it got closer, it didn't seem to be slowing down. "AT..." said Marley nervously. "This has happened once already."

"It'll be okay," said AT, but not very reassuringly. Marley tried to back out of the way, but the car's nose twitched to follow her. At the very last instant, the driver yanked the wheel to the side and slammed on the brakes. The car skidded to a halt inches from Marley's feet. Her gaze met the sunglasses of the driver inside.

The lady removed her sunglasses as Marley stared at her. Amused hazel eyes, an expanse of olive skin, dark hair tucked up into an attractively loose bun. The woman raised a coffee cup in a toast to Marley before swinging herself out of the car. "Well then! That was interesting, don't you think?"

"Yes, very interesting. You almost killed me." Marley's voice was flat.

"It was a test," the woman said. "To be fair, I was just driving carelessly. The curse you're wearing tried to kill you."

AT wandered over. "Hi, Tia. Thanks for coming by on

short notice."

Tia laughed. "Darling, you did me a favor by calling me. There's a lot of interest among my set in this particular situation." Then she put her hands on AT's shoulders. "You've grown. And you haven't been getting enough sleep."

AT shrugged. "So what about Marley? You said something about a curse."

"I brought more coffee, and doughnuts if anybody wants them. How about the little ones?" She waved over AT's shoulder at where the kids piled on the ground. Then she pulled a tray out of her car with two more coffees and a bag of breakfast breads.

"We'll pass," said Marley warily, even as AT took a cup and a doughnut.

Tia smiled at her. "Are you sure? These are fantastic. Good enough for a last meal."

Marley blew out her breath and walked away, back to the twins. She didn't want to deal with another supernatural being who saw her as some sort of toy. She didn't want to deal with *any* of this. She sat down on the ground beside the dozing twins and put her arms around them, just holding them close and trying to center herself.

After a few moments of murmured conversation between AT and Tia, the woman came over and crouched down. "AT tells me you had an encounter with a kaiju last night. I'm sorry to hear that. I want you to know that hurting you is not my interest."

Marley muttered, "Being helpful doesn't seem to be your interest, either."

"Untrue!" Tia shifted position until she was also sitting on the pavement. "Helping people is what I do."

Marley stared at Tia, pointedly inspecting her salon hairstyle, her expensive clothes, her elegant manicure, and, finally, her sports car. "You don't exactly look like Mother Theresa."

Tia gave a little chuckle. "You'd trust me more if I were dressed as a candy striper? Driving a beat-up clunker? No, I think something else is bothering you." She had a friendly, inquisitive look that was so far from the kaiju's knowing smirk that Marley did feel a little better.

She stood up, nestling the girls against the dog Heart, and moved back toward AT. When she looked back, Tia had also risen to her feet but was just standing there, looking at the exhausted girls with her hands on her hips. Finally, she shook her head and joined the two young women.

"Those children need a hot meal, a quiet space, and a long night's sleep. They'll be all right then."

"I wish I could give that to them," said Marley. "But the angel who wants to kill me also wants to... erase them. Or so he told me. Do you know why?"

Tia put her head to one side. "Mmm. Well, they're powerful. When they grow up, I imagine they'll be even more powerful."

"He said they'd be very dangerous. He was trying to tell me about some kind of catastrophe." She remembered the blasted L.A. landscape, the two small figures alone in the desert. *There will not be a world left for them to play in.*

Tia shrugged. "As I said, they're powerful. Men have always considered females with unusual power harbingers of the end. That's been true since the beginning of time." A wry grin crossed her face. "Trust me on this."

One again, curiosity pulled a question out of Marley. "Do you guys actually have a gender? I mean, when you're not..." she waved vaguely around, "physical?"

Tia gave her a long, thoughtful look. "That's a very interesting discussion that I'm not sure we have time for. But if we all survive this, look me up and ask me again. For now, you have this curse on you..."

"Yes. But—" she glanced quickly at AT and decided to

ask anyhow, "Will your help cost me anything? I don't mean to be prejudiced, but traditional narrative is not in your favor."

"Mostly angelic propaganda," said Tia smoothly. "They've always been focused getting people to behave in the way they think is right, even if it requires tricking them. Personally, I think it makes more sense to let people make up their own minds. It's not the action that matters, it's the choice that guides it."

And the road to hell is paved with good intentions, Marley thought, but did not say. She felt the world going thin around her again, and the thought itself seemed shallow. *The path away from the angels is paved with choices.* She felt dizzy.

Tia continued quickly, putting a steadying hand on her arm. "As it happens, I *would* like a favor from you, but I'll help you no matter what." The vertigo faded under the demon's warm touch. "You've made a choice to protect these girls and I like that. Some of my brothers would say that the angel's curse is the natural consequence of that choice, but they're idiots sometimes. Ettoriel's trying to take the easy way out."

"What favor?" Marley breathed, afraid the vertigo would begin again.

"I'd like to talk to the little ones. Present them with a few of their choices." Marley stared at her suspiciously and Tia added, "I'm not asking you to stop protecting them. But even children should be allowed to make choices."

Slowly, Marley shook her head. "Like whether to stick their hands into a fire? Whether to look at things that will give them screaming nightmares? Or run out into traffic? You can't let a child make that kind of choice. They don't have enough information or enough understanding to make it properly."

Tia kept her fingers on Marley's arm, her touch light but steadying. "I expected that answer from you. But I wouldn't encourage that kind of activity. The actions you described aren't so much choices as impulses. To follow one's impulses *can* be a choice, but it rarely is when you're four, and miniature. Or so I've observed. One moment." Her light touch drew Marley over to her car, and her fingers slid down to Marley's hand. Intertwining her fingers with Marley's own, she opened her car door and rummaged around inside with her other hand.

"Aha," she said, and pulled out a folded umbrella. "Let's walk over to that lamp post. What was I saying?"

"You were explaining how children don't make choices, but you'd like to tell the twins about their choices anyhow." Marley walked beside Tia. The demon's grip was light enough that she could pull away at any time, but she was, for now, *choosing* not to. "Why do you have an umbrella?"

"I know; it's August in L.A., right? How long has it been since it rained? But you know how it is, there's that one time your hair is ruined by a downpour and you swear you'll never be caught without one again."

Marley glanced up at the dawn sky. "The only rain we're getting is ash."

Tia smiled, and spun the umbrella in her free hand. "So may I speak with the children?"

"I'd rather you didn't, if you're going to upset them, or make it harder for me to look after them. There's already enough rebellion in the ranks."

Tia pursed her lips, and then glanced up as they passed under the light. "Here we are." She shook open the umbrella and raised it over their heads. "Would you put your hand on the lamp post, please? Like that, yes. In a moment, I'm going to stop suppressing the curse. You may feel a bit of pressure, but you should be perfectly safe." The demon grinned and let go of Marley's hand.

The world flattened until it was lines on tissue paper. The tissue paper stretched taut. It tore.

-twenty-seven-

There was a pop, and a tinkle. Tiny shards pattered against the umbrella and slid off to make a circle of broken glass around their feet. After a moment, Tia shook the umbrella clear and closed it. The light above had shattered explosively. "Sorry about that," said Tia. "The curse pressure was building up and I didn't want to inadvertently trigger an earthquake."

"The world is *breaking* around me?" said Marley, aghast.

"The pressure builds up, but is fully discharged each time it triggers. It might not always be actively dangerous; it might simply be inconvenient some of the time. But if it can't discharge, it's able to affect bigger and bigger things." Tia glanced up in the sky. "I suppose a helicopter passing overhead might fall out of the sky before a fault line shifts."

Marley stared at her in horror. "And this is supposed to... what, kill me? My God, I think I liked the women with guns more."

Tia looked interested. "Guns, really? That's not very angelic. They like to rely on the hand of the divine unless they're being directly threatened."

"There were guns," said Marley firmly. "And Ettoriel protected them after, so I know they worked for him."

"Protected them from...?"

Marley's gazed darted to the pile of children and dogs. "I don't know."

"Ah. Yes. Interesting. Perhaps one of his mortal servants displayed some initiative." Marley thought of Jeremy, and nodded vigorously. "But you protect the children and the children protect you. The difference, of course, being that the children can't protect you from what they don't understand. And their protection is, naturally, rather aggressive. But that, I imagine, is why Ettoriel has chosen this particular curse. If the children think your death is an accident, they may be too confused to get angry."

Marley blew out her breath and stepped away from the circle of shattered glass. "Why does AT like you so much? You're as vague and mysterious as the fairy."

Tia's eyes sparkled. "She was in a situation where her choices weren't being respected. I insisted that situation change. As for the rest... she might tell you the details if you ask. Her father isn't a very nice person."

Marley couldn't help making a face. "You can't just 'insist' here?"

"Here, I can teach. For example, I can teach you what it feels like when the curse is about to trigger, so you can influence *how* it triggers. Did you notice the way you felt before the light shattered? Good. That isn't normal, by the way. You may not be able to protect yourself as you can protect children, but your particular heredity makes you sensitive to rips in the world. I can even give you a small blessing that will allow you to duplicate what I just did in suppressing the curse until an appropriate time."

"Why not just remove it? Can you do that?"

"I might be able to. But I won't. It will fade on its own

in a day or two, so it isn't currently worth my while to do so. Especially since it will be so very educational for you." Tia's teeth flashed again.

"All right. Do that. And then, please go away." Tia raised an eyebrow and Marley plunged on. "You and that other guy, you make me feel helpless and small. All I want to do is curl up and hope somebody else will deal with this. But you won't. And I can't have you distracting me right now."

"Of course," Tia said. She took Marley's wrist between her finger and her thumb, and then tapped two more fingers down in quick succession. "Here is the assistance. The memory of this sensation will activate and deactivate the suppression." A ticklish warmth spread out from her touch, running down to Marley's fingers and up to her chest.

"The suppression will draw upon your own energy, so I suggest only using it when you feel the discharge is imminent." Tia smiled again, but this time it was tight and concerned. "Good luck." She pulled away.

"Wait." Marley stepped after her. "Wait. I know I've been ungrateful, but can I ask something else?"

Tia put her head to one side, her eyes drifting over Marley's shoulder to the kids. She arched an eyebrow.

Marley blew out her breath. "Later. Come find me if we survive the next few days and… something… can be arranged."

"I just want to talk to them, Marley. Just a conversation. But come, what else did you want from me?"

"My friend, Penny, she's involved with this angel. It's hurting her. Corbin says it's destroying her. Is there any way you can free her? Help her?"

Tia pulled out her cellphone and tapped on the screen a few times, frowning. She looked up, her gaze vague and distant.

The moment dragged on. At last, she shook her head. "I've found her, but I can offer her nothing. She's made a choice."

Marley set her jaw. "So? She's been brainwashed or enchanted or something. The choice isn't *good* for her."

Tia smiled gently. "Choosing despite the consequences is integral to humanity. The act of choosing is itself meaningful."

Marley gave the demon a hostile stare. "That is a bullshit philosophy."

Tia's smile faded. "To force her to change her mind would be just another form of 'brainwashing.' Is that what you'd prefer?"

"Can't you just—protect her from the angel's influence somehow? Give her a chance to see herself without a haze of angel love clouding her mind?"

"Maybe. But I won't."

"Because I won't pay for it? I—"

"Marley. No. I won't because this is what she wants. She wants to be part of something bigger than herself. She wants to feel like she has a place in the world, that her life has meaning and purpose. She wants all that and he's giving her that and she's at peace because of it. She doesn't know all the fine details, but she doesn't care to know them either."

Marley's jaw ached. "I don't know where you're getting your information from, but you're wrong. I know her better than that. I'm her friend."

Tia shrugged, put away her phone and folded her arms. "Recall, please, that my 'bullshit philosophy' is why I'm helping you. Get your friend to ask for help, and hell, you might be able to save her yourself. But you want to break her? Apply to the kaiju, not me."

Marley opened her mouth and then shut it again. She took a deep breath. "You're right. Thank you for your help." The words burned.

Tia nodded curtly. "If you don't end up dead, I'll be around to claim what you offered me later." She raised her hand in greeting to AT, who had approached. "I'm just leaving, my dear. Your friend mostly wants heroes, not helpers."

"I want a chance, damn it!" The shout ripped out of Marley before she knew it.

The demon smiled again. "Then take some." She ruffled AT's hair and strode to her car. A moment later, the engine roared to life and the vehicle sped off.

AT looked at Marley anxiously. "Was that not good?"

Marley shook her head. "She was... helpful, I hope. I'm just an ungrateful bitch right now. She's right. I want somebody to deal with all this for me, make it go away. A big strong man to save the day. Branwyn would punch me."

AT said, "Well, I'm strong, and Corbin's a man... I don't know what we'll do for big, though."

"Where the hell *is* Corbin, anyhow?" But Marley thought of Zachariah, and his broad shoulders. Then she looked over at the children, and thought, *But before I learned about princes, it was my mother who fixed things. Is this what happens to moms?*

"Um, yeah, about that. I sent Nod to go look for him. Through the Backworld, you know? That's how I usually get around. Nod hasn't come back. He's not hurt—I'd know if he was hurt again—but something's wrong. I can feel it."

"Like he's been caught and held?"

AT shrugged. "I don't know how that could be, but I guess so."

Marley chewed on her lip. "What would you do if I weren't here?"

"I'd go after him. Both of them. Corbin's smart, but without tons of preparation, he isn't nearly as powerful as I am." AT looked embarrassed as she said this.

Marley raised her eyebrows. "Oh yeah? What makes you so powerful?" And she wondered what "powerful" meant, in this context. Was there a measurement, like with light bulbs? Corbin was only 25 watts and AT was 100? What, she wondered, was she? Or the twins? Zachariah? The angel?

AT hesitated and then matter-of-factly said, "My father is a kaiju. Corbin is third-generation nephilim. That matters, at least for demiurgy and sorcery." She saw the look of incomprehension on Marley's face and added, "Those are the kinds of magic derived from being celestial."

Two different kinds? Whoo-ee! "Would you fight? Do you know how to fight?"

AT's smile was wry and sad. "Oh yes. I mean, I can't take out a celestial myself, but anybody else, hurting a friend of mine? I'd at least try. Probably get my butt kicked, but..." She shrugged. "It's all I can do. I'm not good for much else."

Marley sighed, remember her lesson with Corbin the night before. "I wish we could get our hands on one of these Machine weapons. There *must* be another way to hurt a celestial."

"Senyaza," AT said, instantly. "They use spirit tethers, which I don't know how to create. But it's one reason why the angels hate us so much." Then she sighed. "It isn't a useful answer right now. They've got this major event going down in Europe right now and the local monster hunters are all laid up."

Take chances. Marley closed her eyes, felt the pressure of the angel's curse building around her. "Tia basically told me I can't protect people who don't want to be protected. But AT, you don't have any aversion to being protected by me, do you?"

Confused, AT said, "I'm supposed to be protecting *you*, I think." She added, in a low voice, "I haven't done a very good job."

"Protect me. But let me protect you, too. Maybe that way we can go get Corbin out of whatever trouble he's in." Marley opened her eyes and reached out to AT, pulling her close, wrapping her arms around her in a hug. After a startled moment, AT hugged her back. The teenager seemed so fragile in her arms. She thought she could fight? She wasn't even fully grown. Marley *could* protect her. There was no resistance. Marley felt her power settle over AT like a cloak.

And when Marley stepped away, she knew AT was safe. As long as they stayed close, what could hurt her? And she knew more, too: the dogs were part of AT, somehow, just as the twins were part of each other. She thought she could look deeper, but she didn't want to. The peace that swept over Marley was intoxicating. To know, really *know*, that everybody around her was safe was astonishing. Would the peace last when she took them someplace truly dangerous?

Giddiness swept over her. She remembered good times with Branwyn and Penny, back when she'd been a teenager herself. Action Girl, Smile Girl, and Research Girl, out to cause trouble and save the day. "AT," she said, "Let's go save the boy."

-twenty-eight-

Ⓘt's so white," Marley said. They walked down a matte hallway, all holding hands. "Like a really boring, endless office building. But where are the doors?"

"There are other areas of the Backworld that are much more interesting," said AT. "But they're much more dangerous, too. The folk who live in those places are masters of glamour and you can't trust that anything is real. If you spend long enough there, you stop being able to tell whether you're in the Backworld or not."

If Marley hadn't been holding a child's hand in each of her own, she would have rubbed fingers across her forehead. There were mild tingles in all of the chakra locations Corbin had pointed out, but her forehead actually itched. "Glamour. Fairies?" She had a moment of déjà vu, and tried to remember wisps of dream.

"Yes. But not like the toys... not little pixies. The fae were angels once, too, you know."

Marley shivered. "Bound now, though?"

"Bound first, before any of the others, because they were scary-dangerous. The angels tried to cut them off from the

Sea of Dreams, so they developed new magic, based on the nature of Creation itself. Nobody liked that."

Marley shook her head. Neath, peeking out of her bag, reached up and snagged her wrist with a claw. "Ow! Why are you so aggressive lately, kitten?" She glanced down and stumbled. "AT, hold on. Look at their feet."

The white tile they walked on clouded faintly, like marble. But where the twins had walked, the tile gradually darkened, until the center of each little shoeprint was dull black, threaded with red veins. "Uh," said AT. "That's new."

Kari lifted up her feet to look at the bottom of her shoes. "They're clean," she reported. There was a little popping sound, and Lissa shifted her weight uneasily. AT crouched down, still holding Kari's hand, and ran her free hand over the mark she left behind.

"It's rough. I think it's... eroding." AT stood up and wiped her hand on her jeans.

"Why?" Marley demanded.

AT's brow furrowed, her eyes dark as she glanced at Marley. "I don't know. But let's keep going."

"Yeah. Yeah. So... where *are* the doors?"

"Here and there. I don't use them, though. I've never needed to. I'll open a window when we get to where we're going, just like I did to get us in." The two dogs, Heart and Grim, trotted ahead of them, noses to the ground.

"Will you know what's out there before we go through?"

AT didn't answer at first, and Marley glanced down at the footprints again. Maybe she should be carrying the kids. One on her back, one in her arms; it wouldn't be too bad, and more comfortable than the sack-of-potatoes carry. She remembered the vision from the angel again, the children playing alone in the broken landscape. It *couldn't* be true. So they were powerful, even special. They were sweet kids, too, as innocent as the current situation could allow them to be. But they were a lot more innocent before Zachariah had been stolen from them...

How much more could they take?

"Probably. I have a sense for where we are in Creation as we move through the Backworld, anyhow," AT finally said.

"AT..." Marley paused, trying to sort out what she wanted to ask. It was awkward. But AT shot her a knowing look and it untied her tongue. "You said your father was a kaiju. Do you know him?"

"Yes," said AT quietly. "He was an...involved...father. He'd still be involved now if I let him. He had big plans for me."

That was enough. Nobody said anything else until AT announced, "We're here."

It was an expanse of white hall, exactly the same as the hall they'd been walking down for the last ten minutes. Marley had no idea how AT and the dogs could tell that this location was significant. Heart was sitting alert, nose to the wall, while Grim scratched around the floor as if he wanted to start digging. AT placed her two index fingers together in the center of the wall and drew them apart in a diagonal line. A square of light expanded under her fingers. When it was a couple of feet wide, she stopped and placed her palm in the center. The glowing square chimed.

"It's an apartment building. There's a terrace about halfway up. Corbin and Nod are on the terrace. They aren't alone. I can't see through Nod's eyes. What the hell? It's like he's blindfolded."

"Once we're out, can we leave the window open so that we can get back in again?" The one they'd used to enter the Backworld corridor had closed immediately.

"Maybe. It depends on how long we're out. If there's a convention of celestials out there and we have to run, we can get back in here. Doesn't mean they can't chase us, though."

The giddiness was gone. Marley wasn't entirely sure that

everybody under her protection was safe, now. She hoped it was just the white corridor messing with her senses. But what else could she do? She could feel the pressure from the curse rising. It warped her senses, too. It made everything feel wrong. What would happen if it discharged in here? She glanced down at the dark footprints again. AT had said this place was a passage through the girders of the world.

"Wait a moment before opening the window. I want to get Tia's blessing together. Once I'm ready, we'll go through. I'll find Corbin and see if I can get him away from whatever's got him, while you and the dogs go after... everything else. Distract them. We'll move fast and bring Corbin back here. Once we're in here, we can regroup and figure out what to do next. Since not everybody can access this place like you can, we'll probably have at least a little bit of time."

AT nodded, her eyes distant.

Kari said, "What do we do?"

"Watch the show. I'm going to keep you safe, so you shouldn't have to do anything." Marley made herself smile, and then added, despite herself, "Be careful anyhow. Stay close to me."

Kari didn't protest or make the face Marley expected. She just nodded, looking pale.

Marley took a deep breath and thought of Tia's fingers pressing against her wrist. Her breath caught as the gentle wrongness of the curse faded, and caught again as she felt the magic draw on her. She inhaled again. It felt like the blessing stole a tiny bit of each breath; she was more breathless than she had been after her race to rescue Kari. But it wasn't air itself she lacked, but the energy the air brought. No, she didn't want to maintain this any longer than necessary. Hopefully she'd find a useful way to discharge the curse on the other side of the shining window. "All right," she said.

AT nodded and made the shining square larger, until it

stretched to the floor. Then she pushed her hand into the center and twisted. The surface rippled. She took a step forward, passing through, towing them behind her.

Marley blinked; the late morning sunlight was much brighter than the directionless light of the Backworld corridor. Squinting, she took in their location. They were on a terrace that stretched across a corner of the building, partway up. It was actually divided into two levels, with a metal staircase against the same wall that contained a door into the building. The terrace itself was littered with lounge chairs, many of which had been overturned. Here and there were carefully maintained containers of shrubs and small trees. Along with the ever-present smell of smoke, there was a hint of jasmine in the air. The air on the terrace seemed clean and clear, but around the edges of the terrace, there was a thick yellow haze.

Corbin stood in the center of a circle of tumbled planters, his back to them. Just outside the circle were a handful of other figures. Marley recognized the bulky shape of Absolven right away. The others were blurred and indistinct, as if her eyes wouldn't focus on them. One of them held a long silver leash looped around a black dog's neck; the dog lay with his head flat on the ground. It was a still tableau, although judging from the devastation, it hadn't been moments before.

Corbin spoke to Absolven. "Agreed. If you win, will you carry a message for me? A last request?"

Marley heard AT's sharply indrawn breath. She released Kari's hand and darted forward. "Nod!" she shouted.

The black dog surged to his feet, yanking himself forward. The chain shattered, fragments of silver flashing through the air. Orange clouds detached themselves from the indistinct figures and drifted forward.

Corbin half-turned, and shouted, "No! I didn't—"

An acrid smell of tarmac and carcinogens and exhaust overwhelmed both the wildfire smoke and the jasmine as a wisp of orange blew toward them. It turned, moving less like the wind and more like a ghost. Tendrils reached for the girls, seeming more curious than threatening.

AT whistled, and all three dogs vanished into thin air. Then they burst out of the slivers of shadows along the wall and under the deck chairs. Nod snapped at the inquisitive orange cloud right in front of them.

The orange wisps closest to Corbin's circle moved faster, until they were sharp and jagged with speed, like a cloud of rusty razor blades. The red dog, Heart, leapt to intercept and sailed through one cloud. Bits of fur drifted to the ground behind her as one of the orange elementals shifted direction. Heart shook her head and sneezed. Her fur bristled along her back with effort. Then, starting from the tip of her nose, her body faded, until she, too, was cloudlike. Her teeth glinted and she leapt again.

Nod barked, startling Marley. He danced on his hind legs in front of her and she realized that AT was already halfway across the rooftop garden, heading to Corbin and his captors. Everybody was moving, Corbin and Absolven both bolting forward as the indistinct figures—still indistinct, despite the loss of their cloud elementals—scattered.

Nod snapped his teeth like she was an errant lamb and then whirled away to harry another of the elementals, keeping it away from her. Each of the dogs occupied an elemental, but the fights didn't seem to be as one-sided as Marley had hoped they would be. The smell burned her nose.

Marley moved forward, pulling the children away from the elemental, and then letting them go. *Theyweresafe theyweresafe theyweresafe* and she almost trusted the sense of her power.

"Corbin?" called AT. He was standing inches from Absolven; the big man had his hand up, pressing it against thin air, while Corbin's fingers twitched and moved.

He took a moment to flick a hand at AT dismissively. "Didn't want you here, kiddo." His fingers twitched and stuttered as he coughed, a horrible hacking sound. He gasped, "What did you bring *her* here for?"

"Because I can't be in two places at once," AT snapped. "Hey, you," she said to Absolven. "Bugger off if you don't want to see your own guts."

Absolven's gaze flicked between AT, Marley, and the children. "Hey!" said AT sharply. "We outnumber you. Go away."

"But you are each all alone," said Absolven.

"I don't think so," said AT. She stepped forward, planted her hand on the big man's sternum, and pushed so hard she lifted him up, tossing him back a yard.

Absolven landed gracefully in a crouch. He straightened and raised his hand, beckoning at the figures behind him. They didn't move, but the air shimmered. AT said, "Finish up fast, Corbin."

"They put up a barrier to stop me from leaving. *Us* from leaving, now." He tilted his head toward the roiling hazy wall around the edge of the terrace.

"But you can take it down."

Corbin gave AT another impatient glance. "Not without help, or I wouldn't still be here."

"Well? I can provide a distraction." AT darted forward to knock Absolven back again. This time, he was ready for her. His hand swept up, a triangular blade gleaming in his fist.

But AT trusted her, and AT was safe.

The blade's glare became a flash and Absolven shifted off-balance as he missed his strike. AT grinned humorlessly as she kicked him.

"Ah," said Corbin. "That's your plan." He glanced at Marley directly for the first time. "How's your breathing?"

Marley took a deep breath and realized that it was significantly more challenging than it had been in the Backworld. She wheezed. Corbin nodded. "They're concentrating the toxins from the smoke and smog. They brought Absolven here to finish me fast, but slowly will do the job as well."

"Is there something I can do to help break this barrier?" As he coughed again, she added, "I bet my brand of help would make it easier for you to breathe. Let me—"

"Hell with that," Corbin said. "I'm fine." Marley stared at him in surprise. He went on. "While we're talking, though, I might as well tell you what I found out up here. Hold on." He tugged on something invisible.

Marley was glad she'd resisted activating her Sight; there was enough to keep track of already. The twins were behind her, and AT was harassing Absolven. The teenager grinned, surrounded by a clear halo in the thickening orange haze. The dogs were making plenty of noise elsewhere on the terrace.

"I talked to the Machine that's helping Ettoriel and Absolven. We saw a fragment of it when Absolven showed up at Penny's." said Corbin abruptly. "According to it, the girls represent a kind of singularity or event horizon, obscuring their projections of the future."

"What does that even mean?" asked Marley sharply, thinking again of the vision of the swing in a post-apocalyptic L.A. "Do they *know* the future or not?"

Corbin gave her a pained look. "Does it matter? Ettoriel thinks they do. He might not be interested in breaking the Hush for personal gain, but he'd definitely want to save the world."

Marley took a deep breath. "He thinks there *is* no future. That's what he told me. But you said this Machine is helping him? So it could be lying, too."

"I don't think so. The Machines are hard—dangerous—to understand, but everything I've read says they have no ability to deceive."

Marley shook her head. "I don't—"

"Marley, look out!" shouted AT. She was getting to her feet on the far side of the roof, near the mist-cloaked figures. Absolven was moving towards Marley, hindered but not stopped by the dog trying to trip him.

"Hell," said Corbin. "Run!" He coughed again, even as his hands seemed to blur.

Marley scanned the terrace. "Up the stairs," she called to the girls. "Go, now!" They both took off running. She dropped the bag containing Neath at the end of Corbin's circle, and then dashed off in a different direction, weaving between scattered outdoor furniture. It was hard to run, so much harder than it had been that morning. This time she had to fight to get enough breath.

Helpless cursing from AT drifted across the terrace, and Marley veered to avoid one of the smog clouds. She almost tripped over a hose and grabbed it as she recovered, half-turning to check on her pursuer. He wasn't moving quickly, harried as he was by AT and the dogs, but he seemed inexorable. She backed up, watching him.

"I saw what you did with those birds at the hotel," Marley called. "That wasn't very nice."

"Nice and necessary are often exclusive," the big man replied. "It *is* you protecting them, isn't it?"

"I don't know what you're talking about. Why are you working with Ettoriel?" Her fingers slid over the sprayer trigger.

"His reasons are compelling. And what I have now, he gave me." He paused to pick up AT and toss her into a pile of chairs, then shake a dog off his wrist. He wasn't interested in hurting them any more than a man swimming upriver was trying to hurt the current, and so he made progress, simply because he was much larger than the teenage girl. Blood welled from marks all over his body, but he didn't seem to notice.

"You mean he's your father?" Out of the corner of Marley's eye, she saw a pair of heads peeking over the rail on the upper level of the terrace. The girls had gotten out of the way. Good.

Absolven shook himself violently. "Don't blaspheme, please." Then, like a bird spontaneously taking flight, he leapt for her from twenty feet away.

Marley yelped in surprise and stumbled sideways, a chair scraping across her leg. He thumped to the ground beside her. She scrabbled at the chair and flung it toward the figure looming over her. Then she brought up the sprayer and pressed the trigger, sending a stream of pressurized water into his face. Finally, she flung the sprayer itself at him and scrambled around him on all fours, toward the staircase to the second level.

Even though he was disoriented by her rapid defense, he grabbed at her as she passed just out of reach. His nails elongated into claws; their tips combed through her hair. She flung another chair at him, not looking to see if it hit as she threw herself toward the staircase.

She had to keep thinking, but it was so hard. He was right behind her. One more lunge and he'd have her, and those talons would hurt so much more than Neath's kitten claws. She could hear him breathing.

Halfway up the stairs, Marley clawed at her own arm, trying to force her scattered brain to recall the activation toggle Tia had set on her suppression spell. *Like so.*

The curse struck her. She tripped as the *wrongness* slammed through her and struck the stair beneath her feet. Something metal screamed and buckled. The staircase leaned and sank, and she scrambled up a few more steps on her hands and knees before the other brace tore itself loose. There was a cry and a grunt from behind her as Absolven fell with the bottom half of the staircase on top of him. Then the step

Marley's feet were on disappeared beneath her as the staircase kept on collapsing, and she was left hanging from a crumbling step by her fingers. She scrabbled for a railing that was still connected to the concrete, and it bent under her weight. Frantically, she swung herself up, gashing her forearm on the suddenly jagged metal. Then she leapt for the edge of the terrace, catching it with her fingers as the remains of the staircase fell away from the wall, red rust flaking off long bolts as they sailed past her cheek.

She hung there for a moment, distantly aware of the dogs barking, of AT shouting something, and the twins cheering her on. There was a bit of metal under her fingers, the last remnant of the staircase. Her fingernails hurt. Slowly, she braced one foot against the concrete wall and tried to figure out what would happen if she fell. Broken ankle, maybe, if there wasn't a bunch of jagged rusting metal right beneath her. As it was, it didn't bear contemplating.

The metal heap beneath her groaned and settled. Was it settling? Or was it moving because something was moving beneath it?

The much more human groan below her was a jolt of electricity to her spine. Without conscious effort, she rose over the edge of the terrace like a swimmer surfacing.

She crouched a few feet away from the edge, panting. Lissa came and hugged her, while Kari stayed at the railing, staring over the edge. She hugged Lissa back, then pushed herself to her feet. Her entire body ached. An exercise regimen of reading in the park wasn't enough for fighting monsters, even if she had superpowers.

"Got it!" shouted Corbin, triumphantly. "Get them, AT!" Marley looked over the railing to see Corbin punching the air as he jumped out of his circle. The three mist-wrapped figures on the far side of the terrace spread out. AT spun, looking between Corbin and Marley, and then whistled and raced across the terrace. The dogs met her halfway, and they piled onto one misted figure.

The heap below groaned again, and slid open. Absolven stood up, unsteadily. He inspected himself before tugging a piece of shrapnel out of his arm. Then he raised his bloody face, his blue eyes meeting Marley's.

He said something under his breath. His shape changed, and didn't change. He was still the man, but contained within the man-shape was the griffin, and it was the griffin that cast the shadow. A hooked shadow beak opened, and the shadowy wings flared wide before flapping down heavily. Absolven flung himself up, a huge, impossible jump that had him landing on his feet on the edge of the terrace.

Marley backed away. She didn't have a plan for this. On some level, she'd still believed in things like "people can't fly." She was an idiot. This terrace was smaller and there was nowhere to run. But there had to be a way off this level other than one rusty staircase.

Terror made it hard to think. The claws on Absolven's fingers weren't shadow claws.

"Marley?" said Lissa. The fear in her voice made Marley want to throw herself at Absolven, because it was even worse than the claws.

"Hide. Don't watch," she said to the girls. She took a deep breath and backed up another few steps. Her chest hurt. Instead of chairs, there were ashtrays up here. "Absolven. Don't do this. Ettoriel is wrong."

"You and I, none of our kind should exist," he said, his voice gentle. "There has been so much mercy granted by Heaven, granted for love. They love so deeply. And look what exchanging obedience for love has brought us. I must be better than my father. But I wish you had let them go in the beginning."

Marley's breath hissed between her teeth. "I have to be

better than my parents, too."

"Marley," called Lissa again, and this time there was an insistence in her tone that overshadowed the fear. The twins stood together in the shadow of a table, hands welded together.

Kari shouted, "Go away, bad man! Go away before it wakes up and hurts you!"

There was a cracking sound, all around them. The shadow the twins stood in flooded with crimson. Absolven looked around.

Lissa shook her head. "Too late."

-twenty-nine-

Something clanked below. There was a whirring, crash-ing sound and metal scraped against metal. The air shiv-ered at the awful scratching along the wall, and then a creature formed of broken staircase structure pulled itself over the edge.

It looked like an insect, with six legs made of broken struts, and the steps and railings curved into a thorax. Its head was a tiny knot of twisted metal, barely visible behind a double pair of giant, moving mandibles made of jagged, rust-ed splinters.

The creature vaulted over the railing at the edge of the terrace and then stopped, shifting its legs as if it wasn't quite sure how to use them. The mandibles moved like the grinding of gears.

Absolven leapt away from it, shadow wings billowing out. The metal insect's head whipped around and it rose up on its back two legs and lunged at the big man. One man-dible pierced a shadow wing and Absolven screamed as blood sprayed across the rooftop.

Marley ran to the twins. Lissa had her face covered, while

Kari was staring, eyes enormous. It was the precursor to a wail, she knew. She scooped one child up in each arm, just as Kari started screaming.

Absolven tumbled away from the metal insect, half his shadow indistinct. All of his attention was focused on the creature. It moved toward him, rolling from one leg to another, and he watched it like a cat. Then he dove at it, rolling under it and grabbing one of the metal legs. It bent in his grip and he wrenched at it before rolling away empty-handed. A mandible slashed at his back as he escaped its reach.

Kari wailed again, and Lissa was weeping into her hands. Marley realized that the metal insect traveled within a reddened shadow just like the one that had followed Kari and Lissa, and that now surrounded her. It was part of them, part of their power.

Horror made her legs weak. The twins were no longer *safe*. The bloody shadow invaded their auras, throbbing as though it was alive, bound around them like an umbilical cord wrapped around their necks.

The thing snapped at Absolven, and the dreadful red umbilical pulsed brightly. Marley's vision went dark around the edges.

She put the twins down, slipping away from their grasping hands. Absolven rolled away from the metal insect again and came up in a crouch, grinning fiercely. Two of the abomination's legs were hobbled now. Marley wasn't sure she'd place a bet on who would win. But whichever nightmare won the duel, she was certain the twins would lose. There were burdens that children shouldn't have to bear.

Absolven moved slightly, and Marley charged. Too late, he saw her coming from the corner of his eye, and shifted his attention and his center of balance away from the metal insect. But it wasn't enough. Marley's smaller frame struck him as low as she could, and she pushed and lifted with every aching muscle in her body.

Absolven flipped over the railing at the edge of the ter-
race. He turned the cartwheel into a somersault and then,
mid-air, stretched out to try and catch himself on the edge.
But Marley had surprised him too much, tossed him too far.
His one working wing stretched taut, but it was useless alone.
Marley watched, panting, as he dropped out of sight.

She made herself look down. He dropped like a rock, silently clawing the air. One second, maybe two, and it lasted
forever. And right as he hit the ground, nine stories below, he
vanished.

Moving as though her body belonged to another person, Marley turned around. The metal insect was staring at
the twins, who huddled together where Marley had left them.
"Fall apart," she muttered, willing the artificial monster to
collapse into a junk heap again. Its mandibles moved slowly,
instead.

"The bad guy is gone. I made him go away," she announced loudly. The twins had made the creature out of their
fear and rage and strange power. The bad guy was gone. Reassure them of that and their nightmarish friend would go too,
right?

Beyond the metal insect, where the staircase had once
been, Marley saw a hand and then AT's curly-haired head appear over the edge of the terrace. She pulled herself over the
edge, and Marley wondered if she'd climbed the wall itself.
Then it became much more surreal: Nod followed her over
the edge, and while AT may have climbed, it was clear that
the dog had walked up the wall. Behind Nod came Heart's
feathery red tail, as she backed up the wall, yes, dragging
Corbin by his arm.

Marley blinked and shook off a rush of vertigo as Heart's
orientation changed. Last came Grim, limping backwards
and snarling at a bulbous orange-grey mass: the remaining

pollution elementals, all occupying the same space.

Heart released Corbin, who coughed and brushed himself off. White indentations glistened on his arm where Heart had held him.

AT said, "Is Absolven gone?" She sounded dubious, staring at the metal insect.

"Yes. What do we do about the quit-smoking ads?" Marley said, gesturing at the elementals.

AT dragged her gaze away from the metal insect—*why wasn't it falling to pieces?*—and said, "The dogs'll keep them occupied until they run out of energy. Their makers ran away." She sounded pleased with herself. "What is that thing? Is it...?"

Marley moved to the twins and crouched down to gather them to her. "It's all right."

Neither twin was sobbing now, although tears streamed continuously down Kari's face. They both stared at the metal insect with huge, terrified eyes. Then Lissa dragged her gaze away to put a cold hand on Marley's cheek. "Marley, *it's going to eat us.*"

The bottom dropped out of Marley's stomach. The metal insect's mandibles thrashed together again, over and over. It started creeping forward, each leg twitching, one at a time. .

Marley scooped both children up again. They didn't cling this time, and as distracted dead weight, they were a lot harder to carry. "Corbin? The girls made it. Why isn't it falling apart now that the threat is gone?"

"They're kids. Their subconscious is still doing most of the driving." He snapped his fingers toward the metal monstrosity. "But the Hush shouldn't allow something this huge to exist for very long. Odd."

Then there was no time for words, as the unsteady scraping footsteps of the twins' nightmare burst into an engine-like motion. Marley turned and ran. She headed away from the edge of the terrace, keenly aware of the consequences of one powerful blow. The bulk of the building rose up another two floors. Surely there must be another exit on this level? But all she could find was what looked like a small freight elevator, and the doors would not open.

She banged frantically on the elevator button and then turned her attention to soothing the twins. She desperately wanted to turn around and watch the thing bearing down on her, but children didn't look under the bed for imaginary monsters, did they? They knew they were there and they protected themselves by hiding their heads under the covers. So she huddled with the twins in the alcove of the elevator and whispered every comforting thing she could think of.

The grinding and clattering approached. There was the yelp of an injured dog. Then the sound of metal against metal changed and AT shouted, "Hey! I won't let you have what you want!"

Marley twisted her body to see. AT stood behind the metal insect, holding it back by one of its bent legs. She shed a gentle radiance, illuminated without shadows on her form. But darkness curved away from her, a single deep shadow shaped like a wolf. Her dogs were nowhere to be seen.

The metal insect turned on her. Marley held the hysterically weeping twins close and watched as their nightmare fought the dog girl. The rooftop terrace, already in disarray, was devastated. For what seemed like an eternity, AT dodged and grabbed at the monster, the jaws of her lupine shadow warping the metal struts as if they were as real as her hands. The struts and bars of the rusty exoskeleton were slowly pulled apart, but the essence of the creature kept moving, unfazed, untouchable. Marley felt paralyzed, worried that attacking their nightmare would hurt the children, and terrified of the consequences of not stopping it. She took a deep breath and tried to focus.

The twins weren't *safe*. A monster powered by their own terror could hurt them.

But it was focused on AT, slashing a steel pincer down—

Marley screamed as something invisible impaled her shoulder. Her skin was on fire, her vision all black and red. Something else slashed across her back and she started weeping. She squeezed the panicking twins close to her as she slumped to her knees, gasping for breath. The pain had come from AT. Her protection was fraying, and channeling the damage it couldn't avert back to her. The creature was too strong, or she was too weak. She felt lightheaded, spread thin.

"I'm *so sorry*," came the anguished cry from AT, even as Corbin's arms closed around Marley, supporting the three of them. "I've got to... it's..." AT continued over the clatter and clash of metal.

Marley whimpered, pressing her head against Corbin's arm. She could feel her power dissolving, and it hurt as much as the channeled injuries.

AT spoke again, and this time Marley heard her clearly, as if the words were spoken over a headset. "I don't want your shield anymore, Marley. There's another way."

Marley's remaining protection over the teenager peeled away, and AT was *unsafe*. AT was going to be torn apart. Marley screamed again, in frustration and denial, and surged against Corbin's now-restraining arm. He was saying something but she couldn't understand him, didn't care.

AT shouted, "Father! Help me!"

Marley froze and shuddered as Corbin's arm slackened around her. "Oh no..." he muttered.

For a long moment, the fight between the twins' metal nightmare and AT continued, each slash and bruise on AT leading to the next as she slowed down. But every time it seemed to tire of her and turn back to the twins, she grabbed it, shrieking.

Marley grabbed Corbin's arm. "Why *oh no*? Is something happening? Tell me what's going on!" But Corbin only shook his head, whispering to himself every so often and moving one hand reflexively.

Then a hole in the world yawned open and a masculine figure stepped through. With only the briefest pause to assess the scene, the figure stepped over to where Marley huddled against Corbin with the twins. He knelt down and put a hand on each of the panicking children's faces. Marley stumbled at sudden vertigo as her sense of "safe" and "dangerous" pinwheeled around her. Then the twins, previously rigid and clutching with terror, slumped in her arms.

The metal monster folded in on itself, tumbling into a pile as the blood shadow faded into ordinary silhouettes.

Asleep. The twins were deeply asleep.

Marley gathered them close. AT, crouched on the other side of the pile of metal, covered in her own blood, swayed, and then crumpled into a ball.

As the figure stood up, Corbin stiffened behind her and Marley realized who it was: Severin the kaiju. "*You're* her father?"

Severin gave her only a glance. "Of course not. I heard her call, though, and I knew her father would appreciate the favor of stepping in on his behalf." He stepped over to where AT lay and crouched down again, inspecting her injuries.

"How badly is she hurt?" Marley demanded.

"Nothing some fatherly care won't fix." He picked AT up in his arms and turned away. As he did, a slash in the world opened into a Backworld portal.

"Wait! Where are you taking her?" Marley let the sleeping twins slide out of her arms and tried to scramble after Severin. He gave her an impassive look and then stepped through the gate. It blinked out behind him.

"He's taking her to her father," said Corbin flatly.

"No! She doesn't—how can you just stand there?"

"What am I supposed to do?" growled Corbin. "Do you think you can save everyone? She put herself back into her father's power to save you. To save us." He glared at her. Then he took a deep breath. "He'll take good care of her until she's healthy again. She's safer with him now than anyplace else."

Marley shook her head slowly. "I don't know if you're right. I think..."

Corbin took her shoulders and shook her lightly. "Then it's a fate worse than death! But she chose it, do you understand, because she didn't want us to die. She rejected you because she didn't want you to die." He blew out his breath, staring at her with his eyes slits. "Neither of you have any sense of self-preservation. You have no clue about getting out when you're in over your heads."

"You're still here, too," she whispered.

"That's different," he muttered. His hands tightened on her shoulders again, and she watched the play of expressions on his face. He was very close. A sudden warmth grew from the tangle of emotions roiling inside her—

A warmth that turned to ice as Severin's voice said, "His motives are as selfish as yours, sweetheart."

Corbin dragged his gaze away from her face, although his hands remained on her shoulders. "What are you doing back here?" His voice might have cut steel.

Severin, no longer carrying AT, walked over to where the twins lay. Marley pulled away from Corbin and dashed to interpose herself between Severin and the children.

Impatiently, he said, "I told you before that you're always already there between them and the world. Are you actually going to stop me from waking them? Keeping them asleep would be even more dangerous."

"Won't they wake up on their own?" Marley felt slow and confused, too conscious of the tension that stretched between Corbin and Severin and uncomfortably aware of how Corbin's likelihood of getting hurt rose dramatically whenever Severin was present.

"Yes. They will. Their power will burn away every barrier. And once the fire begins to rage, it's very hard for them to stop it, as you've already seen. Better that they don't feel the need." He quirked an eyebrow. "So I wake them before their power does. Get out of the way."

Her breathing ragged, Marley stepped aside.

-thirty-

Severin crouched before the girls and pressed one hand against each of their foreheads. Their breathing changed, and he stood up and stepped back, very quickly, before they could open their eyes.

Kari sat up, blinking. "I had a bad dream." She saw Severin and pulled back, pushing Lissa to wake her as well. Marley crouched beside them, making soothing noises. Lissa opened her eyes, looking directly at Severin.

He glanced away, fixing his attention on Corbin. Corbin hadn't stopped watching him since he appeared, his body taut and still. Marley was sure that in a moment, a fight would break out.

Her heart in her throat, Marley scanned Corbin, looking for something, anything she could do to stop it. "Don't," said Corbin, and turned his body away. Severin's mouth curved up. Corbin's shoulders twitched and Marley was suddenly sure that Severin was talking to Corbin in his head, just as he'd once spoken to her.

"Don't listen to him," she said, before she could think.

Severin flicked his fingers at her dismissively and whispered: *Run along.*

The girls twisted uneasily under her hands. "No more bad dreams…" muttered Kari. "I don't like him."

There was an electronic trilling. At first she heard the sound as a buzzer: time's up. *All done. Submit your tests now.* Then she jerked and fumbled for her phone. It was Branwyn. She answered it.

"Not a good time," she began.

"It's never a good time lately, is it?" said Branwyn. She sounded tired. "I haven't been having a good time either. Penny is… difficult."

Stricken, Marley said, "Bran, I—I'm trying to help."

"Yeah? From wherever you are? There's a trick. How?" But without waiting for an answer, she went on. "We need to talk about your new friends, Marley. I've been hearing things."

"Does it have to be now? Something really bad just happened to one of my friends, and I'm worried about another."

"Oh," said Branwyn, and the tired anger in her voice was replaced by hesitance. In the background, a deep masculine voice said something, and there was a clunk as the phone changed hands. But the new voice on the phone made Marley stop breathing.

"You were so right, Marley. Branwyn has much more of the action girl in her. She's a bit too busy to help us right now, though. Won't you come over and join us?" It was a voice from her dreams, the piping voice of Tinker Chime. And then the line went dead.

Oblivion buzzed in Marley's ears for a long moment, as she stared at the phone in shock. The world was turning inside out. She wasn't asleep. Then Corbin's hand closed on her shoulder.

"Hey," he said sharply. "What's wrong?" She couldn't answer. She couldn't even find words.

Severin, his voice a growl, said, "Tarn."

Marley's legs collapsed underneath her and Corbin lowered her to the roof. She tried to tell him she was fine. "I—I—" The children clutched her hands, and all she could think of was fairy dolls, suspended from ropes. How long?

Severin appeared in her line of sight, crouching down again. He reached over Corbin to lift her chin. "I'll be around, sweetheart. Hope you can keep it together, because if you can't, if you falter, if you fail, you're mine." He winked. "Just a little motivation for you."

Corbin's hands left her and there was the sound of a scuffle. But even though they were beyond her field of vision, she could still feel them close to her. She could feel Severin's eyes on her, and she thought they'd always be there. Even in her dreams... And finally, oblivion overwhelmed her.

She sat on her bed, Neath in her lap. As she stroked the kitten, it began to grow. "You knew," she whispered. "You knew that he didn't belong in here. Where did you come from, little cat?"

The kitten, now the size of a wildcat, flicked her ears and purred in answer.

The curtains were pulled closed, the door was locked, and there was nothing else in the room with them. And slowly, that absence began to frighten her. The fairy—the faerie—really was elsewhere.

She opened her eyes. She was stretched out on a couch, in an empty lobby. The kids were still holding her hands, kneeling on the floor beside her.

"Faeries," she said. "I've been dreaming of a faerie since this started." She looked beyond the kids to where Corbin was putting away his phone. "Where are we? I have to get to Branwyn. Can you take us through the Backworld?"

"No, I can't. I've called a car. How are you? What happened up there?"

"Using the demon's enchantment while being chased by monsters is exhausting." She tried for a wan smile. It was better than saying she'd fainted from shock.

"I saw that one. And the other new enchantment. Celestial magic. Let me guess—you met Ettoriel, and then AT introduced you to Tia."

"Yes," said Marley. The thought of AT made her want to cry. "Can you remove the curse?"

His look was pained. "I haven't gotten any faster at major workings in the last twenty-four hours. By the time I could remove them, they'd have worn down on their own." He added, "You seem to be managing it, though. Just keep it up. What did you say about faeries?"

"You said there was a faerie glamour on Absolven. I've been talking to a faerie in my dreams since this began."

Corbin regarded her thoughtfully. "How do you know it's one of the fae?"

"Because it was six inches tall and looked like a male version of Tinkerbell? Tinker Chime, he calls himself." She watched as his expression turned dubious. "It was a *dream*," she snapped. "I doubt the inside of my head looks like my childhood bedroom, or that Neath is actually the size of a bobcat." She looked around. "Where is Neath, anyhow?"

"I got her and your bag," said Kari, lifting the sleeping ball of fur in her lap. "Mr. Corbin just wanted to leave her up there," she added accusingly.

Marley glanced inquiringly at Corbin as she took Neath from Kari. He looked irritated. "What I wanted was for these precious darlings not to suddenly race away from me, especially while my hands were full of you." His mouth tightened and he looked out the glass doors at the street beyond.

Kari said, "Marley doesn't leave anybody behind," as if that was all that needed to be said.

"Yes..." said Marley, giving Corbin a thoughtful look.

Then she poked at the sleeping kitten until Neath made a protesting noise and clawed Marley's leg. "Does she look any bigger to you?"

"What about this 'faerie'?" insisted Corbin.

"The entity from my dream, whatever it was, talked to me on Branwyn's phone. She gave the phone to him. He's with her now, and I really don't like that. I wanted to protect her!" And the nasty little voice inside pointed out, *She didn't want to be protected.* "I have to get to Branwyn. She's at Penny's. Where's this car?"

"What do you mean, at Penny's? You mean where I rescued you before?"

"Yeah," said Marley, standing up.

"The house of the girl who is channeling the angel?" Corbin looked downright angry.

Marley's own anger began to trickle back. "How many more friends do you want me to lose to this?"

"This isn't a game, Marley! You can't do anything for them; you can't save them by throwing yourself into danger."

"You don't know that! I have to try!"

"What did you do here? And AT's gone now."

Marley flinched like she'd been slapped, and then said, "I will push you off the balcony, you fuck. I can't believe I traded her for you."

"Neither can I," he snapped. "I didn't ask you to."

"Why the hell are you even helping me?" She stared at him suspiciously. "That asshole Severin said something..."

Corbin narrowed his eyes. "Zachariah used me. He got my friends badly hurt. I need to understand why. And I need to have words with him about his behavior. That's all."

"Oh. So revenge for fallen friends is much better than trying to stop something from happening, than trying to *protect* people. Thanks. Then I'm going after him for Penny and AT. Are you going to get in my way?"

"But *we* hurt AT," said Lissa, her voice very quiet.

The world twisted and stretched. Everything was wrong. The space around her distorted.

The curse struck.

There was a harsh, buzzing noise and the power in the building went out. The half-strength lights faded, and there was the acrid, rubbery smell of an electrical fire. Barely seconds later, smoke trickled out of a vent.

Corbin cursed steadily as he grabbed her stuff and her arm, and started dragging her out of the building. He paused at a fire alarm just long enough to pull it. The clanging helped Marley shake off the aftereffects of the curse striking through her, and she realized that just as Corbin was dragging her, she was dragging the children.

Out on the sidewalk, Kari wailed, "Why do we break everything?" The city street was nearly abandoned; in the distance, a few cars passed and a pedestrian ran along across the street and vanished down the block. It was disturbingly post-apocalyptic.

Corbin's eyes flickered down to the children. "The Machine I summoned didn't mention breaking the Hush. And the Hush doesn't seem to affect their magic at all. That construct was impervious to it. I wonder..." And he trailed off.

Marley remembered what he'd discovered on the roof, about the children being a kind of event horizon to the celestial Machines. She smacked him in the chest, propelling him away from her. "Don't even *think* it," she snarled. "They're *children*."

Corbin looked at her, all angry coiled energy. For a moment, she wondered if she was going to have an actual fistfight with him. Distantly, in the sparking fogs of fear and bravado that now made up what could laughingly be called her mind, she recalled that only a few minutes ago, she'd been *worried* about him fighting with Severin. She *knew* she was being completely irrational, but she could no longer bring herself to care. Being rational hadn't saved anybody.

A black limousine slid up to the curb. The back door popped open. Corbin looked between her and the car, and then he sighed. "Get in."

-thirty-one-

The ride to Penny's house took far too long, and was far too quiet. The girls didn't protest the lack of car seats as they had before. They didn't talk. They didn't play with the buttons in the limo. They didn't even cry. They just sat quietly in their seats, staring dully out the window.

Marley felt like she should address their fears, but her brain was full of sparks that flared and quickly died. She didn't know what to say. She barely knew who she was. She tried to focus on suppressing the curse, so the limo didn't have a catastrophic failure, and she could feel the suppression draining her.

Penny's house looked utterly normal outside. Branwyn's car was parked beside Penny's, and the shades were drawn against the coming afternoon sun. Penny's neighborhood showed more signs of life than the street where she'd found Corbin, although most people remained indoors to avoid the smoke. The fires were so far down the mountain now that she couldn't see much of the orange line, just the black ashes marking where the flames had been.

They emerged from the limo. Corbin paused for a quick

word with the driver, who left the car running. Then he looked up at the charred mountains and blinked. "I think you're right," he said quietly.

"About?"

He shook his head. "Faeries. I know there are other angels involved, but I don't think that was who was on the roof, using the pollution. Fae magic is elemental, and it's governed by the Covenant, not the Hush." She stared at him, and he shook his head. "Let's go see your friend."

But when they knocked on the door, nobody answered. Marley tried the door, and then fumbled for her key to Penny's house. Before she could find it, Kari reached up and touched the knob. There was a click.

Marley squeezed Kari's other hand, and opened the door. "Penny? Branwyn?" she called, as she stepped inside. She didn't expect an answer, and she didn't get one. Dread nearly freezing her limbs, she walked down the short hall to the living room.

It was empty. The whole house was empty. It was perfectly tidy, the model house that Penny's parents wanted it to be. But their model daughter was gone.

"Are you sure they were here?" Corbin asked, coming out of the kitchen.

Marley frowned. "I was sure..." But had Branwyn actually said?

"Marley," said Lissa. She pointed at a delicate transparent sphere, balanced against a photo of Marley, Penny, and Branwyn laughing together. Marley stared at it, frozen, then rushed across the room to snatch at it.

As soon as she touched it, it burst. She saw the room as it had been.

Penny lay on the couch, so pale she seemed transparent. Branwyn stood near her, fierce and angry, facing something that Marley couldn't quite make out. Light bent around it, much like the blurred figures on the roof who had controlled the pollution elementals. "I can't believe she didn't tell me," said Branwyn. Then, overlaid on the scene like a double exposure, a hole in the world gaped open. A winged sprite flitted through it.

The vision faded.

Marley's breathing was ragged. "They took them. Chime took all of them. Zachariah. Penny. Branwyn. We even talked about how faeries steal people."

Corbin said slowly, "Fae elemental magic could be shielding Ettoriel from the Hush. That fire's producing a huge amount of power. But why would they be helping an angel? The Covenant limits them tremendously and they hate the angels for inflicting it on them. And angels hate fae magic because it's parasitical. So... why?"

"Desperation? I'd use whatever power *I* could get right now." She shook her head. "I don't know. I don't understand anything. But I know where to find answers." She knelt down in front of Kari. "You felt the door in the fire once. Can you feel a door to the Backworld where the faeries live?" Slowly, Kari nodded. Marley took a deep breath. "Can you open it?"

Kari hesitated. "Is that where Uncle Zach is?"

"Yes," said Marley, absolutely certain.

Kari's gaze went far away.

In an undertone, Corbin said, "Marley, the valence event is passing soon. Technically, by still being alive, you're winning. In a day or two, you'll have time again."

Marley didn't even look at him, her gaze fixed instead on the patch of air where Kari was staring. He sighed, and said, "Right."

Then Kari touched a point in the air with one finger, and the point flared. It was different from the holes in the world opened by Severin and AT. This looked like lightning, like sparks, like the thin membrane between "here" and "there" was melting and curling from the heat of Kari's touch. It didn't look like a hole that would zip shut again easily. Oh well.

"We'll just step inside and see what there is to see. And we'll come right back out again if we don't like what we do see." Marley wasn't sure if she was reassuring Corbin, the girls, or herself. She held out her hands to the girls and took a deep breath.

Then she stepped through. As she passed through the shattered barrier, Corbin suddenly said, "Marley, wait—"

But she didn't wait. The world on the other side wasn't the white, featureless hall that AT had led her into before. It was a large room, with dim lamplight caressing rich textures. Marley's feet sank into layered carpets, and the spiced air tickled her nose. Shimmering fabric veiled the walls and tinted the light emanating from mirrored lamps set in shallow depressions.

Silhouetted in an arch on the other side of the room was a tall figure with dark hair, broad shoulders, and a familiar profile. It was Zachariah. First Kari, then Lissa, squeaked and pulled away. Before Marley had finished taking in their new location, they were both running forward.

And everything went horribly wrong. Whiteness flared, crackling around the children. Marley screamed as something ripped the twins from her with the force of a tidal wave. A canyon opened between them, and the twins were on the far edge, still moving away from her.

That wasn't Zachariah.

The world turned inside out. The curse struck. Everything became a series of images and unconnected sensations.

The room around her shattered, shards of color and light flying everywhere. A giant invisible hand batted her through the air. She flew backward and then dropped, sickeningly.

She was falling.

Knives sank into her arm. Something yowled.

Without any clear awareness of a transition, the fall through the air slowed like she was sinking through water. Then, as gently as if she'd laid down, she came to rest on a surface. Something warm was on her chest.

Marley couldn't see, blinded by tears. The twins were beyond her protection, although she could still feel them, still sense the awful danger they were in. What had happened?

She remembered AT saying there were things that lived in the Backworld who could control her perceptions. Were the girls really gone? She brought her hands up to scrub at her eyes.

Neath was on her chest, grown to the size of a bobcat again. Marley was lying on a giant velvet pillow tossed against a wall hung with bronze and green. It was the same place she'd stepped into through Kari's Backworld portal, and there was no sign of whatever horror had occurred. She hurt all over, though, like she'd been caught in an explosion.

The twins were nowhere to be seen, but the figure that had seemed so close to Zachariah in silhouette was still present. A single door led from the room, behind him. She could see no sign of the portal that Kari had opened.

Still dazed, she stared up at the man as he moved closer to her. The resemblance to Zachariah went beyond his height and build; he had Zachariah's hair and there was a familial likeness in the features. This man was even more attractive, though, exuding a magnetism that Zachariah barely carried off.

He blew out his breath in a sigh, and then smiled at her. "Come now, stand up. We've waited so long for you."

There was something familiar in his voice, too. It was deeper than Zachariah's, a lazy drawl that didn't seem to expect much of her even as his words encouraged action.

She tilted her still-ringing head, trying to understand

who he was. He looked like Zachariah, yes, but that wasn't where the familiarity stopped. "Who are you?" she breathed.

He held out a hand and flexed his fingers. The air before his hand shimmered, and a tiny winged figure sprang into existence. He bent his hand forward and the figure bowed. He waggled a pair of fingers and the figure opened its mouth in a pantomime of speech.

It was Tinker Chime. Chime, the adorable little pixie, had been a puppet of the man standing before her. He'd done everything he could to lure her into his domain, and as soon as she'd entered, he'd ripped the twins away from her.

Part of her felt she had to get up, rage, attack him. Part of her wanted to weep and shudder in a corner. The rest of her thrust herself to her feet. The oversized cat on her chest fell onto its paws and entwined itself around her legs.

"You took them. You took *all* of them. Zachariah. Branwyn and Penny. The kids. Where are they?"

"Some of them are here, some of them are there. What does it matter now? You've lost them." The bastard's little smirk didn't change.

"No, you've stolen them. There's a difference."

His smile broadened. "Is there?"

Marley paused to consult her guardian sense. The kids were still alive, although in great danger. She thought they were asleep. She had a vague sense that they were *thataway* but had no idea which direction *thataway* was. She nodded at the door behind the man. "Is that the way out?"

"I must inform you there is no way out." His smile twitched.

Marley was tired. She'd been utterly emptied by recent events. But she put her hands on her hips. "Are you trying to be intimidating? Because you're a man who masquerades as a six-inch-tall pixie. Last night I had somebody trying to shred my soul. You're going to have to try harder."

He moved his head to one side, staring down at her. The world went all topsy-turvy again, knocking her off her feet. Something cold and hard caught her around one wrist, then the other.

The world righted itself, with a yank on her arm sockets. This time she was dangling with her toes a few inches above the ground. Her wrists were pinioned over her head, held by, as far as she could tell, a pair of metal hands jutting from the wall.

"Pretty good," Marley panted. Her shoulders hurt and her head drooped.

"I can't just let you go," said the faerie. He sighed again and the light puppet of Chime crossed its arms and tapped its foot. Marley wondered if he always had the puppet out, like a ventriloquist. The thought was unbearably creepy. She shuddered.

Then the little puppet faded away, and the tall man said, "Exhausted, confused darling. If you had found your way here earlier, you could have rested between your downfall and the end of our little play." His eyes slid away from her, finding the cat crouched to one side, growling quietly. "Your damnable guardian delayed things some. Is it a construct of your mother's, perhaps?" His gaze shifted back to her. His eyes were pied, one green, one brown. "But you came, all the same."

"You could have lured me in a lot quicker with an open door and a big sign saying, 'ZACHARIAH HERE'."

"But then we wouldn't have had all those marvelous talks. I enjoyed them, despite that thing." He nodded at Neath again.

"You enjoyed lying to me, you mean. Who the hell are you, anyhow?"

He bowed. "I am Tarn, Duke of Underlight and Master of the Sunset Halls. This is my Velvet Hall, and here is my court."

-thirty-two-

Marley became aware of the feeling of dozens of eyes watching her. The staring was a pressure, a familiar pressure. She'd felt this before over the past few days, at Zachariah's and at Penny's. Invisible eyes, watching her from all directions. But this time the eyes weren't invisible. In the shadows among the hangings on the walls, they glinted.

Marley twisted in the metal grip. The presence of many observers made her feel even more helpless. She wondered if Severin would actually do as he'd threatened, and come to claim her if she failed. She wondered if this Tarn person would let him. Would they fight? She was pretty sure that wouldn't go well for her. Or what if they teamed up on her?

Blackness rolled over her vision. The curse had only triggered a moment ago, but already it was growing stronger again. She didn't have a clear memory of what exactly had happened, in that horrible moment when the twins had been torn away and the world had spun upside down, didn't know what had broken or where, but she'd felt it strike through her. What would it break next time?

Tarn stared at her calmly. Slowly, she became aware of the

rustling sense of expectation among the half-hidden fae in the shadows. They were waiting for something. Was Ettoriel going to come in and finish the job his curse kept almost doing? Was this a strange form of fae torture?

"My arms hurt," she said. "I'm sorry I asked you to try harder to intimidate me."

"You still don't seem very intimidated," Tarn pointed out. "I must say, Action Girl Branwyn was far more... curious... about her situation than you are."

Realization dawned. "You want to *exposit* at me. Oh. You definitely need a cat for that. Neath, you're up. Go snuggle with him." She felt drunk with exhaustion.

Tarn laughed out loud and snapped his fingers. An upholstered footstool appeared beneath Marley's feet, so that while her wrists were still captured, her weight was no longer dragging on them. "It would disappoint us both if you were simply abandoned to languish in captivity. It's so dull in Underlight these days, even in the Velvet Court."

Marley looked around the shadowy room. "Is anything here actually real?"

Tarn moved closer. "I am."

"And them?" She pointed with her chin at the eyes in the shadows. They shifted about, blinking on and off.

"Real enough."

"But this Velvet Court of yours isn't real. That's how you pulled the children away."

"Space is malleable, especially here." He looked around fondly. "It's served us well over the years."

Marley moved her hands back and forth, wondering if she could work them free. What would she do then? Even if she dodged her many watchers and made it to the door, she would still be trapped in this flexible world, with no idea of how to get to the children. No, the only way forward was to play his game. Maybe she could get some kind of concession from him if she kept talking. If she entertained him.

"So, do you believe the girls are dangerous as well? Is that why you're helping Ettoriel?"

Tarn laughed again, a full, rich sound. "I *know* they are dangerous. Their touch will not fade from the substrate of my realm for many years. You did not see it, but when we took them, the world separated around them, like butter from buttermilk."

Marley remembered the white flare she'd seen when the curse had struck and wondered if she had seen the passage of the twins after all.

"Good," she said, and she didn't bother to keep the vindictive pleasure from her voice. "You deserve trouble for helping that bastard."

Tarn dipped his head, as if he didn't disagree with this statement. "It has been a long while since we could do what gave us pleasure." When he looked at Marley again, there was a hunger in his eyes that hadn't been there before.

Marley felt the sudden urge to back away, pressing her shoulders futilely against the wall. "Why do you look like Zachariah?"

Tarn tossed black hair away from his eyes. "Zachariah was never what I'd call a *charming* child, not like your two wards. Even knowing what was at stake, what could be accomplished, he chose to resist my command. But he always did have a knack for predicting the path of games." There was grudging pride in his voice.

Marley blinked and then blinked again. "You're his *father*?"

Tarn smiled again. "His mother was a beautiful, intelligent woman, if easily distracted. Somewhat like you."

"Oh, ew," said Marley, trying to unthink the idea that possibly she reminded Zachariah of his mother. "Next topic! When are you going to let me go?"

"I told you already that I cannot *let* you go." His voice was stiff and strange again, and this time, she caught the subtle emphasis.

"Why do you—" She stopped. *Faeries are like lawyers.* "You're not lying, are you?" *Ettoriel? Who's that? We serve the Dark Lord Tibbersnaufer.* "But in my dream—" She stopped, confused.

Tarn spread his hands. "For a Duke of Faerie to speak untruths within his own realm would be disastrous. All the realm is bound to the truth of its master's tongue. But your dream... What are dreams but lies your brain creates to help it understand a greater truth?"

"But what greater truth?" murmured Marley, mostly to herself.

"You already know it," said Tarn. He raised his gaze, staring off into the distance. "Time is running out. I do hope nothing *unexpected* happens."

"Your puppet lied to me about who you're working with. But why? And it was such a ridiculous lie. Tibbersnaufer. Really?"

Tarn's gaze was still distant. Then it snapped back to Marley. "Do pardon me, but I have to tend to a disruption." He turned to pace through the door.

Marley called, "Wait!" Tarn paused, his head turned just enough to indicate that she had his attention. "Will you at least let Branwyn go? She's got no part of this."

"But she wants a part so very badly," smirked Tarn, as he vanished through the door.

Marley slumped as much as her restrained arms would let her. Then she realized that she wasn't alone just because Tarn had departed. The eyes were still all around her, and now their owners were creeping out of the shadows.

Her first thought was "small goblins," but she realized that though they crouched close to the floor, they were no smaller than her. Nor were they monstrous in appearance. They had wild hair, large noses, and expressive mouths, with slanted eyes, and they moved like dancers emulating animals. Mostly, they seemed male, dressed in rags of silk and fur and feathers, decorated by scars and rainbow-colored tattoos.

One of them, in red silken rags and orange leather, the first from the shadows, loped over to her and stared up into her eyes. On the stool, she was maybe a foot and a half taller than him. Then he ducked his head and pressed his face against her groin, inhaling deeply.

Marley froze in shock, and then kicked up off the stool, trying hard to introduce her foot to his own groin. He dodged to one side, laughing.

"Why don't you do as my lord wishes?" he inquired, when he had his breath back. "It has been so long since we were free to do as we wish. The world misses us."

Marley panted, resting her weight on one foot only, ready to kick again. "What are you talking about? He already has what he wants of me."

He tilted his head, looking at her feet, and then her face. Then he moved closer again. Too close. Reflexively, she kicked out. He caught her foot, as easily as catching a ball. Grinning, he held her foot as she cursed and squirmed, then slipped her shoe off. He tossed the shoe over his shoulder; one of his companions caught it and tried it on his own bare foot.

"Not true. He wants so much more from you." The faerie's voice dropped to a croon. "The sun, the moon, the stars."

"I haven't got the title for those," Marley snapped. She yanked on her foot again, her exhaustion driven away by rising panic. It was just as disturbing to have this strange creature holding her foot as sniffing her crotch. Another one came up alongside her, running a single finger over the small of her back.

Shakily, she said, "If you guys don't back off, I'm going to start screaming. I don't think your lord would like that." That had to be true. He was so polite; there hadn't even been any chains until she'd been rude.

But the faerie holding her foot was still smiling, his strong fingers squeezing its sole. "It rather depends on the screams. He left you here with us quite aware of his actions."

"Tarn!" she shrieked. A third faerie grabbed at the leg supporting her, wrestling it up, while a fourth pried off her other shoe.

"Perhaps we ought to make you one of us," suggested the first faerie. "Show you the nature of our captivity." Her socks came off next. She kicked and twisted and screamed, until she realized that they'd pinioned one foot between three of them and were... tickling it? It was so strange that she gasped and swallowed another scream as she tried to work out what was going on. She couldn't see beyond their wild heads of hair, but she could feel cool, wet, fine lines being traced across the top and sides of her foot, leaving a residue behind.

Were they writing on her? For a moment, she even caught the distinctive whiff of ink. Then she recalled the markings they all wore, and what they'd said finally made it past her wall of terror. *Perhaps we ought to make you one of us.*

Was that even possible? Her memory helpfully supplied the word "changeling" in reply. She shuddered and renewed her fighting, focusing on that foot, on moving it just enough to disrupt the careful inking.

The first faerie looked up at her, his pale eyes hungry. "There are other ways, pretty one, ways you'd like much less."

Marley stared at him, then shook her head. Just let one thing she disliked happen because if she didn't, something worse *might* happen? Hell, no!

"This way," continued the faerie, "you are restrained, and we will drain your power out of you, but your... nature... is untouched. You are not made to suffer." His mouth curved up in a feral, unamused smile.

Marley stared at him in horror. "No! No, I *will* suffer!"

"But how can you? It is such a benign form of captivity. And sometimes we will take you out and let you dance for us. Won't that be fun?" The tickle of the inking moved up her foot to her ankle. "Won't you be grateful for such a minor form of freedom?" He tilted his head to one side, as if listening to something, his gaze growing distant.

Then his gaze snapped back to Marley. She was sure her foot was tingling where the ink had been laid. Was yet another enchantment seeping inside her? Is that why they'd captured her in this way, was that what Tarn wanted? Her magic? Perhaps her powers would be put to use protecting Ettoriel?

She was trapped here. There was no one to hear her scream, no one who cared. All that effort to avoid Ettoriel, and she'd walked right into this hidden enemy's grasp.

A warm finger pressed against her lips, and Marley realized that she'd been whimpering as she stared sightlessly ahead. The first faerie removed his finger, his eyes meeting her own. "You don't like that fate? What would you do to escape it? Lie? Cheat? Betray?"

Hope flared in Marley. *Almost anything. But...* "I wouldn't just let you hurt those children, if that's what you're asking."

He tapped her mouth. "You're a very dense little girl. Carry on, my brothers." He stepped away and looked around. "Where did the sweet kitten scamper off to?"

Marley twitched convulsively as tickling began on her other foot. Where was Neath? Why, after protecting her in so many dreams, had the strange cat abandoned her now? What had Tarn said about her? A construct of her mother's, protecting her?

Tears sprang to Marley's eyes. What a fantasy.

"Hmm," said the first faerie, staring off into a corner. There was a sparkle of light on the carpet that slowly resolved into the wildcat-sized Neath. She flattened her ears and yowled. Her shadow flowed out like spreading ink behind her. It reared up, morphing into a rough human shape.

"Brothers," said the first faerie, warningly. The black shape broke into pieces, light and color streaming out from the cracks. A breeze came from nowhere. Then the shadows flew in all directions, not shadows now but ravens. Corbin stepped into the Velvet Court.

-thirty-three-

Light streamed from both of Corbin's hands, and one eye glowed blue while the other was a black pit. Darkness seemed smeared across his face, and his hair tangled in the wind he'd brought with him.

He pointed with his left hand, silver light dripping from his finger, and the wind smashed into the faeries who held Marley. "Let the girl go," he called.

"You have come into our realm, our power, halfling, a willing visitor," growled the first faerie. "We will add you to our menag—ah!" A raven the size of a hawk had descended on him. More assaulted the faeries holding Marley, so that all she saw was wings, and all she heard was the cries of birds and men. Her feet were released, tickled by feathers.

The metal hands gripping her wrists opened. She fell to the floor, landing awkwardly on exhausted legs that promptly gave out beneath her. A faerie tripped over her and she covered her head and curled up. After a moment, when nobody else stepped on her, she started crawling toward where she'd last seen Corbin.

A hand closed over her arm and hauled her upright. She

struggled tiredly before recognizing the golden glow around Corbin's hand, and raising her eyes to his face.

Up close, she barely recognized him. Something cold and inhuman had settled over his features. He glanced over her and she wondered what had happened to his left eye. Then he raised his golden hand and touched it to her forehead. Something intangible popped free, leaving her feeling, on some metaphysical level, less constricted. The glow on Corbin's hand changed texture, becoming tinged with blue.

"Where is the master of this Court?" demanded Corbin, turning his attention back to the faeries brawling with his ravens. Not just his ravens, either. White lightning soundlessly jumped from faerie to faerie, blinding their eyes and tying up their feet. Perspective skewed, until she wasn't sure if the ravens were larger or the faeries smaller.

"Can we get out again?" she asked Corbin. "However you got here?"

"I don't know," he said in an undertone. "I came on the tail of your cat." She followed his gaze to where Neath was damaging a faerie with spiky purple hair. It looked like she'd grown again. "I'm not ready to leave yet, though. Where are the children?"

"He tricked them away from me, lured them out and did some magic to this place that snatched them beyond my reach," she said angrily. "Out of my range."

"Rather like this," said Tarn's voice, and a cold wind swept through the room, tumbling both birds and the smaller faeries. But there was more to it than that. The cushions and hangings all turned translucent and hard, like a model of a luxurious room carved from diamond. Or ice. Every inanimate thing in the room was now ice or snow, including the walls. Only around Corbin did the material of the room maintain its original character. His hands glowed brightly.

Tarn, standing at the same door he'd departed through,

looked mildly irritated. "My dear, if you wanted more company, you had only to ask. You didn't need to summon this ruffian." He waved a hand and the whole room twisted, the ice flowing and reforming into different structures, until they were in a prison run by the Snow Queen. Fur-lined handcuffs hung on the inside door of the large barred cell that had appeared around them, and a glass cake dome appeared around each of the ravens. A number of unusual implements, all silver and crystal, hung on the wall beside Tarn.

But the new scene barely lasted long enough for Marley to register the details before Corbin lifted his hands and the fittings of the room shattered into whiteness. All was mist, with Tarn and his goblins barely visible through the drifting coils. The ravens cried and flapped through chilly air.

"Do you know what happened when you stepped inside the door?" Corbin asked in a low voice.

"I *told* you. He stole the children."

"I mean when everything exploded. I saw it as the door closed. No? I'll tell you. Three things combined: the nature of this place, the curse Ettoriel placed on you, and your own gift. An enormous amount of power was released. It left marks. Normally, I wouldn't be able to fight a faerie lord, not in his own land, but he must have exerted significant resources to repair the breach you caused."

"Can I do it again?"

He glanced at her and took her hand. "I have no idea."

"What was that you took from me?"

"That enchantment I couldn't identify earlier. A marker for him." He nodded toward where Tarn was tracing delicate shapes through the mist with his long hands. "He's been tracking you."

Marley closed her eyes and felt for the curse, felt for the demon's gift. The curse was there, but still unfocused. The demon's gift—but she was exhausted. She couldn't control it.

"What can you do now that you're here?" she asked quietly. "I want to make him talk. He's been playing with me in my dreams since Zachariah vanished. He's got Zachariah somewhere, and maybe Branwyn and Penny too, and I want to know why. He doesn't have the same motivations as Ettoriel, I know that."

"The dreams explain the mark's purpose, then. Look out," Corbin said, and pulled her to one side. Color was creeping into the mist and swirling along the ground. "Let's walk while we talk, shall we?" He set out in an apparently random direction, towing her after him. Marley thought he'd run into a wall soon, because the room hadn't been that big. But he didn't. The white mist thickened around them.

"What exactly are you doing?" Her body ached all over. It wanted her to lie down and sleep, preferably after a long, hot bath. She ignored it.

"Right now? In layman's terms, I'm interfering with the signal he broadcasts to control the environment. I took the signature from the enchantment he put on you." He raised his blue-tinted hand. "I'm making a lot of spiritual noise. "

Marley nodded, thinking, looking down at her feet. She was wearing shoes again. But she'd felt the ink on her skin. What was real here?

Corbin went on. "You said Zachariah was here? I wonder if we can find him."

"He said Zachariah was his son," Marley said.

Corbin stopped walking to look at her. "Did he really? That explains a lot about the tricky old bastard." It was a moment before Marley realized he was describing Zachariah as old. "Maybe he's just congenitally unable to tell the simple truth. Let's find him and ask."

"If we're going to find somebody, I'd rather find the children. If Zachariah is well, he's not going to stop being well in the next few hours. " And if she could get the girls back this time, she wouldn't hang around L.A. She'd find someplace to run to.

"You're not desperate enough yet, girl," said Tarn's voice from somewhere in the mist. "Your eternal optimism, so human. Your inability to fight back, so like your mother."

"Words are cheap, faerie," called Corbin, and squeezed her hand. "Shall I—"

Light flared around them. Marley jerked so hard she tripped herself, but it was Corbin who twisted and sprawled, as gravity reversed itself for him. A room spread out from the burst of light and they were once again back in the Velvet Court. This time, it was Corbin who was caught up by the metal hands. He kicked and twisted as goblins swarmed him.

Tarn slouched on a throne at the far end of the room. Neath prowled in a cage at his feet. He waved a long-fingered hand. "You failed with the girl, my pets, but look, I give you a second chance with the boy. Do your best work."

Marley lunged forward, without a plan, and banged into a transparent wall. She stared at what she could not see, rage and disbelief warring within her. She wasn't desperate enough? Had all the mist been yet another trick by the faerie lord?

Then Corbin grunted, a sound far more disturbing than any cry he might have made, and she threw herself at the invisible barrier again. If only Corbin would let her protect him. All she wanted to do was keep her friends safe.

Yet how could she fault him for rejecting her? Look how little she'd been able to help AT or the girls. She was useless—worse than useless—to those who had trusted her. Her vision was the stuff of nightmares. If only she could use it aggressively. If only she could fight.

Her skin felt spiky again. Her gaze fixed on Tarn, fully activating the catastrophe vision. He *was* going to suffer soon. He was bound, and he was dancing with dreadful danger, and he was enjoying it.

For a moment, her vision blurred. Logic disjointed, and then she saw clearly again. She couldn't protect without permission. But he was doing something dangerous, and he knew it. He *wanted* to be hurt.

"Enjoy this," she whispered. She reversed her shield and wrapped it around him, so that the spikes were on the inside.

Tarn gasped. The sound, soft as Corbin's grunt, stilled the room. The goblins fell away from Corbin and the hands holding him up released him. He landed on the floor in a crouch, his clothing torn and his skin scratched.

Marley raised her hand to the invisible wall and brushed her fingers across it. It melted away and she stepped forward, watching. Her stomach twisted with nausea even as elation rang in her ears. Tarn's hands clutched his shoulders, his face tilted up. His face contorted, and she was *glad*.

Little noises came from Tarn. Marley drifted closer, straining to hear. Was he begging? She'd begged. Her gorge rose, but she forced it down again. She was doing what was necessary, and her squeamish stomach would just have to cope.

Then she realized that Tarn was laughing. He spread his arms. "Yes. Finally. Such a good girl. Your mother's daughter, but she'd be horrified now."

"Shut up about my mother," Marley snapped. "She abandoned me. I don't want to hear about her." But her gaze moved unwillingly to the caged Neath, who he'd called her mother's construct. The cat sat in the cage, perfectly still, staring at her.

She looked back at Tarn again, who was still coughing with laughter. "What's so funny? It hurts. I *know* I'm hurting you."

"You have bound me utterly," he agreed. "It is glorious. You've bound me so close that no other binding can hold. "

Beside her, Corbin breathed, "I knew it! They *are* invoking the Covenant." Marley glanced at him. He'd clearly understood something, but Marley was still waiting for the dawn.

Corbin saw her expression and went on. "That's like the Hush, but for the fae. My people modeled the Hush after the Covenant. But I thought it was just suppression, not control."

Tarn cleared his throat. "Leave," he said, looking at his passive goblins. A few were stirring uneasily. "Go back to the Feast and await my call. Leave, now!" One by one, they faded into shadows.

"It's much cruder than the Hush. It is both a cage and a bridle. Do you think we'd been hiding in our lands sulking, all these centuries? Only the smallest of part of us could slip the bit," continued Tarn, and his voice was echoing and desolate. "Now Ettoriel has gained the reins, for his wonderful attempt to save the world. The other angels were happy to loan him one of the leashes when he told them he might break the Hush as a byproduct of his heroism. Us, bound to help free the angels!" Laughter bubbled in his voice again, but he mastered it. "He commands us to *aid him*, and so we must. He commands us to *hinder you*, and so we must. He commands us to *reveal nothing*. He commands us to *feed him power* and he does not care how." The laughter escaped, taking away his ability to speak.

"The wildfires," said Corbin. "You've been using the fire as a power source for his magic."

"Clever boy," Tarn said. And he turned his gaze to Marley, looking at her with too-bright eyes, as if waiting for her to understand.

"So you're saying that you didn't *want* to snatch the girls, but you had *orders*."

"Marley—" said Corbin. "The Covenant has restricted them for thousands of years. It's not something they can just opt out of."

"No. Is Ettoriel here, giving orders? This asshole has apparently been creatively resisting him for days, going by my dreams and his ridiculous little alter ego." She glared at Tarn. "Oh, yes, I understand those now, you trying so hard to circumvent his orders. But when you lured me in here by kidnapping my friends, there was no inventive avoidance. You snatched them away without a hint of warning and you *gave* them to *him* and then you started getting *creative*. I bet he was surprised when you handed them over, wasn't he?"

"But so, so pleased," said Tarn, looking at her with liquid eyes. His body was still tense and quivering, like a plucked guitar string.

She turned away. "Yeah. I don't know what you're doing, but you're not on my side. Give me back my friends."

"Your Penny, who is channeling Ettoriel, feeding him with her love, is not here. He took her with him when he took possession of the children."

"Why?" Marley demanded. But even as she asked, she remembered, *My loyal servants will not be lost while I yet endure.*

"He regrets what has been done to her, I believe. Maybe he doesn't want her to burn out alone. I really have no idea. He demanded her and I obeyed."

Marley took a deep breath. "And Branwyn?"

Tarn gave her a smile that made her shiver. "She is in quarters here in Underlight. I would open a passage for you to her, but you have me pinioned."

"Marley," said Corbin urgently. "Is he fighting you? How long can you maintain whatever you're doing? You don't have a power source, do you?"

She glanced at his anxious face, but Tarn spoke before she could. "Why would I fight? When her binding ends, another binding far more distasteful begins."

"And yet you'd still open a passage to Branwyn? Or was that just empty words?"

Tarn's eyelashes fluttered down. He breathed deeply and

then said, "Yes. The angel doesn't care about Branwyn. I took her for my own purposes. As long as I'm not releasing you, the compulsion of the Covenant is uninvoked."

Marley assessed herself. She was so tired, but whatever power the shield drew on seemed untouched by physical and emotional fatigue. She was nauseous, of course—but that could just be physical exhaustion. She wasn't *injured* like she was when the twins' metal nightmare was too much for her protection around AT. Her shoulder and arm burned, remembering it, but the skin had never been broken. She had a gash on her arm, but it was shallow. She was *fine*. And she felt like she could bring the shield back up again. All she had to do was look at Tarn the right way.

"Do it," she said. "Open the passage to Branwyn." And she dropped the shield.

Tarn's reaction was immediate, and so abrupt she almost brought the shield back up again. He spread his arms and lifted his head, then sighed explosively, as if he'd just been punched in the gut. Then he turned, calling, "Branwyn," in a tone of voice Marley didn't like at all.

Beside his throne, a curtain twitched aside. Beyond was a short hallway, leading to a heavy door. "Go and bring her forth, if you wish," Tarn breathed.

"I'll go," said Corbin. "You stay here and watch him."

"I'm not sure that's—" Marley began, but Corbin had already started limping down the hall. He opened the door.

There was a pause, and then a familiar voice shouted, "You! I don't care if *you're* real."

-thirty-four-

S hit!" said Corbin, ducking as something long and metallic scythed through the air where his head had been. He backed up and tripped over his own feet, catching himself on one hand and turning a sprawl into another dodge as the metal cylinder smashed into where his leg should have been.

"Branwyn," called Marley.

Branwyn stepped into the hall and met her gaze, eyes blazing. "They wouldn't dare copy you, would they? What's going on? Is that little winged freak around? I swear I'm going to club *someone* if I don't get some truth." She glanced down at Corbin, who was moving backward steadily while remaining below her eye level.

"I see you're with this scum now, just like the pixie said."

Marley involuntarily glanced at Tarn, who seemed delighted by Branwyn's aggression. "Branwyn, I don't know what he told you, but he's been lying to me, so I think maybe he's been lying to you, too. He's right over here, grinning."

Corbin escaped the hall and straightened up again, moving closer to Marley. "Are you sure this is your friend? And

not another trap?"

"Oh yeah," Marley assured him. There was a reason Branwyn had been Action Girl. Only she would start a conversation with a baseball bat.

"I don't know. You clearly know something about all this crap, and you weren't telling me, just like he said," said Branwyn. She moved out of the hall and looked around. Her gaze lingered on Tarn. Marley bit her lip, and then wrapped Tarn up in her shield again. She didn't trust him. She *couldn't* trust him; he'd all but told her that.

He grunted and twitched, but his smile didn't fade. "My lady," he said, raising his eyebrows at Branwyn.

"I'm not your anything," snapped Branwyn. "You're the pixie? All grown up?" She tapped the cylinder against her hand thoughtfully. It wasn't actually a baseball bat, but an ornate silver and black rod. The ornamentation bore all the signs of Branwyn's style, and Marley wondered if she'd spent her captivity crafting a weapon. Had Tarn actually given her the materials to do that? This place was so strange, she couldn't even guess.

Tarn inclined his head. "All grown up."

"I wonder if it's true that faeries don't like iron," she said and prodded her rod in his direction.

"You'll have to wait until another time to find out, my lady," said Tarn. "Go, speak with your friend. She's worked hard to liberate you from your, ah, studio."

Branwyn gave Tarn a scornful look and turned toward Marley. She wouldn't quite look at Marley, though, her gaze roaming around the room. "Where did the little girls go?"

"Gone," said Marley bleakly. "Stolen."

"Your new friends weren't very helpful, then," said Branwyn, and gave Corbin a nasty look.

"No," said Corbin quietly. "I wasn't."

Marley moved so that Branwyn was looking at her instead of Corbin. "Branwyn, I'm sorry."

"Sorry for what? Sorry for trusting strangers more than your best friend? Sorry for excluding me from the most exciting thing in your life? Sorry for leaving Penny and me when you knew she had something *horrible* wrong with her? Are you going to apologize to Penny, too?"

That, finally, was too much for Marley. A sob ripped its way out of her throat, and she scrubbed her palms at her eyes.

Everybody stared at her. Then Branwyn muttered, "Aw, shit," and moved closer.

"I can't save her, Branwyn. I've tried and tried, but she's found this thing and she... she loves it. It fills her up inside, and she doesn't care that it's hurting her, and she doesn't care that it's taking her away from us. And I couldn't save AT and I couldn't even keep the kids safe—"

Then Branwyn's arms were around her and she pressed her head against her friend's shoulder. "I didn't know how to tell you. I didn't even know what was going on myself."

"Do you now?" asked Branwyn quietly, loosening her embrace to look at her.

"Mostly." Marley lifted her head and wiped her eyes.

She realized suddenly that Corbin was no longer beside her. He'd moved over to Tarn and was speaking to him in a rapid, quiet voice, a furious expression on his face. Tarn spread his hands in apparent helplessness, and looked over at Marley.

Her voice suddenly urgent, Branwyn said, "Sum it up for me? Is it all faeries?"

Marley shook her head. "Sum it up? I inherited a lot more trouble from my birth mother than anybody ever expected." Branwyn gave her an irritated look she knew all too well, and she added, "Seriously. If my mother hadn't been..." she lowered her voice, because it was still hard to say the words to Branwyn, "an angel or something, I wouldn't..." she considered. "Okay, I'd probably have lost the kids the other day when the lawyer showed up to take them. And they'd be done with me."

"Or you wouldn't have been involved at all. Let's ask Zachariah, shall we?" said Corbin sharply.

"I cannot release him from his cell as I did Branwyn," said Tarn. "I am compelled to hold him prisoner." And he looked at Marley with an odd expression on his face.

"Am I failing to play into your Magnificent Bastard plan again?" she asked. Without waiting for an answer, she went on. "But he can have guests, I imagine. I don't see Ettoriel specifying 'no guests.' He's a guy with bigger things on his mind."

"Ettorial might have asked me to kill Zachariah," replied Tarn, "But he didn't want to explore the limits to the Covenant. Yes, he can have visitors. Release me and I will shape you a passage."

Marley thought about snapping *Say please!* but she resisted. As she pulled the shield into herself, dizziness rushed over her. She swayed. But she was *fine!*

Branwyn caught her arm and Corbin was at her side in a moment. "I'm all right," she said impatiently. She stepped away and stumbled. They both caught her this time. She stared down at her hands and then said, "Corbin? Is there anything you can do to help me? Hold off this curse for me? Put together some kind of stimulant spell? Get rid of some of these bruises?"

He hesitated and then said, "I think so. After my friends and I were attacked and I had to bring them back to safety, I kept them alive by linking their health to mine. I can tweak that enchantment so that you can use my energy to do what you need to."

Branwyn gave Corbin a long look up and down. "Because you look so much better off than she does right now. Why don't you link *my* health to hers instead? All I've been doing this whole time is holding Penny's hand."

Corbin started to argue, but Marley said, "Yeah. That's the right thing to do." It was, at least, the only way she had of making things up to Branwyn; if Branwyn wanted to help, she'd let her this time.

Corbin's eyes narrowed. "It'll take longer to set it up on her."

"Work on it while I talk to Zachariah," suggested Marley, which, from his expression, was exactly what Corbin didn't want her to say. She pulled herself away from the two of them and carefully walked toward Tarn.

Behind her, Branwyn said, "So. Curses? Spells? Will there be chanting?"

But Tarn also had something to say. As she passed by him, he murmured, "You realize, of course, that I still can't let you leave my realm. It's one thing to pass here and there within it, and quite another to return to being a thorn in Ettoriel's side."

She glanced at him. "And yet Corbin got in without your permission."

"Do you really believe that?" And he smiled and waved her on.

The passage leading to Zachariah was the hall of an old-fashioned dungeon. At the far end, it opened up into something straight from Hollywood, with a high ceiling, rounded windows, and piles of straw heaped on the floor. There were manacles on the wall and chains welded to staples in the stonework. In one corner, a rough table was set up on a barrel, and two crates served as seats. A chess board was on the table, the pieces carved roughly from bits of wood and stone. There was a game in progress.

Zachariah sat on one of the crates, looking like an actor who had forgotten to go by makeup before getting on set. His black hair was clean and well-groomed, and his face had been recently shaved. He was inspecting the manacle around one ankle. "I suppose I should be glad that I'm not chained to the wall by all four limbs," he said at the sound of Marley's footsteps. But when he glanced up, his eyes narrowed.

"Marley. Where are the girls?"

No surprise, no pleasure, no worry, just the cold question. Marley was reminded all of Corbin's accusations of manipulation. A dozen replies flitted through Marley's head, mostly sarcastic and angry: *I thought they were with you! Girls? Which girls? I gave them to the nice lawyer who said he knew you.*

But what she actually said was, "Where do you think? How did you think I'd protect them?"

Zachariah stared at her, his eyes dark, with barely a reaction. At last he said, "I understand the stage dressing now. Tarn's sense of humor. You're a smart girl, Marley. I was sure you'd come up with something."

"A smart girl with undiscovered talents, eh?" He inclined his head, and something occurred to Marley. "Do you know who my biological parents were? You must, if you're aware of the... nature of my undiscovered talents. Damn you," she finished bitterly.

Zachariah hesitated. "I don't know either of your parents."

"But you knew about me. About... what I could do. What I was. You set me up to protect the kids if something happened to you. You *used* me."

"My original information came from another source." He sat very still, looking at her face. He was just as handsome as ever, although so much had happened to change her perspective now. Tarn's eyes laughed more than his son's ever had.

"And that's why we met? Did you track me down, find me at the park that day, send Lissa and Kari over to me like... like puppies?" Her voice cracked. She couldn't think of the twins themselves right now. She could barely stand to look at Zachariah, he was so calm. Didn't he care about the girls, or were they also part of some bigger plan of his?

"Does it matter now, how and why we met? Now that we are here and they are elsewhere?"

"If you'd talked to me, treated me like a person instead of a... a chess piece... maybe we'd *all* be someplace else right now," Marley snapped.

Suddenly he was standing up and as close to her as the chain, stretched taut, would allow. "You really think so? Because I think that if you'd discovered the truth of your heritage without a reason to ground you, to force you to accept it, you would have run away. I've watched you closely for a long time, Miss Claviger. Anything close to the topic of your birth mother is a wind that inspires storms within you."

Marley flushed. "You're wrong. I wouldn't have run. I wouldn't have abandoned the people who needed me like she did."

Zachariah's eyes were cool. "We are all abandoned children, Miss Claviger. It's lovely to hear about how wrong I was, and if we develop time travel, perhaps you'll have a chance to prove it to me. Meanwhile, here we are. If all you wanted was to blame me, you can now go away."

Marley stared at him and then burst out, "I was worried, *terrified* for you!"

Zachariah looked taken aback. Then, gently, he said, "Tarn has been no more unkind than he was compelled to be. But thank you."

"He's your *father*," said Marley, ignoring the tears that pricked at her eyes.

"That may be why I'm still alive. They can be so very sentimental." He sighed. "Although more likely, he just wanted to resist Ettoriel in some petty way."

"What is going on with him?" Marley demanded. Her anger at Zachariah had earned her nothing but discomfort and confusion, so she refocused on their mutual kidnapper.

"He's so... strange. He says he's no more free than you are, but he's playing at something."

"Tarn does not yet believe all hope is lost, regarding the girls. Ettoriel hasn't yet completed the ritual to disconnect them from Creation."

"How can you possibly know that?"

"He promised me he'd let me know when it was over, and he hasn't done that yet." Zachariah's face was expressionless. "Am I wrong?"

Hope uncurled a leaf in the ruins of angry despair. "No. I can still feel their lives. If I could get out of here and to them, I could protect them again. Ettoriel worked hard to get rid of me—there has to be a reason for that. I'm sure I could stop him."

Zachariah studied her, his gaze roaming from the top of her head down to her feet. "You've met Corbin, I see. I'm glad he's still alive, and helping you."

Confused by the sudden change of topic, Marley said, "He's very angry at you."

Zachariah shrugged, still examining her. "But you've encountered others as well. You're loaded down with the enchantments of interested parties. If you could get to the girls, how would you protect yourself?"

Marley drew herself up painfully.

"I've been doing all right. I was standing right in front of him and he didn't kill me. I don't think he likes getting his hands dirty."

"His hands are very dirty, by now," said Zachariah gently.

"The kids, then. He thinks they're a bomb and he thought hurting me would set them off before he was ready to... end them." She followed the train of thought to its end. "And if he is ready to finish, that isn't protection anymore." She blew out her breath. "Can you do anything?"

He held up his chained foot. "I'm trapped here until Tarn

lets me go."

"Were you tricked?" she asked, broodingly, staring at the manacle.

He hesitated and then admitted, "I was... surprised. I didn't know exactly what Ettoriel had planned, but I knew there would be something."

"Did you have a diary written by their mother?"

"A what?" He looked honestly confused for the first time.

"A diary. I found part of a diary in your study. I think it was written by the twins' mother."

"I did not." His brows drew together and he looked at the door behind Marley.

Marley nodded. "I didn't think so. Her name was Nina, yes?" He nodded and she continued, "Did you know she knew Ettoriel?"

"No. Did the diary claim she did?"

She nodded again. "Did she ever say who the father of her children was?"

A troubled expression passed over his face. "No. Do you think...?"

Marley shrugged. "The diary is unclear." She watched him carefully. "No chance you're their father yourself?"

He grimaced. "She came to me already pregnant, to ask for help I'd promised her when she was younger. But I always saw her as a child. We never had that kind of relationship." He hesitated. "She never talked about their father, but... she didn't die, Marley. She was taken from the hospital after a difficult delivery, and I saw who took her."

Marley's pulse quickened. "Who was it?"

"Not Ettoriel," said Zachariah flatly.

Marley waited until she realized Zachariah wasn't going to willingly say more. "And you think this... kidnapper was the father?"

Zachariah shrugged. "I think he... cared for her. He didn't

say anything about the children, though."

"That's not really conclusive either way," she pointed out.

He spread his hands. "Do *you* think Ettoriel is their father? Does it matter?"

Marley's gaze dropped to the manacle on Zachariah's foot. "I think I need an edge. And that could be it." Her gaze went up to Zachariah's face again. "It isn't just you and me and Corbin involved in this, Zachariah. Not just the people you decided to involve. A girl called AT was dreadfully hurt, and Tarn kidnapped my friend Branwyn, and my friend Penny—" Her voice broke.

Zachariah's face closed up. "I know." That was all. He knew. And apparently, he didn't care.

Marley stared at him, and then turned and walked through the open door, slamming it behind her.

-thirty-five-

Marley walked down the hall and paused next to Tarn. The vision of him imprisoned within the iron maiden of her will was still dominant in her catastrophe vision, and savagely, she slammed it back over him. "You left the diary at Zachariah's house. Is it real?"

Tarn grimaced. "Yes, and hard won."

Marley stalked away from him to where Corbin and Branwyn were consulting. Corbin stepped over to her. The magic that had drenched him when he first arrived in the realm had utterly vanished. "I have the modified spell ready. Did you punch Zachariah in the nose?"

"No. He was chained up. It didn't seem sporting. And it would have been embarrassing to miss and fall over. How do we do this?"

He put his hand on her head. Coolness flooded over her, like diving into a pool on a hot day. She was still tired, still bruised and bloodied, but it felt as if her reserves were deeper, and barely tapped.

Branwyn shivered, without looking up from what she was doing. "Ooh, that feels ticklish. Kind of fun. Like champagne." She'd dumped the contents of Marley's purse out all over the floor, and discovered the Lullaby Plaything. It was no longer a compressed lump of parts, but a barely linked chain of rods and cubes that flowed over Branwyn's fingers.

"What is going on?" Marley demanded. "I thought that thing only responded to nephilim?"

"There was nothing in the documentation about humans one way or the other. We're experimenting. So what did Zachariah have to say for himself?" asked Corbin, his eyes intent on the little Machine in Branwyn's hands. Branwyn was just as focused, with that tiny line on her brow that showed up whenever she was concentrating hard on her artwork.

"Not enough. He set me up to inherit his mess if something unexpected happened. He didn't expect Tarn." Marley shrugged.

Lightly, Branwyn said, "No one expects the faerie inquisition."

Corbin ignored Branwyn. "Did he have anything to say about Ettoriel's reasons for all this?"

"I didn't ask him," said Marley. "Ettoriel's reasons don't matter. And if you think they do...." She flailed wildly for an argument he'd understand. "You're just like Zachariah, not caring about how he got your friends into trouble for his own goals."

"Oh, thank you very much. Except whether this is about the Hush or the Machine prophecy, this is a lot bigger than a couple of people."

"No, it's not. It's about only two people and their combined age is under ten years old. It's about saving who we can save," and once again, her voice broke.

Corbin looked hunted. "I know. I just—" and he cut himself off. "I wish the kaiju wasn't so interested in them. It makes me nervous."

Marley took a deep, shaking breath. *He just wants reassur-*

ance. "I think it's one of those self-fulfilling prophecies. You know how it is. The bad guy tries to prevent something from happening and in doing so causes it. Ettoriel is really afraid of them. Something will go wrong at his little ritual, and that will make something horrible happen. Something will go wrong even if we're not there. But if we *are* there, if the girls aren't alone and forced to protect themselves, we can change things." She stared into Corbin's eyes earnestly, projecting as much confidence as she could.

Corbin sighed. "Good enough." His gaze strayed back to what Branwyn was doing and he frowned again. "That's really impressive. How are you doing that?"

Marley followed his gaze. The Lullaby Plaything had... changed. The cubes had flattened, the spheres had elongated and hollowed out, and the rod structure had stretched into a pyramidal shape. And the catastrophe vision, which had once shown it as something harmless and benevolent, now showed it as decidedly dangerous.

"You said it responded to a person's nature. I'm just being me," said Branwyn, and her grin was nasty. She reached over and picked up the black and silver rod she'd attacked Corbin with, sliding it into the ring at the base of the pyramid. The ring spun at her touch, tightening. She let go of the Lullaby Plaything, and suddenly she was holding a spear with a wicked, glinting three-edged head.

"What a perversion!" said Tarn. He sounded admiring. "A celestial Machine warped to weaponize a human creation. What a lovely toy for you, Marley."

This time, Branwyn's grin was pleased. She brushed damp hair off her forehead and twirled the spear in one hand before presenting it to Marley. "I hear you've been getting into some fights."

Hesitantly, Marley accepted it. The spear was heavier than it looked, seemingly as capable of bludgeoning someone as stabbing them.

Corbin chewed on his thumbnail. "That's just wrong." He looked like someone whose beloved dog had just bitten him.

Branwyn tossed her head and said disdainfully, "It's not *for* you."

"Will it work as a weapon?" Marley asked.

Corbin said, "A celestial's most potent weapon against another celestial is a blade made from a Machine, so... I suppose it would. As a threat, anyhow."

"We could test it," said Branwyn brightly. "Are faeries celestials?"

Everybody's gaze went to Tarn. He stood there, grinning painfully, a sheen of sweat on his skin. He said, "I'd rather not even be near that thing, if I get a vote."

"He did say he couldn't let us out," said Marley dubiously. "And that a faerie duke kept his realm stable."

"Do you know why Machine weapons hurt us?" said Tarn, a little less relaxed than before. A little. "Machines absorb those celestials who study them. Weaponized Machines *eat* us. If you tested it on me, I'd become a part of the weapon and who knows how that would change it?"

Marley said, "We could find out," but she was thinking about the twins, trying to determine their danger state. Bad. It was very bad.

But she could still save them. It had to be possible, or she *would* test the Lullaby spear on the faerie duke. Hysteria, or perhaps madness, gnawed at the edges of her mind. "You manipulated me to get me here, to try to make me *sympathetic*," she spat at Tarn. "How did you *expect* me to get out?"

"The little dog girl was a handy companion for you," Tarn said. "Otherwise... you're clever."

Corbin looked up. "If he expected AT to be able to transition, the curtain must not be totally impermeable."

Marley said, "I wonder if the kaiju could open it. Do you

think he'd hear me if I called, like he heard AT?"

Corbin growled, "Please don't. If not for your own sake, then for Branwyn's."

"What?" said Branwyn, from where she'd been picking up the contents of Marley's bag, assisted, to her bemusement, by two of Corbin's ravens. "Don't you dare suggest I'm some kind of victim damsel to be sheltered."

Marley dizzily imagined the kaiju and Branwyn. The kaiju, Branwyn, Corbin, and Tarn. Bring in Zachariah and she was pretty sure a hole big enough to escape through would be blown right through the world.

That reminded her. She looked around. Neath, still the size of an adolescent lynx, sat nearby, beside the still-shut cage she'd been imprisoned in. The cat was watching her intently, her tail twitching.

"What about the holes the girls made? What about Neath? What about your magic, Corbin?"

"I'm working on it," he said. "Your cat was able to get me in to help you. She doesn't seem to be as... involved anymore."

"I think I surprised her." Marley looked at the cat again and then crossed to Tarn's side. With a flick of her mind, she pulled the inside-out shield off him.

He looked at her, his eyes narrowing, and moved a few steps back, out of reach of the Lullaby spear that she still carried. "If you don't mind... I'd rather be back inside your embrace."

"No, let's talk instead." said Marley, squirming inside at his terminology. "You said something about my cat."

He glanced at Neath, who stretched out on the floor as if considering a nap. "That so-called cat is the independent construct of an angel."

"And what does that mean?"

"A construct is a physical body created by a celestial for interacting with the mortal world in mortal ways. When you saw Ettoriel, you saw his construct. This," he spread his arms, "is a construct. Most of the time, constructs are created purely as hosts for our numina, and channels for our spirit bodies. Such basic constructs must be inhabited to be more than a mindless automaton. With more time and effort, constructs with more independence can be built. "

"How does—" began Marley. But she stopped as a squeak became a creak became a groan. Everything seemed to freeze around her. Her point of view went flying through the air, through a white-burned hole in the curtain. The white became a tunnel that twisted around her like a roller coaster. Then she was looking out of Kari and Lissa's eyes, both at the same time. They were in a bubble of clear air maintained at the midst of a wildfire. At the heart of the bubble was Ettoriel, with wings of light spreading from his back and the strange Ragged Blade in his hands. An iron chain wrapped around one arm. To one side was Penny, and to the other side was the lawyer, Jeremy. Penny was staring at Ettoriel, her eyes huge and dilated.

There was a metal wheel on the ground between Ettoriel and Marley's point of view. And around the core group there seemed to be other figures, ones she couldn't quite make out. *Celestials without constructs?* she wondered, dazed.

"It begins," said Ettoriel, and he sounded sad.

Marley's vision exploded, and she rushed back to her own body. She was on her hands and knees, staring at the old carpet and Tarn's boots. The faerie duke's hand came down and pulled her upright by her arm. He was pale. "It begins," he echoed. "Your friend is too slow."

Marley surged toward Corbin. "Do it! Open it now!"

Corbin looked at her, grinning. Two of his ravens pecked at strands of the carpet, tugging. Whiteness opened as they hopped backwards and Corbin plunged his hand into it. Around his hand, the whiteness became transparent, and then, in the floor, was a hole leading to Penny's living room.

Marley stared at it in horror, remembering the dome of fire and the blazing mountains beyond. "That's not where they are! We can't go there. They're in the heart of some wild-fire up on the mountains!"

Corbin stared at her, his cheer fading. Then he start-ed to mutter under his breath about working unappreciated miracles.

Marley didn't have time to listen. She had to get to them! They were still alive, still whole, but—

"Severin," she screamed. "Kaiju!" Her voice bounced around the Velvet Court as if the walls weren't covered in hangings. Everybody, even Tarn, stared at her, frozen.

But the kaiju didn't appear, and no door opened.

Corbin's left eye began to glow with a black radiance, as it had when he'd showed up in the Velvet Court to rescue her. He stared down at his fingers. Then he spoke. His voice was deeper, rougher, a growl. "Whispering Dark..." The words seemed to linger.

Then the kaiju stepped through the hole in the floor that Corbin had made, pivoting upright as he did. "Such a nice invitation, and from *you*, raven boy—how could I ignore it?"

Marley moved toward him, seizing his attention. "Can you open a gate to where Ettoriel and the girls are? Or other-wise take us there? Now?"

The kaiju's mild gaze swept the room. "Now would be a good time to do that," he agreed. "There will be a price later."

"Get in line," snapped Marley.

The kaiju smiled faintly, although his smile vanished when his gaze moved over Tarn. He spoke softly, but Marley couldn't understand the words. The speech went on and on, sentences flowing over one another.

Tarn said, "*Must* we fight, creature? No, we mustn't. Do what you came to do, and don't try me."

The kaiju looked disdainful. Then he said, in a voice that ate away at Marley's mind, scratching against her consciousness like fingernails on a chalkboard, "*Now.*"

And they were elsewhere.

-thirty-six-

Two little girls lay on a giant bronze gear, side by side. They were bound to both the wheel and each other, by their arms and legs. An angel crouched over them, wings of golden light spreading over him and cupping the ground. The angel held a dagger in his hand—the Ragged Blade—and it was sweeping down to their joined arms.

The girls were paralyzed, staring at the blade with terrified eyes, unable to even cry out. But Marley could hear them all the same, hear them screaming inside for her, for Zachariah. For the mother they had never known.

They *wanted* to be protected. That was part of what made them children.

The Ragged Blade sliced down, and missed, skidding on the burnished surface of the giant gear. The great wings prevented the angel from overbalancing, but was there surprise on that handsome face? If so, it was only for an instant, and replaced quickly by disgust. He stood up, the iron chain uncoiling from his wrist. "Tarn, rectify your failure."

Marley realized she was lying on the ground, amidst

scorched vegetation just inside the fire-free bubble, exactly where the kaiju's transportation had dropped her. Maybe ten seconds had passed since the kaiju had spoken in that voice like acid. But now she was protecting the children again. Now, everything was different.

Now she'd put herself squarely in Ettoriel's way again, and now he had no time to spare. Instinctively, she rolled to one side, feeling for her spear. She'd had it when they transitioned. She scrambled to her feet, looking around wildly.

"Move fast," said the kaiju. But everybody except him seemed to be moving already. Tarn flowed toward her, and if he didn't want to obey the angel, she could hardly tell. A rapier had appeared in his hand and he thrust it at her even as he twisted around to snatch at her as she dodged away. His reach was enormous. She tripped over something and the light changed from golden to fiery. She could feel the heat on the back of her neck, hear the snap of the fire.

Out of the frying pan... She felt around for what she tripped over. Was it a weapon? Her spear? A pointy stick? A rock. A rock embedded deep in the earth. It was so hot it burned her fingers as she scrabbled at it, and she rolled back toward the golden radiance of Ettoriel's wings. The angel was still standing over the girls, ready to strike as soon as Tarn removed the obstacle.

Tarn's fingers caught the back of her shirt. She wriggled, kicking, and it tore away. Then Branwyn said, "Stop." Marley realized her shirt had been cut, and scrambled away.

"Put away the sword," continued Branwyn. She was standing to the left of Tarn, pointing Lullaby at his throat.

"Kill her," said Ettoriel, his golden voice harsh.

Tarn grimaced and moved, turning his sword from Marley to Branwyn. Branwyn didn't even try to dodge, turning a thrust with Lullaby into a stroke that followed Tarn's twisting dodge.

The Machine spearhead stroked the faerie duke's shoulder as lightly as a feather before sliding down across his chest. Where it touched, white fire gushed.

Tarn stumbled, his weapon vanishing. He raised his head, his teeth bared, and his eyes were white fire as well. His uninjured hand came up and the fires around the dome flared, then shrank back as crimson light gathered around his hand.

Neath the bobcat leapt toward his back, all four sets of claws out like she was going to ride him. But instead she passed right through him, as though she—or he—was a ghost. He stiffened, the white fire vanishing from his eyes.

Neath landed, her tail twitching, and in between her claws she held the pixie form of Tarn. Tarn stared at her. "I hate your cat," he muttered, and twitched as the cat placed one paw on the chest of the pixie, her claws pressing into the tiny figure's torso. She gave the man form of Tarn a meaningful look.

Then Branwyn kicked him in the side of the leg, and he fell over. She kicked him again, then knelt on his chest. The crimson light in his hand ran up his arm and started crawling inside his body at the white rents left in his flesh by Lullaby.

"Marley," shouted Corbin, and she jumped as there was a thump behind her, moving just as the Ragged Blade whistled past her. Her scalp felt bare where the long dagger had brushed it. Her fingers closed around Lullaby's haft as Branwyn pushed it into her hand, and she brought it up in time for Ettoriel's second strike. A third strike at her legs, she barely stopped with the Lullaby's Machine point, the clash of the Ragged Blade against the spear making her hands ache awfully.

The ringing from the strike grew louder instead of fading. As Marley retreated, trying to get enough space between herself and Ettoriel that she could think about what she was doing, Lullaby began to sing. Its voice was similar to a glass harmonica, each note sweet and shimmering. Marley could feel them through the haft.

Ettoriel leapt back, his wings assisting his retreat. He stared warily at Marley's weapon, and Marley tried to hold it like she knew what she was doing. Then his eyes flickered to the side, where Branwyn still sat on Tarn.

"You can try killing me, but I might end up killing you instead," Marley called.

"It's only fair," he murmured, and shook out his wings. He stood perfectly still as he looked at her. "I always thought the nephilim were a tragedy, but I never thought they were actually evil. Until now."

Marley blinked and shouted, "Which one of us is trying to murder children?"

Something heavy and bright knocked into her, throwing her off her feet. In her blink, Ettoriel had leapt over to her, his ethereal-looking wings slamming into her.

Her shoulder hit the ground hard. She used the momentum to roll, scrambling back to her feet and thrusting wildly with Lullaby. The crooning of the Machine rose to a scream and she realized she had some space again.

If only I had functional precognition instead of the stupid catastrophe vision. It's ridiculous, she thought dizzily.

But Corbin was beside the girls at the giant gear. The rope that bound their arms and feet fell away at his touch. He scowled down at the paralysis still gripping the children.

"Jeremy!" cried Ettoriel. Jeremy stepped beside Corbin and yanked him off balance.

Marley dragged her gaze back to Ettoriel, resisting the desire to turn her head and check on Branwyn. She couldn't take care of everybody, and to take care of *anybody* right now, she had to concentrate on herself. On her enemy. On the angel trying to kill her. She had to take care of herself.

She narrowed her eyes and dodged randomly to one side.

He raised the hand with the chain, and something white-hot sizzled the air where she'd been standing. *Was that just lightning?*

Ettoriel's face twisted and he closed with her again, slashing with his blade. She bent sideways to avoid it and poked Lullaby at him as she recovered her balance.

This time, to her surprise, the spear caught his arm, leaving behind a burning white line that faded, bright red blood welling from the wound.

Unlike Tarn, Ettoriel didn't seem to be crippled by the touch of the weapon. He didn't even seem to notice. Furious at this failure of her expectations, Marley stabbed at him again, this time sinking the Machine spearhead into his chest. She didn't get it very far in before his hand closed over the haft of the weapon. He yanked it out of her hands and out of him, tossing it to one side. Then he grabbed her hair and pulled her off her feet, bringing his dagger back for a final cut.

A child screamed. The fires, damped down by whatever Tarn had done, roared skyward, and the ground underfoot trembled. Despite the golden glow of the shield around the ritual area, the air sizzled with heat.

The shaking of the ground increased. Marley threw herself to one side, wrenching herself out of Ettoriel's grip and leaving behind a hunk of her hair. She scrambled along the heaving ground toward Lullaby, as Ettoriel cried, "No!"

And a child's voice echoed him. "No!"

Marley looked up as her fingers closed over the spear. Lissa and Kari were both on their feet, beside the bronze gear. A creature made of fire loomed over them, and as Lissa stared angrily at Ettoriel, Kari started tearing the fire creature to cinders.

Marley could feel power beating against the shields she had around the children. The conflict between their desire to lash out and their desire to hide and wait for it to be all over was growing.

"No, Liss," wept Kari. "We're bad. No." Each word rang against Marley's skin.

For a split second, Marley met Lissa's eyes, and she felt the girl's words as much as heard them. "Yes. We are."

"No!" Marley screamed, almost before Lissa had finished speaking, and flung herself back at Ettoriel. "Don't you see what you're doing to them? They were just little girls!"

She slashed at him again and again, and he stumbled backward. Each shallow cut glowed silver before trickling red. Something was wrong. Had stabbing Tarn actually changed the weapon as he'd implied it might? Or was Ettoriel resistant? She paused, panting, and noticed the red smeared all over her own arms. She'd been injured herself, and yet she barely felt it. Branwyn's reservoir of strength sustained her through the connection Corbin had forged.

She remembered that Ettoriel had also forged a connection with one of her friends. Her gaze found Penny. The other young woman was kneeling down, arms crossed tightly over her chest, her head bowed. She was glowing softly. Marley could see each of her chakra nodes, dim and empty. There was a bright shape nestled within her, like Penny's form was projected onto a backlit screen. White rents tore across her form, as if the film projecting her was damaged. White rents that corresponded to the bloody wounds on Ettoriel's body.

"You bastard," she whispered, her spear dipping.

If he'd smiled at her then, calm and superior, it might have reawakened her rage. But he only sighed, like she was a misbehaving child. "You see. If you defend yourself, you destroy your friend. And she is weak. If you hesitate or resist too long, what little remains of her soul will burn just like these mountains. Let me save the world."

"I can't stand by and let you murder them," she whispered. Grief like she'd never imagined swelled within her.

He stepped closer and considered her. "I respect that. I will end you, and then them, and I will keep your friends safe." Almost apologetically, he said, "It's the best way. The only way."

Behind Ettoriel, Corbin kicked Jeremy and crawled over to Penny. He put his hand to his eyes and then pushed his hand against her forehead, just as he had once done to Marley. Penny's top node filled with light. Her head lifted, her eyes widening. She looked at her hands and screamed, high and shrill. Scrambling to her feet, she looked around wildly, dodging randomly. She saw the fire. Ettoriel. The little girls.

Corbin grabbed her arm and said something to her roughly. He shook her, pulled her to one side and turned her so she could see Marley. Ettoriel looked over his shoulder, frowning.

Corbin pulled back his hand as if to hit Penny. And Penny gasped, "Marley, Marley. I don't know what's going on. Please help me."

Marley's soul, stretched as tight as a violin string, sang. Without consciously thinking, she wrapped Penny in *safety*. She was safe, safe from Corbin's hand, safe from Jeremy rising up behind her, safe from Ettoriel's light

dreadfully injured reported the shield but *safe* for now *safe*.

Marley felt thin, just as she had when she'd failed to protect AT, but she didn't care. Penny didn't want what was happening to her, Penny had asked for her help, Penny could be saved. How could Ettoriel stop them? Her friends looked after her and she looked after them, and together they were unstoppable. Joy and defiance exploded out of her, and she screamed wordlessly at the angel.

He spared her only a look and then raised his hands, the Ragged Blade and the iron chain both glinting. He touched the two of them together and once again the air cooled rapidly, as if something was sucking up the energy of the fires.

The audience of ghostly figures watching from the outskirts of the dome of golden light seemed to press in, a ripple going through them that ended with a shape spinning into the dome, made of straight lines and gentle curves, and enclosed by a pair of slowly moving rings. It was the Machine that she had seen once before, the one that Corbin had sought answers from. It hovered, flat side down, over Lissa and Kari, and began to exert a *pressure*.

Marley could feel it through the shield. It wasn't a physical pressure. It was bringing power to bear, not something actively destructive, but something scattered and chaotic. It bombarded her already-weakened shield with noise, confusing her instinctive awareness of threats and safety. She concentrated, trying to maintain her conscious sense of what was a threat and what was not. The Machine was a distraction, not a threat. Ettoriel, blade out, was a threat. Another Machine wheel, identical to the first, settled over his head, and he stepped toward the children.

Her shield faltered.

She wasn't sure if anybody noticed. Could Ettoriel detect the shield before he tried to actually hurt them?

The ground shook again, and a crack opened between Ettoriel and the twins. They'd stopped arguing and were holding hands again, both of them staring angrily at Ettoriel. "You go away," said Lissa. "We're bad. We'll be even more bad."

And Kari said, "I don't like your hat." She pointed at the Machine spinning over Ettoriel's head, and the rings stopped. The ripple from the ghostly onlookers was an audible gasp of horror.

Ettoriel sighed, and closed his wings. The golden dome of light vanished with a whoosh. Red-orange light briefly took its place before white smoke replaced everything with a haze. It invaded Marley's nose but seemed to get stuck at her throat, leaving her easily breathing tainted air. Penny was *safe.* Safe enough. Even flickering, the shield filtered out the worst toxins, the killing heat. But Branwyn started coughing immediately.

Marley looked around wildly as the coughing became choking, and then stopped entirely. She saw Tarn standing, holding Branwyn in his arms, his face bent toward hers.

"You *are* bad," agreed Ettoriel quietly. He was still standing between Marley and the twins, the Ragged Blade at his side. "It's not your fault, though. I can make it all better, if you let me."

Kari muttered, "I don't want to be bad."

Marley advanced on him with her spear up. His back was to her. The Machine over his head was turning only fitfully, like a fan with a dying motor. She could just stab him in the back, and it would all be over.

No. Her shield would not hold, not as thin as she'd spread it, not as damaged as it was by the Machine. It could keep out smoke, but Lullaby destroying Ettoriel was still a threat to Penny. She could see it.

But Tarn had thought there was another way. He'd mentioned a weapon, back when he was Tinker Chime.

"Of course you don't," said Ettoriel to the children, and his voice was as cool and smooth as silk. "Somebody made a mistake, and you've had to suffer for it."

Ah, yes. The faerie *had* provided her with a weapon long before Branwyn and Corbin had, a weapon far more personal and just as dangerous. The spear fell from her hand, Lullaby's song trailing away. *Somebody made a mistake.* "Was it you?" she asked quietly. "Their mother loved you."

Ettoriel froze. She walked around him, so she could look him in the eye. "Her name was Nina. She called you Cat. Did you forget already? Or is this whole thing really about you? About erasing your own mistakes? About forgetting that once you loved someone?"

"It was a trick," he breathed.

"I don't know about that, but I know she really loved you. She would have done anything for you." Marley considered him clinically, then lowered her voice again as she stepped closer. "Did you kill her, too? Was that also to save the world?"

"No!" he said. His eyes, when they found hers, were anguished. "I don't know where she is."

"But you've looked," she said gently. "Are they yours?"

"No!" he said quickly, looking down.

Marley didn't smile, though she wanted to bare her teeth. "You're not sure. Losing your name confused you." He gave her a worried look, his beautiful face twisted up. She continued, her voice just as calm and smooth as his had been. "You don't know. And now you want to kill her children. Not because you want to save the world, but because you can't bear the thought of their existence. And look at what you've brought to bear on such a personal crusade."

"This is bigger than me," he said, and waved vaguely with his dagger, indicating nothing in particular.

"No, it isn't," she said sharply. "It is *only* about you, and the children who could have been yours. The shame and love that *is* yours."

He shook his head. "It doesn't matter." He half-turned toward the twins again.

"Doesn't it? Let's test that," said Marley, lightly, idly. *How long did a valence event last?* "Look at those tiny children. Perhaps they're yours, the result of a world-shaking crime. Maybe it was your crime, your love that brought these children into the world."

Shakily, he said, "Then I should fix it."

"But the real crime's in you," she said brightly. "There's always suicide, but I'm sure that's a crime, too. Let's table that for now. Look at those tiny children. Perhaps they're somebody else's. Maybe she found what you wouldn't give her in somebody else's arms. Maybe after you abandoned her, she was driven to find a replacement. Or maybe she found somebody better."

He squeezed his eyes shut, his entire body rigid.

"We're not done," she said, her voice cutting like a knife. "Look at those tiny children." As if beyond his will, his eyes flickered open again, though he remained coiled like a spring. "Look at them. Look at their faces. Don't they look like her?" She was gambling on his own heart filling in details she knew nothing about. "Can you really kill her children, all that may be left of her, no matter who their father may be? Can you stand a world without Nina?"

She paused, and he said nothing, his eyes fixed on the little girls. "I think," she said finally, "that everything you're trying to stop will occur because you're trying to stop it. That's usually how prophecies seem to work. You're a lot older than me. Maybe you know that, too. Maybe you even want that. I don't know." She stared at his broken face, and felt pity finally stir in her heart. "I really don't know," she repeated.

The fire crackled around them. Her hair was singeing.

At last Ettoriel raised a hand to touch the wheel of light over his head. "I can't—" and his voice cracked. "I can't do this anymore. I'm sorry. I fell from my grace years ago."

Marley's initial burst of elation was cut short as the world suddenly went wrong. *The wrongness was everywhere. The fires were out of focus. The rings of light were the extrusions of some great Machine that arched over them and climbed into the sky. The watching figures complained bitterly.*

Ettoriel's curse, weakened and deprived of tools by Ettoriel's own fire shield, finally found a channel and struck one final time. Her Geometric Sight fully activated, showing her the lines of light twisting around her in a vortex. Something struck her like a hammer. The Sight went out. All her shields vanished.

She crumpled to the ground, staring without understanding; angry words emerged from the roaring of the fire as the ring of watching figures grew larger. **The HUSH. Focus on the HUSH break the HUSH everything can be done but for the HUSH ETTORIEL THE HUSH free us use them there's still time DO IT NOW redeem yourself.**

But the Machine wheel over the heads of the girls lifted and merged with the one over Ettoriel's head, turning onto its edge and growing larger. It drifted down so it was level with Ettoriel's face. "My friend," he whispered, touching it again. "Help me understand."

ETTORIEL screamed the watchers. The sky yawned open and a lightning bolt as thick as Marley's waist struck Ettoriel. For a split second, his entire body was nothing but plasma. Then he and the lightning bolt were gone. The chain he'd been holding, along with the Ragged Blade, dropped to the ground.

Some of the Machine wheel's symbols changed color, and then it vanished as well.

The restless, angry observers remained. Crimson light began to gather in the center of the circle.

Corbin threw himself down beside Marley, putting one arm over her. "You'll be okay," he muttered.

"What about everybody else?" she mumbled. "What about Penny and the girls? What about..." She trailed off. The crimson light was condensing, becoming a humanoid shape with wings. She couldn't remember what she was saying. She was all out. Of energy. Of words. She'd done it all, but apparently all of Heaven was behind Ettoriel, and what could she do against that?

Out of the corner of her eye, Marley saw Severin the kaiju lift his head. His hands were still in his pockets, but a fierce smile stretched his face. "Are we breaking the Hush after all? Oh, please do." He stepped forward, and his footfall shook the ground like thunder. "We *have* suffered terribly under the Hush, haven't we. The angels and the monsters."

The crimson, winged entity paused, a half-manifested, misty form. The kaiju continued, "I would *so* enjoy getting more than a taste of each of you gathered here. A grand council of angels, all agreed! So you just get started with tearing down the Hush, and I'll finish with the spirit tethers." And he pulled his hands out of his pockets and opened them. In each palm was a handful of tiny, glittering balls of light.

The crimson figure fuzzed as the circle of observing entities recoiled away. A few of them vanished completely. Severin's fingers closed over the glittering orbs again. "Oh, come on. It's been so long. How can I eat you if you run away?"

"Good question," murmured Corbin in Marley's ear.

More of the glowing outlines vanished. The crimson figure collapsed into a shower of sparks. Severin paced over to the two remaining figures and leaned toward them, his hands back in his pockets. "Come on," he said again. "Let's do this. We can find out what happens if an angel dies during a valence event. Is their name erased from the Sea of Dreams? It's for science!"

One of the figures spoke, with a voice like an eagle's cry. "My brothers each worry they will be the one who falls before we erase you from the world, lost one. But I would have—"

The other figure interrupted, with a voice like an underwater song. "This has been an informative experiment already. We have much to discuss. Thank you for revealing yourself as part of the equation, lost one." Then it vanished, leaving a little swirl of ashes behind.

The final remaining figure flickered belligerently at Severin for a moment, then faded away. The kaiju snickered, and pulled his hands out of his pockets, shaking dissolving specks of light off them. Then he turned toward Marley on the ground. "Nice job with Ettoriel, sweetheart. I'd never have thought your mother was an angel, with you talking dirty like that."

Marley gagged and threw up on Corbin's arm. Corbin said, "That's okay. I'm okay with that," and raised his voice. "Can anyone do anything about the fire? Before it burns us or I'm forced to do something drastic?"

"Faerie magic, that is," said Severin cheerfully.

Everybody turned to look at Tarn. He'd left Branwyn sitting on the ground next to a huddled Penny as he walked over to where Ettoriel had vanished. Slowly, he bent down and picked up the iron chain from the ground. His hands blistered instantly, but he stared down at it wonderingly. He muttered, "Break the chain."

Marley sat up and wiped her mouth, prickles running down her spine. "Should we...?" she began uncertainly.

"Yeah," said Corbin, heaving himself to his feet.

Tarn carried the chain over to Lissa and Kari, who still clutched each other's hands. He knelt down before them. "I'm so sorry I took your guardian, little ones. It was this chain that compelled me. This chain forced me to do it. And it could be used that way again."

"No," said Kari flatly. "It couldn't." And she touched the chain with her hand.

White light outlined each link. For a moment, everything was frozen. Then, each link in the chain burst, split cleanly into two, and a pile of iron shards fell to the ground at Tarn's feet. Tarn remained kneeling, his head bowed.

Corbin said, "Did she just...?"

Severin said, "Destroy something that it took dozens of celestials to craft? Oh yes! There's fun times ahead, kid. I'm pretty sure faeries one-third freed can cause a hell of a lot of chaos."

"I don't care," shouted Kari. "I want my uncle back! Now!"

The fires around them went out, and in the sudden, howling silence, Lissa said, "Nobody else was putting the fires out and it was hot. Was that bad, too?"

"I don't *care*!" began Kari again, but the world parted like a curtain beside them, and Zachariah stepped out, looking as though he'd just finished showering and dressing for a day at the office.

"You're good girls, both of you," he said, before they double-teamed him.

Tarn stood up, his head still bowed. Marley staggered toward him, and he turned. The smile on his face was as wide and frightening as Severin's grin had been before. "Finally," he breathed. "After millennia... finally." A shudder passed through him, and the faraway look faded from his face. "Thank you, Marley. You were useful in the end. Time for me to go, though. So many things to do! One chain down, two to go." He looked around until he spotted Branwyn, holding Penny's head in her lap. "Sweet, inventive Branwyn. I'll be seeing *you* later." Branwyn stuck out her tongue at him, he blew her a kiss, and then—he was gone.

Marley stared at where he was, still trying to process the last few minutes. She'd confronted Ettoriel with his feelings for the twins' mother. She hadn't stabbed him. If she'd stabbed him, sacrificed Penny, would Tarn still have been able to free himself? Did she really care right now if faeries had been loosed on the world again? What would they do? Maybe Zachariah would know. Zachariah...

"Marley!" cried Corbin, just as he had when she'd been fighting with Tarn, a lifetime ago when they'd arrived at the wildfire zone. It was *so* like a memory that she didn't even dodge as Lullaby's blade skidded up her back. Then the spear thudded to the ground and Severin whirled past her, holding Jeremy in his arms like he was spinning a dance partner.

Jeremy looked charred. Half his hair had been burned to the roots, and he was covered in ash and dirt. But his eyes were furious and feral. "I was going to be immortal," he hissed at Marley. "But you. You and your words... Your lies..." He struggled against Severin's grip.

Severin's face was alight. "Charming. I think I'll take this one. Don't argue; you owe me." He whispered something in Jeremy's ear, and Jeremy's struggles grew even wilder, his expression more enraged.

Exhausted, Marley said, "I won't. Take him away, please." Severin smirked at her, and stepped backward, vanishing behind a world-curtain with his prey.

Marley sat down in the dirt and ashes. It was over. She wanted to find out how Penny and Branwyn were doing, to talk to Zachariah about the twins, to talk to Corbin about the faeries and AT.... But, she thought, she could do that later. There was time. She lay back on the hot ground and looked at the sky, and waited for later.

-epilogue-

later

Marley stood at the bay window of the luxurious room in the private hospital she'd ended up in. She still wasn't quite sure how that had happened; many details were fuzzy in the hours immediately following the fight in the fire. She'd walked down the mountainside, but for how long? And she thought she remembered a giant-sized version of Neath... and there'd definitely been a helicopter. And then the hospital, and kind nurses who helped her bathe and dispensed the very nice painkiller that blew away all the aches that had shown up when Corbin lifted his support charm.

Now Neath slept on the foot of her bed. Penny was in the other bed. She wasn't waking up, but the doctors said she was stable and Marley could see they were right. It was enough, for now.

She turned back to the window and looked at the night.

The red lines still traced the progression of the fire on the mountains, but it was smaller now. The firefighters, and all the technology and determination they brought to bear, were finally winning.

Branwyn bumped the door open and came in with two paper cups of coffee. She handed one to Marley before going to check on Penny. After smoothing their friend's hair, she joined Marley at the bay window. "How are you feeling?"

"They gave me the good stuff, so a lot better than I probably should." Marley wrapped her fingers around the warm cup.

Branwyn gave her a keen-eyed look. "I didn't mean your aches and pains."

Marley sighed. "I know. I'm not the same as I was, you know? The thing behind the anxiety is *real*. It's not just me being... broken. Or if it is, it's something I inherited."

"You're more than what you inherited, though." Branwyn shrugged. "Obvious, but still true."

A little laugh bubbled out of Marley. "So I've heard. I've got to learn how to handle it. I can't just bury it again. But... I think I can."

Branwyn nodded, as if this was the answer she'd been expecting. Then she looked around the room. "So. All this really happened, eh? Wonder if it will help with the rent somehow."

Marley frowned. "Both Corbin and Zachariah have talked to me about that. Corbin said Senyaza would want to talk to me, and they'd pay me for my time. He said they might know something about my birth mother. And Neath the magic cat—which, did I mention, she apparently made? If I can trust what a faerie tells me. Oh, and Senyaza wants to dig into the twins' descent. They like to track bloodlines, I guess." She shook her head. "And Zachariah wants..." She trailed off and stared at her coffee for a moment, until Branwyn touched her arm. "Zachariah wants to pay me to keep on protecting the kids. Be their nanny or governess or something. Their bodyguard." She met Branwyn's gaze, and said fiercely, "I promised them I'd never let them go. And I won't. I fought for them, I saved them, I know it's stupid but they're *mine*. I mean, I don't mind if they're his, too. Not that much, anyhow. But getting paid by *him* to take care of them seems... wrong. He *used* me once already."

"Mmm," said Branwyn, noncommittally. "If you do manage to talk yourself into accepting mere *wages*, go for the bodyguard bucks. They make more."

Marley tried to scowl at her, but another tiny laugh crept past instead. Then she slumped against the chair beside the window. Branwyn raised her cup in a grave toast. "By the way... I did want to ask you about Zachariah and Corbin. I'm guessing Zachariah isn't so high on the Potential Date list right now. But what's up with you and Corbin?"

Marley gave her a blank look. Corbin? But he—realization dawned. Then a slow flush crept up her cheeks. *His motives are as selfish as yours, sweetheart,* the kaiju had said. "We barely know each other. And it's not like we've had time to do anything but run and shout at each other." But she remembered the warmth she'd felt in his presence

Branwyn looked pleased. "Good, good. Don't rush into anything just because he saved your life or whatever."

"I saved *his* life, actually. AT and I." And the scowl returned. AT. Corbin had said she'd be fine and it would all work out, but would it? Her gaze went to Penny again. She realized suddenly that it wasn't all over. She wasn't going back to her old life, with a bit of additional babysitting. Everything had changed, and she could make a difference to more than just a couple of people now. At least, she could if she didn't run away.

"So," said Branwyn, staring at her reflection in the window. "That was some magnificent bullshit you told Corbin and the angel, about the angel causing his prophecy to happen." She looked directly at Marley. "Did you believe it?"

Marley hesitated and then said, "I don't believe in prophecies. Someone told me, 'Men have always considered females with unusual power harbingers of the end.' And I believe that. I've seen that in books, in history. Women and children. Anybody different, really. Everybody from the old order always thinks it's the end of the world when unexpectedly powerful people show up. Those girls will light a fire. I'd like them to be able to decide what kind of fire they light."

"All right," said Branwyn. She sipped her coffee calmly. "I talked to Corbin while you were resting." Marley looked at her in alarm, and she added, "Not about you. It's been a big day for me, too. I wanted to find out more about the faeries, and if they'd be showing up again—"

The lights flickered. Shadows moved around the room, then vanished. Neath raised her head from where she was curled on Marley's bed. Her ears flattened and she rose to her feet, her tail twitching. Marley clutched Branwyn's arm, but before terror could really get a foothold, Neath stalked across the bed to the nightstand and peered at something there, then sat down again and began to wash herself.

Hesitantly at first, then firmly—*not running away*—Marley went to see.

On the nightstand was a glass bubble, like one she'd seen twice before. And it was perched on top of torn-edged piece of paper, upon which an elegant hand had scrawled in silver ink: *For Branwyn.*

Marley stared at it. All the old desire to protect Branwyn flared, then faded away like a dying spark when she remembered Branwyn charging from her prison with an iron bar. This faerie had no idea what he was in for. So, in a voice choked with laughter, she said, "Action Girl, it's for you!"

Branwyn narrowed her eyes. Then she smiled and reached toward the note. Marley moved out of her way.

acknowledgments

Without whom this book would not exist:

Kevin, who put up with everything
Raymond, who supported me no matter what
Neil, who gave me demons
Angie and Gayle, who inspired twins (among other things)

I hope you like what I've done

Everybody else: thank you.

about the author

Chrysoula Tzavelas went to twelve schools in twelve years while growing up as an Air Force brat, and she never met a library she didn't like. She now lives near Seattle with some random adults, miscellaneous animals, and a handy small child or two. She likes combed wool, bread dough, and gardens. She's also a certified technology addict; it says so on her (trademark-redacted) music player.

follow the author

www.dreamfarmer.net
Twitter: @chrysouladreams

www.ingramcontent.com/pod-product-compliance
Lightning Source LLC
Chambersburg PA
CBHW031118210626
46816CB00016B/1690